Praise for Kay Hooper

SLEEPING WITH FEAR

"Readers will be mesmerized." —*Publishers Weekly*

"Hooper's Special Crime Unit novels all have their own unique blend of mystery, suspense and the paranormal laced with a touch of romance. The author is a gifted teller of action-packed stories."
—*Romantic Times Book Review*

"Suspense just doesn't get better than Kay Hooper's novels . . . it's a one-sitting read that will hold you in its grip from beginning to end." —*Romance Reviews Today*

CHILL OF FEAR

"Hooper's latest may offer her fans a few shivers on a hot beach."
—*Publishers Weekly*

"Kay Hooper has conjured a fine thriller with appealing young ghosts and a suitably evil presence to provide a welcome chill on a hot summer's day." —*Orlando Sentinel*

"The author draws the reader into the story line and, once there, they can't leave because they want to see what happens next in this thrill-a-minute, chilling, fantastic reading experience."
—*Midwest Book Review*

HUNTING FEAR

"A well-told, scary story." —*Toronto Sun*

"Hooper's unerring story sense and ability to keep the pages flying can't be denied." —*Ellery Queen Mystery Magazine*

"Hooper has created another original—*Hunting Fear* sets an intense pace. . . . Work your way through the terror to the triumph . . . and you'll be looking for more Hooper tales to add to your bookshelf." —*Times Record News*

"It's vintage Hooper—a suspenseful page-turner."
—*Wichita Falls* (TX) *Facts*

BANTAM BOOKS BY KAY HOOPER

THE BISHOP TRILOGIES
STEALING SHADOWS
HIDING IN THE SHADOWS
OUT OF THE SHADOWS

TOUCHING EVIL
WHISPER OF EVIL
SENSE OF EVIL

HUNTING FEAR
CHILL OF FEAR
SLEEPING WITH FEAR

THE QUINN NOVELS
ONCE A THIEF
ALWAYS A THIEF

ROMANTIC SUSPENSE
AMANDA
AFTER CAROLINE
FINDING LAURA
HUNTING RACHEL

CLASSIC FANTASY AND ROMANCE
ON WINGS OF MAGIC
THE WIZARDS OF SEATTLE
MY GUARDIAN ANGEL (*ANTHOLOGY*)
YOURS TO KEEP (*ANTHOLOGY*)

KAY HOOPER

Something Different

Pepper's Way

BANTAM BOOKS

SOMETHING DIFFERENT / PEPPER'S WAY
A Bantam Book / August 2007

Published by Bantam Dell
A Division of Random House, Inc.
New York, New York

These are works of fiction. Names, characters, places, and incidents
either are the product of the author's imagination or are used fictitiously.
Any resemblance to actual persons, living or dead, events,
or locales is entirely coincidental.

All rights reserved

Something Different copyright © 1984 by Kay Hooper
Pepper's Way copyright © 1984 by Kay Hooper
Cover photo © Jack Hollingsworth/Getty Images

Bantam Books and the rooster colophon are registered trademarks
of Random House, Inc.

ISBN 978-0-553-38522-9

These titles were originally published individually by Bantam Books.

Printed in the United States of America
Published simultaneously in Canada

www.bantamdell.com

10 9 8 7 6 5 4 3 2 1
OPM

Something Different

A writer is only as good as those rare and unrewarded friends who bolster, cheer (or jeer), criticize, question, applaud—or just listen in sympathetic silence. Ideas bounce off these friends, plots are tried for effect, character motivation explored. Discussions go on over the phone; across coffee tables or dinner tables; and in the presence of baffled, bemused spouses.

And you thought I wrote alone.

Pam and Bob, this one's for you.

one

GYPSY HIT HER BRAKES INSTINCTIVELY AND
swerved as the small brown rabbit darted across the road in
front of her car. Satisfaction and relief at not hitting the creature were short-lived, however, as a sudden and savage jolt in-
formed her that her already battered VW had been rear-ended.

Her head snapped back and then forward, banging into
the steering wheel with enough force to give her a brief view of
stars in broad daylight. She found herself fighting various laws
of motion in an effort to bring the car and herself safely to the
side of the road. Her heart lodged in her throat for one flashing
instant, because the side of the road was a narrow strip of dirt
bordering on a sheer drop. And, Gypsy thought, neither she
nor the car had wings.

Sputtering, the VW's engine voiced an unmistakable death
rattle and expired as the little blue car with its bright yellow
daisy decals lurched onto the strip of dirt. Gypsy heard a more
powerful engine rumble into silence behind her. Automatically
and needlessly she pulled up the emergency brake and turned
off the ignition switch.

Although her forehead throbbed painfully, and the sicken-
ing fear at her near-maiden flight over the cliff hadn't quite

faded, Gypsy's thoughts were crystal-clear and crazily detached.

Not again. This could *not* be happening to her again. It was the third time in six months, and poor Daisy was certainly *dead*. Judging by the sound of the impact, not even the best body-and-fender man would be able to pound the dents out. And Daisy's engine had quite definitely been mortally wounded.

Gypsy abruptly became furious at whomever had murdered poor Daisy.

The sound of the other car's door slamming was followed swiftly by a startlingly deep and coldly controlled masculine voice. "Are you all right?" it demanded, and then added icily, "Don't you know that it's illegal as well as unsafe to drive a car without brake lights?"

Gypsy fumbled for Daisy's door handle and struggled out, letting her anger at Daisy's assassin have full rein. "*You* hit *me*, dammit, and Daisy *did* have a brake light—the left one! Now you've killed her—" She broke off abruptly as she got her first clear look at Daisy's assassin. He didn't look like a killer.

He was slightly under six feet tall, wide-shouldered but slender, and finely muscled. His burnished copper hair was thick and slightly shaggy, a bit longer than collar length. Eyes of an astoundingly intense shade of jade-green shot icicles at her. But his obvious anger couldn't hide the shrewdness behind his eyes, and the rigidly held expression only emphasized his marvelous bone structure.

Not a bit like a killer, Gypsy mused....

Recovering from her initial surprise, Gypsy was just about to light into the handsome stranger when he aimed the first thrust.

"My God! I thought the last of the flower children grew up years ago!"

She automatically looked down at herself; there was nothing unusual. Faded, colorfully patched jeans, a tie-dyed T-shirt, ragged sneakers, and a silver peace sign dangling around her neck on a leather thong. She supposed that his description fit, but the thrust didn't go home. In the first place one did not normally dress neatly to perform the errand Gypsy had just completed, and in the second place she didn't much care how she looked—and this man's distaste did nothing to change that.

She rather pointedly eyed his neat, three-piece business suit, spending a long moment gazing at extremely shiny shoes. Then she let her gaze wander briefly to the gleaming silver-gray Mercedes before returning it to his face. Satisfied with his reaction—a slight reddening beneath the tan of his cheeks—she let the matter drop, refusing to correct his first impression.

Dropping the easily assumed dignity, she spoke heatedly. "You hit Daisy from behind, and that makes it your fault!"

He sent a faintly bewildered glance toward Daisy's crumpled rear end, but said shortly, "You had no brake lights."

"Big deal!" she snapped. "If you'd been watching where you were going, you would have seen me swerve to miss that rabbit, and— Oh! Corsair!" Hastily she turned back to her car.

"Corsair?" the man muttered blankly, standing where she'd left him between their two cars and watching her open her car door and extract a bundle of cream-colored fur from inside. As she turned back toward him, he saw that the bundle was a large—a very large—Himalayan cat. Its face, paws, and tail were a dark chocolate color, and its broad face wore what seemed to be a permanently sulky expression.

"Just look at him!" she said angrily. "It's not enough that you killed poor Daisy; you nearly gave Corsair a heart attack!"

To the man's clear, jade eyes, Corsair didn't look as though he'd ever be—or had ever been—startled by anything short of

a massive earthquake. He started to make that observation out
loud, then realized that by participating in this ridiculous conversation, he'd only prolong it.

"Look—" he began, but she cut him off fiercely.

"This is all your fault!"

Jade eyes narrowed in sudden suspicion. "You're certainly
hell-bent to prove this was my fault, aren't you? I'll bet you
don't even— How old are you?" he demanded abruptly.

Gypsy drew herself up to her full height of five nothing
and deepened her glare. "You should never ask a woman her
age! Where did you learn your manners?"

"Where you learned yours!" he retorted irritably.

Into that tense confrontation came a slow, grinding *thunk,*
and Daisy's entire engine hit the ground in a little puff of dust.

Gypsy stared rather blankly for a moment and then began
to giggle. "Poor Daisy," she murmured.

The man was leaning back against the low hood of his
car chuckling quietly, his icy temper apparently gone. "Why
don't we start over?" he suggested wryly. "Hello, I'm Chase
Mitchell."

"Gypsy Taylor," she returned solemnly.

"Gypsy? Now, why doesn't that surprise me?"

"No reason at all, I'm sure." Gypsy sighed, her amusement
brief. "How am I going to get home? Daisy isn't going anywhere without the aid of a tow truck."

"I'll take you. We have to exchange insurance information
anyway." He was looking down disgustedly at the slightly
crumpled hood that he'd just stopped leaning against, then
looked up quickly as a thought apparently occurred to him.
"You *are* insured?" he asked carefully.

Knowing full well that Daisy's lack of brake lights made
her at least partially to blame for the accident, Gypsy had

stopped protesting. "Certainly I'm insured," she responded with dignity. After a beat she added, "At least . . . well, I think I am."

"How can you not be sure?"

"Well, I move around a lot." Unconsciously Gypsy had gravitated closer to the dented Mercedes. "Sometimes the notices from the insurance company get lost in the mail or—" She broke off hastily as she noted a disconcertingly icy storm gathering in his jade eyes. Gypsy loved a good storm, but she wasn't an idiot. "I'm insured. I know I'm insured."

"Right." As pointedly as she had done before, Chase looked from the top of her short black curls to the toes of her sneaker-clad feet. In between he noted a petite but nicely curved figure that in no way belonged to a teenager, and a face that was lovely—with fine bone structure and wide, dreamy gray eyes. "I thought you were about fifteen," he murmured almost to himself, "but I think I was wrong."

Gypsy blinked. "You certainly were." She was neither flattered nor insulted. "By about thirteen years. I'm twenty-eight." She blinked again, and added in a scolding voice, "And that was a sneaky way to find out!"

He grinned suddenly, and Gypsy was astonished at the change it wrought in his stern face. The jade eyes gleamed with amused satisfaction, laugh lines appearing at their corners, and white teeth flashed in a purely charming and surprisingly boyish smile.

"Well, I had to find out," he said. Before she could ask why, he was going on briskly. "Hop in and I'll take you home."

Having always relied on her instincts about people, Gypsy didn't worry about getting into a car with a stranger. Not this stranger. For some reason she instinctively trusted him. With a sigh and a last lingering glance toward the fallen Daisy, she started around to the passenger side of the Mercedes. Then she hesitated and went back to her car long enough to pull the keys from the ignition.

"Shouldn't you lock it up?"

"Why?" Gypsy asked wryly, heading back to the Mercedes. "Daisy isn't going anywhere."

Conceding the point, he got in the driver's side of his car, shut the door, and started it up. "Where to?"

Gypsy pointed along the winding, steadily uphill road. "Thataway. Follow the yellow brick road."

As the Mercedes pulled onto the road and began to climb smoothly, Chase distinctly felt baleful eyes on him. He risked a glance sideways, and found that it was the cat's gaze he was feeling.

Because of a childhood allergy—and no inclination since then—he'd had little experience with cats. But he recognized the expression on this one's face. Only cats and camels could stare through supposedly superior human beings with such utter and complete disdain. It gave him a disconcertingly invisible feeling.

Caused by a cat, it was a hell of a reaction, Chase thought. "Your cat doesn't like me," he observed, eyes firmly back on the tricky business of negotiating the road's hairpin curves.

Gypsy looked at him in surprise, and then glanced down at the cat resting calmly in her lap. Corsair was fixedly regarding one chocolate paw. "You're imagining things," she scoffed lightly. "Corsair's never met anybody he didn't like."

Chase risked another glance, and then wished he hadn't. "Uh-huh. So why is he glaring at me?"

Gypsy glanced down again. "He isn't. He's looking at his paw." Her voice was mildly impatient.

Chase decided not to look again. He also decided that

Corsair was a sneaky cat. "Never mind. Tell me, Miss Taylor—"

"Gypsy," she interrupted.

"As long as you'll return the favor."

"Fine. I hate formality."

"Gypsy, then. Where exactly do you live? I know this road, and it dead-ends a mile or so further up. There are two houses—"

"One of them's mine," she interrupted again.

"Yours?" He sounded a bit startled.

"I'm house-sitting," she explained absently, looking out the window and thinking as she always did, that it was nice to have the Pacific for a backyard. "The owners were temporarily transferred to Europe—six months. I'll be sitting for them another four months."

"I see."

He sounded rather faint, and Gypsy looked over at him in amusement. "I'm not quite as disreputable as I look," she said gently. "I'm dressed like this because I had to take Corsair to the vet."

"And the peace sign?"

His mind obviously wasn't on the conversation, and Gypsy wondered why. "It was a gift from some friends. Sort of a private joke," she explained automatically, gazing at him searchingly. She thought that he had the look of a man who had bitten down on something and wasn't quite sure what it was. Odd. Before she could attempt to probe the cause of his strange expression—Gypsy wasn't at all shy—he was speaking again.

"Do you live around here? When you're not house-sitting, I mean."

"I live wherever I happen to be house-sitting. Before this, I was in Florida for three months, and before that was New England. I like to move around."

"Obviously."

"Not *your* favorite life-style, I see," she said wryly.

"No." Abruptly, he asked, "Do you live alone?"

Gypsy thought briefly of all the bits of information a single woman generally didn't reveal to strange men—like whether she lived alone. However, if she was any judge of character, this man hardly had rape or robbery on his mind. "Usually I don't. A housekeeper usually lives with me; she's a good friend and practically raised me. But she's visiting relatives right now, so I'm on my own. Why do you ask?"

"Just wondering." He sent a sidelong glance her way. "You aren't wearing a ring, but these days asking a woman if she's single doesn't automatically preclude a live-in 'friend.'"

Gypsy looked at him thoughtfully and tried to ignore the sudden bump her heart had given. She'd been on the receiving end of enough male questions to know what that one was pointing to, and it was not a direction she wanted to explore. As handsome as Chase Mitchell undoubtedly was, Gypsy nonetheless told herself firmly that she wasn't interested. At this point in her life, a man was a complication she hardly needed.

And Chase Mitchell would prove to be more of a complication than most, she decided shrewdly. They obviously had nothing in common, and he wouldn't be the sort of man who could fit in with her offbeat life-style.

Frowning, Gypsy wondered at the trend of her own thoughts. Why on earth was she hesitating? Usually she disclaimed interest immediately in order to avoid complications before they arose.

Before she could further explore her inexplicable hesitation, Chase was going on in a smooth voice.

"Of course, you could have a 'friend' who doesn't live with you." It was definitely a question, she thought.

Gypsy answered wryly, "The way I move around?"

"Some men would consider plane tickets a small price to pay," he murmured.

She wondered if that was a compliment, but decided not to ask. With that kind of fishing she was half afraid of what she might catch. Instead, she chose a nice, safe, innocuous topic. "Do you live around here?" she asked casually.

He nodded, his eyes again on the road. The road was still both winding and tricky, but it no longer bordered on the cliffs. Trees hid the ocean now as they progressed further inland. "I've always lived on the West Coast," he said. "Apart from school years, that is."

Gypsy nodded and sought about for more safe topics. "Nice car," she finally managed inanely.

"It was," he agreed affably.

She shot him a goaded glare and immediately became more irritated when she noted that he wasn't even looking at her. "I didn't *mean* to wreck your nice car," she said with dignity. "And if it comes to that, you didn't exactly leave Daisy in great shape, you know!"

"If I were you," he suggested, ignoring the larger part of her accusation, "I'd get another car."

"Well, you're not me. I've had Daisy since I was seventeen; she's a classic. She's also my good-luck charm."

"Judging by the number of dents in her that I can't claim credit for," Chase said dryly, "she doesn't seem to have been very lucky." He was completely unconscious of following Gypsy's lead in using the feminine pronoun to describe Daisy.

Uncomfortably aware of her accident-prone nature, she didn't dispute his point. And she was enormously relieved to see her house as they finally completed the long climb and the road leveled off. She pointed and Chase nodded, slowing the Mercedes for the turn into her driveway.

Her home for the next four months was a sprawling house, modern in design but not starkly so. Lots of glass, lots of cedar. It blended in nicely with the tall trees, and from the back it boasted a magnificent view of the Pacific. But the house next door was by far the more beautiful of the two. It *was* starkly modern, geometric in design, with an abundance of sharp angles and impossible curves. Cunningly wrought in glass, cedar, and stone, it was a jewel utterly perfect in its setting. And the landscaping around the house was among the most beautiful Gypsy had ever seen.

She usually didn't care too much for modern houses, but she loved that one. Glancing toward it as the Mercedes pulled into her driveway, she wondered for the hundredth time who lived there. She'd only seen a gardener who came every day to care for the trees and shrubs.

The thought slipped from her mind as Chase stopped his car just outside the garage. Reaching for the door handle, she said, "You'd better come in; it may take a while for me to find the insurance card."

He nodded and turned off the engine, his eyes fixed curiously on the somewhat battered trailer pulled over onto the grass beside the driveway. "What—" he began.

Gypsy slid from the car before explaining. "That," she told him cheerfully, "contains all my worldly possessions when I move. Aside from Corsair, that is; he rides in Daisy with me." She reflected for a moment as she watched Chase move around to her. "Although I don't suppose one could call a cat a possession."

"Not any cat I've ever heard of," Chase agreed, eyeing Corsair with disfavor. "They seem to be complete unto themselves." He accompanied Gypsy and friend up the walkway.

She fished her keys from a pocket and unlocked the heavy front door. Opening it and stepping inside, she murmured, "I suppose I should warn you."

"Warn me? About wha—" Beginning to follow her inside, Chase suddenly found himself pinned solidly against the doorjamb by two huge paws. Inches from his nose loomed a black and white face in which a grin of sorts displayed an impressive set of dental equipment. It was a Great Dane, and it looked as though it would have considered half a steer to be a tidy mouthful.

A calm Gypsy holding an equally calm Corsair studied Chase's still face for a long moment. "Meet Bucephalus," she invited politely. "He was named after Alexander the Great's horse."

"Obviously," Chase murmured carefully. "Two questions. Is it yours?"

"No; he belongs to the Robbins couple—the ones who live here. Second question?"

"Does he bite?"

"No." She considered briefly. "Except for people who rear-end cars. He makes an exception for them."

"Funny lady. Would you mind getting him down?"

"Down, Bucephalus."

The big dog immediately dropped to all fours, looking no less huge but considerably more friendly. His long tail waved happily and he tilted his chin up slightly in order to wash Corsair's face with a tongue the size of a hand towel. The cat suffered this indignity with flattened ears and silence.

Chase carefully shut the door, keeping a wary eye on the dog. "Any more surprises?" he asked ruefully.

"I shouldn't think so. This way." She led him down the short carpeted hallway. A huge sunken den at the end of the hall boasted a brick fireplace, a beamed ceiling, and an open

L-shaped staircase leading up to a loft. The furniture consisted of an off-white pit grouping with abundant cushions, a large projection television, and assorted tables and lamps.

Gypsy stepped down into the den, set Corsair on the deep-pile carpet, and immediately headed for a corner that was either an afterthought to the beautiful room, someone's idea of humor . . . or both.

Chase followed slowly, staring in astonishment. The corner was partitioned off from the room by an eight-foot-tall bookcase, clearly made from odd pieces of lumber and sagging decidedly in every shelf. It was crammed to capacity. Within the "room" was a battered desk that had seen more mileage than Daisy; it was cluttered with papers, a couple of dog-eared dictionaries, stacks of carbon paper, and a few more unidentifiable items. A ten-year-old manual typewriter sat squarely in the middle of the clutter.

"Your corner," Chase murmured finally.

"My corner," Gypsy confirmed absently, scrabbling through a desk drawer.

Chase wandered over to examine the bookshelf, uneasily aware that the giant Bucephalus was right beside him. Trying to ignore his escort, he scanned the titles of Gypsy's books, becoming more and more puzzled. "I've never seen so many books on crime and criminology in my life. Don't tell me you're also a cop?"

Still searching for the elusive insurance card, Gypsy answered vaguely, "No. Murder." She looked up a moment later to find him staring at her with a peculiar expression, and elaborated dryly, "Murder *mysteries*. I write murder mysteries."

"*You*? Murder mysteries?"

"I wouldn't laugh if I were you. I know ninety-eight ways to kill someone, and all of them are painful."

Chase absorbed that for a moment. "Do your victims lose their insurance cards?" he asked gravely.

"My victims are usually dead, so it doesn't matter. Damn. It's not here."

Chase was frowning. Then the frown abruptly cleared and he was staring at her in astonishment. "No wonder your name rang a bell! I've read some of your books."

"Did you enjoy them?" she asked him politely.

"They were brilliant," he replied slowly, still staring at her in surprise. "I couldn't put them down."

Accustomed to the astonished reaction to her authorship, Gypsy smiled faintly and began to search through the clutter on her desk. "Don't bother telling me that I don't look like a writer," she advised. "I've heard it many times. I'd like to know what a writer is supposed to look like," she added in a reflective voice.

Chase discovered that he had been absently petting Bucephalus and stopped, only to continue hastily when the dog growled deep in his throat. "Can't you tell this monster to lie down somewhere?"

"Tell him yourself. He knows the command."

"Lie down," Chase said experimentally, and was immediately rewarded when the dog flopped down obediently. Stepping carefully around Bucephalus, Chase approached Gypsy and observed her unfruitful search. "Can't find it?"

Gypsy lifted a feather duster and peered beneath it. "It's here somewhere," she said irritably. "It has to be."

"You could offer me a cup of coffee while I wait," he said reproachfully.

"It isn't Tuesday."

Chase thought that one over for a moment. No matter how many times he ran it through his mind, her meaning didn't appear. "Is that supposed to make sense?"

She looked up from her search long enough to note his puzzled expression. "I only fix coffee on Tuesday," she explained.

"Why?" he asked blankly.

"It's a long story."

"Please. This is one answer I have to hear."

Gypsy pulled a squeaky swivel chair out and sat down, beginning to search through the center drawer for a second time. "When I was little," she told him patiently, "I became addicted to iced tea. My mother thought that it was unhealthy, that I needed to drink other things like milk. I hate milk," she added parenthetically.

"So anyway Mother decided to assign different drinks to the days of the week. That way, she could be sure that I was getting a healthy variety. By the time I got around to drinking coffee, the only day left for it was Tuesday. And today isn't Tuesday."

Chase shook his head bemusedly. "When you adopt a habit, it's your life, isn't it?"

"I suppose."

"Well, what's today's drink?" he asked, deciding to go with the tide.

"Is today Friday? Let's see. . . . Friday is wine. Or a reasonable facsimile thereof." She looked up with sudden mischief in her eyes. "Mother doesn't know about that. Poppy—my father—told me that I'd better save Friday for when I grew up. So I did. It's a good thing I listened to him. I like wine."

Staring at her in fascination, Chase murmured, "You seem to have . . . interesting parents."

"To say the least." Abruptly she asked, "What do you do for a living?"

Chase blinked, but quickly recovered. "I sell shoes," he replied blandly.

With sudden and disconcerting shrewdness, she said calmly, "If you're a salesman, I'll eat my next manuscript—page by page."

Chase wondered why he'd lied, then decided that it had probably been due to sheer bewilderment. "I'm an architect."

Gypsy made no comment on the lie, other than a brief look of amusement. "Now, *that* I believe. Residential or commercial?"

"Commercial. I've designed a few private homes though."

"Would you like some wine?" she asked suddenly.

After a moment Chase complained, "You take more conversational shortcuts than any person I've ever met."

"It saves time," she said solemnly.

He decided again to go with the tide. By this time he was beginning to feel like a piece of driftwood being battered against the shore. "Yes, I'd like some wine. Thank you."

Gypsy frowned. "I'd better see if I have any." She rose from the chair and headed for the hallway, saying over her shoulder, "Go through the desk again, will you? I may have missed it."

It took Chase several seconds to realize that she meant the insurance card. With a shrug he sat down in the creaky chair and began searching through the desk.

He'd searched three drawers by the time Gypsy came back into the room carrying two glasses filled with white wine. "Find it?" she asked, handing him a glass.

"No. Tell me something." He waved a hand at the general clutter of her desk. "How can someone so obviously disorganized write such ruthlessly logical and neatly plotted books?"

"Luck, I guess."

Chase lifted an eyebrow at her as she rested a hip against the corner of the desk. "Luck. Right." He lifted his glass in a faint toast, but the expression on his face indicated that he was not toasting Gypsy's answer but rather some wry thought of his own.

"Tell you what." He sighed almost to himself. "Why don't you keep looking for the card? Maybe you'll have found it by the time I pick you up tonight."

"Pick me up? For what?"

"Dinner."

two

"DINNER?" GYPSY LEANED AN ELBOW ON her typewriter and stared at Chase. The reluctance in his voice had been so audible as to be ludicrous, and she fought an urge to giggle. "You don't really want to do that."

"No," he agreed amiably. After a moment he added cryptically, "I've always considered myself an intelligent man."

Was that supposed to make sense? she wondered. "Look, if you're feeling guilty because of what you did to Daisy—" she began, but he cut her off decisively.

"I'm not feeling guilty about Daisy; the accident was more your fault than mine. And taking women out to dinner because I feel guilty isn't one of my noble habits. Do you want to go or don't you?"

Gypsy sipped her wine to give herself time to think. After hesitating, she asked cautiously, "Why are you asking me?"

He stared at her. "You want to hear my motives, I take it?"

"A girl likes to know where she stands."

"Well, my motives are the usual ones, I suppose. Companionship. Interest in a lovely woman. A dislike of eating alone. And," he added wryly, "I think that I should get to know my next-door neighbor."

Gypsy blinked. "You live . . . ?" She gestured slightly and sighed when he nodded. "You've been gone for two months."

Chase nodded again. "Back East working on a project."

"You didn't know Bucephalus," she pointed out.

"I hardly knew the Robbins couple. And I never saw that dog before today. They must have kept him hidden, although how to hide something that big . . . Are you going out with me?"

Gypsy hesitated again, and somewhere in the back of her mind her uncertainty was still nagging her. "Chase. . . ." She was searching for the right words. "If you want a companion across the dinner table, that's fine. If you want a neighbor you can borrow a cup of sugar from, that's fine. Anything more than that isn't fine. I don't want to get involved."

"I see." Chase set his wineglass on top of a dictionary, then took hers from her hand and set it down also. "That's an interesting point."

"What is?" she asked blankly.

"Whether we could become involved with each other. Would Bucephalus protect you?"

Gypsy had the detached feeling that there was something here she was missing totally. Deciding that the simplest course would be to answer his question, she said, "I suppose he would. If I screamed or something."

"Don't scream." Chase rose to his feet and pulled her upright into his arms.

"What're you . . . ?" she sputtered, caught off guard.

"A little experiment," he murmured. "To see if we could become involved with each other." Before she could utter another word, his lips had unerringly found hers.

In that first instant Gypsy knew that she was in trouble. Definite trouble. A fiery tingle began in her middle and spread rapidly outward to the tips of her fingers and toes. It was totally unexpected and frighteningly seductive. And Gypsy couldn't seem to find a weapon to combat the stinging little fire.

Something had kicked her in the stomach; dizziness overwhelmed her, and shock sapped the strength from her knees. Her body seemed to disconnect itself from her mind, her arms lifting of their own volition to encircle his neck. She felt her lips part beneath the increasing pressure of his, and then even her mind was lost. Searing brands moved against her back, pulling her body inexorably against his, and the hollow ache in her middle responded instantly to the fierce desire she could feel in him.

Gypsy was aware of the hazy certainty that she should stop this. Yes. Stop it, she thought. But she couldn't even find the strength to open her eyes, realizing only then that they were closed.

Stop it. In a moment. . . .

The stinging little fire wasn't so little anymore. It was a writhing thing now, scorching nerve endings and boiling the blood in her veins. She could feel her heart pound with all the wild unreason of a captive beast, and it terrified her with its savage rhythm.

She was dimly aware of drawing a shuddering breath when Chase finally released her. Her hands fell limply to her sides and then reached back to clutch at the edge of the desk she was leaning weakly against. Wood. Solid wood, she assured herself. Reality.

She stared at him with stunned, disbelieving eyes, only partially aware that his breathing was as ragged as hers and that the jade eyes held the same expression of bemused shock as her own.

Chase lifted his wineglass and drained it very scientifically. "Scratch one casual friendship," he muttered hoarsely.

Gypsy immediately shook her head. "Oh, no," she began.

"I've been wanting to do that," he interrupted musingly, "ever since you told me about coffee on Tuesday."

She blinked and then fiercely gathered her scattered wits. "No, Chase," she said flatly. "No involvement."

"Too late."

Hanging on to the desk as if to a lifeline, she shook her head silently, ignoring the sneering little voice inside her head that was agreeing with his comment.

"I don't know about you, but I'm not strong enough to fight," he said wryly.

Gypsy silently ordered the little voice to shut up and took hold of her willpower with both hands. "No involvement," she repeated slowly.

He gazed at her with a disconcerting speculation. "I'm reasonably sure it isn't me," he observed, "so what is it?"

For the first time her small work area was giving Gypsy a claustrophobic feeling, and she pushed away from the desk to wander out into the den. She sat down rather bonelessly on a handy chair and watched as Chase followed her into the main part of the room. Since he had a somewhat determined expression on his face, she searched hastily for words.

"Gypsy—"

"Chase, I— Oh, hell." She decided on honesty. "Chase, I've never . . . slept with a man before."

"You haven't?" Something unreadable flickered in his eyes.

"No."

"Why?"

She bit back a giggle, her sense of humor abruptly easing the tension in her body. "A girl used to have to explain why she did; now she has to explain why she doesn't."

"The times they are a changin'," he murmured.

"Uh-huh." She gave him a wry look. "Look, I've spent

most of my life traveling, which isn't exactly conducive to last-ing relationships. Summer flings and one-night stands hold no appeal for me. It's got nothing to do with morality, it's just me. In spite of my footloose life-style, I'm the home and hearth type at heart."

"A ring and a promise?"

Gypsy shook her head patiently. "That's just it: I don't want to get married."

Chase sank down in a chair across from hers and peered at her bemusedly. "You've just done an about-face here, haven't you?"

"Not at all. I'm trying to make a point. The only relation-ship acceptable to me would be a lasting relationship with one man—which, to my mind, means marriage. But at this point in my life I don't want to get married. So...no relationship."

"No involvement," he murmured.

Gypsy felt an enormous sense of relief when he seemed to understand. She also felt oddly disappointed. The resulting confusion left her unusually nervous. What on earth was wrong with her? She had a book to write, and heaven knew that would occupy her for weeks. Why this sudden wish that she had not voiced her "no involvement" policy. Policy? That made her sound like a politician!

"You never gave me an answer."

"What?" She stared at him, trying in vain to read his ex-pression. "Dinner? I...can't. I have a deadline, and I need to organize my notes and get to work."

"You have to eat."

"Yes, well...." She produced a weak smile from some-where. "If you'll take a close look at my typewriter, you'll prob-ably find crumbs inside. I usually eat right over the keyboard."

"You'll get ulcers eating like that," he warned dryly.

Gypsy shrugged and murmured vaguely, "Deadlines, you

know." She hoped that she'd given him the impression her deadline was considerably closer than it actually was. Little white lies never hurt anyone, she reasoned and, besides, she needed time to figure out what was wrong with her.

Along those lines she abruptly changed the subject. "Did you design your house?"

Chase didn't even blink; apparently he was getting accustomed to her conversational leaps. "Yes. Like it?"

"It's beautiful. I've never seen anything like it. Did you design it especially for yourself, or did you just decide afterward that it was for you?"

"It was mine all the way. Shall we talk of cabbages and kings now?" he added politely, doing a bit of conversational leaping of his own.

Gypsy sighed. It was not, she reflected, going to be easy for her to hold her own with this man. He seemed to be extremely adaptable. As unusual as she obviously was in his experience, he had learned quickly how *not* to be thrown off balance by her. "I don't know what you mean."

"You know. Can you cook?" he asked abruptly.

He was using her own tactics on her, damn him! Gypsy sighed again and mentally threw up her hands in surrender. For the time being, at least. "No, I can't cook. Also I can't sew, and I hate washing dishes." If she'd hoped to discourage him with these admissions of unfemininity, she was defeated.

"Nobody's perfect. What's your favorite meal?"

"Spaghetti."

"My speciality. What time would you like to eat?"

Gypsy decided that either the wine, the kiss, or both had addled her wits; otherwise she'd be a lot sharper than she seemed to be at the moment. Was he or wasn't he riding roughshod over all her objections? "I'm working, I told you."

"You have to eat. I'll do the cooking. My place or yours?"

With some vague idea of having the home-team advantage, she said, "Mine. Can you really cook?" She was suddenly dimly astonished to realize that she'd just *let* him ride roughshod over all her objections.

"They teach you to at military schools," he answered absently, his mind obviously on something else.

"You went to military schools?"

"Grew up in them." Gypsy had his full attention now. "My father hoped I'd go on to West Point, but I had other plans."

She'd had little experience with father-son relationships, but she was apparently the type of person that others invariably confided in, so she'd heard many tragic stories resulting from conflicts over career choices. Chase certainly didn't look to be the victim of a tragedy, but her ready sympathy was nonetheless stirred.

"Was he . . . very upset?" she probed delicately.

"He wasn't happy," Chase replied wryly. "I told him I was getting even for all those lonely years spent in military schools."

"Oh, poor little boy!" she said involuntarily. To her surprise Chase flushed slightly. But there was a considering expression in his jade eyes.

"If I were an unscrupulous man, I'd take advantage of your obvious sympathy," he told her gravely. "However, since the last thing I want to do is to begin our . . . friendship with a lie, I'll confess that my childhood wasn't in the least deprived."

"It wasn't?"

"Hell, no." He smiled at her. "The schools were good ones, I had plenty of friends, and Dad visited frequently. He always came and whisked me away to whatever post he happened to be at for holidays and vacations. I was a seasoned world traveler by the age of twelve."

Gypsy had to admit that it didn't sound sad, but she was still puzzled. Chase calmly enlightened her.

"My mother died when I was five, and Dad couldn't very well drag me all over the world with him. More often than not, he was assigned a post squarely in the middle of some revolution. So I went to boarding schools, where I learned to pick up my socks and cook spaghetti. Good enough?"

She nodded slowly. "Sorry to be nosy."

"Not at all. I'm glad you're interested. It'll be my turn to hear your life story tonight." He held up a hand when she would have spoken. "Fair trade. And I *have* to hear more about your parents. What time shall we have dinner?"

She stared at his politely inquiring face for a long moment. "About seven. I guess," she added rather hastily, deciding that she was giving in too damn quickly.

"Fine. I'll come over around six and bring the fixings with me." He rose to his feet and made a slight gesture when she would have got up. "Don't bother. I think I can find the door. See you at six. Oh, and keep looking for that insurance card, will you?"

Gypsy gazed after him, and she felt a sudden pang. Not a pang of uneasiness or uncertainty, but one of sheer panic.

I don't know about you, but I'm not strong enough to fight.

Reluctantly she allowed her mind to relive that...kiss. Kiss? God! Vesuvius erupting had nothing on that "kiss," Gypsy thought. She had never in her life been shaken like that. And Chase had made no secret of the fact that it had shaken him as well.

And that meant trouble with a capital everything.

She rubbed absently at the sudden gooseflesh on her arms, wondering at the inexplicable caprices of fate. Her life was going so smoothly! And she didn't want the status quo to change...not now. Her writing produced enough upheaval for any sane person; asking for more was like asking for a ringside seat at the hurricane of the century.

By the time Chase knocked on her door at six on the dot, Gypsy had come no nearer to an answer. She'd had several hours to think and in all that time, her thoughts had turned continually to that kiss.

She knew that her peculiar life-style and offbeat habits had caused her to miss a lot. She had friends, but not close ones. During high school and college, she'd indulged in the normal sexual experimentation, but a natural unconformity had kept her safe from peer pressure. And she hadn't cared for any man enough to attempt the serious relationship that her own private ideals demanded.

But she had convinced herself over the years that the only things she had missed by her celibacy had been vulnerability and potential heartache. And she knew from experience that it demanded a rare and extremely adaptable person to survive—happily—living with her. To date only Amy, her housekeeper and mother hen, had managed the feat.

Not even her loving and uncritical parents, unusual themselves, had been able to live with their daughter once she'd reached adulthood. And if *they* couldn't do it, what chance had the sane, normal man? Gypsy wondered.

So when she opened the door to let Chase in at six, she was staunchly determined to nip any romantic overtures in the bud. After which, according to all the books on etiquette, the noble warrior would retire from the field in dignified defeat.

The problem was...Chase apparently intended to retire from the field only if carried off on his shield.

"Did you find it?" he asked cheerfully.

Belatedly shutting the door behind him and hurrying down the hall to keep up with his tall form, Gypsy struggled briefly to figure out what he was talking about. "The insurance card? Yes, I found it." She followed him into the modern kitchen, reflecting absently that he looked *really* good in jeans. "It was in Corsair's envelope."

"Corsair's what?" He paused in unloading a bulging grocery bag onto the deep orange countertop, looking at her blankly.

Gypsy was staring at his T-shirt and trying not to giggle. Obviously he wasn't as conservative as she'd first thought. The T-shirt read: THIS IS A MOVING VIOLATION. Above the words was a picture of a leering man chasing an obviously delighted and sketchily dressed woman.

Trying to keep her voice steady, Gypsy finally replied to his question. "Corsair's envelope. You know, where I keep his vet records."

"Oh. I won't ask what it was doing there." He went back to unloading the groceries.

"Uh . . ." She gestured slightly. "Nice shirt."

"Thank you. Is it too subtle, do you think?"

"Depends."

"On what?" He looked at her with innocent mischief in his eyes.

"On whether it's a declaration of intent."

"Bite your tongue." He looked wounded. "I would never be so crass."

Gypsy wasn't about to ask what the shirt was if it *wasn't* a declaration of intent. She decided to leave the question of subtlety up in the air for the time being.

Chase was looking her up and down, considering. "You look very nice," he commented, eyeing her neat jeans and short-sleeved knit top. "But what's this?" he asked, reaching out to pluck a pair of dark-rimmed glasses from the top of her head.

"They're working glasses." She reclaimed them and placed them back on top of her head. "To help prevent eyestrain, according to the doctor."

"Oh." Chase removed the glasses from the top of her head and placed them on her nose. He studied the effect for a moment while she frowned at him, then said, "They make you look very professorial."

She pushed them back up and said briefly, "They make me look like an owl. If you want me to help cook, by the way, the consequences will rest on your head."

Chase accepted the abrupt change of subject without a blink. "You get to watch the master chef at work. Sit on that stool over there."

Gypsy debated about whether or not to dig in her heels. "Those military schools didn't help your personality," she offered finally in a deceptively mild voice.

"I take it you dislike being ordered around."

"Bingo."

"Will you *please* sit on that stool, Miss Taylor, so that I can demonstrate my culinary skill before your discerning eye?"

"Better," she approved, going over to sit on the high stool.

"Trying to reform a man is the first sign of possessiveness, you know." He was unloading the bag again.

"I've taught *manners* to quite a few children," she responded politely, refusing to be drawn.

"Really? How did that come about?" Chase was busily locating what he needed in cabinets and drawers. "I assumed you didn't have any siblings."

"You assumed correctly." Gypsy reflected wryly that he had a disconcerting habit of dangling a line her way and then abruptly cutting bait when she ignored it. "But I like kids, so I usually find a nursery school or kindergarten wherever I'm living and volunteer to help out a couple of days a week."

"So you like kids, eh?" He sent a speculative glance at her as he began to place hamburger in a pan for browning. "I'll bet you'd eventually like to have a houseful of your own."

"You'd lose the bet. I'd make a lousy mother; I'm not planning on having kids at all."

Chase halted his preparations long enough to give her a surprised look. "Why do you think you'd make a lousy mother? Your 'gypsy' life-style?"

She shook her head. "I grew up that way, and it didn't bother me. No, it's my writing. Some authors work nine to five with nights and weekends off, just like an average job." She smiled wryly. "And then there's me. When I'm working, it's usually in twelve- to fourteen-hour stretches. For weeks at a time. I lose pounds and sleep...and sometimes friends. I swear and throw things and pace the floor. Corsair, poor baby, has to remind me to feed him." Her smile unconsciously turned a bit wistful. "What kind of life would that be for kids?"

Chase was watching her with an expression that was curiously still. After a moment he shook his head as if to throw off a disturbing thought. When he spoke, it was about her work habits, and not about her decision not to have children. "Aren't you afraid of burning yourself out?"

"Not really." She spoke soberly. "Notice that I said *when* I'm working. I usually take a break of several weeks between books. I'm healthy and happy—so where's the harm?"

He shook his head again—this time in obvious impatience. "You need someone to take care of you."

"I *have* someone to take care of me—my housekeeper, Amy. The hamburger's burning."

Turning swiftly back to the stove, Chase swore softly. He repaired the results of his inattention silently, then said, "Tell me about your parents. Your mother first; I have to hear about the creator of coffee on Tuesday."

"You're hung up on that." Gypsy sighed. "Well, Mother is an artist—very vague, very creative. She's also a spotless house-keeper, which drives both Poppy and me absolutely nuts; he and I share an extremely untidy nature." She sought about in her mind for a further description of her mother. "Mother is . . . Mother. She's hard to describe."

"An artist? Would I have heard of her?"

"Know anything about art?"

"Yes."

"Then you've heard of her. Rebecca Thorn."

Chase nearly got his thumb with the knife he was chopping onions with. "Good Lord! Of course I've heard of her." Staring at Gypsy, he nearly got his forefinger with the knife. "You come from a very illustrious family."

"You haven't heard the half of it."

"Your father too?"

"Uh-huh. You'd have to be a scientist to recognize his name though. He's a physicist. Disappears periodically and can't talk about his work." She reflected for a moment. "Poppy looks like the typical absentminded professor. He's soft-spoken, very distinguished, and wouldn't pick up a sock if it were made of solid gold."

She grinned suddenly. "It's amazing that he and Mother have lived together in perfect harmony for nearly thirty years. If I didn't know the story behind it, I'd wonder how Poppy ever managed to catch Mother."

"What *is* the story?"

"Never mind."

"Unfair! It'll drive me crazy."

"Sorry, but it's not my story. If they come over to visit, you can ask. They live in Portland."

"I thought they traveled?"

"Used to. Poppy still has to fly off somewhere occasionally, and Mother has her showings from time to time, but they're pretty settled now."

Cutting up ingredients for a salad, Chase glanced at her innocently. "They're so different, yet they get along perfectly?"

Gypsy missed the point. "Usually. Although they told me that there was a definite disagreement before I was born. Mother decided to go on tour when she was six months pregnant, and Poppy protested violently. You'd have to know Poppy to realize how astonishing that is. He never gets mad."

"What happened?"

"Well, Poppy said that he'd be damned if he'd have his child born in an elevator or the back room of some gallery— quite likely, given Mother's vagueness—and that she wasn't going to exhaust herself by trying to give showings in twelve cities in twelve days, or something equally ridiculous. So he planned a long, leisurely tour lasting three months and went with her, and the government was having kittens."

Chase blinked, digested the information for a moment, and then asked the obvious question. "Why?"

"Why was the government having kittens?" Gypsy looked vague. "Dunno exactly. Poppy was working on something for them, and they got very cranky when he took a sudden vacation. They couldn't do much about it, really, since genius doesn't punch a time-clock."

After staring at her for a moment, Chase asked politely, "And where were you born?"

She looked surprised. "In Phoenix. Mother woke up in the middle of the night having labor pains. She got up and called a cab; she knew that she wouldn't be able to wake Poppy—he sleeps like the dead—so she went on to the hospital alone. The problem was, she forgot to leave poor Poppy a note. He nearly had a heart attack when he woke up hours later and found her gone."

Chase had a fascinated expression on his face. "I see. So you were born in a hospital. Somehow that seems an anticlimax."

"Actually I was born in the cab. They made it to the hospital, and the cabbie ran inside to get a doctor. The doctor got back to the cab just in time to catch me. The cabbie—his name is Max—still sends me birthday cards every year."

Chase leaned back against the counter, crossed his arms over his chest, and shook his bowed head slowly. It took Gypsy a full minute to realize that he was laughing silently.

"What's so funny?"

He ignored the question. "Gypsy," he said unsteadily, "I have *got* to meet your parents."

Puzzled, she said, "They'll be here on Sunday for a visit; you can come over then." She had totally forgotten her intention of discouraging Chase's interest.

"Thanks, I'll do that." Still shaking his head, he went back to fixing the salad. A moment later he softly exclaimed, "Will you look at that?"

"What?" She slid off the stool and went over to peer around him.

"Your knife bit me." Chase quickly held his right hand over the sink, and a single drop of blood dripped from his index finger to splash onto the gleaming white porcelain. "Or the Robbinses' knife. Whichever—" He broke off abruptly as a muffled thump sounded behind him.

Gypsy opened her eyes to the vague realization that she was lying on the coolness of a tile floor. A pair of jade eyes, concerned, more than a little anxious, swam into view. She gazed up into them dreamily, wondering what she was doing on the floor and why Chase was supporting her head and shoulders.

He looked terribly upset, she thought, and didn't understand why the thought warmed her oddly.

Then her memory abruptly threw itself into gear, and she closed her eyes with the swiftness born of past experience. "I hope you put a Band-Aid on it," she said huskily.

"I have a paper towel wrapped around it," he responded, a curious tremor in his deep voice. "Gypsy, why didn't you tell me you couldn't stand the sight of blood? God knows I wouldn't have thought it, considering the type of books you write."

"It's not something I normally announce to everybody and his grandmother," she said wryly, opening her eyes again. "Uh...I think I can get up now." She felt strangely reluctant to move, and grimly put that down to her sudden faint.

"Are you sure?" Chase didn't seem to be in any great hurry to release her. "Did you hit your head when you fell?"

"If I did, it obviously didn't hurt me. Help me up, will you, please?" She kept her voice carefully neutral.

Silently he did as she asked, steadying her with a hand on each shoulder until the last of the dizziness had passed. "Are you sure you're all right?"

"I'm fine." Gypsy made a production out of straightening her knit top. "Sorry if I startled you."

"*Startled* me?" Chase bit off each word with something just short of violence. "You scared the hell out of me. How on earth can you write such gory books when you can't stand the sight of blood?"

Patiently Gypsy replied, "I don't have to *see* the blood when I write—just the word."

He stared down at her for a long moment, shaking his head, until the bubbling sauce on the stove demanded his attention. He was still shaking his head when he turned away. "I hope you don't have any more surprises like that in store for me," he murmured. "I'd like to live to see forty."

Curious, Gypsy thought, then shrugged. Turning away, she caught sight of Corsair. The way he was sitting by one of the lower cabinets communicated dramatically. She frowned slightly as she got his cat food out and filled the empty bowl at his feet. "Sorry, cat," she murmured.

"What about Bucephalus?" Chase asked, obviously having observed the little scene.

"I fed him earlier."

"Oh." Leaping conversationally again, he said, "Tell me something. Why is it that the heroes in your books really aren't heroes at all? I mean, half the time, they're nearly as bad as the villains."

"Heroes don't exist," she told him flatly, going back to sit on her stool.

He tipped his head to one side and regarded her quizzically. "You're the last person in the world I'd expect to say something like that. Care to explain what you mean?"

"Just what I said. Heroes don't exist. Not the kind that people used to look up to and admire. The heroes available today are the ones created years ago out of pure fantasy."

"For instance?"

"You know. The larger-than-life heroes who were always fighting for truth, justice, and the American way. Superman. Zorro. The cowboys or marshalls in the white hats. A few swashbucklers. Knights on white chargers. They're all fiction . . . or just plain fantasy."

Chase set the bowl filled with tossed salad into the nearly barren refrigerator. "No modern-day heroes, huh?"

"Not that kind, no. The larger-than-life heroes are either long dead or else buried in the pages of fiction. It's a pity, too, because the world could use a few heroes."

Spreading French bread with garlic butter, Chase lifted a brow at her. "Those words carry the ring of disillusion," he said. "Don't tell me you're a romantic at heart."

Gypsy squirmed inwardly, but not outwardly. "I know that's a sin these days."

"No wonder you haven't gotten involved with anyone."

"You're twisting my meaning," she said impatiently. "I would never expect any man to measure up to fantasy heroes. That's as stupid as it is unreasonable. But there's a happy medium, you know. It's just that...romance is gone. I don't mean romance as in love or courtship. I mean *romance*. Adventure, ideals."

She ran a hand through her black curls and tried to sum up her meaning briefly, feeling somehow that it was important for him to understand what she meant. "Fighting for something *worth* fighting for."

Chase was silent for a long moment, his hands moving surely, and his eyes fixed on them. Then he looked over at Gypsy, and the jade eyes held a curiously shuttered expression. "Heroes."

"Heroes." She nodded. "Now, master chef—when do we eat?"

three

THINKING BACK ON IT THE NEXT DAY, GYPSY
had to admit—however reluctantly—that Chase was a marvelous companion. He'd kept her interested and amused for
several hours, telling her all about what it was like to grow up
in military schools—one prank after another, judging by some
of the stunts he and friends had pulled—and how clients could
easily drive an architect crazy.

And he asked questions. About the different places she'd
lived, about her parents, about how she wrote her books. He
plied her with an excellent red wine, pressed her to eat more
spaghetti than Italy could have held, and then refused her virtuous offer of help in cleaning up the kitchen.

He left on the stroke of midnight... with a casual handshake and a cheerful good-bye.

Not *quite* what Gypsy had expected.

Rising on Saturday after an unusually restless night, she
fiercely put him out of her mind. She fixed herself a bowl of cereal for breakfast, absently noting that she was nearly out of
milk. She fed Bucephalus and Corsair, unlatched the huge pet
door leading from the kitchen out into the backyard, and
rinsed her cereal bowl.

Saturday was juice, so she carried a large glassful out to her desk. Orange juice today; she usually alternated between orange, grape, or tomato juice. Wearing a pair of cutoff jeans and a bright green T-shirt, she sat down at her desk to work.

Two hours later Gypsy discovered that she'd been shuffling papers around on her desk, and had accomplished absolutely nothing.

Physical labor—that's what she needed. Working at a desk was fine, but working at a desk meant thinking, and she was thinking too damn much about Chase Mitchell.

Locating her gardening basket with some difficulty—why was it in the bathroom?—she went out into the front yard. There were several flower beds all bearing evidence that she'd indulged in physical labor quite often during the last two months.

Gypsy was a good gardener. And she had not merely the proverbial green thumb but a green *body*. Flowers that weren't even supposed to be blooming this time of year were waving colorful blossoms in the early-morning breeze. The half-dozen flower beds in the front yard were beautiful.

She glanced around, remembered where she'd left off, then dropped to her knees beside a flower bed ringing a large oak tree at the corner near Chase's property. She attacked a murderous weed energetically.

There was a sudden rustle in the tree above her, and then a metallic sound as a bunch of keys fell practically in her lap. Gypsy stared at them for a long moment. Keys. *Not* acorns. She looked up slowly.

Chase was lying along a sturdy-looking lower limb, staring down at her. He was dressed casually in jeans and a green shirt, open at the throat, and the only way to describe his expression would be "hot and bothered."

"What are you doing?" she asked with admirable calm.

"Getting my car keys," he replied affably.

"Oh, is that where you keep them?"

"Only since I met your cat."

Gypsy's gaze followed his pointing finger and located Corsair, who was sitting farther out on the same limb. The cat's furry face was a study in innocence, and his bushy tail was waving gently from side to side.

Gypsy looked back at Chase in mute inquiry.

Chase crossed his hands over the limb and rested his chin on them, with all the air of a man making himself comfortable. "Your cat," he explained, "has somehow found a way into my house. Beats me where it is, but he's found it. He was sitting on my couch a little while ago—with my car keys in his mouth. I chased him three times around the living room and then lost him. The next thing I knew, he was sitting outside the window, on the sill. When I came out of the house, he climbed this tree. Ergo, I climbed up after him."

"Uh-huh." Gypsy glanced again at the innocent cat. "Why would Corsair steal your keys?"

"You don't believe me?"

"Forgive me. I've known Corsair a little longer."

"He stole my keys."

"Why would he do that?"

"How the hell should I know? Maybe he wanted to drive the car; God knows, he's arrogant enough."

"Don't insult Corsair, or I won't let you climb my tree anymore."

"Cute. That's cute."

"Chase, cats don't steal keys. And Corsair's never stolen anything." Gypsy exercised all her willpower to keep her amusement buried. She waved the trowel about. "What would he want with your keys?"

"He wanted to annoy me. I tell you, that cat doesn't like me!"

"Well, if you keep on calling him *that cat* in that tone of voice, I wouldn't be surprised if he actually did start disliking you. Besides, it's obvious that you know nothing about cats. *If* he disliked you, he'd shred your curtains or attack you when you weren't looking, or something like that. *Not* steal your keys."

"He stole my keys."

Gypsy stared up into stubborn jade eyes. "Of *course,* he did. He just sat down and decided very logically that since he didn't like you, he'd steal your car keys. Then he'd let you chase him three times around your living room. Then he'd let you chase him up a tree—"

"All right, all right!" Chase sighed in defeat. "Obviously I imagined the whole thing."

"Obviously." Gypsy went back to work with the trowel.

There were several rustling noises from above. Then a muffled "Damn!" Then a long silence. Gypsy kept working; another weed poked up an unwary head and she attacked it lethally.

"Want to give me a hand here?"

Gypsy murdered another weed. "A grown man can't get down from a tree by himself?" She had to swallow hard before the question would emerge without a hint of the laughter bubbling up inside of her.

"I'm not too proud to ask for help." There was a pause. "Help!"

She sat back on her heels and looked up at him. She was trying desperately to keep a straight face. "What do you want me to do? Climb up and get you down, or cushion your fall?"

There was a frantic gleam in the jade eyes. "Either way—when I get down, I'm going to murder you!"

"In that case, stay where you are."

"Gypsy—"

"All *right*! What's the problem?"

"I can't look over my shoulder to see where to place my feet. Every time I try, I lose my balance. And stop grinning, you little witch!"

"I'm not grinning. This isn't grinning." Gypsy struggled to wipe away the grin. "It's a twitch. I was born with it."

"Sure. Tell me where to put my feet."

Gypsy swallowed the instinctive quip. "Uh...slide back a little. Now a little to the right. No, *your* right! Now..."

A few moments later Chase was safely on the ground. Gypsy, who hadn't moved from her kneeling position, looked up at him innocently. "That'll teach you to climb trees. What would you have done if I hadn't been here?"

"Perished in agony. I thought you were supposed to be working."

"I told you I worked odd hours."

"What're you doing now?"

"What does it look like? I'm planting weeds."

"You have a sharp tongue, Gypsy mine."

She ignored the possessive addition to her name. "One of my many faults." She tossed him the keys. "Don't let me keep you," she added politely.

Deliberately misunderstanding her, he asked solemnly, "Would you keep me in comfort and security for the rest of my life? I have no objections to becoming a kept man."

The unexpected play on words knocked her off balance for a moment—but only for a moment. She and her father had played word games too many times for this one to throw her. "I won't be a keeper; the pay's not good enough."

"But there are benefits. Three square meals a day and a place to rest your weary head." He sat down cross-legged on the grass beside her, still grave.

"Not interested."

"A live-in proofreader."

"I can read."

"Typist?"

"I'll ignore that." Gypsy weeded industriously.

"That's not a weed," he observed, watching her. The word game was obviously over for the moment.

"It is too. It's just pretending to be a flower."

"What are you pretending to be?"

"A gardener. If you're not leaving, help weed."

"Yes, ma'am." Chase searched through the wicker garden basket, obviously in search of a tool with which to weed. "Why is there a dictionary in this basket?"

"Where do *you* keep dictionaries?"

"One would think I'd learn not to ask you reasonable questions."

"One would think."

"Do you do it deliberately?"

Gypsy gave him an innocent look. "Do what deliberately?"

"Uh-huh." He sighed. "There's a fork here; shall I use it to weed?"

"Be my guest."

"Would you like to have lunch?" he asked, using the fork enthusiastically to destroy a marigold in the prime of life.

Gypsy gently removed the fork from his grasp. "Not just after breakfast, no."

"Funny."

"Sorry." She hastily took the fork away from him a second time. "No more help, please. I don't want Mr. and Mrs. Robbins to come home to a bare lawn."

"Are you criticizing my gardening skills?" he asked, offended.

"Yes."

"Oh."

"No wonder you hire a gardener."

"You made your point. I didn't rub it in that I cook better than you."

"Not better. You cook—I don't. Period."

"Whatever." Chase sighed and got to his feet. "Well, since you won't let me weed, I'll be on my way. Do you need anything from town? I have to run some errands."

Gypsy paused in her work long enough to look up at him. "Now that you mention it—I could use a gallon of milk."

"Is Saturday milk day?" he asked interestedly.

"No, Monday is."

"You're going to drink a gallon of milk on Monday? It'll spoil if you don't."

"I use it for cereal. That doesn't count as a drink."

"Right." He nodded slowly. "Uh . . . what're you doing this afternoon?"

Glancing past his shoulder, Gypsy saw Corsair about to launch himself. "Step back!" she ordered briskly.

Instinctively Chase did so, and Corsair overshot him to land with a disgruntled expression in the grass beside Gypsy. The cat's face seemed to proclaim irritably that not even a cat could pause to correct his aim in midair.

"I told you he didn't like me."

Gypsy swatted the cat firmly. "Leave!"

Corsair stalked toward the house with offended dignity.

"Sorry," Gypsy murmured. "I can't understand it; Corsair likes everybody."

"Everybody but me."

"I may have misjudged you about the keys," Gypsy said slowly.

"Good of you to admit it."

"I'm nothing if not fair."

"I won't comment on that. You didn't answer my question. What're you going to be doing this afternoon?"

"I usually go for a walk on the beach, but I won't know for sure what I'll be doing until then."

"Don't believe in planning ahead, eh?"

"I treasure spontaneity."

"I'll keep that in mind. One gallon of milk coming up." Lifting one hand in a small salute, Chase headed across to his house.

Gypsy stared after him. It occurred to her that anyone listening to one of their conversations—particularly if he or she came in on the middle of it—would be totally bewildered. Neither she nor Chase ever lost the thread. It was as if they were mentally attuned, on the same wavelength.

It was a disturbing thought.

She put more energy into her attack on the weeds, slaughtering without mercy while frowning at the thoughts that flitted through her mind.

She was in trouble. *Definite* trouble. Chase possessed a sharp intelligence, a highly-developed sense of the ridiculous, and an indefinable talent for holding her interest—no mean accomplishment, considering her wayward mind. He was also fatally charming.

Besides . . . she'd always had a thing about redheads.

Gypsy uprooted a marigold by mistake, and hastily replanted it. Damn! She was thinking about him too much. It didn't help to remind herself of that. Long hours at her typewriter had taught her that the mind was a peculiar instrument, given to absurd flights of fancy all mixed up with spans of rational thought.

If only there were a lever that she could switch from ABSURD to RATIONAL. But no such luck.

Her lever was stuck on ABSURD. Or something was. Why else was she kneeling here on the grass and wistfully contemplating a relationship with a man? Particularly *that* man?

"Face it," she told four marigolds and a rose. "You'd drive him crazy inside a week—once you really started to work. And he'd play merry hell with your concentration."

She worked vigorously with the trowel to loosen the soil around her audience. "And you don't want to get involved. You *don't.* Just think . . . you'd have to live in one house for *years.* And he'd expect you to learn how to cook—you know he would. And he wouldn't like whatisits in the refrigerator, or dirty clothes strewn through the house, or cat hair on the couch. Especially Corsair's hair.

"The smart thing to do would be to sink your scruples and settle for an affair," she told her audience, dirt flying like rain as she unconsciously dug a hole at the edge of the bed. "At least then you wouldn't have to go to court whenever he decided that enough was enough. You'd just politely help him pack his suitcases—or pack yours—and call it quits. Nice and civilized."

She frowned as a drop of moisture fell onto her hand. "Oh, for Pete's sake," she muttered angrily, swiping at a second tear with the back of one dirty hand. "It hasn't even *begun,* and already you're crying because it's over!"

Gypsy filled the minor excavation with dirt, dropped the trowel into her basket, and rose to her feet. She picked up the basket and stared down at the colorful flowers for a moment. Then she turned and made her way toward the house.

"Everybody talks to plants," she muttered aloud. "They make good listeners; they don't butt in with sensible suggestions, and they don't warn you when you're about to make an utter fool of yourself!"

Since Chase had arranged to have Daisy towed to a garage for repairs (Gypsy didn't hold out much hope), she was pretty much housebound. Chase hadn't specified any length of time for his "errands," but the morning dragged on with no sign of him, and Gypsy was bored.

She didn't feel like writing. Gardening had palled decidedly. She played fetch with Bucephalus for an hour, but then *he* got bored. She tried to teach Corsair to play the same game; for her pains, she got a stony glare from china-blue eyes and a swishing tail indicative of cold contempt.

"Why do I put up with you, cat?"

"*Waurrr.*"

"Right. Go away."

She watched as Corsair headed for the shade of a nearby tree in the backyard, then glanced at her watch. Twelve o'clock. The morning was gone, and she hadn't accomplished a thing. Wonderful.

Gypsy walked across the lawn to the redwood railing placed about two feet inside the edge of the cliff. She leaned on the railing for a few moments, gazing out over the Pacific and thinking muddled thoughts. Maybe a walk on the beach would clear the cobwebs away.

She followed the railing to the zigzagging staircase leading down to the beach. On the way down, she absently glanced across to the twin staircase leading from Chase's backyard. The beach below was narrow as beaches go, but it was private for a quarter of a mile in either direction. North and south of the private stretch were various small towns, and, of course, other privately owned properties.

But only these two homes possessed the eagle's perch of the cliffs. In this area anyway.

Gypsy loved it.

Barefoot as usual, she walked out to the water's edge and

stood listening to the roar of the surf. It was a comforting sound. A *comfortable* sound. Endlessly steady, endlessly consistent, though at the moment it possessed the disturbing trick of reminding one of one's own mortality.

Frowning, Gypsy turned and walked back a few feet toward the cliffs. She stopped at the large, water-smoothed rock jutting up out of the sand. It was a favorite "place of contemplation" for her, and she sat now in the small seatlike depression in its side.

Mortality.

It was one of those odd, off-center, out-of-sync moments. Gypsy wasn't generally given to soul-searching, but in that moment she searched. And she discovered one of life's truths: that complacency had a disconcerting habit of shattering suddenly and without warning.

How many times had she told herself that her life was perfect, that she had no need to change it? How many times had she asserted with utter confidence that she needed no one but herself to be happy?

Gypsy's frown, holding a hint of panic, deepened as she stared out over the ocean. Had she been wrong all these years? No. No, not wrong. Not *then*. She'd needed those years to work at her writing, to grow as a person.

But had she grown? Yes . . . and no. She'd certainly grown as a writer. And she was a well-rounded person; she had interests other than writing, and she got along well with other people. But she'd never opened herself up totally to another person.

For *person*, she thought wryly, read *man*. No relationships, other than the strictly casual. No vulnerability on that level. No chance of heartache. And . . . no growth?

She was more confused than ever. Who, she wondered despairingly, had conceived the unwritten rulebook on human relationships? Who had decreed long ago in some primal age that total growth as a human being was possible only by risking total vulnerability?

Reluctantly Gypsy turned from the philosophical and abstract to the concrete and specific. Chase.

She was reasonably certain that she didn't *need* Chase—or any other man—to be happy. At the same time she had no idea whether or not that mythical man could make her *happier*.

And for her—more so, she thought, than with most other women—any relationship would be a great risk. She already had one strike against her: She was difficult, if not impossible, to live with. And she wasn't even sure that she could live for more than a few months in one place.

And then there was—

Gypsy's thoughts broke off abruptly as a sound intruded on her consciousness. If she didn't know better...it sounded like hoofbeats. She got to her feet and stepped away from the rock, looking first to the south. Nope—nothing there. Definite hoofbeats, and they were getting louder. She turned toward the north.

The horse was coming up the middle of the narrow beach at a gallop. It was pure white and absolutely gorgeous. The black saddle and bridle stood out starkly, and the metal studs decorating the saddle glinted in the sunlight. And on the horse's back was a man.

In the brief moment granted her for reflection, Gypsy felt distinctly odd. It was as if she'd stepped into the pages of fiction...or into the world of film fantasy.

The rider was dressed all in white—pants, boots, gloves, and shirt. The shirt was the pirate-type, full sleeves caught in tight cuffs at the wrist and unbuttoned halfway down. And the rider wore a mask and a black kerchief affair which hid all his hair. Almost all. A copper gleam showed.

Gypsy took all that in in the space of seconds. And then horse and rider were beside her, and the totally unexpected happened. Gypsy would have sworn that it couldn't be done except by trained stuntpeople on a movie set. Forever afterward, she maintained that it was sheer luck, *not* careful planning, that brought it off.

The horse slid to a halt with beautiful precision, leaving the rider exactly abreast of Gypsy. Then the animal stood like a stone while the rider leaned over and down.

"Wha—" was all she managed to utter.

She was swept up with one strong arm, and ended up sitting across the rider's lap. Through the slits of his mask, darkened eyes gleamed with a hint of green for just a moment. And then he was kissing her.

Ravishment would have been in keeping with the image, she supposed dimly, but the rider didn't use an ounce of force. He didn't have to. He kissed her as if she were a cherished, treasured thing, and Gypsy would have been less than human—and less of a woman—to resist that.

She felt the silk beneath her fingers as her hands came to rest naturally—one touching his chest and the other gripping his upper arm. The dark gold hair at the opening of the shirt teased her thumb, and the hand at her waist burned oddly. The hard thighs beneath her were a potent seduction.

She felt the world spinning away, and released it gladly. Her lips parted, allowing—inviting—his exploring tongue. Fire raced through her veins and scorched her nerve endings. She felt the arm around her waist tighten, and then . . . the devastating kiss ended as abruptly as it had begun.

Gypsy was lowered back to the sand, green eyes glinted at her briefly, and then the horse leaped away.

Dazedly she stared after them. She took a couple of steps back and found her seat by touch alone, sinking down weakly.

The horse and rider had disappeared. Without conscious thought she murmured, "Say, who was that masked man?"

Then she giggled. The giggle exploded into laughter a split second later. Gypsy laughed until her sides ached. Finally she wiped streaming eyes, and tried to gather her scattered wits. In a long and eventful life nothing quite so wild had ever happened to her.

A gleam from the sand at her feet caught her attention, and she bent down to see what it was. She held the object in her hand for a long moment, then her fingers closed around it and she laughed again.

Delighted laughter.

It occurred to Gypsy as she climbed the stairs to her backyard a few minutes later that Chase had somehow found the time to plan that little scene very carefully. Where had he got the horse? And how could he have been certain that she'd take a walk on the beach? The only thing she *didn't* wonder about was the point of it all.

Heroes.

She crossed the yard and entered the house through the kitchen, still giggling. Who would have thought the man would go to such absurd lengths to catch her attention? Why in heaven's name hadn't some woman latched onto him years ago?

Gypsy hastily brushed that last thought away.

There was a gallon of milk in her refrigerator, and no sign of the Mercedes next door. She smiled and went on through the house to her work area. After a moment's deliberation she placed the masked rider's souvenir on the middle shelf of her bookcase. She studied the effect for a moment, nodded to herself, and sat down at the desk.

This time she did accomplish some work. Her notes fell

into place naturally, and she didn't foresee any major problem with the forthcoming book. Aside from pushing Corsair off the desk twice and firmly putting Bucephalus outside after he'd chewed on her ankle for the third time, she worked undisturbed.

"You should lock your doors. Anybody could come in."

It was Chase, back in his jeans and shirt of the morning, and carrying a bag from a hamburger place in town. Before she could say a word, he was going on cheerfully.

"Hamburgers; I didn't feel like cooking. Let's eat." He headed for the kitchen.

Gypsy rose from the desk, smiling to herself. So he was going to play innocent, eh? Well, she could play that game as well. It occurred to her wryly that Chase was rapidly on his way to becoming a fixture around the place ... but she didn't have the heart to send him away.

At least that's what she told herself.

"How do you know I haven't already eaten?" she asked, following him into the kitchen. "It's past two o'clock."

"You've obviously been busy; I guessed that you'd forget about lunch. What's the drink for the day? I forgot to ask this morning."

"Juice. I'm having tomato."

"With hamburgers?"

"With anything. What would you like?"

"The same; I'm always open to new experiences."

Gypsy started to comment on his remark, then thought better of it. She poured the juice while he was setting out their lunch on the bar.

"Will you do something about this dog? I'm going to fall over him and break my neck."

"He's supposed to be outside. Why did you let him back in?"

"I don't argue with a dog that size."

"Right. Out, Bucephalus." She put the dog back out in the yard.

"Salt?" he asked politely, holding up a salt-shaker when they were seated.

"No, thank you." Gypsy tasted the hamburger thoughtfully. "I notice you ordered them both with everything."

"Certainly I did. That way, no one gets offended later."

"Later?"

"When we make mad passionate love together, of course."

"Is that what we're going to do?"

"Eventually."

"Oh."

"You could sound a little more enthusiastic," he reproved gravely.

"Sorry. It's just that I've never heard something like that announced quite so calmly. Or so arbitrarily."

"My military upbringing, I suppose."

"Better learn to rise above it."

"What?"

"Your military upbringing. We've agreed that I don't like to be ordered around."

"I didn't order you around. I just stated a fact."

"That we're going to make mad passionate love together."

"That's right."

"Best laid schemes, and all that."

"Ever hear the one about the dropping of water on stone?"

"Are you trying to say—"

"I'll wear down your resistance eventually."

"I wouldn't be so sure, if I were you."

"But you're not me, Gypsy mine."

"I'm not *yours* either."

"We'll be each other's—how's that?"

"The last thing I need in my life is a man who accuses my cat of leading him up a tree."

"Let's forget about that, shall we?"

"Put down that catsup bottle!" Gypsy giggled in spite of herself. "I'll never forget. That's another of my faults, by the way."

"You seem to have a regular catalog of faults."

"Precisely. Sorry for the disappointment, but I'm sure you can find somebody else to while away your vacation with."

"One of *my* faults, Gypsy mine, is that once I set my mind on something, I never give up."

four

GYPSY THOUGHT ABOUT THAT CALM STATE-
ment during the remainder of the day. As a declaration of intent, she decided, it lacked something. And what it lacked was
a simple *definition* of intent. Just exactly what had he set his
mind on? Her, apparently. But what exactly did he—

Oh, never mind! she told herself irritably. It wasn't going
to do her a bit of good to keep wondering about it.

And in the meantime Chase was making his presence felt.
Not in a big way; he left right after lunch, politely saying that
he didn't want to interrupt her work. But he came back. He
came back four times to be precise—between three and six P.M.
Each time, he stuck his head around the corner of her work
area and apologized solemnly for bothering her. And each time
he asked to borrow something. A cup of sugar, a stick of butter,
two cups of milk, and a bud vase, respectively.

It was the bud vase that piqued Gypsy's curiosity.

"What's he up to, Herman?" she asked her typewriter after
Chase had vanished for the fourth time. Herman didn't deign
to reply. Herman did, however, repeat a word three times. At
least she *blamed* Herman for the mistake.

She was still glowering at Herman ten minutes later, when

Chase returned. He came over to the desk this time, decisively removed the sheet of paper from Herman, and then looked down at Gypsy with a theatrical leer.

"Are you coming willingly, or will I be forced to kidnap you?"

"Coming where?" she asked blankly.

"Into my parlor, of course. My house, if you want to be formal."

"Why should I come to your house?"

"You're invited to dinner."

"Invited or commanded to attend?"

"Invited. Forcefully."

"And if I politely refuse?"

"I'll throw you over my shoulder and kidnap you. Of course, if I'm forced to those lengths, no telling when I'll release you. Much better if you come of your own free will." His voice was grave.

Gypsy sighed mournfully, unable to resist the nonsense. "I suppose I'd better come willingly, then. Do I have your word of honor as a gentleman that I can come home whenever I want?"

He placed a hand on his chest and bowed with a certain flair. "My word of honor as a gentleman."

Since he was still leering, Gypsy looked at him suspiciously, but rose to her feet. "Is this a dress-up party, or come-as-you-are?"

"Definitely come-as-you-are. We'll have a dress-up party later. Better put some shoes on though."

Gypsy silently found some sandals. Corsair was sleeping on one of them and wasn't happy at the disturbance, but she ignored the feline mutters of discontent. Chase was waiting for her in the hall.

He led her out the front door and across the expanse of

green lawn to his house. Since the two properties were separated by only a low hedge, broken in several places, it was a short walk. He opened one of the double doors and ushered her inside.

It was Gypsy's first look inside the house that she had admired so much from the outside. Immediately and wholeheartedly she fell in love with it.

The front doors opened into a huge, open area. The sunken room was carpeted in a deep rust-colored pile, and both the light-colored paneling and the open, beamed ceiling added to the spaciousness. The furniture—a pit grouping and various tables—was modern. There were plump cushions in a deep ivory color, and colorful throw pillows for a pleasant contrast. A combination bookshelf and entertainment center ran along one wall, containing innumerable books, an extensive stereo system, and a large-screen television set.

If the remainder of the house looked like this...Gypsy took a deep breath, dimly aware of Chase's gaze on her. "Did you do the decorating?" she asked finally.

"All the way. Would you like the nickel tour?"

"Please."

The remainder of the house looked *better*. There were three bedrooms, two baths, a large study, a formal dining room in an Oriental motif, a combination kitchen and breakfast nook that Julia Child would have killed for, and a Jacuzzi.

The Jacuzzi occupied a place in half of the redwood deck in back, which stretched from the glass doors opening into the breakfast nook to the identical glass doors opening into the master bedroom. The deck was enclosed by glass around the Jacuzzi, and houseplants abounded, giving the illusion of a jungle scene.

Gypsy stared around her for a moment and sought for a

safe topic. "I thought you weren't good with plants," she managed finally.

"I'm not. But for some reason, houseplants do well for me. This concludes the nickel tour, ma'am. Now, if you'll come back to the dining room with me, dinner will be served."

She preceded him silently, speaking only when they'd reached the dining room. Gazing at the table laid out formally and intimately for two, she murmured, "Now I know why you wanted the bud vase."

Chase seated her ceremoniously and in grand silence, then disappeared into the kitchen.

Gypsy stared after him for a moment, then looked back at the bud vase. After a moment she reached out and gently touched the single peach blossom it contained. Idly she wondered why he'd chosen that particular flower. Did it have some special meaning? She didn't know.

What she *did* know was that, like a person going down for the third time in a deep river, there was little hope of saving her now.

Gypsy had never in her life had pheasant under glass, vichyssoise, or anything else Chase served her that night. She enjoyed it all, but the picture they must have presented sitting at the formal table wearing jeans and casual tops caused her to giggle from time to time.

Or maybe the giggles were caused by Chase's "juice surprise."

"What is this?"

"Juice, I told you. Different kinds."

"Chase, there's more in this than juice."

"So I stretched a point a little. So what?"

"You're disrupting the habit of a lifetime, that's so what."

"It's time to broaden your horizons."

"You sound like a travel ad."

"Sorry."

"This is very good, you know."

"I'm glad you like it. It's—"

"No, don't tell me what it is," she warned hastily.

"Why not?"

"Because if it's snails, I don't want to know about it."

"It isn't snails."

"Good. Don't tell me what it *is*."

"Whatever madam desires. Would madam like more— uh—juice?"

"Chase, are you trying to get me drunk?"

He looked scandalized. "How you could ever suspect—"

"Easily," she interrupted, peering at him owlishly.

"A *baby* has more kick than this stuff," he maintained staunchly.

"Strong baby. Shall I sit here in royal detachment while you clear the table? I'll help if you like, but I hope your china's insured."

"You stay put. I'll clear the table and bring in dessert." He began to do so efficiently.

"What's for dessert?"

"Baked Alaska."

"I'll take a wild guess," she said drily, "that you're a gourmet cook."

"Something like that."

"So tell me, master chef, to what do I owe the honor?"

"Honor?" He placed a delicious-looking dessert in front of her.

"Of having you cook for me."

"I'm trying to seduce you, of course."

Gypsy was vaguely glad that she'd swallowed the first bite before he answered her question. Otherwise, she'd have choked. "I see." She touched her napkin delicately to her lips— mainly to hide the fact that they were twitching. "The way to a woman's heart, and all that?"

Very seriously he responded, "Well, I thought that either the food would get you . . . or the juice would."

She stared at his deadpan expression. How *could* the man look so ridiculously serious? After a moment she began eating again. "I'll say this for you—the approach is certainly original. I don't think I've ever heard the brutal truth used to such good effect."

"Not *brutal*!" he protested, wounded.

She gave him a look.

Chase sighed sadly. "It isn't working, is it?"

"No." She didn't mince words. She also didn't tell him just how well his strategy was working. His straightforward approach was certainly startling, novel in her experience, and if she didn't get out of his house very quickly, she was going to make a total fool of herself.

"Aren't you tired of a predictable life?" he asked persuasively. "Wouldn't you like change, excitement, adventure?"

"Sounds like you're inviting me on a safari," she observed, eyes firmly on her dessert.

Chase gave up—for the moment, at least. Dessert was finished in silence, and then he sent her into the living room with her juice. Gypsy didn't protest, and she didn't try to leave. The juice was beginning to have the inevitable effect on her.

But the inevitable effect on Gypsy was a bit different from what Chase had probably hoped for. Except that she didn't believe Chase had hoped for seduction at all. She had the definite feeling that he'd wanted to keep her off-balance more than anything else. However, visions of seduction or whatever notwithstanding, Chase would probably get more than he bargained for.

The juice really didn't have much of a kick. But then...it didn't take much for Gypsy. It didn't take much, that is, to release the reckless mischief she normally kept tightly reined.

She was going to teach him a lession, Gypsy decided.

When Chase came into the living room after clearing up in the kitchen, Gypsy was prowling the room like a caged tigress. The empty juice glass had been placed neatly in the center of the chrome and glass coffee table.

"Gypsy?"

She whirled around and flung herself into his arms. "I thought you said that we were going to make mad passionate love together?" she questioned throatily, gazing up into startled jade eyes.

Chase had automatically caught her, and now stared down at her as though he'd caught a bundle of dynamite with a lighted fuse. "I did say that, didn't I?" he mumbled.

"Yes. So what are we waiting for?"

"Sobriety," he answered involuntarily.

Gypsy fiercely disentangled herself and stepped back, regaining her balance by sheer luck. "Did you or did you not intend to get me drunk and take advantage of me?" she demanded accusingly.

"Yes—no! Dammit, don't put words in my mouth!"

"You're rejecting me!" she announced in a hurt tone, doing a sudden and bewildering about-face.

"*No*, I'm not rejecting you! Gypsy—"

"Don't...you...touch...me!" she warned awfully when he stepped toward her. "You had your chance, buster, and you blew it!"

For a long moment Chase looked about as bewildered as a man could look. Then the bewilderment slowly cleared, and a whimsical expression replaced it. "Do you like playing with fire, Gypsy mine?"

Damn, but he's quick! she thought wryly. Deciding that there was no graceful way out of the situation, she merely shrugged with a faint smile.

"I could read a great deal into that shrug," he told her.

"Don't imagine things. Thank you for the excellent dinner, master chef, and I think I'd better be going now."

"You're welcome, and I'll walk you to your door."

His easy acceptance bothered Gypsy for some reason. It might have had something to do with the unexplained gleam in his jade eyes. Or it might have had something to do with the fact that he'd twice announced his intention of attempting to seduce her today—and no attempt had yet been made.

The walk across to her front door was accomplished in silence, with Gypsy growing more nervous with every step. Along with the nervousness was a sudden, heart-pounding awareness of the man at her side, and she realized dimly that every muscle in her body was tense.

It was neither dark nor light outside; it was that odd twilight hour. Daylight was colors, darkness was stark black and white, but twilight was elusive shades of gray.

When they reached the front porch, Chase caught her arm and turned her to face him. Gypsy looked up at him instinctively, wary and uneasy. Her heart had recaptured its captive-beast rhythm, and she felt suddenly adrift in a dangerous and unpredictable sea.

"May I kiss you good night?" he asked softly, his hands coming to rest on her shoulders.

Gypsy wanted to say no, sharply and without mincing words. But she wasn't very surprised to find herself nodding silently.

His hands lifted to cup her face, his head bending until

their lips touched with the lightness of a sigh. There was no pressure, no demand. Just warmth and sweetness, and a gentleness that was incredibly moving.

Gypsy felt herself relaxing, felt her body mold itself bonelessly to his. Her arms moved of their own volition to slide around his waist even as she became aware of his hands moving slowly down her back.

If this was seduction, she thought dimly, then why on earth was she fighting it? It was a drugging, insidious thing, sapping her willpower and causing her to forget why she should have been protesting.

A tremor like the soft flutter of a butterfly's wings began somewhere deep inside her body. It spread outward slowly, growing in strength, until she felt that her whole body was shaking with it.

When Chase finally drew away, Gypsy had the disturbing impression that she had lost something. She didn't know what it was. But the tremor was still there, and she was having trouble breathing.

The man was a warlock, she thought.

"Good night, Gypsy mine," he murmured huskily, reaching over to open the door for her.

Gypsy forced her arms to release him. "Good night," she managed weakly, sliding past him to enter the house. She hesitated for a moment, glancing back over her shoulder at him, then softly closed the door.

She went into the den and sat down on the couch, curling up in one corner and staring at the blank television screen. For a long time she sat without moving. Corsair came to sit beside her, his rough purr like the rumble of a small engine. Gypsy stroked him absently. Bucephalus came and lay down on the carpet by the couch.

Gypsy smiled wryly. "What are you two trying to do—

comfort me?" she asked. A canine tail thumped the floor, and feline eyes blinked at her. "Thanks, guys, but I think it's beyond your power."

She sat for a while longer, listening to silence and the whispering voices of reason. But it was the gentle murmurs of desire that tormented her. She finally got up and went to take a long hot bath, hoping that the steam would carry away her problems.

It didn't.

She let Corsair and Bucephalus outside for a few minutes, then called them back in and latched the pet door. She wandered around downstairs for a while, until disgust with her own restlessness drove her to bed. It was midnight by the time she crawled between the sheets, and Gypsy lay there for a while and stared at the ceiling. She finally reached and turned out the lamp on her nightstand, absently moving Corsair off her foot and patting Bucephalus where he lay beside the bed.

Ten minutes later the phone rang. She picked up the receiver without bothering to turn the lamp back on, wondering who could be calling her at that hour. "Hello?"

"Will you dream about me tonight?" a deep, muffled masculine voice asked softly.

Gypsy's first impulse was to hang up. The last thing she needed tonight was a semi-obscene phone caller. But something about that voice nagged at her. It *could* be Chase, she decided finally. Besides, who *else* could it possibly be? So why not play along?

"Of course, I will," she murmured seductively.

"Sweet dreams?"

"As sweet as honey."

"I could make them even sweeter," he drawled.

"Promises, promises."

"Just give me the chance."

"A man should always . . . make his own opportunities."

"And what should a woman do?"

"She waits."

"An old-fashioned lady, I see."

"In . . . some ways." Gypsy was thoroughly enjoying the suggestive conversation.

He chuckled softly. "Sweet dreams . . ."

Gypsy listened bemusedly to the dial tone for a moment, then cradled the receiver gently. " 'Curiouser and curiouser,' " she murmured to herself. She smiled into the darkness for a while.

Then she fell asleep.

Gypsy slept six hours—no more, no less. It was a peculiarly exact habit in a quite definitely inexact person. But apparently her biological clock was set for precisely six hours of sleep and not a second more. And during those six hours, Armageddon could have occurred without disturbing Gypsy.

She dressed and went through her morning routine. She fed the animals and herself, unlatched the pet door, and checked the weather (rainy). Sunday was "dealer's choice" when it came to the day's drink. She decided on iced tea and made a pitcherful.

Since her parents were coming to visit, she unlocked the front door—heaven only knew what she'd be doing by the time they arrived, so they usually just walked right in.

Then she carried a glass of tea to her desk, put a sheet of paper into Herman, and got down to work.

The morning advanced steadily as she worked. The rain stopped and the sun came out. Her canine and feline companions checked on progress from time to time and then disappeared. Gypsy refilled her glass once.

With utter concentration and not a little willpower, she'd

managed to put Chase out of her mind while she worked. And she was glad about that; not even friendship would be possible between them if thoughts of him disrupted her work, and Gypsy knew it. As impossible as she was to live with while she was writing, she was even worse when something prevented her from writing.

Around ten A.M. she heard the sound of a car in her driveway, but continued to work without a pause. If it was her parents, they'd come inside; anyone else would knock.

A few moments later her father came in. He was a tall man, slender and distinguished. His hair was black, save for wings of silver framing his lean face. Mild blue eyes gazed peacefully out from beneath straight brows. And lines of struggle coexisted peacefully with lines of humor on his face.

An interesting face for any artist—and Gypsy's mother had painted it more than once.

Gypsy lifted an absent cheek for his kiss. "Hi, Poppy," she said vaguely.

"Hello, darling." Her father saluted the cheek, and then rested his hip against the corner of her desk. Conversationally he added, "There's a man up a tree in your front yard."

"Oh?" She briskly corrected a misspelled word. "That's Chase."

"An admirer, darling?"

"Neighbor." Gypsy finished a paragraph and briefly debated over the next one before beginning to type again. "Did you ask him why he was in the tree?"

"I didn't want to pry," her sire murmured.

Gypsy acknowledged the gentle remark with a faint twinkle as she pulled the completed page from Herman. "I suppose Corsair stole his car keys again," she explained cheerfully.

Allen Taylor didn't even blink. "When did Corsair start stealing keys?"

"Yesterday. Where's Mother?"

"Helping Chase, I assume. She went to see if he needed help."

"Oh. Half a minute, Poppy; let me finish this page and I'll be through for the day." Gypsy was trying desperately not to think about Chase's first meeting with her mother. But . . . oh, she wished she could be a butterfly poised on a flower out there. . . .

Just as she was pulling the last sheet out of Herman, her father spoke again. He'd wandered over to her bookcase, and now held the masked rider's souvenir in his hand.

"What's this?"

"What does it look like? It's a silver bullet obviously."

"Silver plated," her father corrected gravely.

"It's the thought that counts," Gypsy reproved.

"Oh. Where did you get it?"

"That's obvious too."

"I see." He placed the souvenir back on the shelf.

Gypsy's father was very good at not asking nosy questions.

They had just stepped into the living room when her mother and Chase came inside. And Chase looked so utterly bemused and fascinated that Gypsy wanted to burst out laughing.

Many mothers and daughters look like sisters; Gypsy and her mother looked like twins. The same height, roughly the same weight, the same short black curls and wide gray eyes. They were even dressed similarly in jeans and blue knit pullovers. It was an odd thing, but even if they were in different parts of the country, nine times out of ten Gypsy and her mother would wear at least the same colors on any given day.

Rebecca Taylor, née Thorn, looked eighteen. The only thing that set her apart from her daughter in looks was a single silver curl at her left temple. Her voice was different, slower and richer with age, but her conversation made Gypsy's sound positively rational by comparison. And she never missed a thing.

"Hi, Mother." Gypsy hugged her mother briefly. "I see you've met Chase."

"Yes. Gypsy, you need to talk to Corsair. Stealing keys is a very irritating habit."

"I will, Mother." Gypsy swallowed a laugh as she glanced at Chase. "Poppy—Chase Mitchell. Chase, my father, Allen Taylor."

Still bemused, Chase nearly forgot to shake hands.

It was a fun day. Gypsy's parents had the knack of setting anyone at ease immediately, and they both obviously liked Chase. As for Chase, he'd apparently decided to go with the tide. Although he still tended to blink whenever he looked at Rebecca—particularly whenever she and Gypsy were standing near each other—he was quickly back on balance again.

Rebecca commandeered the kitchen to cook lunch, towing Chase along behind her when Gypsy helpfully mentioned his culinary skill. Allen and Gypsy were almost immediately ordered to make a trip to the store when the cupboard was found to be bare. Corsair and Bucephalus got into the act, mainly by being constantly chased from the kitchen by Rebecca.

When Gypsy looked back on the day, she remembered snippets of conversations, frozen stills from the action.

"Why didn't you tell me that your mother was also your twin? I made a total fool of myself in that tree!"

"There are no fools in my mother's orbit—just interesting people."

"I wish I could believe that."

"Believe it. My mother *expects* to find strange men in trees."

"A sane man would run like a thief in the night."

"Are you sane?"

"Apparently not."

"He's a redhead."

"Yes, Mother."

"Temper?"

"So far, no. But give him time; I only met him Friday."

"I like his eyes. Would he sit for me?"

"Like a shot, I imagine. He likes your work."

"He cooks well."

"Yes, Mother. Military schools."

"Really? That explains it."

"Explains what?"

"He stands and moves like a soldier. Precise."

"I haven't noticed."

"Of course not, darling."

"Mother. . . ."

"I like your Chase, darling."

"He's not mine, Poppy."

"Better tell him that."

"I have. The man's deaf."

"The man has good taste."

"You're prejudiced."

"Slightly. Not that it matters."

"Gypsy, Corsair's sitting in the sink."

"Check his water dish, Mother."

"Chase, why do you keep letting Bucephalus inside?"

"Sorry, Rebecca, but he knocks."

"Do you let in every salesperson who knocks?"

"Only the ones with good legs."

"Chauvinist."

"Dyed-in-the-wool."

"Chase, what were you talking to Mother about? You look strange."

"I feel strange. She just told me the story of how Allen managed to catch her. No wonder you wouldn't tell me."

"Well, it's their story. Don't take it too much to heart, by the way."

"You mean, don't let it give me ideas?"

"Something like that."

"I wouldn't dare. You look like her, but you're not Rebecca. You'd come after me with a gun."

"I'm glad you realize that."

"Military schools don't produce idiots."

By the time Gypsy tumbled into bed that night, she was still laughing softly. The little party had broken up only an hour before, with Chase saying good night along with Rebecca and Allen.

Gypsy pushed Corsair off her foot and turned off the lamp, settling down to sleep.

The phone rang. Gypsy reached for it automatically. "Hello?"

"Did you dream about me last night?"

She smiled into the darkness. "I told you I would."

"Reality's better than dreams."

"Oh, really?"

"I could show you."

"I don't know who you are," she told him serenely.

"I could show you that too."

"It's better this way. Ships passing in the night, unseen."

"But lovers have to meet."

"It would destroy the mystery."

"'But love is such a mystery,'" he quoted softly.

Gypsy found herself automatically quoting the last line of the verse. "And would you be 'such a constant lover'?"

"Eternally, love. Eternally. Sleep well."

Gypsy cradled the receiver slowly, gently. She plumped up her pillow and lay back, thinking whimsical thoughts. About a white horse and a masked rider. About an inept gardener and a marvelous cook. About a late-night caller who quoted obscure poetry and called her love.

About a lover.

---

five

THE OLD SAYING ABOUT TIME PASSING ON winged feet had never meant anything to Gypsy until that next week. The days flew by.

Chase was in, out, and around. Going up the tree after Corsair became a morning ritual; no matter where Chase hid his keys (even under his pillow one night, he said), the cat always found them. Chase began to talk darkly about felines murdered in the night.

He didn't interfere unduly with Gypsy's work, although he insisted on making sure that she ate at regular intervals. So he either cooked, carted in a bag of "take-out" something, or took her out somewhere. He kept her laughing, continued his talk of seduction . . . and never once tried to follow through.

He kissed her occasionally, but Gypsy was never quite sure what kind of kiss it would be or where it would land. A gentle kiss on her forehead, a playful kiss on her nose . . . or a hungry kiss that left her lips throbbing and her knees weak.

Always prone to talk to herself, Gypsy was fast approaching the point of answering herself as well.

And Chase was obviously having problems of his own. He stalked in late Tuesday afternoon, tightly reining the first sign of temper Gypsy had ever seen in him. With what looked like heroic patience he announced, "There's a white cat in my bedroom closet that has chosen to have three kittens in a box containing my new dinner jacket."

Looking up from the page she'd been proofing, Gypsy blinked at him in bewilderment. "Well, what do you want me to do about it?" she asked reasonably.

Chase hung on to control. "Corsair," he explained through gritted teeth, "is standing guard at the closet door, and won't let me near them."

Frowning, Gypsy said reproachfully, "You aren't supposed to disturb newborn kittens."

Chase looked toward the heavens imploringly. Gypsy went on in a puzzled voice. "Why wasn't your dinner jacket hanging up? It should have been, you know."

"I didn't get the chance to hang it up. It was delivered yesterday; I just checked to make sure it was my order and left the open box in the bottom of the closet." He stared at her. "I thought you only had one cat."

"I do. She must be Corsair's girlfriend. I knew he had one around here, but I've never seen her."

"Couldn't we transfer the family over here?"

"With Bucephalus around? She'd only move them back, Chase. Cats are particular."

"Would you like me to tell you how much her nest is worth?" Chase asked politely.

Gypsy wasn't listening. "Chase, does she have blue eyes?"

He blinked. "I don't know. Corsair won't let me close enough to turn on the closet light, and it's dim in there. Why?"

"Well, if she's solid white and has blue eyes, she's probably deaf. I'll bet that's why Corsair's protecting her."

"Deaf?"

"It's fairly common. Some kind of genetic defect, I think."

He stared at her.

"There's cat food in the kitchen," Gypsy murmured, trying not to laugh. "Help yourself."

"Gee, thanks." He left.

Chase apparently became accustomed to his new pets. He gave Gypsy periodic reports and complained of being unable to sleep at night because of squeaks and rustles in his closet. He also made a sort of peace with Corsair, since it was impossible to get to his closet through a hostile cat. But the morning key-ritual continued.

And Gypsy's "night lover" continued to call. More obscure poems were quoted, and the conversations became more and more suggestive. She looked forward to the telephone calls each night and found that she was sleeping better than ever before. The calls were...a nice way to end the day, Gypsy thought.

Whenever he thought she'd been working too hard, Chase pulled Gypsy away from her typewriter. For a meal. For a walk on the beach. She didn't protest because she wasn't far enough into her story to become obsessed by it. But she knew that, sooner or later, Chase would discover a witch with a capital B sitting at the desk where his laughing companion had sat just the day before. She didn't look forward to that day.

In the meantime he kept coming up with things for them to do together. On Thursday afternoon he announced his latest plan.

"It's a masquerade party. In Portland."

"Are you serious? I thought those things went out with hoop skirts."

"I'm serious. It's for charity. So be a good girl and rent a costume tomorrow."

"I'm without a car, remember."

"I'll loan you mine."

"Like to live dangerously, don't you?"

"Always."

Gypsy reflected. "A masquerade. What kind of costume should I get? Or does it matter?"

"It matters. Old West."

"It'd serve you right if I went dressed as Calamity Jane."

"Don't do that. Your gun and my sword would get all tangled up when we dance."

"Your what?"

"Sword."

"What Old West character wore a sword?"

"Wait and see."

"Beast. Just for that, I'll come as a saloon girl."

"With feathers?"

"And sequins."

"Oh, good."

"You'll have to fight the other cowboys off me with a stick," she warned him gravely.

"I'll use my sword. I've always wanted to challenge somebody to a duel."

"Murder?"

"An affair of honor," he corrected nobly.

"Only if he's bigger than you. Otherwise it's murder. And you're talking to someone who knows murder."

Chase perched on the corner of her desk, obviously willing to stay and talk for a while. "So tell me, what's the perfect murder weapon?"

"No such animal." She chewed on a knuckle thoughtfully, her chair leaning backward until it was in imminent danger of going over. "I've always wanted to use the jawbone of an ass as a murder weapon. Interesting, huh?"

"I think that's been done."

"Not recently."

"You'd know better than me."

"Naturally."

"What's your plot in this book?"

"I don't talk about them until they're finished."

"That's cruel. You know I'm a mystery buff."

"No exceptions."

"Orders from the muse?"

"I suppose."

"I'll rig a Chinese water torture."

"Go feed your cats."

"That's 'the unkindest cut of all.' "

Gypsy drove Chase's car—*very* carefully—into Portland on Friday to get a costume. She toyed with the idea of finding the briefest saloon-girl costume possible, but discarded the notion.

She wanted something else.

She found the something else in the first costume-rental shop listed in the Yellow Pages. So far, Chase had seen her in nothing but shorts or jeans, and she wanted to wear something feminine. And what could be more feminine than a long dress with a hoop skirt?

Gypsy didn't question her desire to look feminine. She wasn't questioning anything these days. And that was a bad sign. But she didn't want to question *that* either.

The boxes were loaded into the trunk of the Mercedes, and Gypsy left the rental shop. She ran a few errands in Portland, and then headed back toward the coast. It was late afternoon when she arrived back home.

She parked Chase's car in his driveway and collected the boxes from the trunk, absently putting the keys in the pocket of her jeans. Chase was nowhere to be seen; she shrugged, then carried the boxes across to her house.

She hung the costume in her bedroom, put away the few odds and ends she'd bought, and then settled down in the living room with the book of poetry she'd found in a used bookstore. Obscure poems and poets. Her "night lover" had her on her mettle, and she wanted to refresh her memory. She ended up going through two more books from her shelves, discovering a treasure-trove in Donne and Shakespeare.

"What *are* you doing?"

"Reading poetry. You did say that the masquerade is tomorrow night, didn't you?" She looked up from her cross-legged position on the floor to peer at Chase over the tops of her study glasses.

"Tomorrow night it is." He slid his hands into the pockets of his jeans and leaned against the bookcase, gazing down at her with a smile that looked as if it were trying hard to hide. "Do your murderers read poetry to their victims at the eleventh hour?" he asked gravely.

Gypsy pushed the glasses back up her nose. "Are you kidding?" She narrowed her eyes expressively. "My murderers stalk their victims on cloven hooves."

"Mmm. Then why are you reading poetry?"

"I like poetry, peasant."

"I beg your pardon, I'm sure."

Gypsy pulled off the glasses and waved them magnanimously. "You're forgiven."

"Thank you. There's another pair on top of your head."

"What?"

"Another pair of glasses."

That explained his trying-not-to-smile expression, Gypsy thought. She pulled off the second pair and set them absently on the bottom shelf of the bookcase.

"Does it take two pairs for you to read poetry?" he asked politely.

"Never mind."

He went on conversationally. "I've counted eight pairs of glasses scattered throughout this house. All in strange places. Like the pair I found in the refrigerator yesterday."

"I wonder why I put them in there?" Gypsy murmured, more to herself than to him.

"I haven't the faintest idea, and I don't think I want to know."

"Smart man."

"But what I *would* like to know"—he pointed at the corner of her desk, where a new acquisition was sitting—"is why you got *that* during your trip into Portland."

That was a statue of an eleven-inch-tall Buddha with a clock in its stomach. A broken clock.

Gypsy ran her fingers through her black curls and gave him a harassed look. "I asked myself that. *What do you want with a Buddha with a clock in his tummy?* No answer. I must have been possessed. There was a garage sale, and somehow or other . . . Anyway I paid five bucks for it." She shook her head darkly.

Chase reached down and pulled her to her feet. He removed the glasses from her hand and tossed them lightly onto the desk. Then he caught her in a tight bear hug. "Gypsy," he said whimsically, "I can't tell you what a delight you are to me."

She pulled back far enough to look up at him blankly. "Because I bought a Buddha?"

He laughed. "No, because you're you. I thought we'd cook out tonight; how do you like your steaks?"

"Cooked." Gypsy made no effort to disentangle herself from his embrace.

"There goes that sharp tongue again, Gypsy mine. You shouldn't sass your elders; you're liable to get paddled."

"Are you my elder? I didn't know."

"I'm thirty-two, brat."

"Methuselah."

He swatted her jean-clad bottom lightly. "How do you like your steak?"

"Well done. And stop hitting me!"

"It'll teach you not to sass me." Chase was unrepentant.

"I'll sic Bucephalus on you!" she threatened.

"I've been slipping him snacks for days now; that dog loves me like a brother."

Gypsy pushed against his chest, curiously pleased when she couldn't budge him. "Leave! People over thirty can't be trusted."

"That slogan went out of style years ago."

"Only because the people saying it reached thirty."

"Are you sassing me again?" he demanded.

"For all I'm worth."

He bent his head and kissed her suddenly. But it wasn't a gentle kiss. It was demanding, probing, possessive, and just short of violent. He kissed her as though he wanted—needed—to brand her as his for all time. The kiss lasted for brief seconds only, but Gypsy felt as though every nerve in her body had been lanced with sheer electricity.

Chase stared down at her. "Are you through sassing?" he asked hoarsely.

Gypsy nodded mutely, wondering dimly when she was going to start breathing again.

"Good." He lowered her gently to her former position on the floor. "You finish reading your poetry. I'll yell when I get the grill going."

She nodded again, and watched him turn away. When he'd gone, she gazed blindly down until a line of Donne's jumped out at her from the open book before her on the carpet. "Take me to you, imprison me. . . ."

Why did it suddenly make her ache inside?

He called again that night, and their conversation took a turning point. No longer seductively suggestive, it was filled with gentle whimsy.

It was somehow easier to open up to a husky voice on the telephone, easier to admit to and show vulnerability. Alone in her bedroom, lying in the darkness, she could be the sensitive woman who mourned the loss of heroes. . . .

"I've missed you," he breathed softly. "The sound of your voice haunts me, and yet I can't hear enough of it."

"You don't know me," she murmured in reply.

"'Twice or thrice had I loved thee, before I knew thy face or name,'" he quoted tenderly.

Gypsy smiled into the darkness. He'd read Donne as well. "You don't know me," she repeated.

"Then tell me what I should know."

"I don't . . ." Her voice trailed away.

"Do you love rainbows?" he asked gently.

She smiled. "Yes."

"And the sound of rain in the morning?"

"Yes."

"Do you wish on stars?"

"I do now," she whispered, tears springing to her eyes.

"Then I know all that I should know," he said.

"Do you believe in unicorns?" she asked him.

"I do now," he replied.

"And life on other worlds?"

"Yes."

"And . . . heroes?"

"And heroes."

"I don't think you're real," she told him with a shaky laugh.

"I'm real, my love. Flesh and bone, heart and mind . . . and soul. And my soul aches for you."

Gypsy felt her heart stop for a moment and then pound on. What could she say to that? What could she possibly say?

But he didn't expect a response.

"Sleep well, my love. And dream of me."

She did.

It took Gypsy two hours to get into her costume late the next afternoon. She wasn't really accustomed to dresses of any kind, and even less to dresses fastened with tiny hooks and eyes, and beneath which were rather puzzling undergarments.

She had decided to stretch a point with the costume; otherwise, she'd have had to wear something like calico if she wanted to be authentic. And since she had a hunch about Chase's costume, she felt free to stretch a point. Besides—*Old West* covered a lot of territory.

Gypsy giggled over the shiftlike garment and the frilly bloomers, but the corset presented a problem. She had a small waist, but she'd been astonished at how much smaller it appeared after the assistant at the costume shop had laced her up in the corset. Being Gypsy, she'd had the corset included without a single thought as to who would lace her up at home.

She finally put it on backward, laced it up, and then spent a few comical moments holding her breath and tugging. With the strings finally tied in a fierce knot, she collapsed on her bed, flushed and breathless.

No wonder the pictures of women in that era always looked so stiff, she thought. And no wonder genteel ladies were constantly swooning.

But once the dress was on, Gypsy understood why women had sacrificed comfort for the dictates of fashion.

The dress was black silk, and it rustled softly whenever she moved. Worn over a wide hoop—Gypsy had giggled for ten minutes after seeing herself in shift, bloomers, corset, and hoop—it was low-cut and off-the-shoulder. The corset nipped in her waist to a tiny span, and lifted her breasts until it seemed that a deep breath would get her arrested. She wasn't worried though; she could barely breathe anyway.

The dress was wicked for any era, and instantly branded her a scarlet woman in the era it pretended to belong to. The colorful splash of fake emeralds at her throat and dangling from her ears, however, loudly announced that she—or rather, her character—possessed wealth, and wealth could open doors even for scarlet women.

Gypsy had worked long and hard with her makeup, but was still faintly surprised to find that she had actually achieved a seductive look. The emeralds lent her gray eyes a green gleam, and the careful shading she'd done gave them a catlike slant. And the scrap of black silk that would serve as a mask only emphasized the seductive look.

"I look like a hussy," she told Corsair, who was sitting companionably at the foot of her bed, watching her. He'd stopped constantly guarding his family since Chase had proved to be reasonable.

"Is this what's called playing with fire, cat?" she asked him wryly.

Corsair yawned.

"Don't let me keep you awake," she begged politely.

By the time Chase knocked on the front door, Gypsy had donned the floor-length cloak and fastened it securely to hide the low neckline of her dress. Not that she was nervous about the cleavage, but there was no need to startle the man right off the bat, she decided mischievously.

Gypsy opened the door and gazed silently from the black-booted heels to the top of a Spanish-style hat. Her hunch had been right on target: He was dressed as Zorro.

"Are you going to run around tonight slashing *Z*'s in the woodwork?" she asked him solemnly.

"Only if someone maligns your honor," he replied with equal solemnity and a deep bow.

She started to warn him that just about anyone would malign her honor once they got a good look at her dress, but decided to await developments.

"Black suits you," he noted critically, head to one side as he studied her masked face. "As a matter of fact, you look beautiful. Why are your eyes green?"

Gypsy flicked a dangling earring with one finger. "It's the emeralds. And thank you."

"You're welcome. It's a long drive to Portland, so we'd better get started. Just as soon as you tell me where you left my car keys."

"Car keys. . . ."

It took Gypsy half an hour to locate the keys; she'd left them in the pocket of her jeans and had forgotten to return them to Chase. He waited patiently while she searched, but every time she passed him, he fingered the hilt of his sword and gave her a threatening look.

The sixty-some-odd-mile journey to Portland took less than an hour.

"Do you know what the speed limit is?"

"Of course, I know."

"No wonder you killed Daisy."

"Funny. Besides, it's this damn sword; it keeps stabbing me in the foot."

"You're supposed to be wearing it on your *left* hip."

"Why?"

"You're right-handed."

"Oh. Remind me to change it around when we get there."

"Right. Are you sure you'll be able to dance in that thing?"

"Of course I will." There was a pause. "The couples dancing near us'll have to watch their step though."

The masquerade was being held in a huge recreation center on the outskirts of Portland. The charity involved was one for needy children. From the looks of the size of the crowd that had turned out, whatever goal had been set for this fundraising event, it had been reached easily. Costumes were varied and ranged from the sublime to the ridiculous. Royalty from the Court of St. James vied with those of other European countries, and clashed with various fuzzy creatures from recent movies and assorted fairy-tale and nursery-rhyme characters. There was even one giant of a man who was dressed as Paul Bunyan, and kept wandering around asking if anybody'd seen his ox.

Refreshments had been set out along one wall, and the buzz and laughter of a hundred conversations filled the tremendous room. A small band of musicians tuned their instruments screechily in one corner.

Gypsy winced at a particularly discordant clash as Chase, standing behind her, removed her cloak and handed it over to the cloakroom attendant. "Are we supposed to be able to dance to that?" she asked wryly, turning to face him.

Chase's mouth fell open.

Suddenly remembering her dress, Gypsy fought to hide her smile. "Didn't know I was so well blessed, did you?" she asked him gravely.

His eyes lifted to her face, and he laughed. "Gypsy, you say the damnedest things!"

"What's a little bluntness between friends?"

"Oh, I wholeheartedly approve. Of the bluntness—and the dress. Shall we check out the refreshments?"

"Yes. I'm dying of thirst, but I won't be able to eat anything."

"Why not?" He took her arm and began leading her toward the refreshments.

"I'll tell you about it someday." Her voice was rueful.

He looked at her curiously. "Now you've got me wondering."

Gypsy thought of her afternoon's struggle, and her lips twitched. "Never mind."

"Gypsy . . ."

"Hang onto your sword, will you? You just stabbed that Louis in the shin."

"I wondered why he was glaring at me." Chase handed her a cup of punch with his free hand. "And don't try to weasel out of it; why can't you eat something?"

Gypsy glanced furtively around to make sure no one was close enough to overhear. "It's my corset," she told him in a stage whisper.

"Your what?"

"My corset. I can barely breathe, much less eat." Gypsy thoroughly enjoyed the struggle going on on his face.

After a moment he set his own cup of punch on the table, released his death grip on the hilt of his sword, and solemnly measured the span of her waist with both hands. "Yep. It's definitely smaller."

"Looks great to me," announced a strange masculine voice over Chase's left shoulder.

Chase turned suddenly, stabbing another Louis (or was it the same one?) in the shin as he greeted the tall man who'd come up behind him. "Jake, the last I heard, you were building something in Texas."

"Surprise! I finished building it."

Introduced to Jake Thomas a moment later, Gypsy's first impression was that Chase's builder friend was an absolute nut.

He was big and rawboned, his size and obviously cheerful personality perfectly suited to his lumberjack costume. It took Gypsy only a moment to realize that he was the Paul Bunyan in search of his ox.

"You're the one who writes those mysteries Chase is always raving about, aren't you?" Jake asked Gypsy after the introduction.

Gypsy looked up at Chase in surprise, only to find him gazing studiously into space. "Well, I write mysteries," she answered Jake.

"You don't look it," Jake told her gravely, and at her expressive grimace, added, "You've heard that before, I take it?"

"Innumerable times."

A black cat wandered up just then, holding on to her long tail to avoid having it stepped on. She was about Gypsy's size, with a petite figure and blond hair escaping from beneath her ear cap. And she had large blue eyes that looked dumb but were obviously lying.

"Jake, how dare you leave me in the clutches of that King George? He kept bumping me with his stomach and stepping on my tail."

Laughing, Jake introduced Gypsy to his fiancée, Sarah Foxx. Chase she obviously knew, since she stood on tiptoe to kiss his cheek lightly.

"You write mysteries?" Sarah asked in surprise, studying Gypsy. "You—"

"—don't look like it," the other three chorused.

"I seem to be redundant," Sarah observed wryly.

"That's all right," Gypsy told her. "I'm getting used to it."

"I'll bet." Sarah gave her a friendly grin. "That's the price you and I pay for looking as if we can't string two words together."

Gypsy looked interested. "What do you do?"

"I'm a psychologist."

Gypsy felt an immediate affinity for the other woman. "Isn't it terrible? That nature played this awful trick and made us look dumb, I mean?"

"Yes, but it has its advantages. People are always bending over backward to do things for us because we look so help-less."

"There is that," Gypsy agreed thoughtfully.

Chase sighed in manful long-suffering. "Don't you two start talking about the failings of mankind, or Jake and I won't get to dance."

Sarah looked solemnly at him and said, totally deadpan, "You and Jake can dance if you like. It might look a little odd, but if *you* don't mind . . ."

"Cute, that's cute." Chase took a giggling Gypsy firmly by the arm. "Dance with me, Gypsy mine, before Sarah puts us both on her couch."

The musicians had struck up a waltz, and he swept her regally out onto the floor. One *ouch!* and two muffled *dammit*'s followed them.

"Chase, you're going to have to take off that sword."

"Zorro without his sword? Don't be ridiculous."

"They'll throw us out."

"They can't afford to refund our money."

"You're making enemies."

"We're supposed to be dancing in romantic silence here."

"How can we dance in romantic silence with curses following us all around the floor? See? You just stuck Louis again."

"He'll learn to keep out of my way."

"Chase—"

"All right, shrew! I'll take it off and let the cloakroom attendant keep an eye on it. But you're coming with me. I don't want anyone stealing you away from me."

"Who'd want to do that?"

"Louis. Revenge."

"Thanks a lot."

"You're welcome."

six

LOUIS OBVIOUSLY WASN'T IN THE MARKET
for revenge that night. As a matter of fact, he kept a respectful
distance from Gypsy and Chase—sword or no sword. A couple
of braver souls attempted to cut in on Chase, but retreated in
some confusion when Zorro sneered at them.

Between dances Gypsy and Chase stood talking to Jake and
Sarah. The two couples were apparently on the same wavelength; there was none of the normal awkwardness or guard-
edness of new acquaintances. By evening's end Gypsy knew
that she had two new friends.

She was also a bit unnerved to realize that her response to
Chase during the evening had been very much like Sarah's to
Jake; teasing, playful, bantering. It shouldn't have surprised
her, since the same type of thing had gone on since the day
she'd met him. But it did surprise her.

It surprised her because she had never looked at their relationship objectively—from the outside, so to speak. But in
comparing them to the other couple, the similarities were startling. It was as though she and Chase were lovers of long
standing. Companionable, playful, teasing, they reacted to

each other with the certain knowledge of two people who were very close.

It gave Gypsy food for thought.

The party broke up around midnight, with invitations extended and accepted for a barbecue at Chase's house on Sunday afternoon, and the two couples went their separate ways: Sarah and Jake to the apartment they shared in Portland, and Gypsy and Chase toward the coast.

It was silent in the car for most of the trip, a companionable silence that neither chose to break. Gypsy was occupied by various thoughts and by the rumbling in her stomach; she had eaten nothing since breakfast, and was by now heartily cursing the binding, uncomfortable corset. She was also beginning to wonder how on earth she was going to get out of the thing; she'd never been very good with knots. And along the same lines was her dress; the tiny hooks and eyes had been nearly impossible to fasten, and she wasn't at all sure that she could *un*fasten them without tearing the rented costume.

A solution occurred to her, and Gypsy considered it idly. Dangerous. Definitely dangerous. Playing with fire for sure. She wondered why she wasn't at all concerned any longer about burning her fingers. It might have had something to do with the kiss Chase had bestowed during the unmasking at the party. It had been a definitely fiery kiss—a first cousin to Vesuvius. Her lips were still tingling.

And after that . . . why worry about burning her fingers?

Chase parked the Mercedes in his driveway, and they walked across to Gypsy's door. She located her key in the string purse dangling from her wrist, and Chase unlocked the door.

"Is the evening over, or are you going to ask me in?" he inquired politely.

"The evening is young. Besides, I have a favor to ask. Come in, please."

"A favor?" Chase followed her into the dimly lighted den, his cloak and mask landing beside Gypsy's on one of the chairs. "Your wish is, of course, my command."

"I'm so glad. It's a . . . delicate favor."

"So much the better." Just as she turned to face him he caught her in his arms. A faint, lazy smile lifted the corners of his mouth. "Gentlemanly courtesy aside, though, I'm afraid I have other things on my mind right now."

"Chase—"

He kissed her, and Gypsy promptly forgot all about the favor. She might have been vague, but she wasn't stupid; what woman would pass up an opportunity to revisit Vesuvius? She felt his hands lifting, the fingers threading through her black curls, and her own arms lifted to slide round his waist. His lips toyed with hers for a brief moment; gentle, sensitive. And then he abruptly accepted the unconscious invitation of her parting lips, deepening the kiss in a sudden surge of curiously yearning hunger.

Gypsy abandoned herself to sensation. A part of her stood back and watched, both disturbed and fascinated by the woman who gave herself up totally to addictive sensations. She felt one of his hands move to caress the side of her neck lightly, his thumb rhythmically brushing her jawline; his free hand slid slowly down her back, over bare flesh that tingled at the touch. The warmth of his mouth seduced, impelled, made her forget everything except the need to have more of this. . . .

The phone rang.

Gypsy wanted to ignore it. She *tried* to ignore it. But it was ringing persistently, and finally Chase raised his head with a groan.

"Oh, Lord! And we were doing so well too!"

She stared up at him, dazed, for a long moment, then firmly got a grip on herself. A warlock. He was definitely a warlock. She moved toward the phone as he reluctantly released her. Clearing her throat as she lifted the receiver, Gypsy managed a weak "Hello?"

"You've been out!" a wounded male voice accused sadly.

Gypsy slammed the phone down so hard and fast that she nearly caught her fingers beneath it. "Oh, God..." she whispered to herself, appalled. A stranger? Some nut had been calling her, and she'd—

"Who was that?" Chase had come up behind her and began to nuzzle the side of her neck.

"Uh... wrong number." She was glad he couldn't see her face; it probably scaled the limits of human shock.

He chuckled softly. "You obviously have no patience with wrong numbers; somebody's ears are still ringing."

Apparently not; the phone began ringing again.

Gypsy didn't move, she just stared at it silently.

"Persistent devil." Chase made a move toward the phone. "Want me to...?"

"No!" Hastily Gypsy picked up the receiver, trying to ignore Chase's startled look. "Hello?"

"Darling, why did you—"

"I can't talk now," she interrupted hurriedly, and hung up before another word could be uttered. There was a dead silence from behind her. She decided not to turn around.

"Should I ask?" he inquired finally in a mild voice.

"No." Gypsy sought hastily for something to divert his mind. Although why she should feel so guilty...! And who the *hell* had been calling her all this time? she wondered. "Uh... Chase, about that favor...?"

"I'd forgotten. Other things on my mind, I'm afraid." His voice was disconcertingly formal. "What is it?"

Gypsy mentally flipped a coin. She lost. Or won. Or maybe, she thought miserably, it didn't matter either way. She arranged her face and turned to gaze up at him. "Would you please help me get these clothes off?" she requested baldly.

It diverted his mind.

Chase blinked at least three times, and Gypsy could definitely see some sort of struggle going on beneath his tightly held expression. And then he relaxed, and she knew that she had won after all. A jade twinkle was born in his eyes.

"I thought we were doing well," he murmured.

Gypsy fixed him with a plaintive look. "I don't think I can get them off by myself. The dress has tiny hooks and eyes, and the corset... well, I tied the strings in a knot. And I'm not very good with knots," she added seriously.

He sat down on the arm of the couch and folded his arms across his chest, bowing his head and laughing silently.

"It's very uncomfortable!" she told him severely.

"Sorry." He wiped his eyes with one hand. "It's just... dammit, Gypsy—Cyrano de Bergerac couldn't romance you with a straight face!"

"Oh, really?" She lifted a haughty brow at him.

"Really." He pulled her into his lap, and both of them watched, totally deadpan, as her hoop skirt shot into the air and poised there like a quivering curtain.

She turned her head to stare at him. "You may have a point."

"Yes."

"This never happens to heroines in the movies."

"Uh-huh." Chase looked as though his expressionless face was the result of enormous effort and clenched teeth.

"They *never* get stuck in their dresses," Gypsy persisted solemnly.

"God forbid."

"Or lose control of their hoops."

He choked.

"Or have to put their corsets on backward."

Chase bit his bottom lip with all the determination of a straight man.

"Or ask a man, with absolutely no delicacy, to take their clothes off." Gypsy reflected a moment, then amended gravely, "Except a certain kind of heroine, of course."

"Of course," Chase agreed unsteadily.

There was a moment of silence, broken only by a peculiar sound. Gypsy looked down at her tightly corseted stomach disgustedly. "Or have stomachs that growl like volcanos," she finished mournfully.

It was too much for Chase. He collapsed backward on the couch, pulling Gypsy with him, unheeding and uncaring that her hoop was doing a fan dance in the air above them. He was laughing too hard to notice. So was Gypsy.

She finally struggled up, fighting her hoop every step of the way and sending Chase into fresh paroxysms of mirth. Sitting on the edge of the couch and clutching the hoop to keep it grounded, she requested breathlessly, "Please unfasten this damn dress—it hurts to laugh!"

Gaining a finger-and-toe-hold on his amusement, Chase rose on an elbow and began working with the tiny fastenings of her dress. They were undone much faster than they'd been done, and she was soon rising to her feet and wrestling yards of material up over her head. When she emerged, flushed and panting, she tossed the dress carelessly onto a chair and looked at Chase.

No man had ever beheld a woman stripping with more appreciation, she decided wryly. Chase was all but rolling on the couch, and if a man could die laughing, he was clearly about to.

She posed prettily, one hand holding the bare hoop and the other patting tousled curls in vain. The vision of herself in shift, bloomers, corset, and hoop obviously affected Chase just as it had her.

"I thought all men liked to see women in their underwear," she said provocatively.

Chase gathered breath for one sentence. "Take it off," he gasped. "Take it *all* off!"

Gypsy placed hands at hips and affected a Mae West drawl. "You think I do this for free, buster? There's a cover charge, you know."

He laughed harder.

Uncaring of the ludicrous embellishments of fake emeralds dangling from her ears and around her neck, and delicate black high-heeled slippers, Gypsy discarded—with some difficulty—the hoop and went over to sit on the couch beside Chase. He'd struggled to a sitting position and was once more wiping his eyes.

"Pity you left your sword in the car," she said, struggling with the stubborn knot on her corset.

"Sorry," he murmured unsteadily. "I didn't know you'd need it."

Gypsy sighed, kicked off her slippers, and sat back, giving Chase a pleading look. "D'you mind? If I don't take a deep breath in the next few seconds, I'm going to be the first woman of the twentieth century to suffocate because of a corset."

Not bothering to hide his grin, Chase reached for the stubborn knot. "In the twentieth century?" he queried gravely.

"You can't make me believe that nobody ever died in one of these things. The lengths women go to for fashion!"

"You should try wearing a sword," he said.

"No, thanks. Besides, swords were for self-defense, not fashion. How could a woman defend herself with a corset?"

"It obviously gave her an edge in defending her honor," he pointed out, tugging at the stubborn knot. "I don't understand how the population of the world managed to increase during this stage of fashion."

"Carefully," she murmured. "Ouch!"

"Sorry. Maybe we'll need the sword after all. Could you inhale a little?"

Gypsy gave him a look reserved for those persons one step below the moron level in intelligence. "Are you kidding?"

"Cyrano would definitely find it an uphill struggle," Chase murmured wryly. "What are those things called?" He gestured.

"Bloomers."

There was a moment of silence, then Chase said carefully, "I see."

Gypsy crossed her ankles and linked her fingers together behind her neck, affecting a pose of comfort. "If my father were to walk in right now . . ."

"Yes?" Chase asked politely.

"Well, think about the picture we're presenting. Here I am in a very undressed state, with a man dressed all in black and bending over me in a very suggestive and villainous pose. . . ."

"Do you want to sleep in your corset?"

"I was just making conversation. It's not easy to sit here calmly and watch you trying to take my clothes off, you know."

"And you not even struggling! What's the world coming to?" he said in a shocked voice.

"Terrible, isn't it?"

"Definitely." He sighed. "I'm going to have to cut the strings."

"Oh, no, you don't! This thing's rented."

"What could a couple of strings cost?" he asked reasonably.

"It's the principle of the thing. Could you just try a little while longer? Please?"

"You like watching me suffer," he accused wryly.

"Are you suffering?" she asked interestedly.

"I'm dying by inches. I've been struggling to keep my hands to myself all night, and now here I am. You're at my mercy, dressed in a corset, bloomers, and some kind of top that I can see right through—"

"Keep your eyes on the corset," Gypsy muttered, embarrassed for the first time.

The jade eyes gleamed with mischief—and something else. "You're blushing," he announced, chuckling.

"I am not. If my face is red, it's due to lack of oxygen. I'm telling you—this thing's killing me!"

"Then you'll have to let me cut— There! That's got it. Now you can breathe again."

Gypsy took a deep, ecstatic breath while he removed the corset and tossed it on top of the dress and hoop. "Air!" she murmured blissfully. "Both lungs full. If you ever take me to another masquerade," she added flatly, "I'll go as a writer."

"I'll remember that." Chase's mind didn't seem to be on what he was saying. His left hand was resting on her flat stomach, separated from her skin only by the almost transparent linen of her shift. His jade eyes, darkening almost to black were gazing into hers.

Suddenly wordless, Gypsy watched as he leaned toward her slowly. She wondered dimly at the abrupt cessation of laughter, of humor. And marveled at how quickly her heart had leaped to a reckless rhythm. And then all academic wonderings ceased, faded into nothingness.

His lips touched hers lightly, and Gypsy was just about to abandon reason willingly when she felt him shaking with silent laughter. He lifted his head, then dropped it again abruptly, resting his forehead against her stomach.

"Poor Cyrano," he murmured helplessly. "Oh, poor Cyrano!"

Gypsy was bewildered for a moment, but then she both felt and heard her empty stomach rumbling. So much for the fires of ardor! she thought. "Sorry," Gypsy said with a sigh. "I haven't eaten since breakfast."

"So I gathered." He rose to his feet, still chuckling, and offered her a hand. "Come on, Pauline."

"As in *The Perils of* ?" she inquired dryly, accepting the helping hand.

"Well, you've got to admit that you're batting a thousand," he pointed out ruefully. "I don't know what you've got in the fridge, but—"

"Tons of stuff," she interrupted, leading the way to the kitchen without a thought of her decidedly strange hostess outfit. "I called a takeout place this afternoon with a huge order; I had a feeling I'd be starving by the time we got back. Chinese food."

"At two A.M.?" Chase protested weakly.

"When do *you* eat Chinese food?" she asked politely, busily removing various boxes and cartons from the refrigerator.

He sighed. "Another stupid question."

"Can you get that pitcher of tea?"

"Tea on Sat— No, it's Sunday, isn't it? And here I thought you were breaking with tradition willingly."

"Have an egg roll."

"Might as well." He sighed again. "My plans for the evening seem to be all shot to hell."

"Sorry."

"You sound it. Pass the soy sauce, please."

Half an hour later, Chase finally spoke again, diverting Gypsy's thoughts from her stomach and lungs—both full and content for the first time in hours.

"Gypsy?"

"Mmmm?" She bit into her third egg roll with relish.

"Could you at least button the top button?"

Startled, she instinctively looked down to see that her shift was displaying more of her charms than her dress had. Before she could say anything, he was going on conversationally.

"It's not that I hate looking, you understand. But since the end result of this Chinese culinary retribution is bound to be acute indigestion, I don't think I really need to add skyrocketing blood pressure to my sleepless night."

Gypsy hastily buttoned the top button. "Sorry."

"Think nothing of it," he begged politely. Five minutes later he rose abruptly and left the kitchen without a word. When he returned, he was carrying her black cloak, which he dropped around her shoulders. "Not enough coverage," he said gruffly.

She fastened the cloak, hoping that he didn't think she'd been deliberately teasing him. "Chase, I'm sorry. I didn't mean—"

"I know," he said with a sigh, resuming his seat. "If I've learned anything about you, Gypsy mine, it's that the obvious answer is never the correct one."

"Is that good or bad?"

"I'll answer that question when *I* find out the answer."

Gypsy followed him to the front door some time later, feeling curiously vulnerable and not sure why. She held on to the cloak and gazed up at him as he opened the door, wondering if he was disappointed at the unplanned turn the evening had taken. She couldn't tell from his expression.

"Remember the barbecue tomorrow—I mean, today. Jake and Sarah will be at my place around three."

She nodded. "I'll remember."

"It's been . . . an unusual evening, Gypsy mine." He grinned suddenly. "I don't think I ever enjoyed an evening half as much in my life. Has anyone ever told you that you're something different?"

"No." The relief in her voice was obvious even to her.

"An oversight, I'm sure." He bent his head to kiss her quickly, adding in a whisper, "And you look cute as hell in bloomers." With a cheerful wave he vanished into the night.

Gypsy slowly closed and locked the door, smiling to herself. She went through the house to the kitchen. She cleaned up in her usual manner, dropping cartons into the trash can and anything not made of paper into the sink. She let Bucephalus and Corsair in from the backyard, fed them (ignoring Corsair's irritated grumbles at being left outside for so long), and went up to bed.

"You hung up on me," he told her sadly.

Gypsy rubbed sleep-blurred eyes and stared at her bedside clock. She'd been in bed half an hour. "Who *are* you?" she demanded, by now more angry and frustrated than horrified.

"I'm yours, my love—"

"Stop it!" she snapped.

"You're angry with me?"

"What do you think?" she asked witheringly. "Some *nut* calls me every night, and I'm supposed to be entranced?"

"Last night you—"

"Last night," she interrupted, "I thought I knew who you were."

"But you know who I am," he murmured whimsically. "We meet every night in your dreams."

"Quit it!"

"You belong to me."

"I'm calling the police."

"Mine."

She hung up. Hard.

The phone rang. And rang. Gypsy finally picked it up with a rueful sense of great-oaks-from-little-acorns-grow. Why had she ever started this?

"'The day breaks not, it is my heart,'" he whispered.

"Stop quoting Donne, dammit," she ordered.

"So cruel. . . ."

Gypsy could feel herself weakening. Whoever he was, this man had seen the vulnerable side of her. And she wondered dimly why she was so sure that he had shown her a side of himself that no one else had ever seen. It had to be Chase. But how *could* it be? Nothing made sense!

"Stop calling me," she heard herself pleading.

"Would you ask me to stop breathing? It's the same, my love. The very same. I'd die. I love you."

"Don't love me. I . . . I'm in love with someone else." She cradled the receiver gently.

In the darkness of her bedroom Gypsy slid from the bed and dressed in jeans and a sweat shirt. She barely heard the phone begin to ring again as she left the room.

With Bucephalus as escort she went through the house to the kitchen, and then out into the yard. She crossed to the stairway down to the beach. Moments later she was sitting in her favorite seat and gazing out over a moonlit ocean, the big dog at her feet. She listened to the muted roar of the surf; she looked up to count the stars, wishing on a few; she might even have cried a little bit.

She thought about loving Chase.

Gypsy wasn't quite herself at the barbecue later that day. She might have been developing a cold after sitting on a windy beach for the better part of a cool June night. Or it might have been lack of sleep. Or it might have been a last defensive gesture in a battle lost for good.

Whatever it was, Chase and her two new friends obviously noticed.

Being Gypsy, she couldn't pretend that everything was fine. She couldn't hide her almost nervous silences in response to Chase's teasing. She couldn't recapture the light bantering of the past days. And she couldn't help but stiffen at his lightest touch.

As the barbecue progressed his jade eyes began to follow her with an anxious, puzzled expression, and he asked her more than once what was wrong. She always answered with a meaningless smile and a swift change of subject.

By the time Gypsy picked her way through the meal of excellent barbecued ribs, baked potatoes, rolls, and crispy salad, Sarah had obviously seen enough. Laughing, she ordered the men (who had cooked) to do the cleaning up, seized Gypsy's arm in a companionable grip, and led her across the yard to the railing at the cliff.

"If you'll forgive an old, outworn cliché," she told the other woman ruefully, "the atmosphere between you and Chase is thick enough to cut with a blunt knife. You two have a fight? Or am I being incurably nosy?"

Having seen more than enough of the ocean the night before, Gypsy turned her back on the view and leaned against the railing. She smiled slightly and murmured, "No to both questions."

Sarah was silent for a moment. "Forgive me if I'm probing—a psychologist's stock-in-trade, I'm afraid—but can I help?"

"Is your couch free?" Gypsy managed lightly.

"For a friend in need? Always." Sarah leaned back against

the railing and pulled a pack of cigarettes and a lighter from the pocket of the man's shirt she was wearing over a halter top. "Dreadful habit. Want one?"

"Thanks." Gypsy accepted a light.

"I didn't think you smoked," Sarah said.

"I quit three years ago."

"Uh-huh. But now . . . ?"

"Am I on your couch?" When Sarah nodded with a smile, Gypsy murmured, "I need a temporary crutch, I suppose." She blew a smoke ring and concentrated on it.

"Why?"

"To keep from falling flat on my face. Although I think it's too late to prevent that."

"Falling as in 'in love'?"

"Are you that perceptive or am I that obvious?" Gypsy asked wryly.

"A little of both. You watch him when he isn't watching you. And another woman always knows." She paused. "You're scared." It was a statement.

"Terrified," Gypsy admitted almost inaudibly.

"Why? Chase is a wonderful man." She smiled when Gypsy looked at her. "I've known him longer than I've known Jake; he introduced us."

Gypsy wondered suddenly—an inescapable feminine wondering—and Sarah obviously understood; her smile widened.

"No, there was nothing serious between Chase and me. Just friendship. He's been searching ever since I've known him. Last night I realized that he wasn't searching any longer."

Gypsy fixed all her concentration on grinding the stub of her cigarette beneath one sandal.

Sarah went on slowly, thoughtfully. "He's been lonely, I think. His upbringing . . . well, he missed a lot. Don't get me wrong—Chase and his father have a very good relationship. But he missed being part of a family. He missed the carefree, irresponsible years. I don't think he's ever done a reckless thing in his life."

Gypsy, thinking of a masked rider on the beach, smiled in spite of herself.

Sarah was obviously observing her closely. "Or maybe I'm wrong about that. You've been good for him, Gypsy."

Gypsy moved involuntarily, not quite sure that she wanted to hear this; not quite sure she could stand to hear it.

"You've unlocked a part of his personality." Sarah's voice was quiet and certain. "He was so relaxed last night, so cheerful and humorous. I've never seen him like that before. And he looked at you as if you were the pot of gold at the end of the rainbow."

"Please . . ." Gypsy murmured.

"What is it? What's the problem?"

"Me," Gypsy said starkly. "I'm the problem. I'm afraid— very much afraid—that I'll ruin things between us."

"How?"

"My writing." Gypsy showed Sarah a twisted smile. "He doesn't understand—and I don't think you will." She fumbled for an explanation. "Sometimes I get . . . obsessed. The story fills my mind until there's no room for anything else. For days or weeks at a time." She laughed shortly. "A friend with a couple of psychology courses under his belt told me once that I had a split personality."

"No," Sarah disagreed dryly. "Just an extremely creative mind. One out of every ten writers goes through roughly the same thing." She smiled when Gypsy gave her a look of surprise. "Creative minds fascinate scientists and shrinks; research has been done, believe me. You're not alone."

It was strangely reassuring, Gypsy thought. "But can Chase

adapt to those kinds of mood swings? Sarah, I'm an absolute shrew! My own parents couldn't live with me once I started writing. And I'm no bargain when I'm *not* obsessed! I can't cook, I hate housework, I'm untidy to a fault—totally disorganized."

"Has any of this bothered Chase so far?" Sarah asked reasonably.

"No. But we're not living together."

"I'll bet he's around a lot though."

"Yes, but it's not the same."

"True." Sarah lifted a quizzical brow. "You won't thank me for pointing out that you're crossing your bridges before you come to them."

Gypsy sighed. "Meaning that all these rocks I'm throwing in my path may turn out to be more imagined than real, and why don't I give it a chance?"

"Something like that."

"Let's drag out another cliché. I'm afraid of getting hurt."

"Welcome to the human race." Sarah's voice was as sober as Gypsy's had been.

"Close my eyes and jump, huh?"

"Either that—or don't take the chance. And spend the rest of your life wondering if it would have been worth it." After a moment of silence Sarah added softly, "Some smart fellow once said something about it being better to have loved and lost. . . . I have a sneaking suspicion that he knew what he was talking about. But I don't think you'll lose."

"Why not?"

"Because I think you'll find that Chase is as adaptable as a stray cat. I think you'll find that he'll treasure the laughter *and* the fights, that he may even make it easier for you. I know he'll try."

"And I couldn't ask for more than that," Gypsy said softly.

The two women smiled at each other, and Gypsy added wryly, "Keep a couple of hours of couch time open, will you, friend? I just may need them."

Sarah laughed. "I'll do that. But I don't think you'll need them. Shall we join the menfolk, friend? Jake should be swearing a blue streak by now; he hates cleaning up as much as you do."

"*Nobody* hates it as much as I do."

"Better hang on to Chase, then. With him it's sheer habit."

"Military schools have their uses."

And on that light note they joined the men.

seven

GYPSY RELAXED A BIT DURING THE NEXT few hours. She was still thoughtful, introspective, but able to respond naturally to Chase. And she no longer stiffened when he touched her. Chase was patently relieved, although obviously still puzzled.

A late afternoon shower sent them inside around five, where they sprawled in various positions in the den and commenced a spirited game of charades. Sarah was the hands-down winner with her comical silent rendition of "My Old Kentucky Home" and received a standing ovation from the others. A fire was kindled in the fireplace as the rain continued outside, and Sarah and Jake went happily to raid Chase's kitchen for popcorn.

Gypsy sat silently on the couch, trying not to think too much about the jade eyes gazing up at her. Chase was lying on the couch with his head in her lap, and she could feel the steady beat of his heart beneath the hand resting on his chest. She stared into the fire.

"All day long," Chase said in a musing voice, "I've had this weird feeling, Gypsy mine."

Reluctant to meet his eyes, Gypsy nonetheless looked down. "About what?" she asked lightly.

"It's hard to explain." Chase toyed absently with her fingers. "As if . . . Juliet was about to shove Romeo off the balcony. As if Cleopatra told Marc Antony to walk the plank of her barge. As if Lois Lane asked Superman to take a flying leap."

Gypsy couldn't help but smile.

"As if you were trying to find some way of saying good-bye to me, Gypsy mine," he finished quietly.

She felt the utter stillness of the room, the level, searching gaze of his eyes, and her smile died. She shook her head slowly. "No."

He lifted her hand to cradle it against his cheek. "I'm glad." His voice was husky. A faint twinkle lighted the darkness of his eyes. "Besides—I wouldn't let you run me off with a loaded gun. Don't you know that by now?"

"Masterful," she murmured in response, her free hand unconsciously stroking his thick copper hair.

"Always." He pressed his lips briefly to the palm of her hand. "Which reminds me, about that phone call last night . . ."

Gypsy's faint smile remained. This was one subject she had been prepared for. "What about it?"

"That's just it: what about it? Why do I get the feeling I have a rival for your affections?"

"Sheer imagination."

"Will you tell me who it was?" He wouldn't be put off.

"Can't. I don't know myself." Her smile widened at his skeptical look. "I swear. It was my—uh—mystery lover. He calls every night." She carefully studied Chase's blank look; if he was acting, he deserved an Oscar, she thought wryly.

"Have you called the police?" he demanded.

"No." Gypsy wasn't about to explain *that*.

"Gypsy—"

"He's harmless, Chase. Besides . . . I like him."

Chase stared at her. "Maybe *I* should start calling you," he muttered.

"Maybe you should. And muffle your voice a bit."

"What? Why?" He looked thoroughly bewildered.

"Never mind." Gypsy looked up as Sarah and Jake entered with the popcorn. "Oh, good. Popcorn!"

Both the rain and the other couple had gone by eleven that night, after a late supper of leftover barbecue and a shoot-'em-up western on television. After Sarah and Jake had driven off, Gypsy felt more than a little let down when Chase solemnly offered to walk her home. She wondered irritably if he was trying to drive her crazy, then thought of the night before with a smothered giggle. Well, maybe he had cause!

As soon as they stepped out onto the porch, Chase stopped her with a frown. "You'll get your feet wet." As though she were contemplating a walk across crushed glass, he added, "Sandals are no protection." He swung her easily into his arms and started across the darkened lawn.

Gypsy linked her fingers together at the nape of his neck. "Let me guess." Her voice was grave. "Sir Walter Raleigh? The White Knight?"

"The former."

"No cape to lay across a puddle?" she asked in a wounded voice.

"No puddle," he pointed out. "And the cape's rented."

"Details, details," she said airily.

"Don't pick on me when I'm trying to be heroic," he complained mildly.

"Sorry. Shall I change the subject, Walter?" She felt his

arms tighten, and added hastily, "I'll change the subject. I've been meaning to ask you what you named your cat."

"She's not my cat, she's Corsair's cat. And he can have her back whenever he wants her."

"Uh-huh. The mailman told me Friday that you'd been asking around to see if she has a home hereabouts. And you ran an ad in the paper too."

"Busybody," Chase muttered.

Gypsy ignored the interruption. "So you found out that she's homeless?"

He sighed. "Not anymore."

"I thought so. What did you name her?"

If a man could squirm while walking and carrying a grown although pint-size woman, Chase squirmed. "Cat."

"Try again," she requested solemnly.

He sighed again. "Angel. Dammit."

Gypsy bit back a giggle. "Those blue eyes get 'em every time," she said soulfully.

Not really uncomfortable, Chase laughed softly. "Corsair's obviously been talking to her; she thinks she's a queen. I've moved the family into one of the spare bedrooms, and she keeps trying to move them back. One of us is going to give up sooner or later."

"Bet I know which one."

Chase dipped her threateningly over a very wet hedge. "And just which one do you bet it'll be?" he asked politely.

"Angel, of course." Gypsy giggled. "I have every faith in your perseverance, Walter."

"Smart lady." He stepped onto her front porch and set her gently on her feet. But he didn't release her. "Busy tomorrow?"

Gypsy managed to nod firmly, even though she couldn't seem to make her fingers remove themselves from his neck. "I have to work. I've fallen behind."

"My fault?" he asked wryly.

"No. The first half of a book is always slow." She hesitated, wanting to warn him of what would surely come, but dimly aware that it was something he'd have to find out for himself.

"You'd better get some sleep, then." One finger lightly touched the faint purple shadows beneath her eyes. "You look tired."

"I'm not." Gypsy felt heat sweep up her throat at the hasty reply. But the truth was that she *didn't* feel tired. She felt on edge, restless, and sleep was the last thing on her mind.

Unfortunately Chase apparently wasn't picking up undercurrents tonight.

"Good night, Gypsy mine."

He kissed her. On the nose.

Leaning back against the closed front door after he'd gone, she automatically turned the deadbolt and fastened the night latch.

Dammit.

She frowned as Bucephalus came into the hallway and wagged a long tail at her. "Out?" she queried dryly. Bucephalus woofed softly.

Sighing, Gypsy went through the house to the kitchen, letting him out and Corsair in. "You're wet, cat," she muttered. She looked at the few dishes in the sink, mentally flipped a coin, and turned away from them. She dried Corsair and fed him, then let Bucephalus back in and dried and fed him. Gypsy ignored the dishes. Again.

Restlessly she took a long shower, changing the water from hot to cold halfway through and musing irritably over the untruth of certain remedies. She killed time by washing her hair, then stood naked in front of the vanity in the bathroom as she dried it with her dryer.

She stood there for a long moment after the buzz of the

dryer died into silence, staring into her own eyes. Resolutely she mentally flipped another coin.

The gown was in the bottom drawer of her dresser—just where Rebecca had placed it on one of her visits.

"You might need it, darling."

"I have the only mother on the West Coast who advises her daughter to go out and seduce a man."

"Surely not. Look at the statistics."

Silently Gypsy slipped the gown over her head. It was white silk, nearly transparent, and as form-fitting as a loving hand. Delicate lace straps were almost an afterthought to hold up the plunging *V* neckline. The silk was gathered slightly just beneath the *V,* then fell in a cascade of filmy material to her feet.

The matching peignoir was long-sleeved, made of see-through lace to the waist and silk from waist to floor. It tied in a little satin bow just at the *V* of the gown.

Gypsy slipped on the high-heeled mules and studied herself in the dresser mirror, a bit startled. Normally she wore a T-shirt to bed; seductive silk nightgowns had never been a part of her wardrobe. This one suited her, however. The stark whiteness emphasized her creamy tan and raven's-wing hair, and turned her eyes almost silver. Almost.

She scrabbled through three drawers to find the bottle of Christmas perfume never opened, locating it finally and using only a drop at the gown's *V* neckline.

"I'm going to feel like an absolute fool if this doesn't work out," she muttered to herself, leaving her bedroom after a hurried glance at the clock. It was just after midnight, and she didn't want to be around if her "night lover" decided to call tonight.

She left the pets in the kitchen, closing the back door behind her but not locking it. Who knew when she'd be back?

She stood on the porch for a few moments, gazing over at Chase's house; only a few dim lights were on. Gypsy stepped off the porch . . . and her courage deserted her.

Only half aware that her high heels were sinking into the wet ground with every step, Gypsy began to pace back and forth. She held up the long skirt as she walked, absently addressing whatever shrub or flowering plant happened to be handy.

"*Now* what? Do I go over and ask to borrow a cup of sugar? In this outfit? Not exactly subtle, Gypsy. Why don't you just hit the man over the head with a two-by-four?"

She frowned fiercely at an inoffensive holly bush. "So what if he rejects you? You're a big girl—relatively speaking. You can handle it. The world won't come crashing down around your ears if the man laughs at you. Will it?"

Since the holly bush remained mute, she paced on. A rosebush listened meekly to her next strictures.

"You're a grown woman, dammit! Why don't you act like one? You're only *technically* innocent, after all. You've probably seen things he's never seen! Why, you spent an entire summer observing the D.C. plainclothes cops, and if *that* didn't show you life, I don't know what would!"

The rose didn't venture a response, so Gypsy started to turn away. But she nearly fell. Regaining her balance, she looked down slowly. She was standing completely flat-footed: both heels had sunk completely into the wet earth.

Using words her mother had never taught her, Gypsy stepped out of the shoes. Still holding her skirt up, she bent over, wrestled the shoes from the clinging ground, and flung them angrily toward the house.

"A grown woman," she muttered derisively. "Just call me Pauline!"

Courage totally gone and ruefully aware that she couldn't pull off a seduction even if somebody drew her a diagram, Gypsy abandoned the idea. It would have to be up to Chase, she decided. And if she'd said "No involvement!" one time too many, then that, as the man said, was that.

Miserably wide-awake, Gypsy finally headed for the stairs leading down to the beach. Why waste her outfit? Let the moon have a thrill.

It was unusually warm for early June, and she briefly debated a moonlight swim before discarding the notion. It wasn't all that warm. And she didn't feel like swimming. She felt like sitting on her rock and crying for an hour or two. Or three.

Blind to everything except inner misery, she made for her rock as soon as the stairs had been successfully negotiated. But normal vision took over when she reached the rock. There was a white towel lying on it.

Gypsy picked up the towel slowly, blankly. Had someone left it here, or—Chase! Swimming alone? She turned quickly toward the roaring ocean, a sudden fear filling her sickeningly. It drained away in waves of relief as she saw him.

The huge orange moon, hanging low in the sky, silhouetted his head and shoulders as he moved toward the beach. Gypsy watched, hypnotized by the unforgettable sight of him rising from the ocean as raw as nature had made him.

He was all wild, primitive grace, curiously restrained power, she thought. His wet flesh glistened in the moonlight; rippling muscles were highlighted, shadowed. It was as if the Creator had begun with a jungle cat and then decided to mold a man instead from the living flesh. He was bold and strong and male, Gypsy felt—a living portrait of what a man could be. And Gypsy's heart nearly stopped beating.

She fixed her eyes on his shadowed face as he stopped

before her, automatically handing him the towel with nerveless fingers. "You shouldn't swim alone," she said, wondering at the calm tone.

"I know." His voice was husky. He slowly knotted the towel around his lean waist.

Gypsy tried in vain to read his expression; the moon behind him prevented it. "Why did you?"

"I flipped a coin. Swimming won over a cold shower."

"They don't work, you know." She laughed shakily. "Cold showers, I mean."

"Have you tried?" he murmured, one hand lifting to brush a curl from her forehead.

She nodded. "Tonight. It didn't help."

His hand moved slowly downward, the knuckles lightly brushing along the plunging *V* of her gown until he was toying with the little satin bow. "And . . . you were coming to me, Gypsy mine?"

Gypsy swallowed hard, mentally burning her bridges. "I— I was. But I lost my courage."

"Why?"

He was nearer now, and she could see the catlike gleam of his jade eyes in the shadowy face. What was he thinking? "Because . . . I was afraid. Afraid you'd laugh at me."

"*With* you, yes. At you, never." His voice matched the muted roar of the ocean in its infinite certainty. His fingers abandoned the bow to slide slowly around her waist, his free hand lifting to cradle her neck. "You're so lovely. I thought I'd dreamed you. And now I'm afraid I'll wake up."

Gypsy felt damp, hair-roughened flesh against her palms, aware only then that she'd lifted her hands to touch his muscular chest. The pounding of the surf entered her bloodstream; the moonlight blinded her to reason. "If you wake up," she breathed, "wake me up too."

Chase made a soft, rough sound deep in his throat, bending his head to kiss her with a curiously fervent hunger. She could feel the restraint in his taut muscles, the fierce desire he couldn't hide, and a fire ignited somewhere deep in her inner being. Her arms slid up around his neck as Chase crushed her against his hard length, and Gypsy gloried in the strength of his embrace.

She met the seductive invasion of his tongue fiercely, her fingers thrusting through his thick hair and her body molding itself to his. Hunger ate at her like a starving beast, stronger than anything she'd ever known before.

In a single blinding moment of understanding, of clarity, she realized why she was taking this chance, why she was willing to risk pain. It was simply because she had no choice. This—whatever it was—was stronger, far stronger, than she was.

Chase lifted his head at last, breathing roughly, harshly. She could feel his heart pounding against her with the same untamed rhythm of her own. Staring up at him with dazed eyes, she realized that she was trembling, and that he was too.

"Let me love you, Gypsy mine," he pleaded thickly. "I need you so badly, so desperately . . ."

It wasn't in Gypsy to refuse, to protest. It just wasn't in her, she realized. She tightened her arms around his neck, rising up on tiptoe to press shaking lips to his, telling him huskily, "I thought you'd never ask. . . ."

He kissed her swiftly and then swung her up easily into his arms, heading across to the stairs leading up to his backyard. Surprisingly he chuckled softly. "I wouldn't dare try making love to you on the beach, sweetheart," he murmured whimsically. "One of us would be bound to get bitten by a sand crab . . . or something."

Gypsy found herself smiling. "Just call me Pauline."

"I'd rather call you mine." His arms tightened as he climbed the stairs, her slight weight obviously not bothering him in the least. "Fair warning. . . . I'm playing for keeps." He stopped at the top of the stairs, looking down at her as if waiting for her to change her mind . . . or to commit herself.

She fought back a sudden unease. "Can we talk about that tomorrow?" she asked softly, her lips feathering along his jawline.

"I'm not sure." His voice had grown hoarse. "I think I should have it in writing with you, sweetheart. You're so . . . damn . . . elusive!"

"Not really," she murmured, fascinated by the salty taste of his skin. "But if you keep standing here, it's going to start raining or something, and ruin the mood. . . ."

Rather hastily Chase headed for the deck. "You're so right, Pauline!"

Gypsy laughed, but her laugh faded away as he carried her through the glassed-in half of the deck to the sliding glass doors leading to his bedroom. The doors were open, and he brushed aside the gauzy drapes and carried her inside.

His bedroom was lighted only by a dim lamp on the nightstand. The covers were thrown back on the king-size bed, evidence of his inability to sleep. The room was definitely a man's room: solid, heavy oak furniture, earth tones—a place for everything and everything in its place. But there was a curious sensitivity in the unusual seascapes on the walls; they were lonely, bleak, riveting in their otherworldly aloneness.

Gypsy noticed little of the room; her full attention was focused on Chase. She could see his face clearly now in the lamplight, and the undisguised need gleaming in his jade eyes held her spellbound. She'd never seen such a look in a man's eyes before, and it made her suddenly, achingly aware of the hollow emptiness inside herself.

He set her gently on her feet beside the bed, his fingers lifting to fumble at the little satin bow. "Gypsy...I want you to be sure," he said roughly, as if the words were forced from him.

Shrugging off the lacy peignoir, she said unsteadily, "The only thing I'm sure of is that I'm glad I found you on the beach tonight."

His eyes darkening almost to black, Chase bent his head to touch his lips to hers as if she were something infinitely precious. His hands brushed the lacy straps of her gown off her shoulders, and Gypsy felt the cool slide of silk against her flesh as the gown fell to the deep pile of the carpeted floor. Her arms slid up around his neck, the searing shock of flesh meeting flesh sending tremors through her body as he crushed her against him.

His hands moved up and down her spine, pressing her even nearer, his mouth exploring hers as if he could never get enough of her. Tongues clashed in near-violent hunger as Gypsy matched his need with her own. She lost herself in that moment, something primitive possessing her with the strength of a fury.

Gypsy felt she wasn't close enough to him, could never be close enough, and the realization was maddening. She fumbled with the towel at his waist, flung it aside, just before he lifted her into his arms, placed her gently on the bed and came down beside her. Gypsy looked up at him, her eyes heavy with desire, watching as his gaze moved slowly over her body.

"So perfect," he murmured huskily. "So tiny and perfect...." He bent his head, capturing the hardened tip of one breast with fervent lips.

Her senses spiraled crazily as his hands and lips explored. She was floating, being pulled inexorably in a single direction, and the current was too strong to resist. She felt the sensual abrasiveness of his hands, the heated touch of his mouth, and moved restlessly in a vain effort to ease the tormenting ache inside her.

"Gypsy. . . ." He rained kisses over her face, her throat; he took her hand and placed it on his chest. "Touch me, sweetheart. I need your touch. . . ."

Eagerly, driven by curiosity, by a starving sense of not knowing enough of him, she touched, explored. She felt the thick mat of dark gold hair curling on his chest, the muscles bunching and rippling with every move. Her fingers molded wide shoulders, traced along his spine, slid around to marvel at his flat, taut belly.

"I didn't know," she whispered, almost to herself.

"What?" he breathed, his mouth slowly trailing fire along a path leading him downward. The sensitive skin of her lower stomach quivered at the touch.

Gypsy gripped his shoulders fiercely, biting back a soft moan. "That a man could be so beautiful," she gasped.

"*You're* beautiful," he rasped softly, his fingers probing gently, erotically, until they found the heated center of her desire. "So sweet, Gypsy mine. . . ."

She was only dimly aware of her nails digging into his flesh, her eyes wide and startled at sensations she'd never experienced before. A strange tension grew within her, winding tighter and tighter until there was no bearing it. "Chase. . . ." she pleaded hurriedly, desperate to reach some unknown place, frantic to tap the critical mass building inside her frail body.

"Yes, darling. . . ." He rose above her, his breathing as rough and shallow as hers, eyes blazing darkly out of a taut face. With almost superhuman control he moved gently, sensitively.

Gypsy knew that he was being careful, trying not to hurt

her. But the primitive fury possessing her burst its bounds, es-caping with the exploding suddenness of a Pacific storm. She took fire in his arms, as wild as all unreason, giving of herself with passionate, innocent simplicity. She drew him deep inside herself fiercely, caught him in the silken trap of woman un-leashed, held him with every fiber of her being. He was hers. For one brief, eternal moment he was hers, and she branded him. . . .

Gypsy barely stirred when Chase drew the sheet over their cooling bodies. Nothing short of a massive earthquake would have budged her from his side, and she didn't care how obvi-ous that fact was to him. She felt drained, contented, and very much at peace.

"Gypsy?" He was raised on one elbow, gazing down at her with a sort of wonder in his eyes.

She looked up at him, smiling, much the same wonder shining in her eyes. Without thought she lifted a hand to touch his cheek, her smile turning misty when he held the hand with his own and gently kissed the palm.

"Rockets," he murmured whimsically, smiling crookedly at her. "And bells . . . and shooting stars . . . and earthquakes."

"You're welcome," she told him solemnly, reaching for humor because she felt the moment was almost unbearably sweet.

Chuckling, he drew her even closer, arranging her at his side and wrapping his arms around her. "You're quite a lady, Gypsy mine."

She decided that his shoulder had been expressly designed for pillowing her head. "Well . . . I wasn't such a total slouch as a seductress after all, was I?"

"Honey," he laughed softly, "you've been seducing me since the day we met."

"Have I? Then why did you keep on talking about seducing *me*?"

"Encouraging you. I thought it was time you—uh—spread your wings."

"That was big of you."

"I thought so. After all—I'm a great supporter of the quest for human knowledge. And experience."

"Will you give me a reference?"

"Not a chance. We'll keep all your experience in the family."

"In the family?"

"No summer flings, Gypsy mine. I warned you. For keeps."

Gypsy was silent for a long moment. It warmed her that Chase should be so set on making a commitment, but it also disturbed her.

"Gypsy?" There was a thread of anxiety in his deep voice.

"You don't know what I'm like," she said softly. "You really don't know, Chase. I'm afraid . . . afraid I'll ruin things."

"Your writing?"

She nodded mutely, staring across the lamplit room at one of the lonely seascapes and wondering suddenly if there was a very lonely man behind Chase's cheerful facade.

"We can work it out, honey," he told her in a voice of quiet certainty. "I know we can. If you'll just give us a chance."

"How will you feel," she persisted tonelessly, "when I start ignoring you—maybe for days at a time? When I can't stand to be touched or bothered in any way? When I snap at you for no good reason? When I work around the clock?"

"We'll work it out," he repeated quietly.

"But what if we can't?" Her voice sounded afraid of itself.

"If we both make an effort, there's nothing we can't do. I promise you, sweetheart."

"I need time," she whispered. "Time to be sure." After a moment she felt his lips moving against her forehead.

"Then we'll take all the time you need." His hands began wandering beneath the covers, and he abruptly lightened the mood. "Meanwhile back at the farm . . ."

"Chase . . ." She swallowed a giggle, wondering how he could have her near tears one moment and giggling the next.

"I'm hooked on you, Gypsy mine; you'll just have to accept that."

"Take your hand off my derriere, sir!" she commanded with injured dignity. "Or I shall retaliate!"

"Please do," he invited politely.

Luckily she just happened to discover his weakness. She tickled him and was immediately rewarded when he choked back a laugh.

"Gypsy—"

"Ha! You're ticklish! I knew there was a chink in the armor."

"I'm bigger than you, sweetheart," he warned, struggling to keep her hands away from ticklish places.

"Not if you're ticklish." Gypsy feinted and lunged with happy abandon, breaking through his defenses from time to time. "If you're ticklish, you're at my mercy!"

"Stop that, you witch!" He choked, making a vain attempt to pin her down to the bed. "I'll tickle you until you can't breathe," he promised threateningly.

"Go ahead." Gypsy launched another sneak attack, smiling with evil enjoyment. "I'm not ticklish."

"What?" He looked horrified. "Not at all?"

"Well . . . there is *one* place."

"I'll find it," he vowed determinedly, hastily blocking her newest line of attack. "If it takes me the rest of my life!"

"Until then—" She commenced a two-handed, hell-for-leather attack.

"Gypsy!"

eight

"CHASE, YOU CAN'T *DO* THAT IN A JACUZZI."

"Says who?"

"Me. We'll drown."

"It's a chance in a million. I'm willing to risk it; how about you?"

"I have to get out. It's nearly noon. We've wasted the entire morning."

"Wasted?"

"Well..."

"You look so lovely...like Circe, rising from—"

"I hope you've got your legends mixed up," she interrupted tartly.

Chase was suspiciously innocent. "Why?"

"Circe turned men into swine, *that's* why."

"Sorry. Who do I mean?"

"I haven't the faintest idea."

"Helen of Troy?"

"'The face that launched a thousand ships'? I don't look that good, pal."

"You launched my ship," he pointed out.

"It's not hard to launch a leaky canoe."

"I'll get you for that!"

"Chase! Stop it this instant! I'll tickle you! I swear, I—"

There was a long silence, broken only by the bubbling water, and then Gypsy's voice, bemused and breathless.

"Well, what do you know . . . you *can* do that in a Jacuzzi."

Chase headed into Portland after lunch to return their costumes, leaving Gypsy hard at work behind the typewriter. Half expecting to be dreamy-eyed and thoughtful after their first night together, she was more than a little surprised to find that she was able to keep her mind on writing. In fact, she turned out page after page that more than satisfied her own critical standards.

It was enough to spark a faint hope. If, somehow, Chase stirred her to write *better*, then perhaps the obsessions were a thing of the past. At least she could hope they were.

Daisy was delivered around four, and Gypsy was walking in a slow circle around the car when Chase pulled into the drive and began unloading the Mercedes.

"Groceries," he announced cheerfully. "Both our cupboards are bare. I see Daisy arrived safe and sound."

Gypsy automatically accepted the bag he handed to her. "Chase, you had her painted. And *all* the dents are out—not just the ones from the Mercedes."

"Looks pretty good, doesn't she?" Chase studied the little blue car critically. "I told them to reapply the daisy decals."

Still staring at him, Gypsy protested, "But she's got a whole new interior. New carpet, newly upholstered seats. Chase, the insurance didn't pay for all of that."

"Daisy deserves the best." He kissed Gypsy on the nose and headed for the house.

"Why?" Gypsy asked blankly, following behind. "And why

haven't you had the dent taken out of the Mercedes? It's a *sin* to drive a dented Mercedes."

"The dent is a memento," he told her gravely, unloading the groceries in the kitchen. "And Daisy deserves the best because she introduced us. We probably wouldn't have met otherwise; until you came along, I never paid attention to neighbors."

"Oh." Gypsy thought that over for a while.

"I hope you like lobster."

"Love it. You're *never* going to get the dent taken out?"

"That Mercedes will go to its grave with the dent."

Gypsy helped Chase put away groceries. "I bet Freud could have had a field day with that," she murmured finally.

"I wouldn't doubt it. Through for the day?"

She blinked, remembered her writing, and nodded. "With the book. But I got a set of galleys in the mail, and I have to proof them. They have to go back in the mail tomorrow."

"Without fail?"

"Without fail."

"How long will it take you to proof them?"

"Couple of hours. Give or take."

"Ah! Then we'll have plenty of time."

"Time for what?" she asked innocently.

"To cook lobster, of course," he replied, totally deadpan.

"Let a girl down, why don't you."

"Never."

"Besides, I don't cook. Remember?"

"I'll cook. You'll keep me company. What is this?" He was holding up a covered plastic bowl taken from the refrigerator.

Gypsy crossed her arms and leaned back against the counter. "I don't remember what it started out to be. Now it's a whatisit."

"Come again?"

"A whatisit." She smiled gently at his bafflement.

"Is it alive?" he wondered, prudently not lifting the lid to find out.

"Probably." Gypsy choked back a giggle. "I warned you that I wasn't a housekeeper."

"I seem to remember that you did." Chase stared at the mysterious bowl for a moment, then placed it back in the refrigerator.

"Lack of courage?" she queried mockingly.

"Common sense. No telling how long that thing's been growing in there; it might bite by now."

"Superman would have looked."

"Superman would have thrown it into outer space."

Gypsy sighed mournfully. "They just don't make heroes like they used to."

"Pity, isn't it?" He lifted an eyebrow at her.

She crossed the room suddenly and wrapped her arms around his waist, hugging fiercely.

"Hey!" He was surprised, but clearly pleased. "What did I do?"

"You made Daisy beautiful." She hugged harder, rubbing her cheek against his chest. "Thank you."

"Superman would have gotten you a new Daisy," he said gruffly, returning the hug with interest.

"Superman wouldn't have known I wanted *my* Daisy. You did."

"I won out over Superman?" he asked hopefully.

"Hands down. Let Lois have him."

Chase turned her face up gently, gazing down into misty gray eyes. "I think the lobster will wait awhile," he murmured.

"Lobsters are tactful souls. . . ."

Gypsy didn't get around to proofing the galleys until nearly midnight. And she only managed to get started then because she flatly refused to share Chase's shower.

"You'll be sorry. . . ."

"And you're a menace!" Gypsy carelessly discarded the caftan she'd been wearing all evening and climbed into bed. Ignoring her audience, she pulled the covers up, arranged them neatly, and drew the galleys forward. "I absolutely *have* to read these. Go take your shower."

There was a moment of silence, and then Chase said in a laughing voice, "I'd much rather watch you."

Gypsy was hanging half out of bed, fumbling beneath it and muttering to herself. "Ah!" She righted herself, rescued the sliding galleys, and held up a pair of her reading glasses in one triumphant hand. "I knew they were there somewhere."

"You keep a pair under the bed?" Chase asked politely.

"Where do—"

"I know," he interrupted ruefully. "Where do *I* keep glasses?"

"Am I in a rut?" she wondered innocently.

"No, sweetheart." He bent over the bed to kiss her lightly. "You're the last person in the *world* who could ever be in a rut."

"Close the door," she called after him, polishing her glasses on the sheet. "I don't need steamy galleys."

"If it's *steamy* you want—"

"Don't say it!"

The closing bathroom door cut off his laugh.

Smiling to herself, Gypsy began to read the galleys. She was vaguely aware of the shower going on in the bathroom, but concentrated completely on the job at hand. Until the phone rang.

Gypsy quickly picked up the receiver, only half her mind on the action. "Hello?"

"You were gone again last night."

She cast a baffled, harrassed look toward the bathroom door. Dammit, it *had* to be Chase. "I told you to stop calling me!" she said fiercely.

"'I am two fools, I know, for loving, and for saying so,'" he breathed sadly.

He was quoting Donne again.

Gypsy pushed the glasses to the top of her head and tried to think. "Don't call me again—and I mean it this time!"

"I dream of you," he whispered. "I dream of a voice like honey, of sweetness and gentleness. I believe in unicorns and heroes, and I wish on stars."

"Quit it," she said weakly.

"I created a dream-love, and she's you. She's the first flower of spring, the first star at night, the sun's first ray in the morning. She's a song I can't forget, a light in the darkness, and I love her."

"*Please,* quit it," Gypsy moaned desperately.

"Dream of me, love." The phone clicked softly.

Gypsy cradled the receiver. She nudged Corsair off her foot, not even noticing when he immediately resumed his favorite sleeping place. Undecided, she looked toward the bathroom door, then shook her head.

"No," she murmured to Corsair, or to Bucephalus beside the bed. "If I went and looked, he'd be there. And I don't think I could take it." She gazed into Corsair's china-blue eyes bemusedly. "I might well be in love with two men—and one of them's faceless, nameless, and probably a nut!"

When Chase came out of the bathroom a few minutes later, she was chewing on the earpiece of her glasses and staring into space.

Chase, a towel knotted around his waist, came over to the bed. He picked up Corsair, got Bucephalus by the collar, and escorted both to the door, shutting them out in the hall. When he turned around, he looked at Gypsy for a moment, then asked politely, "You'd rather they slept in here?"

"Hmmm?" She blinked at him.

"The pets." He crossed to sit on the foot of the bed, adding, "You were frowning at me."

"Cheshire cat," she murmured absently.

It was his turn to blink. "Earth to Gypsy?"

She stirred, finally giving him her full attention. "I wasn't frowning at you—I was just frowning."

"Why?"

Gypsy looked at him for a moment. "Seemed the thing to do."

Chase gave up. He shed the towel and climbed into bed beside her. "About finished up?" he asked seductively.

"About at the end of my rope," she confided seriously.

He propped himself up on an elbow and stared at her for a long moment. "You're just full of cryptic comments tonight, Gypsy mine."

"Uh-huh." Gypsy dumped the galleys on the floor beside the bed, dropping her glasses on top of them. "I'll do these in the morning. *Early* in the morning before the mailman comes. Don't let me forget."

"Perish the thought. . . ."

The galleys were late.

The next few days were interesting to say the least. Nights were alternately spent in Chase's house or Gypsy's, although days were generally spent at Gypsy's since she flatly refused to "clutter up" Chase's lovely den or study with her stuff.

She worked during the day; her story was still shaping without an obsessive urge to work constantly. Chase made several trips into Portland, where his office was located; he was officially on vacation, but since his was a one-man office, and since he was designing a house for Jake and Sarah, the trips were necessary.

But he was usually somewhere nearby. Gypsy would look up occasionally to see him stretched out on the couch reading, or hear him whistling in the kitchen. And he always made sure she ate regularly.

"I'll gain ten pounds if this keeps up!"

"Ten pounds on you would just be necessary ballast."

"Funny man. That 'ballast' won't be able to fit into my jeans."

"Have another roll."

With Chase, every day—and certainly every night—became an adventure. Gypsy never knew what he'd do next.

"What *is* that?"

"The mating call of whales."

"Really? I didn't even know you had an aquarium."

"Cute. It's a record. To set the mood."

"And I thought we were doing so well."

"Change is the spice of life, Gypsy mine."

"Right. Where's the water bed?"

"Damn. Knew I forgot something."

Gypsy discovered that it was definitely nice to have a man around. She was as mechanically inept as she was forgetful, her usual method of fixing anything being a few swift kicks or thumps.

"Chase, where are you?"

"In the kitchen feeding your pets."

She headed for the kitchen, announcing without preamble, "Herman's *e* is sticking, and it's driving me crazy. Can you do anything?"

Chase nearly lost a finger since he was giving Bucephalus a

steak bone and looked up at the crucial moment. He stared at Gypsy for a second, then apparently deduced that Herman was the typewriter. "I'll certainly try," he told her, accepting named typewriters without a blink.

Ten minutes later Gypsy was happily typing again. "My hero," she murmured absently as Chase straightened from his leaning position against the desk. He touched her cheek lightly and said, "That's all I ever wanted to be, sweetheart."

Gypsy looked up only when he'd left the room. She stared after him for a long time, eyes distant and thoughtful. Then she bent her head and went back to work.

Chase came in late one afternoon to find her pounding the keys furiously and wearing a fierce grimace that didn't invite interruption.

"Gypsy—"

"Hush!" she said distractedly, hammering away at her top speed, which was pretty impressive. "Someone's about to get killed."

It was half an hour before her assault on Herman ceased. Gypsy straightened and rubbed the small of her back absently, reading over what she'd written. Only then did she become aware of a presence. She looked up to find Chase leaning against the bookcase and watching her with a faint smile.

"Hello," she said in surprise. "How long have you been there?"

"A few minutes. I tried to interrupt you, and you told me to hush."

"Oh, I'm sorry," she muttered, horrified.

He chuckled softly. "Don't be. I knew it was the wrong time but, to be honest, I wanted to find out what you'd do. And if that was the worst, we're home free, sweetheart."

Gypsy pushed her glasses up on top of her head, never noticing that the pair already there fell to the floor behind her.

She looked curiously at his trying-hard-to-hide grin. "We'll have to wait and see, won't we?" she murmured in response to his comment.

"If you say so. What would you like for dinner?"

Gypsy's "night lover" continued to call whenever she and Chase were spending the night in her house. Chase was always around, but never in the room, and her suspicions were growing by leaps and bounds. It was much easier, she admitted to herself ruefully, to believe that it was Chase; otherwise, she was quite definitely in love with two separate men . . . and *there* was a wonderfully cheering thought!

A few days later, suddenly and with no warning, her book became an obsession. It wasn't too bad at first; Chase found wonderfully unique ways of getting her away from the typewriter for a break or a meal or sleep—and all without causing her to lose her temper once.

"Gypsy?"

"Not now."

"You have to help me—it's desperately important!"

"What then?"

"My zipper's stuck."

"Chase!"

"It got you away from the typewriter."

"I know, but really!"

"Now that you're *here*—"

"You're incorrigible!"

Or:

"Gypsy?"

"*What?*"

"You have to help me."

"What's desperately important now?"

"I have to get my car keys."

"Chase, you've been up that tree every morning for weeks; you should know the way by now."

"Corsair went up a different tree. Sneaky cat."

"I'll bet you told him to."

"How could I? He doesn't listen to me. Come now, Gypsy mine, just a moment of your time. I don't ask for much, after all."

"Stop sounding pitiful; it won't wash."

"It was worth a try."

He found her outside one morning, sitting cross-legged on the ground and methodically pulling up handfuls of grass.

"Why are you mangling the lawn?" he asked sweetly, sinking down beside her.

Gypsy was fixedly watching her hands. "I've painted myself into a corner, dammit," she muttered irritably. "And now I don't see . . ."

"Let the paint dry and repaint the room," he advised cheerfully, obviously without the least idea of what she was talking about.

She froze, lifting startled eyes to his. "Wait a minute. That just might work. I could— And then—" She reached over to hug him exuberantly. "You did it! Thank you!"

Chase followed her into the house, murmuring, "Great. What did I do?"

Chase managed to get her away from the typewriter all day the following Sunday by inviting her parents to have dinner and spend the afternoon at his house. Gypsy was inclined to be temperish about it at first; in fact, it was the first time she really snapped at him—and it upset her more than it did Chase.

"*Why* did you do that? I can't stop working for a whole

day! I'll never get this book finished, dammit, and it's all your fault!"

"Gypsy—"

"You've messed up my whole life!"

"Have I?" he asked softly.

She stared at him and her anger vanished. Quickly she rose from her chair and went over to him, wrapping her arms around his waist. "Why do you put up with me?" she asked shakily.

"Well, you're just an occasional shrew," he told her conversationally. "And I always did prefer tangy to sweet."

"Chase—"

"Cheer up. You haven't seen *my* worst side yet."

"Do you have one? I was thinking of having you canonized."

"Saint Chase?" He tried the title on for size. "Doesn't sound right, somehow. We'll have to think it over. Come along now, Gypsy mine; we're going to prepare a feast for your parents."

"We?"

"This time you get to help."

"Help do what? Kill us all? Face it, pal—I have absolutely no aptitude for cookery."

"You can slice things, can't you?"

"You're going to let me have a knife?"

"On second thought I'll do the slicing. You can set the table and keep me company."

"As I asked once before, is your china insured?"

"Since the day after I met you."

The entire day was fun laced with nonsense, and Gypsy thoroughly enjoyed it. She always enjoyed her parents' visits, but Chase's presence made it even better. He got along very well with both of them, accepting Gypsy's definitely unusual parents with clear enjoyment.

And they just as clearly approved of him:

"Mother, what were you and Chase in a huddle about?"

"Nothing important, darling. Are you working on a book? You don't look as tired as usual."

Knowing her mother, Gypsy accepted the change of subject. "Chase makes me rest."

"Your father is just the same with me. When's the wedding?"

"Are you and Poppy getting married again, Mother?"

"Gypsy . . ."

"He hasn't asked, Mother."

"Nonsense, darling. He doesn't have to."

"Etiquette demands it."

"Write a new rule. Ask him."

"I'm an old-fashioned kind of girl."

"Stubborn. Just like your father."

"Poppy, where are you going with that ladder?"

"Corsair stole *my* car keys. He's on the roof; Chase is going up after him."

"Oh. Chase had a ladder all this time? I'll get him for that; I've been helping him out of trees all week."

"Corsair?"

"Chase."

"Oh, I like him, darling."

"Corsair?"

"You're worse than your mother. Chase, of course."

"Stop smiling at me, Poppy."

"I like smiling at you; fathers do that, you know."

"Yes, but it's *that* kind of smile. A definitely parental Father-always-knows-kid-and-don't-try-to-hide-it kind of smile. Unnerving."

"You're misreading my expression. This is my I-want-to-dandle-a-grandchild-on-my-knee-one-day smile."

"Poppy—"

"I'll take the ladder to Chase."

"Do that."

"Did you get Corsair off the roof?"

"After a merry chase, yes. Your cat has a devious mind."

"I've been meaning to tell you. If you'd only stop playing his game, he'd stop too. He never would have gone up a tree a second time if you'd only ignored him the first time."

"I needed my keys."

"He would have dropped them. Eventually."

"Uh-huh."

Days passed and Gypsy became more and more wrapped up in her book. The clutter on her desk, composed of notes on odd sheets of paper, reference books, and assorted alien objects like the Buddha, grew until it was nearly impossible to find her or Herman in the middle of it. Chase pulled her from the muddle for meals but otherwise left her strictly alone.

Gypsy made a tremendous effort and firmly stopped work-ing at midnight every night. She'd never held herself to any kind of fixed schedule before, and was agreeably surprised to find that it didn't seem to be interfering with her creativity. If anything, it helped; she always stopped before she got too tired now.

Besides . . . she cherished the nights with Chase. He

showed her an enchantment she had never before known, and she loved him more with every day that passed. Neither of them ever put their feelings into so many words, and she had a suspicion that Chase wouldn't say a word until she did. He'd said that he was "playing for keeps" and was leaving the rest up to her.

But Gypsy still wasn't ready to commit herself fully. She was still uneasy, still worried that his patience would run out.

And it did.

As the book neared its completion Gypsy warned him that the midnight halts were at an end. The last few days of a book were written in a white-hot headlong rush, interrupted by nothing except a catnap when the typewriter keys blurred before her eyes. At that point Gypsy was driven by the need to just *finish* the thing, and there was nothing else she could do.

It went on for three days. Gypsy ate little and rarely left her desk. She catnapped on the couch at odd hours, then took showers to refresh her mind before going immediately back to work. She was dimly aware of Chase, but not distracted by his presence. As for Chase, he was always around but didn't intrude.

Three days. At two A.M. on the fourth day, the headlong rush came to a crashing halt.

Gypsy found herself jerked suddenly to her feet, banging both knees against the desk's center drawer, and quite thoroughly and ruthlessly kissed.

"Do I have your attention now?" Chase demanded hoarsely.

She blinked up at him, a bit startled by the suddenly unleashed primitive man. Clearing her throat carefully, Gypsy barely managed a one-word response. "Yes."

"Good!" He lifted the glasses from her nose, dropped them on the foot-high clutter on the desk, and then threw

Gypsy over his shoulder with one easy, lithe, far from gentle move.

"Chase!" Dangling helplessly, she realized that he was carrying her into the bedroom.

"*Don't* have me canonized!" he snapped.

"Chase, what're you—" She bounced once on the bed, looking up with wide eyes as he joined her with a force that stole her breath. "Chase?"

He kissed her with a roughness just this side of savagery, a bruising impatience that stripped away all the civilized layers of the mating game. His hunger was voracious, insatiable. Restraint was gone, gentleness was gone; there was only this crucial need, this desperate hunger.

Gypsy had believed that she could never be surprised by his lovemaking, but she discovered her mistake. And after the first moment of shock, she responded with a mindless need to match his own wild hunger.

It was silent and raw and indescribably powerful. They loved and fought like wild things compelled to mate once and die, their movements swift and hurried and uncontrolled. Something primal drove them relentlessly, pushing them higher and higher, until they soared over the brink in a heart-stopping, mind-shattering release. . . .

Floating in a dreamy haze, Gypsy was lying on her back close beside Chase. She felt his arm, heavy across her middle, heard his rough breathing gradually steady. She wanted to smile all over. Eyes closed, she felt rather than saw Chase raise himself on an elbow, felt his gaze.

"Honestly," she murmured in an injured tone, "you could have just asked, pal. I mean—I think they used to call it ravishment."

"Gypsy . . ."

Startled by his hesitant, anxious voice, her eyes snapped

open. She looked up at him, searching his concerned face and darkened eyes, realizing in slow astonishment that he was really worried. She wasn't about to let *that* go on.

Sliding her arms up around his neck, she allowed her inner smile to show through. "You should get creative more often."

The jade eyes lightened, but he still looked anxious. "You really don't mind?" he asked in a low voice. "I didn't mean to be so rough, honey."

Gypsy rather pointedly traced a long scratch on his shoulder with one finger. "We both got a little carried away. Let's get carried away again . . . real soon."

He chuckled softly, apparently realizing that she wasn't the slightest bit upset by ravishment. "You should be mad, Gypsy mine; I interrupted your work."

"With a vengeance," she agreed dryly. "But I forgive you. I only had a few pages left to do anyway."

"To finish the book?" When she nodded, he said ruefully, "That close to the end and I stopped you. . . . You should be furious."

"No, but I am *curious*. What finally pushed you over the edge? I mean, you've been Saint Chase for weeks."

"I'm not quite sure." He paused, then went on firmly, "Yes, I am sure, dammit. I was jealous."

"Jealous?" Gypsy was startled. "Of what?"

"The book. The typewriter. The desk. Everything standing between you and me. I was lying here in bed—alone, I might add—and suddenly decided that enough was enough."

Gypsy frowned uneasily, and he immediately understood her worry.

"Honey, I really don't think that your writing will get between us. It only happened tonight because . . . because you're still so *new* to me." His voice deepened, roughened. "You're like a treasure I stumbled on by accident—I want to keep you to myself for a while. I want to—to hoard my riches until I'm sure I won't lose them."

She tried to speak past the lump in her throat, but found it impossible.

"Still..." He was suddenly rueful, obviously trying to lighten the atmosphere. "The White Knight wouldn't have approved."

Tightening her arms around his neck, Gypsy swallowed the lump and said huskily, "The White Knight doesn't know what he's missing. And neither does his lady."

"Hey..." He smiled down at her. "I win out over the White Knight too?"

"He's not even in the same race."

Chase kissed her gently, murmuring, "You're running out of heroes, Gypsy mine."

"I hadn't noticed...."

---

nine

DUE TO ONE THING OR ANOTHER—AND Chase fit into both categories—Gypsy didn't finish her book until late the next day. As always, the book was too fresh in her mind for her to be objective about it. She only knew that she was satisfied.

She woke the next morning with the disquieting sensation that something was wrong, and it took only seconds for her to realize what it was. Chase wasn't in bed with her. She listened to the silent house for a moment, then slid out of bed and put on one of his T-shirts. By this time both their wardrobes were pretty equally divided between the two houses.

She padded soundlessly through the house until she reached the doorway of the living room. There she stopped, leaning against the wall and watching him with quiet eyes.

He was sitting at her desk, the chair pushed back to accommodate his long legs. Dressed only in cutoff jeans, hair still tousled from sleep, his head was bent over the last few pages of Gypsy's manuscript. He'd obviously been there for some time.

When he'd read the last page, Chase turned it facedown with the others in a stack on the corner of the desk, his expression thoughtful. He looked up suddenly a moment later, as though sensing her presence. Gazing at her, he murmured, "I think it's the best thing you've ever written."

Gypsy came across to him, sinking down on the carpet at his feet with her folded hands resting across his thigh. "Why?" she asked, her voice as soft as his in the early-morning hush.

Chase reached out to stroke her tumbled curls absently, frowning slightly in thought. "Certain things haven't changed—from your other books, I mean. It's ruthlessly logical, neatly plotted, with unexpected twists and turns. But your *characters* are different. Especially the hero." Chase smiled suddenly. "He's the type you want to stand up and cheer for. Not an *anti*hero like the others, but a human hero with strengths and weaknesses. He's smart but not cynical, idealistic without being a fool. And he has a fiendish sense of humor. You'll have to make him a continuing character, sweetheart—readers will love him."

Gypsy smiled, more than content with the critique. "I'm glad you think it's good."

"It's more than good, Gypsy mine. It's terrific. A sure bestseller." He leaned forward to kiss her lightly, remaining in that position as he gazed into her eyes and asked casually, "Want to go to Virginia with me?"

"Virginia?" She was still smiling. "What's in Virginia?"

He seemed to hesitate for an instant. "A project they want me to do."

Her smile faded slightly. "They?"

"The city fathers in Richmond. The project I worked on for two months was for them. Now they want a big shopping mall."

Dimly Gypsy realized that it would be a professional feather in Chase's cap. "When do you have to be there?"

"I'm supposed to meet with them Friday afternoon."

"That's tomorrow," she said slowly. "How long—I mean, will you have to be there for months?"

"Not at this early stage. We'll be talking about budgets and designs—that sort of thing. Guidelines have to be ironed out before they commit themselves, and before I commit myself. It'll take days. Weeks, if they're as slow as last time."

He was still smiling, but there was a curiously blank look in his eyes, as if he were deliberately hiding his thoughts. "Come with me?"

"I can't."

"Jake and Sarah'll watch the houses for us." He was still casual.

She shook her head. "That's not it. The book's finished, Chase, but the manuscript isn't. I have days of retyping to do."

"I see." His eyes remained blank. "Can't type in Richmond, I guess?"

Gypsy felt strangely shaken by his light tone, disturbed by the shuttered gaze. "Would it be worth the bother to carry all my stuff out there?" she asked uncertainly. "You said it might just be days, and—"

"You're right, of course." He sat back, looking down at her with a glinting smile. "Then I go alone." Softly he added, "You're still not sure about us, are you, Gypsy?"

Before she could answer, he rose to his feet and pulled her gently to hers. "I'll catch an afternoon plane today; I'll need time to check out the proposed site tomorrow before the meeting. And since I have a few things to take care of in Portland before I leave— I'd better get a move on, I guess. Want to help me pack?"

"You're leaving right away?" she asked weakly.

"After breakfast. I'll cook if you'll pack for me. Deal?"

Two hours later he was gone, leaving Gypsy at the door with a light kiss and a cheerful wave.

His eyes had still been blank.

"Well, dammit...." Gypsy muttered miserably to herself, watching the Mercedes disappear from sight.

Days passed, while Gypsy worked to retype her manuscript. She worked long hours, but not because the story drove her; she worked because something else was driving her.

Chase called every evening around eight to report progress (none, from the sound of it). He was casual, cheerful. He didn't once call her Gypsy mine or sweetheart or honey. He didn't talk about heroes.

So Gypsy threw herself into her work. She worked so fiercely that the manuscript was retyped and on its way to her editor by the middle of that week. And then she was at loose ends, struggling to find things to do. She gardened. She washed Daisy three times in two days. She used the key Chase had left her to let herself into his house and take care of Angel and the kittens. She watched television. She read poetry.

Poetry. If it hadn't been for her "night lover," Gypsy didn't know what she would have done. He called every night around midnight. Gypsy always listened intently, trying to pin down the voice, trying to convince herself it was Chase. But she just wasn't sure. And she was too fearful of a negative answer to ask if it was him.

"'Come live with me and be my love,'" he invited softly one night.

Lying in bed in darkness, Gypsy smiled to herself. "Will you show me 'golden sands and crystal brooks'?" she murmured.

"I'll show you... the ones inside myself," he vowed. "I'll show you all the things you have to *believe* in before you can see them. Will you let me do that, love?"

She laughed unsteadily. "You haven't shown me *you*."

"I'm one of those things that has to be believed first, love. If you believe in me, then I'm real."

"Like unicorns?" she whispered.

"Like unicorns. And heroes."

Gypsy tried desperately to deny the emotions welling up inside of her. "I can't believe in you," she told him shakily. "I—"

"You must believe in me, love. Without you I can't exist."

"Don't say that. . . ."

"Dream of me, love."

Gypsy found herself pacing the next night. Pacing restlessly, endlessly. She had talked to Chase only an hour before; a casual, meaningless conversation. Why was he doing this to her? He was deliberately holding back a part of himself, and—

She stopped dead in the center of the room, her lips twisting suddenly as the realization slammed at her. "Idiot!" she breathed softly to her usual audience of Corsair and Bucephalus. "Of course, that's what he's doing. He's showing you what it's like, you fool! You've spent weeks huddled inside your own stupid uncertainties, while he waited patiently for you to—to grow up."

What was she *really* afraid of? Gypsy asked herself. Not that they couldn't live together—they could. Not that her writing would come between them—because, dammit, she wouldn't let it.

"Drag out the cliché, Gypsy," she told herself softly. "You're really afraid of getting hurt. You told yourself for years that you didn't want to get involved, and when it finally happened, it scared you to death. For the first time in your life, you let someone close enough to see you. And now . . . ?"

Facing the fear squarely for the first time, she realized slowly, gladly, that it was fading into nothingness. Chase would never hurt her—not intentionally. And being seen by him was a very special thing indeed. She only hoped that it wasn't too late to tell him.

Gypsy's heart thudded abruptly as a sudden painful question presented itself. It pounded in her head, slammed at walls already crumbling, leaving panic in its wake.

What if she lost him?

Not the vague, elusive worry of "someday," but the concrete realization that life was uncertain at best. What if he never came back? What if she never saw him again, was never given the chance to say . . .

One glance at the clock and Gypsy was sitting on the edge of her bed and reaching for the phone. It was midnight in the East; he'd be at his hotel. She placed the call and listened as his phone rang, her only thought that "tomorrow" was sometimes too late.

"Hello?"

"I miss you," she said starkly.

"Do you?" He was guarded, his voice still and waiting.

"Chase . . ."

"You sound upset." It was a question.

"I'm lonely." She laughed shakily. "For the first time in my life, I'm lonely. Are you— When are you coming home?"

He sighed. "Looks like another few days."

Gypsy closed her eyes, knuckles showing white as she gripped the receiver. "I don't think I can wait that long."

"Gypsy?"

"Nothing's right." Her voice was hurried, half blocked by the lump in her throat. "Nothing's the same. The house seems empty. . . . Bucephalus isn't eating. . . . I can't find my glasses. . . . The Buddha fell off my desk, and he's shattered, just shattered. . . . Corsair goes from room to room, and he can't seem to find what he's looking for—"

"Gypsy—"

"Angel moved her kittens back to your bedroom," she went on disjointedly. "And some kind of bug's attacking the roses. I washed dishes last night because I didn't want to be messy, and I picked up all the clothes on the floor. . . . It rained all day. . . . My bed's so big . . . so empty. . . ."

"I'm catching the first plane home," he told her, his voice oddly unsteady.

"But your work—"

"Never mind my work. You're more important. I'll be home tomorrow, honey."

"I'll be waiting," she promised huskily.

"Good night, Gypsy mine."

"Good night."

Gypsy cradled the receiver gently, staring across the room blindly.

"You're more important."

Her mind flashed back to an earlier inner resolution not to let her writing come between them, and she felt a sort of wonder. Somehow, without her being consciously aware of it, the two most important things in her life had softly changed places. From now on, she knew, nothing would ever be as important as Chase.

As for her writing . . . Gypsy shook her head ruefully. It had been right there in front of her all the time, and she'd never seen it. But Chase had. He'd told her that her fictional hero was "the kind you want to stand up and cheer for," and she hadn't realized the importance of that.

She could imagine heroes now. Human heroes; fallible, but heroes nonetheless. And Chase had given her that. Chase and her "night lover."

Gypsy frowned suddenly. It was Chase. Period. She'd go on playing the game as long as he did, and just stop questioning. And one day, when they were old and gray and rocking side by side on a vine-covered porch, she'd ask him. And if he didn't say yes . . . she'd hit him with her cane.

"Do you believe in unicorns, love."

"Yes," she whispered.

"And heroes?"

"And heroes."

"And . . . me?"

"And you." Her voice was tender.

"We'll find those 'golden sands and crystal brooks,'" he told her with impossible sweetness. "We'll follow rainbows until we find the pot of gold. And when it storms outside, when the world goes crazy, we'll have each other."

"Never alone," she murmured wonderingly.

"Never alone. Sweet dreams, love. . . ."

Gypsy was restless, on edge. She was bursting to tell Chase how she felt, and the morning dragged by with no sign of him. She washed Daisy again and cultivated two flower beds, and *still* he didn't come.

She wandered around the house, trying to rehearse what she wanted to say. But she knew ruefully that—rehearsals notwithstanding—heaven only knew what would come out of her mouth when the moment came.

It was after two when she finally left the house, wandering out to the edge of the cliffs and sitting down on the grass at the top of the steps. She stared out over the ocean, her mind empty of everything except the wish that he would come to her.

She didn't hear him coming, but was instantly aware when he knelt on the grass just behind her.

"Gypsy?"

She twisted around abruptly, her arms going around his neck with blind certainty. She felt his arms holding her tightly, felt the smooth material of his shirt and the heavy beat of his heart beneath her cheek.

"I've found a new kind of hero," she told him breathlessly. "A kind I never knew existed."

"What kind?" he asked gently, holding her as if he would never let her go.

"He makes me laugh. And he doesn't mind that I'm messy and can't cook. He fixes Herman and helps me find my glasses and cooks marvelous meals for me. He makes me stop work to help him down from trees, even though he's got a ladder. He does impossible things in Jacuzzis and plays music made by whales, and thinks I'm a treasure he stumbled on by accident. He puts up with a huge dog and an invasion of cats, and keeps a dent in his Mercedes. And he's so very patient with me...."

"Gypsy..." Chase turned her face up with gentle hands, looking down at her with glowing jade eyes.

"I love you," she told him fiercely. "I love you so much, and if you can only put up with me—"

"Put up with you?" His voice was an unsteady rasp. "God, Gypsy, don't you realize what you mean to me?" He rubbed his forehead against hers in a rough movement. "When we first met, I didn't know whether to kiss you or have you committed. Within six hours I knew that I wanted you committed—to me. For the rest of our lives. I love you, sweetheart."

"Chase..." Gypsy closed her eyes blissfully as his lips met hers. She was dimly aware of movement but was not troubled by it, responding with all the love inside herself to the sweetness of his kiss. When her lashes finally drifted open again, she discovered that she was lying on her back in the soft grass, with Chase lying close beside her. His lips were feathering lightly along her jawline, teasing the corner of her mouth.

"Why did you leave me?" she asked huskily, knowing the answer but needing to hear it from him. "Why were you so— so indifferent?"

"I was gambling, Gypsy mine," he murmured, lifting his head to gaze into her eyes. "You still weren't sure about us, and I was going crazy trying to think of some way of proving to you that we belonged together. So I decided to leave, suddenly and with little warning. I hoped you'd miss me. But driving away that morning was the hardest thing I've ever done in my life. These last days have been hell," he finished roughly.

Gypsy touched his cheek, a gentle apology for the pain of his uncertainty, and her senses flared when he turned his head to softly kiss her palm.

"Everything happened so fast that morning," she said. "You didn't give me a chance to stop and think; you were just gone."

His smile was twisted wryly. "If I'd given you a chance to think, honey, I would have given myself one as well. And I never would have gone. It was like taking bad-tasting medicine; I had to get it over with quickly."

"And . . . the project in Richmond?" she asked softly.

"Oh, it was real. They called me a couple of weeks before I left. The project's on, by the way. There are still a few details to be hammered out, but the contract's being drawn up now. Would you like to spend the winter in Richmond, Gypsy mine?"

"I've never been to Richmond." She smiled up at him, and then the smile turned wondering. "I just can't believe it," she said almost to herself. "I'm so hopeless to live with, and yet you—"

"Honey..." He shook his head with a faint smile, and went on slowly. "You brought something different into my life, something special. There aren't enough hours in the day for me now, because every one brings something new and exciting. Don't you realize how fascinating you are just to *watch*?"

He kissed her lightly on the nose, one finger tracing the curve of her cheek. "The way you blink like a startled kitten when you're surprised. The way you absentmindedly put on one pair of glasses while another's on the top of your head. The way you explain something totally ridiculous with all the reasonableness in the world.

"You accept the absurd without a blink and make the commonplace seem fascinating. You have a mind as sharp as a razor, and yet you can never find whatever you're looking for. You have a penchant for naming objects and talking to them—and about them—as if they were people. You're prone to collect strange things like Buddhas, and the urge to collect them honestly bewilders you." He smiled tenderly at her. "And when I'm with you, I feel as if I'm on the world's biggest roller coaster—exhilarated and breathless."

Gypsy tried to think straight. "But I can't cook, and I'm not a housekeeper."

He kissed her suddenly, as if he couldn't help himself, and she realized that he was laughing silently.

"How you do harp on that," he chided gently. "Do you think I give a damn that you don't cook and aren't a housekeeper? So what? I couldn't write a book if you took me through it sentence by sentence. I couldn't create a hero you'd want to stand up and cheer for—"

"Yes, you could," she interrupted breathlessly, the emotions inside of her threatening to burst their fragile human shell.

Chase hugged her silently, a suspicious shine in the jade

eyes. "The point is," he went on huskily, "that I don't have to 'put up' with you at all, honey. I love everything about you. You're beautiful inside and out. Warm and giving, humorous and ridiculous, and passionate. You fill my days with laughter and my nights with magic. From the moment I saw compassion in your lovely eyes for the lonely little boy I might have been, I knew that I'd found the woman I've been looking for all my life. The treasure I stumbled on by accident . . ."

"I love you, Chase," she told him shakily. "I was so empty when you left, so alone. I realized then that if I never wrote another word, it wouldn't bother me—but if I never saw you again, I'd die. I was so stupid, so stupid not to see it sooner!"

"My love," he murmured, kissing her.

Long moments passed, the silence broken only by the muted roar of the ocean, the soft twittering of birds, and murmurs of love.

"I really hate to break the mood," Gypsy said at last, her voice grave, "but I think we'd better get up."

"Why?" he lifted a brow at her. "No neighbors."

"Neighbors are closer than you think." Gypsy made a slight, restless movement. "Uh . . . I believe you put me down on an ant's nest."

Chase began to laugh helplessly.

She grinned up at him. "Just call me Pauline!"

Still laughing, Chase got to his feet and helped her up. "I believe I've mentioned it before, sweetheart, but even Cyrano would have a hell of a time trying to romance you!"

"Are you glad you've got me instead?" she asked politely.

"I can't believe my luck." He began enthusiastically brushing her down to remove possible ants.

"Chase?"

"What?"

"I was lying on my back. Not my front."

"So you were, so you were." He grinned at her, linking his hands together at the small of her back as they stood close together.

"You're impossible!" she told him severely.

"Can I help it if I can't keep my hands off you?" he asked, wounded.

"Dignity," she said austerely, "should be our uniform of the day."

"That uniform won't fit either one of us."

"We must strive to cultivate dignity," she insisted solemnly.

"Why?"

"Because we're grown-up adult people, that's why."

"Are we?" Chase frowned thoughtfully. "I don't think so."

"We'd better be, if we're going to get married. Are we going to get married?"

"Of course we are."

"I wondered. You never said."

"I was waiting for you to ask me."

Gypsy thought of her mother's advice, and bit back a giggle. "Never let it be said that I didn't do what was expected of me. Shall I make an honest man out of you? I think I shall. Will you marry me?"

"You're supposed to get down on your knees and swear undying love," he pointed out critically.

"Can't I stand and swear undying love?" she asked anxiously. "The ants, you know."

"I'm willing to stretch a point," he allowed graciously.

"Thank you." Gypsy tightened her arms around his neck and looked up at him soulfully. "My darling, you're everything I didn't dare hope to find, everything I looked for in my dreams." The light mockery fell away from her slowly as she gazed at the lean face that meant so much to her.

"I can face the worst of life with you beside me, and enjoy

the best of life as I never would without you. I'd do anything
for you, pay any price for your love. I'd willingly give up everything that ever mattered to me if you asked it of me. I'd follow
you through the fires of hell itself." Her voice became suddenly
unsteady, but not uncertain. "I'll love you until I die . . . and after. Will you marry me, my love?"

Chase drew a deep, shuddering breath, his arms tightening
fiercely around her. "Yes, please," he said simply.

Gypsy swallowed the lump in her throat and smiled tremu-
lously up at him. "Now we're betrothed," she said gravely.

"And a very short betrothal it'll be, love," he told her firmly.
"I hope you hadn't planned on a big wedding."

"What? With my *Perils of Pauline* luck?" Gypsy was honestly horrified. "I wouldn't dare! I'd trip over my train, or drop
the flowers—or the ring—"

Chase was laughing. "You probably would, Gypsy mine.
So we'll have a nice quiet wedding as soon as it can be
arranged. Would your parents mind if we were married at the
office of a justice of the peace?" A whimsical expression crossed
his face as he thought of Gypsy's parents. "Stupid question,"
he murmured.

Gypsy was grinning up at him. "My parents wouldn't
mind if we were married in the middle of Portland during rush
hour—just as long as it's legal."

"Mmmm." Chase lifted an eyebrow. "Dad won't be able to
get leave to return to the States for the wedding, so you'd better be prepared for a second ceremony—in Switzerland."

"Switzerland?" she mumbled.

"Uh-huh. Nice place for a honeymoon, don't you think? I
can watch you wrap Dad around your little finger, and then we
can spend a few weeks seeing all the places the tourists miss.
We'll even rent a chalet—that way we won't have to bother
about DO NOT DISTURB signs. How does that sound?"

Gypsy frowned at him. "Why do I suddenly get the feeling that you've had this arranged for quite a while?"

Chase looked thoughtful, the jade laughter in his eyes giving him away. "I couldn't say—unless it's because you know me so well, sweetheart."

"Chase!"

He chuckled softly. "Guilty—and I don't regret it a bit. Actually I called Dad during one of those hellish nights in Richmond and told him that I was bringing my bride to the Alps as soon as possible, and would he please rent a chalet for us?" Chase looked reflective. "I'm sure I sounded a little wild. Anyway Dad can't wait to meet you."

Gypsy realized that her mouth was open, and hastily closed it. "Oh, Lord," she murmured.

"He already knows you from your books," Chase was going on cheerfully. "We share an addiction for mysteries. As a matter of fact, we both agree that you're number one; we each have your books hardbound, and guard them jealously."

"You never told me that," she mumbled, suddenly remembering Jake's comment about Chase's "raving" over her books.

"You never asked." He kissed her nose; it seemed to be a favorite spot for him. "How many children shall we have, Gypsy mine?"

She blinked. "You like your questions loaded, don't you?"

"Never answer a question with a question," he chided gravely. "I was thinking of three. That's a nice, uneven number. However, I absolutely *insist* on being consulted over the names. Otherwise, our children will end up with names like Vladimir or Shadwell or Zenobia or Radinka. Or Bucephalus."

"I didn't name him!" Gypsy objected, trying not to laugh.

"I have my suspicions about that," Chase told her darkly.

Gypsy giggled, and then sobered. "Three," she murmured, and then looked up at Chase with sudden vulnerability and uncertainty in her eyes. "Our children. . . . Darling, I'd love to be a mother, but do you think—"

He laid a gentle finger across her lips, cutting off doubts. "Our children will cherish their mother all the days of their lives," he assured her huskily. "They'll come to her with their laughter and their tears, because she'll laugh with them and cry with them. She'll be the type of mother who'll gather all the neighborhood kids at her house for an impromptu party or a picnic, and she'll never run out of games or stories. It'll be a disorganized home, filled with laughter and love, and innumerable pets—and I wouldn't miss it for the world!"

After a moment of drowning in the warm jade depths of his eyes, Gypsy murmured softly, "In that case, three won't be enough."

He kissed her nose again. "I'm open to negotiations, darling."

"Why don't we try out that Jacuzzi of yours again?" she suggested solemnly. "It should be a good place to . . . negotiate."

"Great minds. We could—"

"So here you are! I turn my back for an instant, and just look at the trouble you've gotten into!"

The authoritative voice—rather like the screech of a disturbed crow—caused Chase and Gypsy to step hurriedly apart, their expressions those of guilty children caught with their entire arms in a cookie jar. They turned toward the house, Gypsy with resignation and Chase with astonishment.

"Is *that* Amy?" he asked Gypsy in a comical aside.

"Uh-huh." Gypsy didn't dare look at Chase for fear of coming unglued. "Hi, Amy," she said in a stronger voice. "You turned your back for more than an instant, you turned it for *weeks*. Of course, I got into trouble." Chase poked her with an elbow, and she continued obediently, "Amy, this is Chase. The trouble I got into."

After a rather desperate look at Gypsy, Chase produced a winning smile. "Hello, Amy. It's nice to meet you finally, after—"

"You have a last name?" Amy demanded tersely, never one to possess scruples about interrupting other people in the middle of their sentences.

"Mitchell," Chase supplied in a failing voice.

Gypsy was coming unglued.

Amy was six feet tall in flat shoes (which she normally wore) and built like a fullback. She had long hair worn in a no-nonsense bun and as red as a fire engine, snapping blue eyes, and the kind of face artists drew on Vikings. That face had character; it also had the trick of looking like a scientist's face in the act of dispassionately studying the latest bug under a microscope.

She might have been any age between forty-five and sixty-five, and looked about as capable as a human being could look without resembling a computer. She had no waist, and there was more of her going than coming, all of it tightly bound in gasping blue jeans and a peasant blouse. And her voice would easily wither a Bengal tiger in his tracks.

"So you're Mitchell. Rebecca told me about you." She looked Chase up and down with cold suspicion.

Recovering from that inspection—when Amy looked at you, he decided, your bones felt scoured—Chase hastily decided on a strategy. Exposure to Gypsy and her parents had taught him nothing if not that unpredictability was "a consummation devoutly to be wished." So he decided on a fast charge through forward enemy positions.

Stepping forward, he caught Amy around her nonexistent

waist with both arms, planted a kiss squarely on her compressed lips, and said in a conspiratorial whisper, "You'll have to excuse us for a while, Amy; Gypsy and I are going to negotiate in a Jacuzzi."

He released her and turned to pick up a laughing Gypsy and toss her lightly over his shoulder. When he turned back, he saw that Amy's face had altered slightly. There was the faintest hint of a possibility that there *might* have been a twitch of her lips which an optimistic man would have called the beginnings of a smile.

"Negotiate what?" she asked. (Mildly for her, Chase decided, although a grizzly bear would have happily claimed it as a lethal growl.)

"Important things," Chase told her solemnly. "Like the number of children, and names for same . . . and cabbages and kings. You will excuse us?" he added politely.

"Certainly." Her voice was as polite as his, and her deadpan expression would have moved a marble statue to tears. "Supper's at seven—don't be late."

"We wouldn't think of it," Chase assured her, carrying his future bride over his shoulder and striding toward the deck at the rear of his house.

As he went up the steps to the deck Chase swatted a conveniently placed derriere, and said despairingly, "I was expecting a *motherly* sort of woman!"

"I know you were!" Gypsy was laughing so hard, she could barely speak. "Oh, God! Your expression was priceless!"

"Why didn't you warn me, you heartless little witch?" he demanded, setting her on her feet beside the Jacuzzi. The gleam in his eyes belied his fierce frown.

"And miss that little scene?" Gypsy choked. "I wish Poppy could have seen it; he'd have dined out on that for a month! Oh, darling, you were perfect—Amy loves you already."

"How could you tell?" Chase asked wryly, and then a sudden thought apparently occurred to him. "Gypsy . . . is Amy going to live with us?"

"Of course she is, darling," his future bride told him serenely.

Chase raised his eyes toward heaven with the look of a man whose cup was full. More than full. Running over.

"Don't worry." Gypsy patted his cheek gently. "If you're good, she'll only come after you with her broom once a week or so."

"Gypsy?"

"What is it, darling?"

"You're kidding?"

"No, darling."

"Gypsy?"

"Yes, darling?"

"I'll never survive it."

"Of course you will, darling." She smiled up at him sunnily. "My hero can adapt to anything. That's one of the reasons I love him."

"News for you, sweetheart," he murmured, kissing her nose. "Your hero has feet of clay."

Gypsy smiled very tenderly. "That's another of the reasons I love him."

"My Gypsy," he whispered. "My love."

They were late for supper. But Amy didn't fuss.

ten

THE SHRILL DEMAND OF THE TELEPHONE
finally roused Gypsy, and she felt a distinct inclination to swear
sleepily. They'd flown half around the world the day before,
from Geneva, Switzerland, to Portland, Oregon, with only
brief layovers. Gypsy wasn't even sure what *month* it was—
never mind the day. She was suffering from lack of sleep, a
horrendous jet lag, and the irritating conviction that she'd forgotten *something* in Geneva.

And now the phone. It was only a little after eight A.M.—
the birds weren't even up, for Pete's sake!

Gypsy half climbed over Chase to reach the phone; he was
dead to the world and didn't move. She fumbled for the receiver and managed finally to lift it to her ear, murmuring,
"What?"

"You've been gone," a soft, muffled masculine voice told
her sadly. "For weeks . . . and you didn't tell me. . . ."

Gypsy slammed the receiver down and sat bolt upright in
bed, staring at the phone as if it had just this moment come to
life. Now, *that* was a hell of a thing to wake up to in her condi-
tion! She had to ask Chase. She had to know.

Chase stirred and looked up at her with sleep-blurred eyes.

"You look like a house fell on you," he observed, muffling a yawn with one hand. "Who was that on the phone?"

Shock tactics, she decided, might have some effect.

She snatched the sheet up to cover her breasts and stared at Chase in patent horror. "We have to get a divorce. Immediately," she announced in a very firm voice.

Chase raised himself on his elbow and stared at her with sleepy courtesy. "We just got *married* a few weeks ago," he pointed out patiently. "Are you tired of me already?"

Gypsy struggled hard to maintain her expression of shocked indignation. "I've married the wrong man! I fell in love with a voice over the telephone, and now I find out that it wasn't you at all. Get out of my bed!"

Chase was soothing. "You probably had a bad dream. Jet lag will do that to you. Lie down, sweetheart."

"I want a divorce."

"I won't let you divorce me. I like being married. Besides, my father would stand me in front of a firing squad if I lost you. He's telling half of Geneva about his daughter-in-law, the famous writer."

"Well, if that's the only reason you want to hang on to me, I'll go and see a lawyer today!"

"It's Saturday."

"Is it? Monday, then."

Chase pulled her down beside him and arranged them both comfortably. "Not a chance. Amy loves me. And Corsair's coming around. You'd never find anyone as adaptable as me. Besides, we've already arranged to house-sit in Richmond for the winter."

With an inward sigh Gypsy abandoned her ploy to find out if Chase was really her "night lover." "Did we say hello to Jake and Sarah last night?" she asked suddenly. "I seem to remember something about it."

Chase laughed. "Well, sort of. I was carrying you, and you waved at them and asked how they liked my Jacuzzi. I think you were sound asleep at the time."

Gypsy frowned. "Were they over here, then? Shouldn't they have been at your place?"

"Our place," Chase corrected. "And they were over here keeping Amy company until we arrived. Jake's determined to win her over," he added with a chuckle. "He says he wants the friendship of any woman who can defeat him at arm wrestling."

Gypsy accepted this information without a blink. "Oh." She yawned suddenly and changed the subject again. In an injured tone she said, "It's inhuman to drag a person halfway around the world. If man had been meant to fly—"

"He'd have wings?" Chase finished politely.

"No. He'd have a cushion tied to his rump to make up for airport lounges," she corrected disgustedly. "I seem to have spent eons in them, and my rump *hurts*!"

Chase patted it consolingly. "You'll recover. And, besides, whose fault was it that we made the trip in one fell swoop?"

"Mine, and don't rub it in." Gypsy sighed. "Can I help it if I wanted to get the whole thing over with as quickly as possible?"

"No, but you could have warned me before we went over that you had a phobia about flying."

"It isn't a phobia, it's just an uneasiness," she defended stoutly.

"Uh-huh." Chase grinned at her. "Tell me what the Swiss Alps look like from the air."

"I can't."

"Why not, sweetheart?"

"Because I had my eyes closed, and you know it, dammit!"

Chase laughed at her expression. "Seriously, honey, we

should have taken Dad's suggestion: gone overland to Bordeaux and then taken a ship."

"Across the Atlantic?" Her tone was horrified.

They'd had this same discussion in Geneva, and Chase laughed as much now as he had then. "It beats me how you're willing to fly over an ocean, although you hate flying—but you aren't willing to sail across an ocean, although you love swimming."

"A plane's faster," Gypsy said definitely.

"So?"

"So don't make me explain my little irrational fears. I warned you long ago that I was no bargain, but you just wouldn't listen. So now you have an irrational wife."

"I have a wonderful wife," Chase corrected comfortably. "And I have Dad's stamp of approval to verify it. I thought he was going to cry when you hugged him that last time at the airport. You definitely made a conquest there."

Gypsy smiled. "I love your dad. He reminds me of Poppy—very quiet, but with a deadly sense of humor."

"Mmmm. I think you've about got him talked into settling in Portland when he retires. You can work on him some more when he comes over for Christmas."

"It'd be nice to have both families nearby," she agreed, then frowned as part of his remark set up a train of thought. "Christmas. That reminds me—before we left for Geneva, I saw you and Mother come in here with a package all wrapped up. It looked like a painting. Somehow or another, I forgot to ask you about it."

Chase laughed silently. "That's my Gypsy—give her enough time, and she'll get around to it eventually!"

Gypsy raised up on an elbow and stared down at him severely. "Stop avoiding the subject. What have you and my mother been up to?"

"That question sounds vaguely indecent," he murmured.
"Chase!"

"I have a shrewish wife," he told the ceiling, then relented
as the gleam in her eyes threatened grievous bodily harm.
"Take a look behind you, shrew," he invited. "On the wall—
where you were too much asleep last night to notice it."

Gypsy twisted around to look. Then she sat up and looked
a while longer. Then she looked at Chase as he sat up beside
her.

He smiled. "Rebecca painted it for me. Although she said
she didn't know why I wanted it—since I was bound to end up
with the original. I asked her to paint it that Sunday I invited
them for lunch. And we left it here because I knew we'd spend
our first night back in this room."

After a moment he added softly, "I didn't know she'd put
me in it."

Gypsy looked at the painting again. Her first thought was
that Rebecca must have seen the seascapes in Chase's bedroom
and, with her usual perception, decided to paint another
seascape which would blend in . . . and yet stand out. Because
this painting wasn't bleak or lonely.

The central figure was Gypsy. She was wearing the silk
nightgown and leaning back against the rock jutting up behind
her, staring out to sea. Above her were storm clouds, curiously
shaped, as if Nature had been in a teasing mood that day, bent
on luring mortals out to sea. The clouds were wispy, insubstan-
tial; their dreamy visions seen only by those who cared to see.
There was a unicorn leaping from one cloud, a castle topped
another; a rainbow cast its hazy colors over the ghost-ship sail-
ing beneath it, a ghostly pirate at its wheel. There was Apollo,
driving his sun behind dark clouds; there was a masked figure
on a white steed; there was a knight climbing toward his
cloud-castle.

And there was Chase—real, substantial. The view caught him from the waist up, half hidden by the rock Gypsy was leaning against. And Chase wasn't looking out to sea at the siren-visions of clouds. He was looking at Gypsy, and his face was soft with yearning.

Gypsy took a deep breath, realizing only then that she'd suspended breathing for what seemed like eternal seconds. "I never stop wondering at Mother's perception," she murmured almost inaudibly. She looked again at the cloud-heroes, seeing in each one an elusive resemblance to Chase.

"She saw it, Chase—she saw it all. I was looking at visions of heroes and seeing you without realizing it."

"And I was looking at you," Chase murmured, bending his head to kiss her bare shoulder.

"I'm so glad you're a patient hero," she whispered, smiling up at him as he lowered them both back to the comfortable pillows.

Chase grinned faintly. "An original hero, anyway. What other man would have scoured Geneva—of all places!—to find a Buddha with a clock in his middle?"

Gypsy giggled helplessly. "Did you see your dad's face when we carried it in? And when you told him very seriously that your watch had stopped?"

"He looked even more peculiar when we opened the other boxes," Chase noted ruefully. "Such odd souvenirs for a honeymoon: an abstract wooden sculpture of a knight on horseback, a bogus nineteenth-century sword—complete with scabbard, a hideous little genie-type lamp covered with tarnish. . . . You'd do great on a scavenger hunt, sweetheart."

"*You're* the one who fell in love with the sword," Gypsy pointed out calmly.

"A memento of our courtship," Chase said soulfully.

"Right. Just don't try to dance while wearing it."

"As long as you don't try to conjure a genie from that lamp."

"Why not?" she asked in mock disappointment.

"I shudder to think what'd pop out."

Gypsy sighed. "You're probably right."

"And speaking of being right"—he patted her gently— "I've been meaning to tell you that the Swiss cooking did wonders in adding that extra ballast you needed."

"Uh-huh." Gypsy twisted slightly for a view of her blanket-covered posterior. "Too much ballast, if you ask me. Just look! I'm getting broad in the beam!"

He choked on a laugh. "Your beam looks great to me."

"Flatterer."

"The choice of words was yours." He drew her a bit closer. "Besides, you still weigh no more than a midget. I'll have to fatten you up some more before we go to work on Radinka or Shadwell."

Gypsy started laughing. "You're hung up on those names! I thought you just used them as a terrifying example of the names I'd come up with on my own."

Sheepishly Chase murmured, "They kinda grow on you though."

"No, Chase," she told him firmly.

"I suppose not. Still—"

"No."

"No?"

"Definitely no. I'd be a widow as soon as the kids realized what you'd done to them."

He sighed. "My first opportunity to come up with some really creative names," he mourned sadly.

"Exercise your creative powers by naming Angel's kittens. Or you can name the Mercedes. Or we'll get a dog—"

"We already have one," Chase told her casually.

Gypsy lifted her head to stare down at him. "We do?"

"Uh-huh. Bucephalus."

"But he belongs to the Robbinses—"

"Not anymore. Remember when we called before the wedding to explain about Amy being in sole charge of the house while we were gone?" When Gypsy nodded, he went on. "You had to leave the room because Rebecca wanted to talk to you about flowers or something. Anyway, I was talking to Tim. It seems he's been offered a two-year position, which could turn out to be permanent, in London starting next year. Bucephalus would have to spend six months in quarantine, and he'd be miserable. So Tim offered to give him to us. I accepted—for both of us."

Gypsy smiled. "That's wonderful. Now we have a head start on our family."

Chase began to nuzzle her throat. "Mmmm. Would you care to start working toward the rest of our family, Gypsy mine?"

"I thought you'd never ask," she murmured, feeling that delicious tremor stir to life inside her. Then she smiled, and said almost to herself, "Gypsy mine; you've called me that from the first. Were you that sure of me, darling?"

"Not sure. Hopeful." Chase pulled her easily over on top of him and smiled up at her whimsically. "I've never been one to search for rainbows, but you were my dream." He hesitated, then added very softly, " 'So if I dream I have you, I have you.' "

A thousand and one thoughts tumbled through Gypsy's mind.

"What is it, love?" Chase asked gently. "You're giving me a very peculiar look."

Gypsy carefully searched her memory of events. She was almost sure— Yes, she *was* sure! Her "night lover" had called only twice when Chase was actually in the room, and on both occasions, she'd hung up on him before he could say more than a few words. What if . . . what if she *hadn't* been so quick to hang up? Would she have discovered that it had been a tape-recorded message? Held up to the phone by a helpful friend, perhaps?

"You're staring at me, love. Somewhat fiercely, I might add."

"Chase . . ."

"Yes, love?"

"You just quoted Donne."

"Did I, love?" He was smiling slightly, the jade eyes veiled by sleepy lids. "The man obviously had a way with words."

"Chase."

"Hmmm?"

"It was you. It *was* you . . . wasn't it?"

"What was me, love?"

Gypsy tried to ignore wandering hands. "The phone calls. It had to be you. Wasn't it you?"

"I don't know what you're talking about, love."

"Chase, you *have* to tell me! I'll go nuts, and—" A startled giggle suddenly escaped her.

Jade eyes gleamed up at her, filled with laughter. "Ah-ha! I finally found your ticklish spot. You're at my mercy now, love."

Gypsy choked back another giggle, trying to ward off his tickling hand. "Chase! Stop that! And tell me it was you, dammit! Darling, I have to *know!*"

"What was that, love? Didn't quite catch it."

"Chase!" she wailed.

He smiled.

Pepper's Way

one

WANTED: MAN. Must be over six feet tall and weigh at least two hundred pounds. Must own large house on considerable acreage. Must like animals. Must have job with flexible hours. Preferably single. Call Pepper.

HE WOULDN'T HAVE GIVEN THE AD A SEC- ond glance if he'd found it in the personals column of some trashy magazine. It certainly sounded typical of that kind of publication. And yet . . . Thor looked at the ad for the fifth time in as many minutes. Well, he fit all the requirements. And he was dying to find out what kind of woman would place such an ad in a large daily newspaper.

He'd seen the ad every day this week, and had grown more and more curious. And since he knew very well that the newspaper in which the ad was running didn't pander to lonelyhearts or practical jokers, he couldn't help but wonder exactly what it was all about. A publicity stunt or something. Had to be. But if it *wasn't* . . . well, then, what was it?

He possessed two overwhelming sins, neither of which was appropriate in his profession: curiosity and a love of the absurd. Sighing, he reached for the phone and dialed the number printed after the name Pepper.

"Hello?"

It was a sweet, childish voice, presently filled with suspicion. She sounded as though she might possibly be five years old . . . on her next birthday.

"Pepper?" he asked cautiously.

"Yes?" Definitely wary now.

"I'm calling about your ad," Thor began.

"Oh, Lord—another one! Listen, I'm pulling that ad tomorrow, so forget it! I've been listening to obscene suggestions all week, and I'm fed up! So, whoever you are, get your kicks somewhere else!"

The voice, he reflected, was still sweet and childish, but this was definitely no little girl he was talking to. Curiosity grew. Mildly, he told her, "I didn't call to make obscene suggestions."

"You didn't? Then what do you want?" she demanded.

"I thought it was a matter of what *you* wanted," he murmured. "A man over six feet tall, two hundred pounds—and so on."

"Do you fit?" she asked, still suspicious.

"Yes."

"How old are you?"

"Does that matter?"

She sighed, irritated. "I've had calls from four high school quarterbacks this week, and I didn't like any of their questions."

"High school is definitely behind me," he responded, then asked in spite of himself, "What did they ask you?"

Clearly aggrieved, she said, "Well, one of them asked if I like leather. The other questions weren't repeatable."

Trying not to laugh, Thor said, "Your ad is a bit . . . suggestive."

"It is? But I spent so much time on the wording just to get the proper effect!" she wailed softly.

"The effect you got was far from proper. What, by the way, is the ad all about? You'll notice," he added virtuously, "that I'm not leaping to conclusions."

"I'll bet you leaped to plenty before you picked up the phone," she muttered, and then sighed again. "You see, it's my dog."

"Your dog?" Thor echoed.

"Uh-huh. My landlord found out. That is, he'd known that I *had* a dog, but he got all upset with me last week. Said something about not realizing that I fed it hay. Anyway, I can't keep my dog in this apartment anymore."

"I see." The matter was, indeed, becoming plainer to Thor. "Which is why you advertised for a large man with a house in the country."

"Right." She sounded relieved. "I mean, a small man would feel intimidated by a Dobe, don't you think?"

Thor, whose mind couldn't instantly identify *Dobe* to conjure a picture, agreed wholeheartedly. "Certainly. I suppose you'll want to know how large my house is?"

"You mean, you're interested?"

"Of course." Thor looked around at his large, spotless living room and heard his housekeeper banging pots in the kitchen. Ah, well. He could keep the dog outside; he needed a watchdog anyway. Pepper's voice intrigued him; he would have offered to look at a Bengal tiger if she'd asked. "Are you selling the dog, or—"

"Oh, no!" She was shocked. "I wouldn't do that!"

So she was just finding the dog a good home. Odd how some people felt better about giving away their pets rather than selling them. "I see. Well, Pepper—" He hesitated. "I'm sorry, but you didn't tell me your last—"

"Oh, everybody calls me Pepper," she assured him cheerfully. "Who are *you,* by the way?"

Thor found himself smiling. "Thorton Spicer. My friends call me Thor."

"I'll bet you have red hair."

Surprised, he confirmed her guess. "Yes, I do, but how did you know?"

"Vikings," she said cryptically, then went on as if no explanation were necessary. "Do you have a large house?"

"Four bedrooms, two baths, living room, den, study—"

"That sounds perfect! Land?"

"Fifteen acres." He was growing more and more amused. But he warned himself not to develop a mental picture of Pepper; whenever he did that, he was always disappointed. Of course, his mind was already busy drawing. Pepper, it decided arbitrarily, was about five feet tall with blond hair and big blue eyes. He told his mind not to be so damn sure. She was probably six feet tall with black hair and played hockey.

"Perfect!" The little breathless voice sounded delighted. "Oh, but, you'd better—"

"See the dog," he finished dryly. "Yes, perhaps I'd better. I'm heading into town this afternoon; if you'll tell me where you live, I'll stop by."

She gave him clear, precise directions to her apartment building, which rather surprised him; she had sounded a bit feather-headed. Then she finished with, "You can't miss it"— which made him immediately distrust the directions. But he promised to drop by around three o'clock.

Before she could respond, there was a loud crash from her end, and she said hurriedly, "Oh, heavens! Brutus! What're you—? Look what you've done! Um, I'll see you at three."

Thor found himself listening to a dial tone, and assumed in

amusement that the last sentence had been intended for him. He hung up the phone, chuckling quietly. Well, it would certainly be interesting meeting Pepper. And he *did* need a watchdog. Brutus? He scaled his mental image of a Dobe up a few inches. Obviously a large dog. And why did the name keep ringing warning bells in his mind?

"Your lunch is getting cold," Mrs. Small told him dourly from the doorway of the room.

Mrs. Small wasn't. By any stretch of the imagination. She was only a little over five feet tall, but made up for the lack in other areas. All other areas. And she was the exception to the rule that all plump people were jolly souls. In five years Thor had never seen her so much as smile. He'd even given in to the lesser side of himself and tried a few practical jokes, only to be told coldly that he was too old for such nonsense.

Thor looked at her now and decided not to tell her about the possible addition to his household. "I told you not to bother," he said instead.

"No bother, as long as you eat it."

He wondered vaguely if Mrs. Small would ever call him by his name. Either of his names. She never had. He was almost terrified of the woman. "I'm coming," he said hastily, noting that her habitual frown was assuming thunderous proportions.

She deepened her glare, nodded briefly, and turned away.

Thor sighed and got to his feet. He headed for the dining room—Mrs. Small would *never* feed him in the kitchen!—wondering if Pepper would live up to his mind's optimism.

At exactly three o'clock Thor was standing before the door marked 3-B and silently bracing himself to be disappointed. He looked down at his neat dark slacks, white shirt, and sport jacket, and thought wryly that most people probably didn't care how they dressed to meet a dog. But then . . . he was meeting a woman. At least he hoped she was a woman.

He made a mental note to write to the friend from his college days, who now ran a rather lucrative dating service. If Jim hadn't tried inserting peculiar ads in newspapers, he was missing a good bet. . . .

Thor knocked on the door. A deep-throated "Woof!" and various other indefinable sounds came from within. Then the door swung open.

"Come in," a sweet, breathless voice invited. "If you're Thor, that is."

"I'm Thor," he managed, stepping inside automatically. The door closed behind him while he tried to collect himself. It wasn't easy; his mental picture of Pepper had been uncannily on target.

Since she was in socks only, he could gauge her height nicely; if she was stretched on a rack for ten minutes, she might possibly be five feet tall. Her hair was so light that *silver* was the only color that could describe it, and it fell nearly to her hips. Her face was finely drawn and delicate, and flattered the word *beautiful*. Only her eyes varied from his image, and he was glad they did; plain blue could never begin to compare with that glorious pale violet.

And—though tiny she certainly was—the mature and somewhat startlingly voluptuous curves filling out her jeans and knit top belonged only to a woman.

"I'm glad you found the place," she was telling him in that ridiculously intriguing little-girl voice. "Would you like to sit down, or—"

A loud thump from somewhere in one of the other rooms interrupted her, and she half turned from Thor, exclaiming fretfully, "Oh, damn, he got out!"

Before Thor could ask the foreboding question in his mind, a two-pound fury hurtled across the carpeted floor, uttering a hysterical yapping sound, and attached itself ferociously to his trouser leg. On closer inspection the fury turned out to be a Chihuahua that would have had to be dipped in milk and rolled in bread crumbs to weigh two pounds. It was light brown in color, and obviously possessed the temper and general disposition of a drunken marine.

In patient silence Thor shifted his weight onto his unencumbered leg and raised the other about a foot off the floor. The fury clung tenaciously, growling and trying fiercely to bring down its intended prey, entirely unperturbed by the fact that it was hanging in midair. Thor returned the foot and attached dog to the floor and lifted his eyes to Pepper. She was, he noted, looking down at the tiny dog with a fondly exasperated expression.

"What's it doing?" Thor asked politely.

Pepper looked up, surprised. "He's attacking you, obviously. He's an attack dog."

Thor looked hard for mockery on the lovely face, and found only solemnity. "Oh. Do you mind calling him off?"

"Well . . . I can't."

"You can't?" Thor decided that if both Pepper and this Lilliputian canine thought that it was an attack dog, who was he to argue? "I thought there was a command to call them off."

"There is," she agreed cheerfully. "It's 'break.' But Brutus ignores it; he always has."

Incredulously Thor dropped his gaze to the tiny creature. "*This* is Brutus? You can't tell me your landlord objects to this little mite!"

"Of course not. *Fifi's* the problem."

"Fifi?" Thor decided that he had wandered through Alice's

mirror by accident. The scary part was that he was enjoying it. "Uh . . . where's Fifi?"

Looking surprised again, Pepper half turned and gestured toward the couch a few feet away. Thor's gaze followed her pointing finger, and he immediately understood her surprise; his only excuse for having missed seeing the creature until now was that he'd been too fascinated by Pepper to look at his surroundings.

"Fifi" was a respectably sized mountain of short gleaming black and tan fur, quivering from pointed little ears to stub of a tail. It was lying on its belly with its face thrust underneath the couch, and a quick and rough calculation told Thor that it would be nearly three feet tall on all fours.

It was a full-grown and heavily muscled Doberman pinscher, which Thor had always considered one of the wickedest-looking dogs in creation. And it weighed every ounce of a hundred pounds.

The landlord's horror, he reflected, was now perfectly clear. He tried to picture the expression on Mrs. Small's face when she saw Fifi and hastily abandoned the effort when the first fleeting image came to his mind.

"Fifi?" Pepper called softly, and the dog quivered even more, not moving an inch.

"What's it doing?" Thor asked curiously.

"She's hiding."

"What's she hiding?"

"Herself."

"But I can see—"

"Shhh!" Pepper made a hasty gesture to silence him. "*She* thinks she's hiding. Since she can't see you, she thinks you can't see her."

Thor decided to let that pass; for the life of him, he didn't know how to respond. He realized suddenly that he was still being savaged. "Look, can you get this dog off my leg? I'm going to look a little peculiar walking around with him attached to me like this."

Pepper looked down at Brutus, frowned for a moment, then stepped closer. She bent over and swatted the tiny dog firmly on the rump. Immediately he whirled to contend with the surprise attack, and she snatched him up and tucked him under her arm. Apparently still blind with rage, Brutus was on the point of sinking his teeth into her arm when her voice stopped him cold.

"Don't . . . you . . . dare," she told him in an unexpectedly icy tone.

Pointed ears that were overlarge on the tiny head perked up, and there was such a ludicrously expressive "Oh, it's *you!*" look on the dog's face that Thor burst out laughing. Brutus immediately threw a snarl his way, clearly trying to save face.

"What do you feed him—gunpowder?"

"Of course not. I told you he was an attack dog." She waved a hospitable hand toward the small living room they were literally standing in. "Why don't you sit down? On the couch there, by Fifi. She'll come out once she gets used to your voice."

Thor went over to the couch, making a lengthy detour around Fifi's ample rump to sit a prudent distance away from her. He was taking no chances.

Pepper sat across from him in a chair, holding the ever-growling Brutus firmly in her lap. "Are you still interested?" she asked wryly.

Looking at her instead of the dog, Thor murmured, "More than ever."

If she heard anything in his voice to suggest that it was she, rather than her dog, that Thor was interested in, Pepper didn't show it on her face. She was completely natural, and obviously didn't possess a single coquettish bone in her body.

And she didn't, Thor reflected thankfully, weigh him with a speculative and unnerving eye, as so many women seemed to do these days. He wondered suddenly if she were as old as her body suggested.

"How old are you?" he demanded abruptly.

Pepper seemed neither surprised nor offended by the question. Instead, she released a long-suffering sigh. "*Et tu, Brute?* I'm twenty-eight." At his obvious surprise she added dryly, "I have to carry a special police identification card because nobody ever believes that. Shall I show it to you?"

Thor grinned. "No need; I'll take your word for it."

"Thanks. And you never told me how old you are, by the way."

"Thirty-four. And nobody *ever* disbelieves that."

She studied him with a total lack of self-consciousness. "I can see how they wouldn't," she said ingenuously. "You have a rough sort of face; it has a history."

Thor immediately felt at least ten years older than he was. History? Glancing aside to collect his thoughts, he found himself under scrutiny from a pair of panicky brown eyes that widened in even greater panic and then disappeared. Fifi was hiding again. Thor looked at Pepper, and she shrugged, giving him a rueful smile.

"She'll get used to you."

"She's a coward," he observed dryly.

"Well . . . I guess you could say that. She barks once and then hides."

Thor remembered the deep-throated bark he'd heard. "Uh-huh. Some watchdog she's going to make."

Pepper smiled at him happily, the bottomless pools of her violet eyes oddly riveting. "Are you saying that you want her?"

He didn't even hesitate. "Definitely. But I don't know about taking her with me today. She's so nervous, and my car—"

"What kind of car do you have?"

"A Corvette."

Pepper winced. "That'll never do. Tell you what. I have a van, so why don't I do the relocating? We can come tomorrow."

Convinced that Pepper wouldn't abandon her pet totally, Thor nodded and smiled. "Sounds great. You can help her with the—uh—transitional period."

"Wonderful! What time tomorrow shall we come?"

"Any time after noon."

"We'll be there." Pepper looked down at the huge, quivering dog, and smiled fondly. "I'm sure she'll be braver in the country."

Thor blinked and then looked down at the dog as well. He'd nearly forgotten about Fifi. "Uh...yes. I'm sure she will be."

---

two

GRAY EYES, **PEPPER THOUGHT, LEANING BACK**
against the closed door and staring absently across the room.
He had gray eyes. Combined with his red-gold hair and deeply
tanned skin, the gray eyes were startling. They were also sharp,
intelligent, and held a lurking twinkle.

Releasing her pent-up breath in a long sigh, Pepper bent to
set Brutus on the floor. She saw that her hands were shaking
and wasn't surprised by that. But she was surprised by her reaction to Thor Spicer. At twenty-eight she'd ruefully decided that
she would probably remain unattached, because she had not,
in all her travels, met a man whose voice set her heart bumping
and raised goose bumps on her flesh.

Almost reluctantly she lifted an arm and examined her
lightly tanned skin. Uh-huh. Gooseflesh. And heaven knew her
heart was bumping against her ribs as though she'd been running.

Still leaning against the door, she watched Fifi rise, shake
herself, then wag a happy bobtailed rear end and follow Brutus
toward the kitchen and their food dishes. Pepper shook her
head slightly. What had her *brilliant* newspaper ad gotten her

into? Simply because she'd wanted to find Fifi a good home with a kind man . . .

The truth floated into her consciousness gently, unthreateningly: like most of the schemes and plans her active mind spawned, this idea had looked innocent and logical on the surface. Experience had taught her that her "logical" plans generally possessed hidden pitfalls. However, she'd never given up her scheming just because of a few minor stumbling blocks.

Cal's voice surfaced suddenly in her mind, a little desperate and a lot wild: "You're dangerous, you know that? You're *ruthless* and, God, who'd guess it by looking at you?"

Pepper grinned to herself. That had been wailed at her just moments before Cal's wedding to Marsha five years ago, and just after a long and somewhat involved courtship in which Pepper had played a vital role. Matchmaker. She was good at that.

After all, Cal and Marsha were still married, and very happily so from the looks of it. And the other matches she'd engineered over the years were still going strong, not a divorce or separation in the lot.

This time Johnny's voice popped into her mind: "Let's all band together and get Pepper settled; it'd be poetic justice! She's the only one of the gang still footloose and fancy-free."

Absently Pepper moved over to sink down on the couch, drawing her legs up and tucking her feet under a cushion. The gang was indeed all settled. Most within driving distance of one another in the Northeast; she, herself, was the farthest north at the moment, living in Maine. Her original college crowd numbered nearly a score—and that wasn't counting the strays she'd happened across on her travels and brought home to be matched with her friends.

Ruthless? She thought about that for a moment. Certainly

she was ruthless. But she would never do anything to hurt a friend—which was probably why she had so many of them. She was also a helluva lot smarter than she looked, and perfectly capable of taking care of herself even in the turmoil of Third World countries.

So, being a smart and ruthless lady, she had never yet hesitated to go after what she wanted, be it a seat on a booked airline or some trinket requiring haggling in a language she didn't speak.

But a man? No, she'd never gone after a man. Heaven knew she had plenty of male friends spread out over the world. But no gooseflesh. Until now.

She grinned to herself. "Okay, Pepper," she murmured out loud, "how do you propose to do the thing? And never mind the idea. The idea is dumb...and dangerous." She brooded silently for a moment.

"He's interested. That was obvious. I don't know why, but he is." She winced as Fifi clambered up onto her lap—all hundred pounds of her. Stroking the sleek fur, Pepper gazed sternly into mild brown eyes. "He didn't want you, old girl. I'm sure he'll give you a good home, and love you once he gets to know you. But curiosity brought him here. He wasn't interested in a hundred-pound lap dog. However...he *said* he wants you. I wonder if he realizes I won't totally abandon you to a stranger?"

Fifi whined what could have been taken for an agreement.

"I wonder exactly how far his interest goes?" Pepper mused to her sympathetic canine friend. "He doesn't look like the home-and-hearth type. I was right; his face has a history. That little scar above his left eye...And he looks tired. I wonder what he does for a living? Something out in the weather. That's not a swimming-pool tan, and his hands have seen rough use. And he's strong."

Fifi saluted her mistress's cheek with a tongue the size of a hand towel and smiled all over her face.

"Thank you," Pepper told the dog dryly. "I'll certainly try to justify your faith in me." She managed to worm her way out from under Fifi, knowing from experience that it was much easier to move herself than to move the huge dog. Absently she paced over to the sliding glass doors that opened onto her balcony. Then, turning away a moment later, she caught her reflection in an ornate mirror on the wall and paused to study herself critically.

"If only you were a few inches taller," she told the frowning reflection mournfully. "And brunette. And busty." She turned sideways and stuck out her chest experimentally. The experiment wasn't a complete success; she looked decidedly off-balance and rather ridiculous.

Sighing, Pepper turned away from the reflection and assumed her normal posture. "Face it," she told herself aloud in a firm voice. "You'll just have to do the best you can with the material available."

She paced restlessly around the room, only vaguely noticing that Brutus had returned from the kitchen and taken up a heel position, pacing along beside her like a diminutive sentry. She thought back over the years, reviewing the personalities and appearances of various men who'd crossed her path and expressed a preference for pint-size blondes.

Pepper had received more than one proposal during the past ten years and quite a few propositions, none of which she'd felt even mildly tempted to accept. For the most part, she reflected, men tended to treat her like a kid sister, but the ones who had felt romantically inclined had certainly tried hard enough to arouse the same reaction in her.

Self-confident without being at all vain, Pepper was always surprised by interest from a man; it was never something she expected. Generally content with her own appearance, she nonetheless fell prey to wishful thinking whenever confronted by a tall, graceful brunet woman. She was ruefully aware that it was impossible to be either graceful or striking when one was possessed of a snub nose and less than five feet of height.

The desire to change both characteristics had never been more than wistful . . . until just a few minutes ago . . . when she had opened the door to admit Thor Spicer. At that moment she had wanted desperately to grow six inches and acquire a thin, aristocratic nose.

The shrill demand of the phone yanked Pepper from her thoughts just then, and she went over to an end table to lift the receiver.

"Hello? Oh, hello, Mr. Jacobs. Well . . . yes, I still have the dog, but— Yes, I know when I sublet the apartment I agreed— Yes, but— Mr. Jacobs, if you'll just let me tell you— I *know* how long it's been— Look. I'm trying to tell you—"

She felt an unaccustomed anger growing inside of her as she listened to the annoyed and repetitive voice of the building manager. And the idea she had firmly discarded, she realized later, began prodding her subconsciously . . . or at least that's how she excused herself forever afterward.

"Mr. Jacobs. Mr. Jacobs! Enough with the threats, all right? Nobody's complained to me about the dog except you, and I think— What? There's no need to be abusive! Fine. Fine. But you'd damn well better not rent this apartment to anyone else, because Miss James has a lease and it's paid up for months! And another thing: You're responsible for her furniture until she returns from Europe. I'll call her attorney tomorrow, and he'll be over to inventory every stick of furniture and every ornament in the place. And every bit of it had better *be* here when she gets home! Good-bye!"

Pepper slammed down the telephone and spent a few moments breathing quickly and feeling mildly surprised at her own anger. By nature she was a peacemaker and not given to outbursts—least of all with someone who had every right to be angry at her. She sat down on a chair and looked thoughtfully at her waiting canine audience.

"I believe I just burned my bridges," she told them slowly. "With a vengeance. My friends, we're about to embark on an all-out frontal assault. We're going to storm the battlements . . . march on the citadel . . . with banners flying and cannons at the ready." She giggled suddenly, nervously, at her own imagery, then sobered.

"I only hope that laugh I saw in his eyes was for real. Otherwise he's going to repel this invasion with the greatest of ease!"

Thor found himself going to the front window for the tenth time in as many minutes, and swore softly. But he didn't leave the window. He stood looking out over his neatly manicured front lawn and thinking absently about the hours spent raking leaves over the past week. A calming pastime, and one he enjoyed whenever he was home. He'd be home now for several weeks. Time enough, he thought, to get to know a tiny blonde with the most incredible violet eyes he'd ever seen.

A motion on the edge of his line of sight caught his eye, and he turned his head to see Lucifer's sleek black head lift above the split-rail fence bordering the yard. The stark white diamond in the center of the stallion's forehead pointed toward the house, and he seemed to be watching intently. Thor pulled one hand from the pocket of his jeans and swept the drapes aside, giving the horse an indication of his presence.

Immediately Lucifer shied violently away from fence and house, a movement prompted by spirit rather than fear. He patrolled the fence for a few moments, head high, nostrils flaring, and long black tail held like a banner of pride, looking toward the window as if in invitation. Then he took off in a burst of speed, galloping toward his open stable in the little hollow below the house.

Thor felt a sudden uneasiness. Other than himself, Lucifer hated every living thing, and dogs topped his list of enemies. How he would react to "one of the hated" living with his master, Thor didn't even want to guess. He comforted himself with the reminder of Fifi's cowardice; she probably wouldn't go near the pasture, he decided. He hoped.

He started to turn away from the window when a motion from the opposite direction caught his attention. And as soon as his eyes focused on the predominantly white object, he realized that Pepper had arrived to effect the relocation of her pet.

She'd said she had a van, he remembered, but... "Good Lord," he murmured to himself, fascinated. Anyone, he decided, who could call that vehicle a van was prone to vast understatement. He made an absent mental note to remember Pepper's penchant in that regard and then stared at her vehicle again.

In the first place, it was not a van at all, but what was commonly called an RV—a recreational vehicle. And it was thirty-five feet long. Custom built from the looks of it, it boasted tinted windows along the sides; cheery bumper stickers and more prosaic state travel stickers were plastered everywhere; a blue and white awning was rolled up and tied in place above the door; and the whole was liberally splashed with mud.

Wondering how a woman as tiny as Pepper could wheel that monster into his driveway so neatly, Thor left the window and headed for his front door. And if he'd been fascinated yesterday, he was even more so now. From childhood he'd been drawn to the offbeat, the unusual—and it had led him into trouble more than once. It could, he knew, be leading him into trouble now. But the realization didn't cause him to falter.

He enjoyed trouble. Usually.

Shutting the front door behind him, Thor left the house and went down the walk to the paved driveway. He enjoyed the ludicrous contrast of his sleek Corvette and the hulking monster Pepper had parked behind it. The side door of the RV opened just as he reached it. Brutus leaped out first, lifting a lip at Thor but not wasting time with an attack because of his obvious desire to explore new surroundings.

Pepper got out of the vehicle in a no less sedate manner, jumping down without bothering to use the built-in step. Thor almost sighed aloud at the lovely picture she made in her neat jeans and pale blue sweater, her long hair caught up in a casual ponytail. And he forwent polite greetings out of the necessity to give a hasty warning.

"Better not let Brutus go near the pasture. If he attacks Lucifer, he'll learn how to 'break' the hard way."

"Lucifer?" she questioned over her shoulder, somewhat occupied with half lying inside the door of the RV and hanging onto the collar of a reluctant Fifi.

"My horse," he murmured, watching the struggle with interest and silently betting with himself on the outcome.

He lost the bet. Pepper emerged victorious from the struggle, hauling the hundred-pound dog out of the vehicle. Fifi immediately hid her face behind the woman, quivering.

"Is the name descriptive?" she asked, one delicate eyebrow rising.

" 'Fraid so."

Pepper looked around quickly and spotted the tiny dog near the rear of the RV. "Brutus, heel!" she ordered in that disconcertingly icy voice of command, and the voice was heeded as Brutus came to sit by her ankle.

"I thought he didn't obey," Thor noted in surprise.

"He obeys everything but 'break,'" Pepper told him cheerfully. "And I think he only ignores that because he likes attacking." Before he could respond, she was speaking once again in that little-girl, breathless voice that utterly fascinated Thor.

"Just look at the trees! They go on practically forever. You know, after I lived in a desert for six months, I learned to absolutely *adore* trees. I guess you can never know how much you will miss something until it isn't there."

"I guess." Thor watched her reach back to shut the door of the RV, feeling his mind drift gently into that bemused sphere that Pepper seemed to carry around with her. "You lived in a desert?"

"For a while. Never really liked it though. No trees. And I hate camels. What a beautiful house! I love the bay window. And that rock chimney! Is the fireplace rock?"

Trying not to laugh, Thor followed Pepper as she began to explore the outside of the house and the yard. "It's rock," he barely had time to answer, and then she was off again.

"Is that the barn down there in the hollow? Of course. What a beautiful horse! He looks so proud. Do you ever show him? Oh, I love your patio! What do you cook in that barbecue—a whole steer? Heel, Fifi, and stop being so silly; no one's going to hurt you! Out of the shrubs, Brutus, and heel, blast you!"

Having given up on his intention not to laugh, Thor just enjoyed the stroll around the house. He listened to Pepper's questions but didn't again try to answer them, content just to watch her profile and hear the lovely sound of her voice. And he wondered to himself if it would be possible to get to know this woman in a few short weeks.

And then her words penetrated, and he felt slightly bewildered for a moment to hear her voice his thoughts.

". . . and it'll only be for a few weeks, after all."

They had completely circled the house by then, coming to a halt back where they'd started beside the vehicles. Thor blinked and tried to concentrate. "I'm sorry. You were saying . . . ?"

"That it'll only be for a few weeks, three months at the most," she responded cheerfully. "When Kristen comes home, I'll be on my way again, so it's just until then. That English breeder carried her off with him just for the season, he *said*. Anyway, I think that paved area beside the garage will be perfect for the van. But we never discussed rent. I'll be quite happy to pay what the apartment was costing, if that sounds reasonable to you."

"Rent?" Thor managed blankly, wondering with an unfamiliar sense of desperation when he'd lost the thread of the conversation.

She looked surprised. "Of course! I mean, I wouldn't think of parking the van on your property and living here for weeks without paying rent. I'll need bathroom privileges too. I can hook up to that outside receptacle for power, but it's really not practical to hook up the water or septic tank for such a short time, don't you think?"

With her inquiring violet eyes on his face, Thor could only answer in one way. "Uh . . . of course. It's not practical at all."

Pepper nodded. "That's what I thought. Here, let me go ahead and park the van in place, so it'll be out of your way. Stay!" she ordered the two dogs firmly, casually guiding Thor's hand to grasp Fifi's collar. And then she opened the RV's door and climbed inside.

Thor found himself leaning back against the hood of the Corvette, holding a quivering Doberman by the collar and staring down at an obviously hostile and watchful Chihuahua. He lifted his gaze to watch Pepper, looking absurdly childlike through the driver's window, maneuver the RV expertly into place beside the garage without once getting into the grass or near his car.

Bemused, bewildered, and ruefully convinced that he'd wandered back through Alice's mirror, Thor was conscious of only one thought: It couldn't be this easy!

It can't be this easy, Pepper thought a little wildly, parking her van neatly beside the garage. She felt a giggle rise in her throat and let it emerge. Oh, his face! The poor man; she really should be ashamed of herself for barreling over him like a steamroller!

He'd taken it well, though, she thought in amusement. A blank look and then a blink—and then she'd seen that really marvelous gleam of laughter rise in his eyes.

And she didn't regret a thing. In fact, she'd never before been so glad that she'd followed her instincts and jumped headfirst into a situation without a lot of planning. Of course, it was quite possible that nothing would ever come of it.

Pepper felt something in that moment that she'd never felt before. A surge of emotion blocked her throat, and she hesitated for a minute before leaving the van.

What if nothing came of it?

A gambler at heart, and quite prepared to pay whatever price was demanded for the chances she took, Pepper was fully and completely conscious for the first time of just what she was doing. She had never gambled for such high stakes, or bet so heavily on herself.

The game—for now, at least—was blindman's bluff. Each bit of knowledge and understanding she could gain of him would light a dim candle, and with those candles she would have to find her way. The more she learned, the brighter the light to see by . . . to see if what she'd instantly felt for him was real . . . and to see if he could learn to feel the same for her.

Pepper squared her shoulders and reached for the door. Well, she had played more dangerous games—more dangerous to life and limb, that is. Not more dangerous to the heart. Danger didn't bother her. If one risked nothing, one gained nothing, after all.

So she was risking everything, her whole self, on one throw of the dice. And if what she felt was real, she meant to chase Thor as long and as far as it took. Until he caught her.

Emerging from the van and crossing over to where Thor and the pets waited, Pepper choked back a laugh at his still-bemused expression. She quickly began to speak. "You know, it's a good thing you answered my ad yesterday. My landlord called right after you left and threw me out. Wasn't that mean of him? He was supposed to give me more time."

Thor roused himself from some inner speculation. "I meant to ask why you lived in an apartment at all. Since you have the RV, I mean. Or isn't it yours?"

"Oh, it's mine." Pepper bent to pick up Brutus, tucking him under an arm. "The apartment wasn't though. Not really. I sublet it from Kristen, primarily so that I could take care of her furniture and things while she was in England."

"A friend?" he guessed, feeling his way.

"A good friend. We met at Madison Square Garden in New York a couple of years ago at a dog show."

Thor glanced down at Fifi, who was sitting beside him and looking less nervous than he'd yet seen her. Then he looked at Brutus. "Which one were you showing?"

"Oh, neither. I was handling another friend's Great Dane. Kristen was handling a Dane, too, for a client of hers. We got our leashes tangled on the way to the ring, and one thing led to another. We've been friends ever since."

Thor nodded as if the meeting made perfect sense to him. "I see. Uh . . . why don't we go inside the house? I n— that is, I'd like to have a drink."

He thought that he saw a quick gleam of laughter in her eyes, but it was gone too rapidly for him to be sure. She looked anxiously from one dog to the other, then back up at his face.

"The dogs are very well mannered, but—"

"They're invited too." Thor sighed and started up the walk, automatically retaining his hold on Fifi's collar. "My housekeeper is off today, so she can't object."

"You have a housekeeper?" Pepper was walking beside him. "What's she like?"

Thor didn't answer until he'd opened the front door and stood aside for her to precede him. "Difficult," he pronounced finally.

Pepper halted in the doorway to give him a mischievous smile. "Ah. Your home is her castle?"

"Something like that." He followed her into the entrance-way and shut the door behind them before releasing Fifi. A bit uneasy, he watched Pepper set Brutus down on the carpeted floor. "If he attacks me again . . ."

She looked back at him in surprise. "Of course, he won't. This is your house, not his. He may be a bit protective around the van once he realizes that we're staying here, but he won't attack you inside your own house."

Thor watched the little dog guardedly for a moment, then realized that Pepper knew what she was talking about. Brutus showed no disposition to savage his host, but set about immediately getting acquainted with the house.

"Let's have that drink first," Thor murmured finally. "Afterward I'll show you around the house if you like."

"I like." She smiled and then obeyed his slight gesture, preceding him and stepping down into the sunken den. Looking

around the neat room, Pepper sighed with pleasure. It was decorated in shades of brown and rust and contained the comfortable overstuffed furnishings appropriate for a big man. "I don't
know about the rest of the house, but this room is terrific."

"Glad you like it." Thor moved toward an unobtrusive bar
in the corner by the bay window and sent a questioning glance
toward her. "What's your poison?" he asked, his mind only
half on the query as he realized how right she looked in his
home. It was a very disconcerting observation.

"Oh, whatever you're having."

He paused for a moment. "I'm having whiskey. Straight."

"Fine." She laughed at his expression. "Thor, I'm old
enough to drink, you know. In fact, those who know me best
claim that I have a cast-iron stomach." Wandering over to
stand before the lovely rock fireplace, Pepper continued to
smile at him. He seemed to be concentrating on fixing the
drinks, and his next abrupt question nearly caught her off
guard.

"Why did you advertise for a 'preferably single' man?"

Pepper waited to answer until he looked at her and appre-
ciated the wry expression on her face. "Well, I hardly think a
wife would welcome my camping out on her doorstep, do
you? Of course... there's always the possibility of a girlfriend
or fiancée objecting." It was a question, and Pepper didn't
bother making any bones about it. The stakes were too high.

Thor picked up their glasses and carried hers across to her.
When he handed her the glass, he shook his head slightly, and
there was a tiny smile in his eyes. "Not in this case. My job
takes me away from home too often to encourage... long-
term relationships."

Pepper was quick to hear the note of constraint in his deep
voice, so she passed on asking the next logical question. So he
was touchy about his job, eh? Well, she could find out about

that later. She raised her glass in a slight toast. "Then there's no problem."

His glass clinked softly against hers. "No problem at all."

She knew very well that he realized she hadn't initially planned on moving herself as well as the dog out here, and hoped that her mention of the landlord's having thrown her out would cover that. However, the whole situation was still full of holes, and her biggest hope was that Thor simply wouldn't question it.

Feeling suddenly breathless under the gaze of steady gray eyes, Pepper turned away and went over to sit down on the comfortable couch. The phone on the end table beside her set up a train of thought, and she looked across at Thor. "By the way, do you mind if I let my friends know where they can reach me by phone?"

"Of course not."

She grinned. "It's only fair to warn you. They're a talkative bunch. I'm liable to get calls pretty regularly. I'd hate to tie up your line."

Leaning against the mantel and watching her with a faint smile, Thor shrugged. "That's okay. I have another line in my bedroom for . . . important calls."

Again Pepper let the subject pass without a question, although she nearly had to bite her tongue to do it. "Great. Oh—we never settled on the rent."

"There's no hurry." Glancing toward the doorway, he found himself under scrutiny from Fifi's ridiculously worried brown eyes, and had to chuckle. "Unlike your former landlord, I won't kick you off the place."

"Whatever you say." Pepper sat back and sipped her drink slowly, wondering how to say what had to be said. She hesitated to assume an interest that had not yet been put into words, but she would have been less of a woman than she was to misinterpret the look in Thor's gray eyes.

His seemingly offhand remark about his work had told her two things, and she was sure that one meaning, at least, had been deliberately sent her way. He probably hadn't realized that she'd picked up some undercurrent concerning his job. Definitely, though, he had meant her to understand that long-term relationships weren't a part of his plans.

That didn't daunt Pepper; either he would change his mind or he wouldn't. And this man, she knew intuitively, would neither be pushed or led down the aisle. He would take that trip of his own free will, or he simply wouldn't go. And she wouldn't have had it any other way.

"You're very beautiful," he said suddenly, and immediately looked surprised, as if he hadn't intended to say those words aloud.

Pepper felt her heart give a bump, and sternly tried to control it. He had given her the opening she needed, and she had to take advantage of it. She looked down at the drink in her hand, then steadily back at him.

"I'm not very comfortable with oblique comments, Thor. I'm not very good at tiptoeing verbally around a subject. And since this situation is a bit out of the ordinary, well . . . I'll be blunt." She felt herself smiling wryly. "My friends say I'm good at that."

"Not interested, huh?" he asked lightly, but Pepper could feel his sudden tension. She didn't answer the question directly.

"I have rules, Thor."

"Rules?"

She looked at him steadily, and the honesty in her eyes told him that she was serious, that she meant whatever she was about to say.

"Rules. They're my rules, and they have nothing to do with morality. It's only that I know what would or wouldn't work for myself. And an affair wouldn't work for me."

"I see. Commitment."

Pepper dropped her gaze to the glass in her hand, and when she went on, her voice was quiet, musing. "There have been occasions during the last ten years when the opportunity was there. But something inside of me always said that what was right for the moment wouldn't be right for long. And I don't like regrets. Life's too short for regrets."

Watching her, Thor felt suddenly that there was a very definite reason for her last almost inaudible sentence. Her eyes were hidden from him, but her face was very still, and her voice seemed to have come from a great distance. She had some reason to avoid regrets, he thought, and wondered what it was.

She looked up suddenly, the violet eyes blurred for a moment. Then they were clear, and she was speaking in the same quiet, thoughtful voice as before.

"Commitment...yes. Something that's right for more than just the moment. Usually when people talk about a commitment between a man and woman, they mean marriage. Well, marriage seems to be entered into very lightly these days by a lot of people. But I don't happen to believe marriage is something you decide on with the idea in the back of your mind that it's a contract easily and amicably dissolved in court if it doesn't work. When I say 'till death do us part,' I expect to mean just that.

"And I *am* looking for that kind of permanence, Thor. I don't know if I'll find it—how can I know that? But one thing I do know: If I climb into a man's bed, or he climbs into mine, it has to be with the knowledge that I think I've found what I'm looking for. And he has to feel the same way."

She laughed suddenly and shortly in wry amusement. "And

if that puts me in the company of dodos and dinosaurs"—she lifted her glass in a slightly mocking toast—"then here's to things past . . . but not forgotten."

After a moment Thor lifted his glass in an answering toast. In doing so, he was silently complimenting her honesty. But, more than that, he was admiring clear-sighted knowledge. She knew what she wanted, and she was unwilling to settle for less. And how many people, he wondered, were that lucky? How many people were spared blind searching because they had the foresight, the certain knowledge, of what they were searching for?

He watched her sip her drink, remembering suddenly the stillness of her face and the remark about no regrets. That expression had been oddly in contrast to his first impression of her. But, then, he had been constantly revising his first impression with every moment spent in her company. And the question that escaped him now was a little rueful, and more than a little bemused.

"How many women are you, Pepper?"

She looked at him, something unreadable flickering in her eyes. And then she was smiling, her smile as twisted and rueful as his own. "As many as I have to be." She finished her drink and set the glass down on the end table beside the phone.

"That admission is a challenge to any man," he pointed out softly. "Like looking at a diamond with countless facets, or a puzzle with countless pieces. Something that has to be—must be—understood."

"Some puzzles can't be solved because they're interpreted different ways by different people." Pepper looked intently at him, determined in her innate honesty that he wouldn't think her rules were easily overcome. "Like the Lady and the Tiger. If you were that man, Thor, and you opened the door your princess had told you to open, what do you think you would find?"

Thor looked at her searchingly, aware that she was telling him something. And he felt that what she was trying to tell him was important. Slowly he said, "I think if I opened the door she told me to open, I'd find the lady behind it."

Pepper rose to her feet, sliding her hands into the pockets of her jeans and shaking her head slightly. "And I think you'd find the Tiger. Princesses—women—were ruthless in those days, Thor. We still are. Abstract reasoning doesn't appeal to us much. We decide things by feelings more often than not. Our own feelings."

"What are you telling me?" he asked bluntly. "That your rules are yours, and therefore inviolable?"

Pepper laughed suddenly. Only a few candles had been lit, but already she saw her way clearly. And, true to her nature, she stepped forward boldly to begin the journey.

"What I'm telling you, Thor, is—*be warned*. If you decide to study the diamond's facets, or put the puzzle together, you may be biting off more than you can chew. Lord, we're mixing metaphors right and left. Because while you're looking for solutions, I might very well decide that you're just what I've been looking for."

Thor was slowly beginning to smile. "And so?"

"And, so, I'm a ruthless woman. I hate to lose." Pepper smiled at him very sweetly. "I'd chase you to hell and back, O god of thunder. And not even Odin—or your magic hammer—could save you."

three

THOR'S LAUGH BEGAN AS A RUMBLE DEEP inside his chest, growing slowly into the delighted sound of pure enjoyment. She'd flung the gauntlet at his feet, the little witch! She'd neatly picked up his earlier hint of no long-term involvement, flatly laid down her own rules, and then gently dared him to match wits with her. Challenged him . . . and he'd never had a more intriguing challenge.

Still chuckling, he put his empty glass down on the mantel and moved slowly toward her with the unthinking grace of a cat. "You realize, of course," he told her conversationally, "that I can't possibly ignore your challenge."

"The thought did occur," she murmured, watching his approach and still smiling. Not quite as calm as she appeared, Pepper was tautly aware that this would be the moment of truth. In the next few minutes one of two things would happen. Either she would know that she'd been wrong about her feelings for this almost stranger—in which case she would fold her tent and steal quietly away—or she would discover that the feelings would indeed be there. And there would be no turning back.

"I've always loved challenges. I would have wanted to

open Pandora's box," he said, halting less than an arm's length away and looking down at her with lazily smiling eyes.

"Never know what might jump out at you," she warned softly, tilting her head back to look up at him.

Thor reached out slowly, one large hand nearly encircling her neck, his thumb brushing along her jawline. "I think," he murmured as his head bent toward hers, "I'll take my chances."

Pepper didn't know what she had expected. A pleasant tingle, perhaps. A firecracker or two. She'd even wondered if Marsha had been right with her "Bells, my dear—ringing their little clangers off." But, being realistic, she had expected nothing so drastic. Just a sign, a preview of marvelous things to come.

What she got was the main attraction, and she very nearly forgot who had challenged whom.

For a still, timeless moment his lips rested on hers with the weight of a feather and the force of a sigh. Warm, undemanding, faintly questioning—and she was astonished at her response. The shivering tingle began somewhere near her middle, sweeping outward in ripples of curiously hot-cold sensation. She was only dimly aware of her hands leaving the pockets of her jeans and sliding up around his neck, helpless to prevent her lips from parting and inviting his exploration.

And the hot-cold sensation blazed suddenly white-hot, sizzling through her veins and scorching nerve endings as he abruptly accepted her invitation. His lips slanted across hers with driving hunger, demanding, compelling, sapping the strength from her legs.

Pepper was conscious of an aching emptiness within her, a throbbing hollowness she had never felt before. It seemed to fill her being, hot and hurting with an unfamiliar pain. She felt driven to be closer to him, hungry to touch him and have him touch her.

The sensations frightened her in their intensity; they swept aside logic and rationality to leave only raw emotion. But what frightened her even more was that the raw emotion was stronger than fear, stronger than her ability to fight it. She couldn't break away from him even with her instincts for self-preservation clamoring a desperate warning.

Those instincts told her that she'd met her match this time, that the stakes were higher than she had known. Her challenge had left her vulnerable to an intensity of feeling she'd not been prepared for, and she wondered dimly what price would be demanded of her this time for the reckless chance she had taken.

Then the fire in her veins blazed over fear, and she was conscious only of her need for this man. She had no strength left, no power over her own body. She was weightless and adrift on a churning sea, and there was no life preserver to save her from drowning. . . .

Thor's lips left hers as she was going down for the second time, and he drew a deep breath as if he, too, had nearly drowned.

Pepper stared dazedly into storm-clouded gray eyes and, incurably honest, said exactly what she was thinking. "Pandora's box. I think we're both in trouble."

"I think you're right," Thor said a bit raggedly. "Good Lord, for such a little thing, you pack one hell of a punch, lady."

"You know what they say about dynamite." She wondered idly how she could possibly be having a perfectly rational conversation while looking eye-to-eye with a man who'd just demonstrated the Fourth of July in the middle of October. . . . Eye-to-eye? That wasn't right!

Leaning a bit sideways, Pepper looked down and realized only then why she felt so weightless: she was being held a good foot off the floor for Pete's sake. Returning her gaze to Thor's still-bemused face, she requested politely, "Could you put me down, please?"

"No," he said simply.

Pepper stared at him. "Why not?"

Thor kissed her very lightly. Then he kissed her lightly again, wearing the pleased expression of a man who has discovered a wonderful new hobby. "Because, like Brutus," he murmured, "I ignore the command to 'break.'"

She bit her lip to hold back an ill-timed giggle. "I did say please."

"I can't seem to hear that either. Although, if it were stuck in the right sentence—"

"Forget it, chum." She unlocked one hand from his hair and waved a threatening finger beneath his nose. "Remember the Alamo!"

He lifted an eyebrow. "No quarter?"

"No quarter. No mercy. One of us is going to break. And, as the man said, it ain't gonna be me."

"Want to bet?"

"We already did."

"True."

"Are you going to put me down?"

"No."

"You're vulnerable, you know. There are pressure points in your neck. And, of course, I could always resort to the old both-hands-clapped-to-the-ears trick. It shatters the eardrums, I'm told."

Thor looked at her consideringly. "You've learned to take care of yourself."

"Yes." She didn't elaborate.

"I get the feeling you've had an interesting life."

"Perhaps. But, interesting or not, I have no intention of discussing my past while dangling in the air."

"Will you discuss it if I put you down?"

"Maybe."

"Uh-uh." Thor shook his head. "If I've learned anything at all about women it's that 'maybe' means a variety of things, none of which is 'yes.'"

"You've learned that, huh?"

"I've also learned that in these days of women's lib and whatever, a man needs every edge he can find or steal. And since I happen to be considerably larger than you, I plan to use that advantage every chance I get."

"Are you going to turn me over your knee?" she asked interestedly.

"Don't give me ideas."

"Wouldn't think of it," Pepper drawled. "Never give the opposing side a gun; it leads to uncomfortable things. Like defeat."

"You don't like to lose?"

"Not if I can help it." She stared at him and frowned. "We seem to have digressed somewhat from the point."

"What was the point?" He kissed her again.

Pepper fought for breath and cleared her throat determinedly. "The point. Ah. This macho attempt to use your muscles—that's the point. It's unfair."

"'All's fair in . . .' Well, you know the rest."

"'Love and war,' if I remember correctly. And it's going to be the latter with a vengeance if you don't put me down."

Thor looked virtuous. "It was your challenge, therefore I choose the weapons. It's a rule."

"Look, I'm not used to this altitude, and I'm getting dizzy. Why don't we sit down and discuss the rules?"

Thor appeared to think about her request, then nodded, making a complicated maneuver that ended with him sitting on the couch and Pepper sitting in his lap.

"This wasn't quite what I had in mind," she noted dryly.

"It's what I had in mind. You were saying something about rules?" He seemed to find her ponytail fascinating, winding the silky hair around his hand and apparently watching light play on the silvery strands.

Or maybe, she thought wryly, he was adding insurance to the arm resting across her lap. Since he obviously didn't intend to let her escape, Pepper, characteristically, got on with the matter at hand.

But it was damnably hard to ignore the hard thighs beneath her. . . .

"The rules. Well, you said it was up to you to choose the weapons, but any contest of physical superiority ends right here."

"Oh?"

"Definitely. It's too unequal. Brute strength wins out in the end, and we both know it," she said seriously.

He looked at her for a long moment. "That's a lesson usually learned in a hard school; my curiosity about your past is growing by leaps and bounds."

Pepper felt a peculiar little mental shock and wondered silently at his perception. But she wasn't ready to talk about hard schools or pasts, and skated over the subject lightly. "When one is pint-size, it's a lesson easily and quickly learned. So—no physical domination, okay?"

In an odd little gesture his free hand lifted to lie along the side of her neck, the thumb moving gently beneath her ear. His expression was totally and completely serious. "I'd never hurt you, Pepper. That's one thing you can always be very sure of."

Swallowing hard—for some reason there seemed to be a lump in her throat—Pepper decided to accept that for agreement. "Fine." She decided to lighten the atmosphere. "And since that washes out your strongest weapon—no wordplay intended—what do you choose instead?"

Thor's lazy smile indicated an approval of her light question, but his reply made her realize suddenly that her own strategy was marching inexorably over quicksand.

"Honesty."

"I see." She wondered where her own unwary steps had led her, and how he defined honesty. "No punches pulled. No quarter asked . . . or granted."

"You said it first." He was still smiling, but watchful now, gray eyes probing. "No quarter. No holds barred. And since honesty is the weapon"—his smile grew—"I'll be the first to employ it. Tell me something, Pepper. Were you looking for a place to park your RV for a few weeks? Or were you looking for a home for Fifi?"

"Dammit." Pepper was torn between a desire to laugh and an urge to hit him with something. "That's not a fair question!"

He shook his head reprovingly. "You can't cry foul whenever something doesn't suit you. Come on now, 'fess up! Your gauntlet was well hidden, but you were bent on challenge yesterday, weren't you?"

Pepper felt a smile tugging at her lips. This was honesty with a vengeance! "Well, since you obviously aren't taking to your heels, I'll admit that I could have found somewhere else to park the van."

"Not good enough."

"You want your pound of flesh, don't you?"

"Something like that."

"Beast."

"To the core. Well?"

"All right!" She glared at him; her expression was part

mockery and part amused exasperation. "I was . . . interested. Satisfied?"

He was openly grinning now. "It'll do. Damn, you must have been *born* with a poker face; you certainly didn't give anything away yesterday. I figured you didn't have a subtle bone in your body."

"You call this subtle?" Pepper looked at him with a lifted brow. "If my fellow women found out about this, I'd be drummed out of the sisterhood."

"What sisterhood?" Thor looked puzzled.

Pepper decided that if he wanted honesty, he was going to get it. It was a tactic that, according to theory, was guaranteed to give most men nightmares, but she was intuitively certain that it was the right one with this particular man. Not total honesty, of course. There would always be guarded areas of any individual's privacy in which intrusion would neither be forgotten nor forgiven. She sighed. Oh, well, he knew that as well as she. Honesty in *intent,* though—well, that was different.

"News for you, pal," she told him with a gentle smile. "Women have always done the chasing; we just never let you guys know it. Subtle, you see. Which is why the sisterhood would disown me if this got out."

Thor stared at her for a long moment. "What have I gotten myself into?" he murmured.

"Trouble." She bit back a giggle. "With a capital *T* and a capital all the other letters too. You've opened a Pandora's box, remember."

"What about you?" The intent, probing expression in his gray eyes belied his easy smile. "Aren't you putting yourself in a vulnerable position by admitting interest so early in the—uh—game?"

"You mean, 'what price honesty'?" Too serious, she

thought, and gave him a light answer. "Well, I've always paid my own fare. And, besides, it seems to me that a lot of the problems in human relationships arise out of trying to hide what's painfully obvious." She smiled a little. "I'd be an idiot to deny interest after the way I reacted to your—uh—physical response to my challenge. Wouldn't I?"

Something flickered in Thor's eyes, an expression that might have been admiration or approval—or bewilderment. When he spoke, his voice was a curious combination of all three emotions.

"I asked for honesty, but I didn't really expect it, Pepper. The closer I look at the puzzle, the bigger and more complicated it gets." Almost whimsically he added, "Are you real? Or will I wake up and find you were a dream?"

Pepper didn't delude herself into thinking that the question meant what it seemed to mean: that her honesty made her more imagined than real, something he'd needed but never expected to find. She wasn't that complacent about herself or that certain of him. So she simply answered the first question and tried to ignore the second.

"I'm real. And you'd better remember that honesty's a double-edged sword; it cuts both ways. You have to be honest too."

"And so?"

"And so . . . the chase is on. Do you feel hunted?"

He appeared to consider the question seriously. "Oddly enough, no. I suppose because I feel certain that you'd chase, but not trap. And *I'd* be a fool if I weren't flattered by your . . . interest."

Pepper was honestly surprised. "Why?"

Thor was clearly amused. "My ego, I guess. I've never been chased by an angel before."

Instead of taking the remark as the compliment it was obviously intended to be, Pepper was shaken by it. "Thor... don't put me on a pedestal. I'd lose my balance. I'd fall off."

In that moment Thor felt a curious need to reassure her. He didn't know why, but the need rose with a certainty not to be questioned. And he didn't question. He simply drew her closer, resting his chin against her hair and wrapping both arms around her. "You look like an angel," he told her quietly. "I don't expect you to be one. In fact, I wouldn't know what to do with an angel."

Pepper was surprised by his reaction to her plea, but warmed by it. She wanted him to think of her as a flesh-and-blood woman, not the china doll some men wanted her to be. A china doll was placed on a shelf and displayed proudly; it was rarely touched or even held. Pepper had discovered in the last few minutes just how much of a woman she was, and she didn't want to risk the loss of Thor touching and holding her.

Wary again of being too serious, of delving into too many unfamiliar emotions, she tried to lighten the mood. "You said something about giving me the nickel tour," she murmured, highly conscious of his big arms around her.

"It's gone up to a dime," he responded gravely. "Inflation, you know."

"Really? Well, I guess it'll be worth it."

"That remains to be seen."

"True." She made an experimental attempt to remove herself from his lap, both relieved and disappointed when he allowed her to get up. "Lead on."

Thor rose to his feet slowly and stood looking down at her for a moment. "I am flattered, you know," he said suddenly.

Pepper was deliberately obtuse. "Just because I think the tour'll be worth a dime?" she asked lightly.

"No." He touched the tip of her nose with one finger. "Because I'm being chased."

"It's early days yet," she told him wryly. "This time next week you may be running in fear for your very life."

"Somehow I don't think that's likely. In the meantime, however... This, ma'am, is the den. And, if you'll come this way..."

The house was beautiful. Downstairs was the living room, den, study, kitchen/breakfast nook, formal dining room, and one of the three bathrooms.

The rooms were spacious and airy, decorated—Pepper's discerning eye for such things told her—professionally, but with instructions to lean toward comfort rather than style. The furniture was composed of sturdy woods and comfortable cushions, nothing delicate or spindly. Colors varied from room to room, mostly earth tones brightened by greens and blues.

The study held her interest the longest, particularly since she was looking for clues to the man himself, and experience had taught her that work areas in the home offered the most insight for those who cared to look.

It was carpeted in deep brown, paneled in birch, and filled with bookshelves that were filled, in turn, with books of every type. Pepper could find no preference that would aid in her deductions, except that he seemed to have a fondness for mysteries. The huge oak desk in one corner was neat; no clutter of papers or objects to indicate that work was done there.

Two high-backed chairs were grouped with a table and reading lamp in another corner. In the center of the large room was a game table, suitable for card games or jigsaw puzzles, or whatever. It was bare.

In the remaining corner was a baby grand piano. Gleaming a velvety black, its polished surface spoke of loving care, but whether that was due to Thor or his housekeeper, Pepper couldn't tell. She touched a sparkling ivory key with one finger and wondered silently.

"You play, I gather," she said aloud.

"Indifferently. How about you?"

"When I get the chance."

"Feel free."

"Thanks; I just might take you up on that."

They left the matter there and went on with the tour. The laundry room held no interest for Pepper, but a good-size room with a door through to the garage did. It was bare except for a storage cabinet and a large deep sink, and appeared not to be in use.

"What's this?"

"In the plans it's called a mudroom."

"You don't use it for anything?"

"No. Why?"

Pepper eyed the size of the room, paying close attention to the sink. "I was just wondering . . . well, if you don't need it for anything, d'you mind if I use it while I'm here? I promise to leave it just as I found it."

Thor looked at her curiously. He wondered why she needed a large bare room, but decided that the reason would become apparent in time. "I don't mind. Help yourself."

"Thanks." Pepper smiled a little, wondering how he would react to the second invasion he would suffer shortly. She hoped it would be humorously; never before, she was reasonably sure, had a man been the victim of such an honestly declared and inwardly devious chase.

If nothing else, she thought with humor, her methods were original. She was being totally honest in her goal—permanence—and utterly absurd in her methods. One of them would win . . . or Thor would murder her, resulting in a sort of victory by default.

"Why the Mona Lisa smile?" Thor asked a bit uneasily.

"Oh—no reason. Is the tour taking us upstairs now, or shall I imagine the rest?"

"Heaven forbid. After you." He gestured for her to precede him, still wondering about that smile but lacking the nerve to ask again.

They went up the staircase in the entranceway so she could view the four bedrooms. They were accompanied by Fifi—who'd been with them from the first of the tour, and by Brutus—who'd caught up with them in the kitchen. All the bedrooms were beautifully decorated, one containing a huge king-size waterbed. There was a central bathroom opening into the hall, and another off the master bedroom.

That room itself was the largest, and possessed a tremendous oak four-poster bed that Pepper would have needed a stool to climb onto. It looked like an antique, along with the long dresser and tall chest of drawers. The room also boasted a walk-in closet, and the bathroom contained a sunken bath deep enough to satisfy a giant.

Passing up the opportunity to call him a sybarite, Pepper made only one remark. "Awfully big house for only one person," she murmured as they were going back down the stairs.

"Mmm. I like space."

She considered his reply as they went back into the den. And a glance around at the room made her remember that she'd seen few indications of "personality" in the house. No clutter or mess, which merely indicated that he was either very neat or that his housekeeper was. More surprising—and perhaps more revealing—was the lack of personal touches.

The prints and paintings throughout the house were ambiguous as to taste, mostly landscapes and seascapes. No adventurous abstracts or romantic portraits, no favored artist. There were few ornaments, and what there was seemed more the touch of a decorator than a declaration of personal taste. Where were the souvenirs of places visited? Photos of people related or known?

Pepper wondered just how often his job took him away from home. Now, she asked herself, which one of them was putting a puzzle together? She or Thor?

"Another drink?" he asked, pulling her from speculation.

"No, thanks." She slid a hand into her pocket, absently retrieving a worry-stone and beginning to "worry" it rhythmically.

Thor watched her curiously for a moment, then stepped closer and caught her wrist. "What's this?"

Realizing only then what she'd been doing, Pepper opened her hand and watched him lift the smooth stone to examine it. "It's a worry-stone," she said.

Thor turned the object in his fingers. It looked like quartz and was roughly two inches from end to end and about a quarter of an inch thick. Oval in shape and smoothly polished, it was flat on both sides and had a slight depression in one end which was, he saw, perfectly suited to be rubbed by a thumb.

He placed the stone back in her palm, his fingers lingering on hers. "Are you worried about something?"

Rather hastily Pepper slid the stone back into her pocket. "Of course not. I quit smoking a few years ago. Some people chew gum—I play with a worry-stone."

"I see." He didn't look convinced.

Pepper decided to change the subject. "Look, it's almost suppertime, according to my stomach's clock. I think I'll take advantage of those liberated tendencies you blanketed us females with and ask you to share my meal. I can bring some stuff over from the van, since your dining room's larger than mine. Or else we can go somewhere. If you're interested, that is."

"I'm interested. But why don't we just make do with whatever's in the kitchen here? Mrs. Small usually keeps the place stocked."

"Fine with me. What were you planning to have tonight?"

"A TV dinner."

Pepper lifted a brow at him. "Is that your usual fare?"

"On Mrs. Small's day off it is."

She shook her head mournfully. "It's disgraceful to reach your advanced years without being able to cook."

Thor decided to ignore the first part of her sentence. "Don't expect me to be perfect. I suppose you can cook?"

"Yes."

"Well, that was a flat answer."

"You asked a flat question," she reminded him.

"No modest disclaimers, huh?"

"We're being honest."

"So we are," Thor said.

"Will Mrs. Small mind us invading her kitchen?"

"We just won't ask her."

"Devious man."

The rest of the evening was companionable, and if they felt the undercurrents, neither mentioned it. They observed a tacit agreement not to delve any further into their sudden relationship, treading instead around lighter topics with the wariness of fencers. They talked casually about various subjects in the curious give-and-take probing of new acquaintances, neither giving much away.

What emerged was that Thor preferred blue and enjoyed football and soft pop music and hated snails, while Pepper loved the color wine-red and also enjoyed football and pop music and could take or leave snails. Both agreed that Maine was a beautiful state and that the latest best-selling novel was fascinating and that neither nervous Dobermans nor inquisitive Chihuahuas belonged in kitchens.

After a totally deadpan preparation of hot dogs and French fries by Pepper and a joint clean-up in the kitchen, a murder mystery on television topped off the evening. Thor sided with the detective while Pepper seriously defended the murderer's motivations.

Pepper firmly dissuaded him from walking out to the RV with her, refusing his offer to help in hooking up the vehicle to his electrical supply and condescending only to accept a flashlight. After a comically grave handshake she thanked him solemnly for the meal, the flashlight, and the place in which to park her van, gathered the dogs firmly to heel, and strolled off into the darkness.

A while later, as he was lying in bed and staring up at a darkness-distorted ceiling, Thor wondered how on earth such an emotional and challenging afternoon had turned into a disconcertingly calm and companionable evening. Questions floated around in his mind, their answers beyond his reach because he didn't yet know Pepper well enough to even guess.

Was her honesty as real as it seemed? Had she indeed decided that he might be what she was looking for and, if so, how did he really feel about that? What had happened in her life to teach her that brute strength always wins in the end? Why the worry-stone? What events in her life had shaped a woman who could challenge a man with honesty and humor?

The last question occurred just as he was dropping off to sleep, and it bothered Thor more than all the others.

Why had she not invited him for a nickel tour of her own home? In fact, without being in the least rude, she had made certain that he had not seen the inside of the RV. Was it because it contained some of the pieces he needed to put the puzzle together? And while Thor was suddenly, if sleepily, consumed with an intense desire to do so, he knew that he wouldn't set foot inside the vehicle without Pepper's invitation.

The thought followed him into dreams in which distorted RVs loomed mockingly and spewed forth countless jigsaw puzzle pieces while a cowardly Doberman looked at him with panicky brown eyes, a savage Chihuahua attempted to maul him, and the maniacal laughter of Odin fell derisively on the ears of a hapless, earthbound god of thunder. . . .

Rising earlier than usual after a restless, disturbed night, Thor decided to take the coward's way out and leave home before Mrs. Small arrived for the day. He would have dearly loved to be a fly on the wall during the meeting of his housekeeper and Pepper, Brutus, and Fifi; at the same time, the thought of likely chaos sent him out of the house after a breakfast of coffee.

Feeling both guilty and amused, he fed Lucifer and then cranked the Corvette as quietly as possible, noting that Pepper's RV was hooked up to his garage and seeing no sign of the dogs. Presumably then, she was still asleep.

He'd given her a key to the house the night before and told her to treat it as her own, and her Mona Lisa smile of the day before came suddenly back to haunt him. What would he find when he returned?

Pushing the useless speculation from his mind, Thor backed the low-slung Corvette out of the driveway and headed toward town. He had errands to run, he assured himself silently. And he'd left Mrs. Small a note to explain Pepper's presence. Sort of explain anyway.

"Coward," he muttered aloud.

When Thor parked the Corvette in his driveway later that afternoon, he saw that the only difference in the appearance of his home was the presence of Mrs. Small's little VW. He felt relieved that she hadn't, apparently, quit, but wondered what kind of reception he would get from her. Steeling himself, he headed for the front door.

As the door swung inward he heard a deep-throated "Woof!" and saw Fifi disappearing in the direction of the kitchen. As he closed the door behind him, he saw Brutus sitting squarely in the middle of the entranceway and lifting a lip at him.

Thor stood staring down at the tiny dog. "Make up your mind, pal," he told Brutus calmly. "Either you accept me or you don't; we aren't going through this little charade every time we see each other."

The lip descended to cover pointed teeth, and Brutus returned the stare. Then he got up, wagged a tail, and trotted off after Fifi. Feeling mildly pleased with himself, Thor followed the canine parade.

When he reached the kitchen door, he felt tremors in the very foundation of his world. Mrs. Small was smiling. *Smiling.* And even as he watched and listened in incredulous fascination, he heard her laugh for the first time in five years. It was an odd, deep laugh, seemingly rusty from disuse, but it was definitely a laugh.

She was leaning against the refrigerator and stirring something in a large mixing bowl, unperturbed by the Doberman trying to hide behind her as she listened to Pepper's cheerful little-girl voice. And Pepper was sitting on the end of the counter wearing jeans, ridiculously small boots, and a red and black plaid shirt over a black sweater.

Thor watched her gesture to illustrate some point he wasn't taking in, wondering dimly how she had managed to pile all her hair on the top of her head to achieve that tousled, impossibly sexy look. Then she glanced toward the door and saw him, breaking the trance he seemed to be swimming in.

"Hi, Thor," she said casually.

"Hi," he managed.

She tilted her head to one side like an inquisitive robin. "Are you all right? You look strange."

"I'm fine," he murmured, deciding not to explain that he'd expected a mushroom cloud and gotten Alice's mirror instead.

He wasn't sure he understood it himself.

four

BEFORE ANOTHER WORD COULD BE SPO-
ken, a head popped out of the doorway to the hall leading to
the mud and laundry rooms. It was a masculine head roughly
seventeen years old, with an attempt at a mustache, fairly long
brown hair, and the mild brown eyes of a hopeful spaniel.

"Jo Jo's done, Pep. Want me to start on Dickens next?"

While Thor was pondering the meaning of these mysterious
words, Pepper answered cheerfully, "Give him a few more minutes to settle down; Mrs. Shannon just brought him a little while
ago. I'll take care of Jo Jo while you work on Ladama's nails."

"Right." He vanished.

Pepper slid down off the counter, using every ounce of her
control to keep from laughing at Thor's bewildered expression.
Studiously refusing to look at him, she smiled at Mrs. Small in-
stead. "After I've finished, I'll go and dig out that recipe, Jean.
You may not be able to find all the ingredients around here, but
I have most of the raw spices."

Mrs. Small nodded. "I'd love to try my hand at it."

"Great. See you later." With a wave to Thor Pepper disappeared through the doorway.

He stared after her. Jo Jo? Dickens? Ladama? He looked at Mrs. Small. *Jean?*

Cryptically Mrs. Small said, "Sukiyaki. Authentic. I'll need to borrow her wok though." She turned back to her mixing bowl with an absent "Move, Fifi." As the Doberman shifted slightly sideways and continued to regard Thor with uneasy eyes, the housekeeper added even more cryptically, "A little Japanese village."

Shaking off the growing conviction that this was a continuation of his wild dream, Thor headed purposefully for the mudroom. He didn't know what was going on in his house, but he meant to find out.

The mudroom had been transformed. Along the garage side of the wall were several wire kennels of various sizes, four of them occupied by three poodles and a cocker spaniel. On a makeshift table sat a disdainful collie whose paw was being bent over by the strange young man with the attempt at a mustache. A collection of bottles sat on the wide counter beside the sink, along with several crumpled towels and a stack of neatly folded ones.

Another table, this one entirely professional, had been set up on the other side of the sink. On shelves beneath it were three hair dryers; a variety of electric clippers, brushes, and combs; and a tasteful selection of narrow, colorful ribbons. On the top of the table stood a silver-gray miniature poodle, eyes half closed in blissful enjoyment as two brushes were worked steadily through his thick coat.

Wielding the brushes with the casual, easy precision of an expert was Pepper. She didn't look around as the door opened, but simply said firmly, "Out, Brutus."

Thor looked down to see the tiny Chihuahua turn stiffly and stalk from the room. He shut the door and leaned back against it, staring again around the room. "What the hell?" he muttered.

"Thor, this is Tim." She gestured toward the young man with the nail clippers, still without looking around. "Tim, our host."

Tim looked up briefly. "Hi." Then bent again, his full attention back on the collie's nails.

"Hi. So this is what you wanted the room for?"

"Obviously. You don't mind, do you? It's Kristen's business, you know. She had a little place in town, but since the lease was up, I decided to work out here instead."

"Does Kristen know?" Thor asked dryly.

"No. But then, she thinks she's coming back to the States."

"And she isn't?" Thor pulled fragments of conversation into his mind. "I thought you said you planned to move on in a few weeks."

Pepper glanced at him, wondering in amusement if he was beginning to feel trapped. "That's what I plan. I think Kristen will come back only to pack up her things. That English breeder had something permanent in mind when he swept her off, I just know it. They'll be happy together."

Thor pondered the information. "I see. Did you—uh—introduce them, by any chance?"

"Sort of. You don't mind about this, do you?"

A neat change of subject, he decided. "No. No, if Mrs. Small doesn't mind, then I don't."

"Jean loves dogs."

"I didn't know that," he mumbled.

"Mmm. Anyway, we'll be out of your hair within a few weeks." Pepper sent an amused glance his way. "So you don't have to panic."

"I wasn't," he told her, sending a glance toward the

younger man and hoping that the conversation was too cryptic for him to follow.

"Of course not. The thought of my moving in bag and baggage doesn't daunt you a bit, does it?"

Thor decided to use one of her tricks and change the subject. "What's this about a little village in Japan and sukiyaki?"

She was blandly casual. "Just a recipe I picked up a few years ago. I'm about to turn on the clippers here, which will make conversation totally impossible. And I think Jean has your lunch ready."

Thor smiled wryly at the far from subtle hint. "Okay, okay. No help from you in the god of thunder's quest, I take it."

Pepper chose a set of clippers and plugged them into the outlet beside the table, giving Thor a limpid smile. "Fair is fair. When the quarry turns to confront his huntress . . . well, who knows?"

His smile went a little crooked. Respect for her grew as he realized that the lady was far from dumb. She saw that, however willing he was to be chased, he wasn't yet ready to explain his reasons for running. With a slight inclination of his head that was half acceptance and half salute, he murmured, "Just call you Diana."

"Goddess of the hunt?" she queried lightly, demonstrating a knowledge of Greek as well as Norse mythology.

"Goddess of the hunt. Join me for lunch?"

She shook her head slightly. "I have to finish up my friends here before five."

"You have to eat," he reminded.

"I usually skip lunch."

"Bad habit."

"I never claimed to be perfect. See you, Thor."

Giving in to the nudge, Thor sighed softly and left the

makeshift grooming parlor, hearing the clippers begin to buzz loudly.

Mrs. Small—Thor couldn't bring himself to think of her as Jean—served him cheese enchiladas, and since it wasn't her habit to experiment with "foreign" fare, he looked at her questioningly.

"Mexico," she responded in answer to the look. "Pepper's recipe. Authentic."

Thor sampled Pepper's recipe. "Delicious," he said honestly. Before Mrs. Small could return to the kitchen, he decided to do a bit of unscrupulous digging. "When was she in Mexico?" he asked casually.

"Last year." The housekeeper picked up a china vase from the sideboard and apparently decided to take it back to the kitchen for a wash rather than a dusting. "The same time as you were there."

Thor looked up quickly. "Does she know I was there?"

"Didn't mention it." She left the room.

Staring after her, Thor wondered which of them hadn't mentioned it—Pepper or Mrs. Small. His housekeeper had never struck him as the type to talk about her employer, but he wasn't sure, after today, that she wouldn't answer a direct question if Pepper asked. And he couldn't help but wonder if Pepper had decided to do a bit of unscrupulous digging as well.

He also wondered about her presence in Mexico. Clearly the lady had done a bit of traveling; the recipes from Japan and Mexico, and she'd mentioned spending six months in a desert with camels. Not that she'd put it that way, of course, but *desert* and *camels* suggested Arabia or northern Africa, both of which he, too, had spent time in.

She hadn't traveled the world grooming dogs, he knew. So what *did* she do? Was she wealthy? Heaven knew she neither looked nor acted it, but he'd quickly learned not to stick any kind of label on Pepper, and that RV hadn't come cheap.

It was another piece to the puzzle and he didn't know where to fit it.

Five o'clock had just passed when the last of the dogs had been picked up by admiring owners and Tim had left with the girl-friend who'd come to get him. Pepper finished cleaning up the mudroom, leaving it neat before wandering out into the kitchen. An appetizing scent led her to the oven, where she dis-covered lasagna bubbling away.

Pepper grinned faintly, noting that the lasagna recipe and the ones for cheese enchiladas and sukiyaki were tacked to a small cork board above a counter work area. She hoped that Thor didn't mind this culinary experimentation, since Jean seemed determined to try every recipe in Pepper's rather crowded recipe box.

Still smiling, she left the kitchen. Both Thor and Jean had told her to treat the house as home, and she felt no uneasiness about doing just that. Besides, she had to find the pets; they seemed to have disappeared in the last few hours.

The muffled roar of the vacuum cleaner told her that Jean was finishing up the bedrooms upstairs, but no other sound led her to the pets or Thor. Puzzled, she went from room to room, ending up in the empty study. Nothing. She crossed to the window with a view of the pasture, pulled the heavy drapes aside and looked through.

And she couldn't help but grin.

Fifi sat off to one side, wary and keeping her distance as she watched Thor throwing a small stick for Brutus to fetch. The difference in size of Thor's six-feet-three two-hundred-pound frame and Brutus's seven inches and less than two pounds was utterly ridiculous. But both seemed oblivious to the comical aspects of their game.

Pepper watched for a few moments, then rose on her tiptoes to look down toward the hollow and Lucifer's stable. The bottom half of the Dutch door was closed, she saw, and the stallion shut inside. So . . . Thor really was worried about his horse hurting the dogs. She'd have to do something about that. Tomorrow. Maybe before Thor woke up in the morning.

Pleased that Thor was making an effort to get friendly with her pets, but wondering if it was only because he wanted to save wear and tear on his nerves, she turned away from the window. The baby grand in the room drew her like a magnet, and she went over to sit on the padded bench.

Her fingers moved over the keys lightly, fluidly. She played a bit of Mozart from memory, then began a soft pop song that was a favorite of hers. The piano was beautifully tuned, and Pepper lost herself in the enjoyment of having the chance to play. Leaving her piano behind was the one sacrifice she'd had to make in launching her gypsy life-style.

The words to the song formed in her mind, her throat, and she allowed them to escape softly. Only then did she realize that it was a love song about a woman who loved beyond all reason and feared to lose that love. It wasn't a sad song, oddly enough, but one filled with determination. And, even as she was singing, Pepper wondered in amusement at the proddings of her subconscious.

The last notes trailed away into silence, and the sudden sound of a husky masculine voice threw her into confusion for one of the few times in her life.

"Was that meant for me?"

Startled, she swung around on the bench. Thor was standing in the doorway, leaning back against the jamb with his arms crossed over his broad chest, and something in his eyes made her almost too breathless to answer.

"I thought you were outside," she managed to say after a few moments of silence.

"Ah. Then it wasn't meant for me?"

He wasn't going to let her avoid answering, dammit. "I thought you were outside, I told you. The song was for me. I don't like advertising my lack of voice."

"Fishing?" he inquired with a lifted brow.

Pepper was honestly surprised. "Of course not."

"Then," he told her calmly, "you don't know ability when you hear it. You could sing professionally."

She blinked at him. "I could? Uh . . . I question your taste, but thank you for the compliment."

"You play beautifully too."

"Thank you," she said gravely, staring at him.

"And you look sexy as hell with your hair piled on top of your head like that. I meant to tell you earlier."

She blinked again. "You're feeling *very* complimentary" was all she was able to say.

"I'm also feeling unusually protective," he said conversationally. "So I guess I'd better know how you feel about that. I mean, do you object to my feeling protective, or is that one of the qualities you're looking for?"

"Would it matter?" she asked in sudden amusement, assuming that eventually he'd get around to the real point he wanted to make.

He considered her question. "I doubt it. I don't seem to be able to control it. However, if you object—women's lib or whatever—then I'll see what I can do about it. *Do* you object?"

"Not really. As long as it isn't taken to extremes. I mean, if you accept that I'm not helpless, we'll get along fine."

"I accept that."

"Wonderful. And so?"

"What kind of heat does that RV have?"

The point? she wondered. "I have a kerosene heater. Why?"

Thor frowned. "I don't like that."

"They're perfectly safe," she offered, still amused.

"I suppose. But . . . there's a cold front moving through tonight, and I won't sleep a wink. Why don't you move into the house?"

Ah. The point. Pepper bit back a giggle. "You take your time in getting around to the point, don't you?"

"I'm serious," he scolded, but there was a grin working at his mouth.

"What brought this on?" she asked dryly.

"It's getting chilly outside, and I wondered. I could be callous and say that I don't want my house burning down along with your RV, but that didn't occur to me until just now. Actually it's you and the mutts I'm worried about. Humor me. Move your things in here."

"Thor—"

"God knows, there's enough space. Pick any of the bedrooms—I won't even exclude mine. I won't even charge you rent. Just keep giving Mrs. Small those wonderful recipes and sing for me from time to time."

"Thor—" she tried again, but he cut her off once more.

"The mutts too. If you feel obligated or something, we'll work out a fair trade of services. I mean—uh, no, I didn't mean that the way it sounded. I'll make you wash dishes or something. . . ."

Pepper was laughing.

"That object you see protruding from my mouth," he told her ruefully, "is my foot. Be gentle with me; I've never asked a woman to live with me before."

She choked off a last laugh. "You haven't, huh? I never would have guessed. I think your ulterior motives are showing."

"Bite your tongue. I'm trying to be gallant."

"With the accent on the last syllable?"

"Right. Chivalrous," he said.

"It also means flirtatious."

"Just so, Diana."

"Mmm." Pepper stared at him. "Let's fall back on honesty, shall we? Thor, do you know what you're doing?"

"You think I'm being reckless?"

"Suicidally reckless. If you're counting on the home-team advantage, I should warn you in all fairness that I never need a cheering section."

Thor started to laugh. "You know, whenever we're together, the metaphors fly so thick and fast that I can barely keep up. Cheering section? I thought this challenge was just between you and me."

"You know what I mean."

"It's scary to admit it, but yes, I think I do."

"Why scary?"

"You're beginning to make sense to me; that'd scare any sane man."

"Thanks a lot."

"You're welcome. And we're digressing again. Will you move in?"

Abruptly serious, she asked slowly, "Do you really think that would be a good idea?"

He nodded, still smiling but clearly serious. "Yes. We've got—what?—a few weeks before you either catch me or fold up your RV and steal away. We should make the most of that time."

Pepper felt a smile tugging at her lips. "You really do like the idea of being chased, don't you?"

"I told you, it panders to my ego," he returned solemnly, and then relented because of the suspicious look on her face. "Okay, okay. It may be unmacho to admit it, but yes, I'm getting a hell of a kick out of the whole thing. Although I haven't seen any real evidence of chasing yet."

"Haven't you?" she murmured with another Mona Lisa smile.

He stared at her. "Am I being manipulated?" he demanded suddenly.

She gave him a "Who, me?" look of innocence.

"I think I am," he told the ceiling in mock despair. "And I thought it was all my idea."

"But it was," she told him gently. "That's the subtlety of it."

"You're dangerous."

Pepper started laughing, unable to keep a straight face after his look of sham horror. "I've been told that before. But in this case I'll confess that I hadn't planned on moving into your house. That's a bit too blatant even for my taste."

"I'm glad you admitted that. Honesty I can deal with, but subtlety unnerves me."

"I'll keep that in mind."

"Do that. Are you moving in?"

"Thor—"

"Humor me."

She stared into his smiling gray eyes. "If you'll accept a promise from me," she said seriously.

"What are you promising?"

"I'm promising not to complicate your life—more than you can stand anyway. And I'm promising that you won't have to tell me to go. If you get tired of the game"—she smiled slightly—"or take to your heels in earnest, I'll know. I want you to understand that you won't have to ask me to leave."

Gazing at her, Thor realized dimly that this was the first time either of them had admitted that the game would have an ending, and that it might not be a happy one. "Are you moving in?" he repeated steadily.

"Are you accepting the promise?"

"If I have to," he said unwillingly.

"You do."

"All right then." Thor shook his head. "This is the strangest chase I've ever heard of. Why aren't you attacking me and tearing my clothes off?" he demanded mournfully.

Approving of the brighter atmosphere, she said reprovingly, "That's what happens when I catch you."

"Then why the hell am I running?" he demanded in bewilderment.

They stared at each other for a moment, then both burst out laughing.

"Tuck away your gallant manners, will you?"

"I just offered to help."

"Thor, I'm bringing over some clothes and that's all. They won't be heavy and I can manage nicely on my own, thank you very much."

"You might trip in the dark."

"Thor."

"Why don't you just admit that you don't want me in your RV and be done with it?"

She was slipping, Pepper decided, if it was as obvious as all that. She turned and leaned back against the closed front door, staring up at Thor. He wanted honesty, she reminded herself. "All right then. I don't want you in the van."

"Thanks a lot."

"Sorry."

"Afraid I'll steal the silver?"

"None to steal."

"Afraid I'll find puzzle pieces?" he asked more seriously.

His perception caught her off guard, and for a moment she was silent. Without realizing that she was doing it, Pepper reached into a pocket of her jeans and brought out the ever-present worry-stone, her thumb moving rhythmically in the depression. "Every time we turn around," she murmured, "we seem to be stumbling over honesty."

Thor noticed her unconscious gesture, but didn't comment on it. "That's a good thing to stumble over," he said instead.

She nodded slightly. "As long as one of us doesn't fall." Before he could respond, she was going on evenly. "Okay, then. I came into your home, Thor. And I looked for clues."

"To me?"

"To you. I found a beautiful house. I didn't find clues. I didn't find you."

"I see." He gazed at her steadily. "But I'd find you in the van?" When she hesitated, he said flatly, "I won't step inside the door without your permission, Pepper. I promise you that."

She nodded again and said almost unwillingly, "You'd find me, I think. I've never looked at myself the way you do— pieces of a puzzle, I mean. But if that's what I am, then all the pieces are there. That van is my...anchor. My lifeline. Something to come back to. Someplace to store memories. Home. I believe that everything I am is in that van."

Thor took a deep breath and released it slowly. He reached out a hand, grasping hers and stilling the busy thumb. "I won't go inside without your invitation," he told her, rewording his earlier promise.

Pepper looked up at him, the honesty in her violet eyes neither a weapon nor a plea, but a simple frankness, a calm integrity that brushed aside games and left only truth. "If I ask you, it'll be because I want you to see me. With no veils, no shields, nothing hidden. I'll want you to see everything that I am. Do you understand what that will mean?"

His hand tightened around hers. He bent suddenly and kissed her briefly, a kiss that was curiously rough, almost a protest against what couldn't be denied. "Yes. I know what it will mean." His gray eyes were almost violently stormy, his voice taut.

She pulled her hand from his slowly, still unaware of the worry-stone as she slipped it into her pocket automatically. "Shall I get my things?" she asked him quietly.

"Get your things." As she turned to open the door he added, "Pepper...no matter what happens between us, I want you to remember something. You have valid reasons for your rules. I have valid reasons for mine."

She paused to look back at him, alarmed by the raw sound of his voice. What had they begun? What had they unleashed that had the power to disturb them both this way? Whatever it was, the intensity of it frightened her. "I almost wish...I hadn't challenged you," she told him, and she had never been more honest.

His smile was tight. "I almost wish I hadn't accepted your challenge. But I think we both know there's no going back now."

"Yes. That's what frightens me." She went out, closing the door softly behind her.

"It frightens me too," he murmured, staring at the door's carved panel as if it offered answers. "Dammit to hell, Pepper, why can't I tell you to leave?"

Coming back up the walk a few minutes later, Pepper glanced in the den window, where the drapes had yet to be drawn. She saw Thor sitting in a chair before a newly kindled fire, with Fifi sitting at his feet. The Doberman's long, aristocratic face was turned toward him, her chin on his knee as he pulled absently and rhythmically at her small pointed ears.

Pepper smiled at the dog's acceptance of Thor, but then she got a look at his brooding face, and her smile died. She stood for a moment, looking in and ignoring the breeze that had turned to a chill wind.

Whatever was building between her and Thor, it was happening too fast. They barely knew each other. It had to slow down, she thought desperately. If the headlong rush continued, it would stop only with a painful impact, injuring one or both of them beyond time's ability to heal.

It had not been a part of her plans, she thought dimly, this wrenching of the senses and the heart. She had thought love a warm and gentle emotion, not something that left senses bewildered and unfulfilled bodies aching long into the night. Not something that hurt and frightened. For the first time in her life she wanted to run away.

But she couldn't.

Pepper squared her shoulders and continued up the walk to the front door. Light, she reminded herself. Keep it light. No more soul-searching. Whatever is happening you obviously can't control. So don't look back, and don't look ahead. Light your candles one at a time, and just keep going, dammit.

It was good advice.

She only hoped she could follow it.

Carrying an armful of clothes and with a heavy duffel bag slung over her shoulder, she closed the front door behind her with a thud, not surprised to see that Thor was already in the entranceway.

"Here, let me," he said, reaching out to slip the bag off her shoulder.

Pepper let it go with relief. "Thanks. It's heavier than I

thought." She nodded at Fifi, who was standing at heel by his side. "I see you've made a conquest."

Thor looked down in surprise, having obviously been unaware of Fifi's presence. "So I have."

"I hope you're prepared for her to dog your steps—no pun intended."

He winced. "I'm glad that was unintentional; it's a lousy pun."

"So what do you expect at nine o'clock at night after a delicious meal of lasagna and three glasses of wine?" she asked practically, beginning to climb the stairs and relieved that he'd followed her light lead.

"Better puns. You did say you wanted the waterbed, didn't you?"

Pepper turned in the appropriate door and flipped the light switch. "Can't you tell?" she asked casually, dumping the armful of clothes down on the bright orange comforter.

Thor halted in the doorway, staring at Brutus. The little dog was lying calmly in the center of the bed, front legs crossed and big eyes blinking sleepily in the light. "How did he know?" Thor asked blankly.

"Experience." Pepper laughed. "When I visit friends here in the States, he usually goes with me. And if there's a waterbed, that's where I sleep."

Shaking his head, Thor set the duffel bag on a chair by the door. "Don't tell me Fifi will expect to sleep with me?" he asked uneasily.

"Not unless you invite her to," Pepper answered solemnly. "She's a lady."

"Cute."

"I'm serious. She won't come up on the bed unless you call her. Not while you're awake anyway."

"Great." Thor sighed, looking down at the large dog sitting patiently at his side. Then he looked back at Pepper, his eyes restless. "Do you play chess?" he asked abruptly.

"Yes," she replied, surprised.

"Then how about a game? If you're not too tired, that is."

All of Pepper's instincts told her to turn in early and let the night and sleep take the edge off tension, although she didn't think they would. But there was a faint, almost unwilling plea in Thor's eyes, and she couldn't ignore it. "Sure. I'd like to take a shower first though."

He looked relieved. "Same here. But I have to go turn Lucifer out of his stall first; he hates being shut up all night. So I'll meet you downstairs in about an hour?"

"Fine."

She watched him wave with apparent cheerfulness and head back downstairs, Fifi at his heels. Absently hoping he'd remember to leave the dog inside, she searched through the jumble of clothing on the bed until she'd found her robe, then went into the bathroom adjoining her new bedroom.

Habit born of spending a great deal of time in an RV with a small water tank made her shower brief. She dried off quickly, then donned the floor-length velour robe, zipping the front up to the base of her throat. It was sapphire in color and had heavy batwing sleeves. It was not, she thought judiciously, a seductive garment, and that seemed perfect at the moment. Looking from the inside out, Pepper never realized that the enveloping garment lent her a tiny, rather fragile appearance; an appearance that some men would find far more sexy than bare limbs and cleavage.

She took down her hair and brushed the silvery strands; then, after a moment's hesitation, put it back up and studied the effect in the slightly fogged mirror over the vanity. Odd.

Thor had called the hairstyle sexy. Dispassionate scrutiny convinced Pepper that she looked like a dolled-up Pekingese.

Shaking her head in bemusement, she left the bathroom. Five minutes and an upended duffel bag located her slippers, and then she headed downstairs. She heard Thor whistling in his bedroom as she went down the hall. Well, at least he sounded cheerful, she noted with amusement.

Pepper went into the den and knelt in the deep-pile carpet before the blazing fire. Watching the flames leaping, she followed her own advice about avoiding soul-searching. Instead, she looked as objectively as possible, at the behavior of her and Thor since her "challenge."

"We pretend it's a game," she realized slowly, speaking aloud in the quiet room. "We pretend...and we drag in metaphors and puns, and toss the challenge back and forth...." And then, she also realized, something real pulled at them. And they faced each other in an unguarded, off-center moment filled with an intensity both wanted to back away from. In those moments lurked the danger.

No wonder laughter inevitably followed those moments, she thought ruefully. That intensity scared the hell out of both of them, and laughter was a natural channel for fear.

Pepper was under no illusions as to the traditional belief that men walked boldly into danger. Most walked boldly, certainly, but few went unafraid. There wasn't *that* much difference between the sexes. Unfortunately and unfairly, men were trained by environment, heredity, and too many generations of being "strong and silent" to present a fearless face to the world.

She shook her head at the follies of trapping people into roles, then bit back an ironic laugh as she remembered that both she and Thor were playing roles they'd shaped for themselves. Games. And she wondered which fact they would face first: that they were playing a game—or that it wasn't a game at all.

A sudden sound brought her head up sharply, and Pepper frowned as she listened intently. It had sounded like a muffled howl, she thought. What on earth . . . ?

With only that warning and an instinctive knowledge of what might have happened, Pepper barely had time to prepare herself for a hundred-pound Doberman, soaking wet and quivering with anxiety, bounding into her lap.

"Oh, Fifi," she murmured unsteadily. "You didn't."

"She sure as hell did!" Thor announced irately from the doorway.

five

HOLDING FIFI WITH BOTH ARMS AND AB-sently aware of the water soaking the front of her robe, Pepper stared at the doorway. Thor stood there, dripping, with only a towel knotted at his lean waist.

And the towel was slipping.

Being a graduate of a California university and having been a traveler for years, Pepper had viewed men in various stages of undress. She'd seen men on beaches wearing little more than moral support, and a curious visit to one rather infamous night spot in Europe had boasted a star attraction who'd scorned even that minimal covering. If she'd felt anything on such occasions, it had been a mild analytical interest. In her opinion most men—like most women—looked better with a judicious draping of material here and there.

But Thor's towel seemed to her a sinful crime against nature.

Impressive with his clothes on, he was far more so without them. Powerfully muscled without being overly so, he was deeply tanned, and there wasn't a spare ounce of fat on his large frame. The thick mat of hair on his broad chest was gold, arrowing down his flat stomach to disappear beneath the towel. And the hands-on-hips glaring stance prompted an image of a virile god of thunder.

Pepper's mouth was suddenly dry, and her ability to breathe easily seemed impaired. With a wrenching effort she tore her eyes away to look down at the trembling dog in her lap. She was very grateful that Thor was too angry to pick up the tremulous desire within her.

"Why didn't you warn me?" he was demanding.

"Sorry." She was also grateful for the amusement warring with awareness inside of her. "Uh . . . Fifi likes communal showers. I forgot."

"I'll bet." Thor hitched absently at the towel.

Pepper looked hastily away again. "I swear. Look, you go finish your shower in peace while I dry her off. You're—uh—dripping all over the carpet." She cursed the last sentence silently as he looked down and seemed to become aware of how he was dressed. Or not dressed. And when he gazed at her again—she couldn't seem to stop staring at him—she could see the sudden awareness in his eyes.

"Pepper . . ."

Damn, she thought. Oh, damn, how are we ever going to get to know each other with this . . . this combustion between us? Heaving Fifi off her lap with a strength born of desperation, she got up quickly and grasped the dog's collar. "I'll just go and—" She broke off abruptly and made tracks for the makeshift grooming parlor and the towels used for her canine clients.

Thor stared after her for a moment, then cursed softly and headed for the bathroom upstairs to finish his interrupted shower.

By the time Pepper got Fifi dry and calm again, a glance at her robe told her that she had suffered quite a bit in the dog's wet retreat. The sapphire velour was clinging to the curves beneath it, the material too wet for a hasty drying. She swore under her breath, ordered her pet to stay in the den, and went back upstairs to her bedroom.

It wasn't so much *finding* another robe as choosing between those she had, and the choice took a few moments. Out-and-out seduction had never been a part of her plans, and the last thing she wanted tonight was to spark the highly combustible feelings between her and Thor. But since she liked the gliding feel of silk next to her flesh even in winter, her night-time wardrobe was somewhat limited in the area of concealment.

She finally chose a violet silk nightgown a bit less transparent than the others available. It was floor-length with spaghetti straps and a moderate *V*-neckline, the material slightly gathered beneath her breasts. Over it she donned a matching negligee with a tie closing and long sleeves with wide cuffs at the wrists.

Pepper returned to the study ahead of Thor, and was frowning down at Fifi when he entered the room.

"I'll get the chessboard and set it up on the coffee table in front of the fire—" he began as he came in, but he broke off abruptly. His eyes glided over her new outfit as he automatically finished turning back the cuffs of his blue-and-black plaid flannel shirt.

"Instead of that," she said casually, moving away from the fire's golden light and making a mental note not to stand there again in a silk nightgown, dammit, "if you have a deck of playing cards somewhere around, why don't we try a few hands of poker? It's a little late to start a chess game."

"Poker," he murmured abstractedly. He shook his head, obviously to rid himself of another thought, since his next words were agreement. "Okay. There's a new deck and some chips in the study. While we're at it, we might as well finish off that wine. Why don't you get the wine and glasses while I get the cards?" Before she could respond, he was out of the room.

Pepper silently went to fetch the wine. She didn't suspect Thor of trying to deprive her of inhibitions, since she'd told him at dinner that her head was as hard as her cast-iron stomach and that the only effect wine had on her was to sharpen her wits. And since she liked wine, she had no argument with his suggestion.

A few moments later both were seated on the floor on either side of the coffee table, Thor leaning back against a chair and Pepper against the couch. Their wineglasses were at their elbows, and Thor was opening a new deck of cards.

Pepper glanced down at Fifi, where the still-nervous dog lay beside her, and couldn't help but laugh. "You've lost ground; the poor girl was frightened half to death by that bellow of yours."

Thor followed her gaze and grinned ruefully. "Her sudden entrance into my shower didn't do me much good, either. She just barged right in. I thought you said she was a lady!"

"Only where her sleeping habits are concerned."

Shooting a quick look across the table, Thor half opened his mouth to comment, then apparently thought better of it.

Dryly Pepper said, "No need to be discreet; that's one unasked question I'll answer."

"What did I hesitate to ask?"

"If Fifi's owner shared the—uh—same trait?" Pepper asked with a grin.

"Sharp, aren't you?"

"I try. To answer: yes."

"A lady . . . but only where sleeping habits are concerned?"

"If you accept the traditional definition of ladylike behavior."

"Now you've got me curious."

"Good."

"No elaboration?"

"Oh, I don't think so. I think I'll just cut bait. You should be nicely hooked by now."

Thor started to laugh. "Dammit, Pepper!"

"Honesty's a wonderful thing, isn't it? What stakes shall we play for?"

"Sky's the limit. Shall I bet my house?"

"Better not."

"Are you challenging me again?"

"In spades . . . if you'll forgive another bad pun."

"I won't forgive that one. Cut for the deal?"

"Right."

"Ten of clubs."

"Queen of hearts. I deal." Pepper began to shuffle the deck. "I hope you can afford to drop a bundle," she told him demurely. Briskly, skillfully, slender fingers flying, she dealt the hand.

Thor leaned his elbows on the low table and stared across at her. "I think I should have held out for chess."

Pepper picked up her cards. "Bet."

He sighed and pushed a couple of chips to the center of the table. "Sky's the limit, I said. Why do I get the feeling I'll regret it?"

Nearly two hours and quite a few hands later, Thor laid down a straight and stared at Pepper. "Well, go ahead—I know you'll beat it."

She laid down a full house, aces over queens, and grinned as she raked in the pile of chips to add to her considerable winnings.

"Damn, you're good."

Pepper smiled and slid two fingers beneath the tight cuff of her negligee, removing an ace of hearts from its hiding place. With a professional snap, the card landed in front of Thor.

"I also cheat," she told him placidly. "Not ladylike at all."

"Damn," he repeated blankly, staring down at the card and then at her. "When did you swipe it?"

"While I was dealing."

"I watched your hands," he protested.

"Mmm. I learned from the best."

"Don't tell me. Monte Carlo?"

"Actually no. They knew him in Monte Carlo; he couldn't play there."

Thor groaned. "You're a cardsharp!"

"Has a nice, dishonest ring to it, doesn't it?"

"Your checkered past."

"You're fishing now."

"With every line I can find. Look, d'you mind furnishing just one small piece of the puzzle gratis? I'm stumbling around in the dark here."

Pepper felt a tiny mental shock as his imagery matched her own. Stumbling in the dark? Aware now of what happened in these off-center, unguarded moments, she could literally see the clear-cut limits of their roles becoming hazy. She picked up her glass, sipping the cool wine and wondering despairingly why she had to constantly wave puzzle pieces at him in challenge.

"Off the top of my head, or d'you want to ask a question?" she heard herself ask abruptly.

"Question."

"Time out for a question from the peanut gallery," she mocked lightly.

"Cute."

"Well. Fair trade then. If I answer your question, you have to answer mine."

"All right," he said slowly.

"So ask."

"An honest answer?"

"If I can."

"Pepper—"

"All right! An honest answer."

Thor reached a hand across to cover the restless fingers worrying her wineglass. His thumb swept lightly across a long, thin scar across the back of her hand. "How did that happen?"

Surprised, Pepper looked down at the scar for a moment and then back at him. "Oh. That."

"Uh-huh."

She frowned at him. "I could say I fell down on something when I was three."

"You could. It might even be true. Is it?"

Pepper sighed. She didn't want to appear mysterious, but unless she supplied several of the puzzle pieces, that was probably the way her answer would sound. Still . . . he'd asked. And she'd promised to answer.

"I was cut."

"How?"

"That's two questions," she said evasively.

"No, it isn't. I asked *how* that happened; you just told me *what* happened."

"You're splitting hairs."

"Pepper."

"Oh, all right." She pulled her hand from beneath his and stared across at him. "I was cut with a knife."

It was Thor's turn to frown. "An accident?" He'd noted that she hadn't said she cut herself.

"You could say that," Pepper drawled. "I certainly didn't mean for it to happen."

"Worser and worser," he muttered. "And you still haven't told me how it happened."

She took a deep breath. "Someone wanted to take something away from me."

"A mugger?" he guessed.

Pepper hesitated for a split second. "Close enough."

"Pepper—"

"My turn," she said hastily.

"Dammit. All right, what's your question?"

She nodded toward the small scar above his left eye. "How'd you get that?"

"What?"

Pepper reached across the low table to touch the scar lightly with her fingertip. "That." And was disconcerted when he immediately caught and held her hand. She wondered why she had the odd feeling that he'd known what she was referring to; why she thought that he'd wanted her to touch him. Wishful thinking?

Thor chuckled softly. "Believe it or not, I *did* fall—out of a tree when I was seven."

Pepper started to laugh. "It figures!"

He was smiling, but he didn't laugh with her. Instead, he watched her with eyes gone a curiously metallic silver. "You and your damn rules," he said softly.

She felt his hand tighten around hers, her own amusement fading. The tingling awareness within her grew and spread with the suddenness of a brushfire. She heard her own voice, husky and unsteady, and wished that she'd shown sense and turned in early. "I warned you."

"You warned me. Sporting of you. Diana, goddess of the hunt, dropping me into a maze and turning loose her hounds.

And such strange hounds." He sent an oddly expressionless glance toward Fifi. "A neurotic Doberman and an attack-trained Chihuahua."

"You didn't have to accept the challenge," she reminded him.

"Oh, but I did," he told her abruptly. "It was like waving a red cape at a bull to force an instinctive reaction."

"I can still leave," she said, after swallowing the lump in her throat.

Thor released her hand and leaned back against the chair, folding his arms across his chest. "No, you can't. We both know that. One way or another, the game has to finish. But what happens to the loser, Pepper?"

"That . . . depends on who loses."

"I know what happens if I lose. What happens if you do?"

Pepper saw where his thoughts had headed, and the ease of her understanding startled her; it was as though they were attuned somehow. They both understood that if she lost, it would be because she'd broken her rules and accepted his—a short-term relationship with no strings and no promises. And she understood then that Thor had realized she could be hurt by that.

She smiled faintly. "If I lose, I'll just drive off into the sunset. Remember what I promised. You won't have to ask me to leave."

"Dammit, Pepper," he said roughly.

She got to her feet, looking down at him and still smiling. "Don't worry about me, Thor. I'm a survivor. And I'm always ready to pay the price for any chance I take."

He was suddenly up and around the low table, catching her shoulders and looking down at her probingly. "How many times have you paid a price for taking a chance?" he demanded. "The scar on your hand—was that a price, Pepper?"

She shook her head, trying not to be so stingingly aware of his touch. "No, not really. The end result of taking a chance, I suppose, but—dammit, don't box me in!"

"What d'you think you're doing to me?" His voice was fierce. "Hell, Pepper, every time I turn around, there's a wall! I don't want to get involved with you, but I can't seem to help myself. I want to know everything there is to know about you. I want to get inside that puzzle that passes for your mind. Dammit, I want to carry you upstairs and make love to you, and that scares the hell out of me because I don't think I'd ever be able to forget you after that. I don't think I'll be able to forget you anyway. . . ."

"Do you want to forget me so badly?" she asked unsteadily, staring up at him and nearly hypnotized by the nerve pulsing erratically beside his mouth.

"I have to," he breathed huskily. "Dammit, I have to . . . but I don't think I'll be able to. . . . God, Pepper, what're you doing to me?"

Before Pepper could answer that unanswerable question, he pulled her abruptly against him, his hands sliding over the cool silk covering her back, and sought her lips hungrily. Hunger, a strange, soul-deep hunger welling up inside of him had taken control, and Thor could no more fight it than he could ignore it.

She was on fire and weightless again, some distant part of her mind aware that he'd picked her up and placed her on the couch; another more primitive part of her mind was aware of the unfamiliar weight of his body lying half on hers. He was heavy, and she absorbed the weight of him in wonder; it should have been uncomfortable, but it wasn't. It felt right.

It didn't occur to Pepper to resist, and even if it had, her body's desires would have overwhelmed logic. As it was, both her mind and body seemed to have become two strangely disconnected things. Her mind was hazy, floating like a leaf in a fast-moving stream; her body was being bombarded by sensations it had never experienced before, and all her nerve endings seemed to have short-circuited.

She felt his fingers fumbling blindly with the tie closing of her negligee, pushing the silk aside to find the lace and silk of her gown's V-neckline. His lips followed the fiery brush of his fingers, exploring the lightly tanned flesh above the edging of lace. One of his hands rested on the back of her neck, the fingers moving in her hair; the other hand moved with rough gentleness to cup a throbbing breast warmly.

Her own fingers tightened in his hair, then loosened and moved down to grip his shoulders. Mindlessly her head tilted back against the hand holding it. Eyes fiercely closed, she wondered hazily if this was love, knowing somehow that it was. She wanted more of him than she could ever have, needed more than he could or would give to her. And the sadness of that brought the sting of tears to her eyes and pulled her wayward mind back into her aching body.

"Sweet," he was murmuring hoarsely against her skin. "God, you're so sweet! Don't stop me, Pepper. . . ."

"I won't," she breathed unevenly, realizing only then what she was saying, realizing that he would know too. She'd told him that lovemaking for her would mean that she'd found—or believed she'd found—what she'd been looking for in a man. And it was too soon, far too soon, to tell him that, but it was true, and she was too honest to pretend.

His head lifted, and Pepper saw slate-gray eyes staring down at her, cloudy, oddly uncertain. Pepper touched his face with hands that were shaking a little, giving him the honesty he'd demanded—and now wished she could consign to hell.

"I can't ask you to stop. I don't want to, Thor."

Thor gazed into the bottomless pools of her violet eyes,

seeing the shine of tears that only a part of him understood. And a frustration greater than any he'd ever known gnawed at him relentlessly. He heard what she was telling him—and he wasn't ready either to break his own rules or to ask her to break hers.

Stalemate.

Pepper knew his decision almost the moment he made it, knew that he was going to leave her. He was running, and she still didn't know why.

He got to his feet slowly and stood for a moment looking down at her, his face taut and eyes restless. Then, with a smothered sound that might have been a curse, he turned on his heel and started for the front door.

She didn't try to call him back. Sitting up, she saw him grab a jacket from the brass coat tree in the entranceway and heard the door close quietly. She waited for long, tense moments, but there was no roar from the Corvette.

Pepper swung her legs off the couch and got up, bending over the coffee table long enough to stack the cards neatly and place the chips back in their caddy. Then she picked up their wineglasses and carried them to the kitchen before going silently upstairs to her room.

The Doberman had followed her, but hesitated in the doorway to the room, whining softly. Pepper looked down at her for a moment, then smiled wryly. "You too, eh? Come on in, girl. I won't close the door all the way. You can go to him when he comes in." Fifi lay down in front of the chair by the door, still whimpering.

Pepper moved about the room for a few moments, putting her clothes away neatly and wondering if she'd be packing them back up tomorrow. Oddly enough she didn't believe that Thor wanted her to leave. She'd seen the conflict in his eyes tonight, and knew that something—perhaps his own set of rules, or something else—was having a tug of war within him.

She had to wait and find out what...or who...would win.

Going to the window to draw the drapes, she automatically looked out and down, seeing the moonlit shapes of Thor and his stallion by the fence. She gazed out for a moment, then drew the drapes. She slid between the sheets of the wide bed, pulling the quilted comforter up and reaching to turn out the lamp on the nightstand.

The water moved gently beneath her for a few seconds as she got comfortable and Brutus moved to his accustomed place near her feet. Then everything was still and quiet.

She didn't think she'd sleep. Her body was aching as if she were coming down with the flu, and her mind was, for once, too weary to tear apart the events of the evening, analyze them, and try to make sense of it all. The only thing she was certain of was that time seemed to have slowed to a crawl, and she'd lived a whole emotional lifetime in a little more than two days....

She slept, and she dreamed, oddly, of the occasion during which she had acquired the scar that seemed to fascinate Thor. In the dream she was running through the narrow streets of London, fog hampering her sense of direction, tensely conscious of the pounding footsteps of the man chasing her. Her good hand gripped the briefcase; the cut hand had been bound on the run with a handkerchief and was throbbing with every step. And then she rounded a corner and it was all right, doubly all right, because there was a bobby and there was the house, she recognized that peculiar gate, and she could finally stop running, and damned if she'd ever carry gems again....

Pepper woke with a start to see dawn's gray light creeping through the narrow crack in the drapes. Her eyelids felt scratchy, sure evidence of a restless night. And she'd moved all the way to the other side of the bed, which was easy to do on a waterbed but was, she noted, further evidence of disturbed sleep. The house was silent, and Brutus was sitting up and looking at her expectantly, his tail thudding softly against the comforter and saying "Out."

Within a few minutes Pepper was up and dressed in jeans and a thick, bulky sweater of pale pink. She splashed water on her face in the bathroom, noting the red-rimmed eyes and realizing wryly that she looked as though she'd sobbed her heart out during the night. She hadn't, of course; that was just the way she inevitably looked after a bad night.

She brushed her hair and left it to fall, straight and shining, past her waist, then donned her suede ankle boots, tucked Brutus under an arm, and quietly went downstairs. Fifi joined them just as she opened the front door, and she took a moment to reflect that Thor, too, had left his bedroom door ajar so the dog could get in.

Standing on the front porch, she watched the dogs race around in the chill morning air for a while, sharply calling both to heel when she heard Lucifer gallop up to the fence to investigate the strange goings-on. Then she took the dogs to meet Lucifer.

It took less than an hour to convince the stallion that she was his friend; it took nearly another hour to coax him to accept the dogs. Born with a gift for handling animals, Pepper was patient and soft-spoken with the horse. And wary. She knew horses—and particularly stallions.

She didn't use carrots or sugar cubes or any other enticement, and she never lifted a hand against the horse. But by the time she'd slid off the fence and onto Lucifer's back for a wild gallop around the pasture, they were friends. The stallion was well trained, responding to the slightest pressure of her knees, and a few moments' experimentation bore out her guess that he knew voice commands as well. After that it was downhill all the way.

The sun was well up and warming the frosted ground by the time Pepper climbed up to sit on the top rail of the fence and watch the fruits of her efforts. Lucifer and Fifi were engaged in a playful game of chase at the moment; the Doberman, while cowardly with people, was perfectly cheerful with other animals, and was both quick enough and strong enough to give the stallion a run for his money. Brutus, disdaining lesser pursuits, was down in the hollow investigating the stable.

Pepper enjoyed watching the games, interested as always in personalities—whether or not they were animal or human. She was so caught up in her observation, in fact, that she totally missed the sound of a strange car pulling up in the driveway. But she didn't miss the strange masculine voice.

"Who're you, for God's sake?"

She swung around on the fence, nearly losing her seat, to find herself under scrutiny. Before she could respond, he was speaking again.

"Well, well, well. Don't tell me Thor's been caught at last!"

"I'm working on it," Pepper said involuntarily.

Laughter immediately lit the stranger's golden eyes and filled his deep voice. "Then *you* I've got to meet! D'you mind coming away from that fence for the introductions? Lucifer and I are old enemies."

His name was Cody Nash, and he was a golden man. His thick hair was golden, his tan was golden, his remarkable eyes were golden, and his deep voice held the rough beauty of raw gold.

She pegged him at about Thor's age, although the classical

bone structure of his handsome face would probably, she decided, never really show age. Like Thor, he was a tall man, but a couple of inches shorter than Thor and more slender. He was innately charming, friendly, funny, and possessed the kind of looks that had probably broken hearts for years.

Pepper liked him. She liked him immediately and instinctively. Oddly enough, he asked the question Thor hadn't asked, which was, "Pepper what?" She went through the story of how she'd gotten her name, wondering in amusement when it would occur to Thor that he didn't know her entire name. Cody was delighted by the story, returning the favor by explaining that his name had come from an old western novel that his father had been reading in the fathers' waiting room at the hospital.

"So you're a friend of Thor's?" she questioned as they stood a couple of feet back from the fence and watched the canine-equine games.

Cody grimaced slightly. "I think so anyway. We've known each other since we were kids."

Pepper wondered at the answer. Just as she'd picked up constraint in Thor's voice about his job, she heard the same thing now in Cody's voice. And her mind came up with a possible answer. "Did you two have a falling out over some girl?" she asked lightly.

"If only it were that simple," Cody said wryly.

She looked at him inquiringly, not wanting to ask outright but intensely curious.

Abruptly Cody asked, "Were you serious about—uh—working on Thor?"

"Very much so," she answered steadily.

He looked at her for a moment, then nodded slightly. "I see you are. Well, then." His gaze went out over the pasture . . . or over the years. "We were friends all through school, through college, and just normally competitive over girls—the way all boys are after a certain age. But there was nothing serious for either of us. That was in Texas."

Pepper looked at him, startled, but didn't interrupt.

"After school we drifted apart a little—and that's normal too. We had different jobs, and both of us traveled. Thor settled down up here after his parents died; I was still traveling quite a bit. Whenever I wound up in the Northeast, I dropped in. We still tried to take each other's money at poker and kept up a running chess game for a while.

"But gradually—" Cody broke off and shook his head slightly. "I don't know. Something changed. Thor...Thor wasn't the same. Oh, not unfriendly. Just not overly friendly. Let's just say that I wasn't encouraged to keep dropping in on the spur of the moment."

"But here you are," she murmured.

"Here I am." He laughed a little ruefully. "I turn up every few months whether he likes it or not. I don't always catch him at home, but when I do, I usually stay a day or two."

"Why?" she asked bluntly. "I mean, why d'you keep coming around?"

"He's my friend," Cody said simply.

Pepper stared at the serious man beside her for a moment, then looked out over the pasture. She thought that she might be seeing a different Thor today because Cody was here, and she wasn't sure she wanted that.

Certainly she wanted to know Thor in all his moods, but she was afraid that this one was going to disturb her. Things were bound to be strained between her and Thor after last night, and any additional tension was not going to be fun to deal with.

She wasn't able to give another thought to this problem, though. A tiny brown fury suddenly erupted from beneath the bottom rail of the fence, yapping hysterically and launching himself with murderous intent at Cody's ankle.

"Hell's bells!" Cody stared down at his would-be assassin in lively astonishment. "I'm being savaged!"

From behind them a laconic voice said, "Welcome to the menagerie."

six

THE NEXT FEW MINUTES WERE RATHER
full. While Pepper was rescuing Cody from the clutches of the
wantonly protective Brutus, Thor, with a totally deadpan
expression, explained Brutus's attack training. By the time
Pepper had the growling Chihuahua tucked under her arm and
while Cody's bemusement was holding him silent, Thor suddenly took note of the other pet cavorting in the pasture with
his killer horse.

"What the hell—?"

"It's all right, Thor; I introduced them."

"You what?"

"Introduced them. They're friends now. I didn't want you
to have to keep shutting Lucifer in his stall whenever the dogs
were outside, so I—"

"Pepper, that horse is a killer! And he hates dogs."

"He doesn't hate our dogs." Pepper took no notice of the
pronoun, and Thor was too upset to notice, but Cody filed it
away in his bemused brain. "Stop fussing, Thor. He's a very
well-trained horse. Did you train him? The slightest knee-
pressure, and—"

"You rode that horse?"

"Well, just once around the pasture, but—"

Thor erupted. He swore violently and at great length, mostly in English but with a smattering of Spanish and what sounded like a few words of Arabic. He poured wrath over Pepper by the bucketful, and for ten solid minutes never once repeated himself.

Cody stood with arms folded across his chest, staring at his friend with an expression somewhere between the mildly astonished and the totally stunned, from which Pepper gathered that Thor didn't often explode.

As for herself, Pepper stood listening politely and waited for him to run down. Having heard quite a few explosions in her time, she was well aware that this one had been detonated by anxiety along the lines of You-could-have-gotten-your-stupid-self-killed-you-idiot-and-why-the-hell-didn't-you-have-more-sense?

She was enjoying it thoroughly.

He finally began repeating himself, and Pepper decided that it was time to interrupt. "Jean's here," she said, cheerfully breaking in on a sentence calculated to make her hair stand on end. "I think I'll go help her with breakfast. You'd better feed Lucifer, Thor, if you can pry him away from Fifi. And send the mutt on up to the house so I can feed her. See you." She strolled off toward the house, still carrying Brutus tucked underneath an arm.

Venturing to intrude on Thor's fulminating silence, Cody said mildly, "She's quite a lady, Thor. Where'd you find her?"

Thor dragged his glare away from Pepper's retreating back and fastened it onto Cody's hapless person. "Oh, shut up!" he snapped violently, and stalked away to feed his killer horse.

After the emotional tumult of the day before and his sleepless night, Thor was in no mood to deal with the sudden arrival of Cody. And Pepper's recklessness where Lucifer was concerned hadn't helped. And, though she'd been her normal cheerful and absurd self, he'd taken note of the red-rimmed eyes; the image of her crying herself to sleep last night haunted him.

By the time he and a prudently silent Cody entered the house, Thor had himself under nominal control. The slightest spark, and he knew he'd go up like a rocket though.

Ordered cavalierly into the dining room by Mrs. Small, he found that his and Cody's breakfast consisted of omelets.

"Spanish. Pepper's recipe. Authentic," Mrs. Small told him, plunking the plates down on the table.

"Well, where is she?" Thor asked irritably.

The housekeeper looked down her nose at him. "In the kitchen. She's—"

"Tell her she can damn well get her butt in here and eat with us," Thor ordered. "No more skipping meals."

Mrs. Small lifted an eyebrow at him, then returned to the kitchen.

A moment later Pepper came in bearing a plate. "Omelets," she announced mildly, "are cooked one at a time. I was fixing mine." Sitting down at Thor's left hand, she looked across the table at Cody and added solemnly, "He's so masterful."

Cody's laugh changed itself to a hasty little cough, and he bent his attention to his omelet. Thor, feeling a bit like a fool, glared down at his food and dug in.

"My Spanish omelets are very spicy, you know," Pepper said conversationally just as both men reached hastily for water glasses. "Cayenne pepper." She ate calmly without recourse to her water.

"You don't say?" Cody wheezed.

"Unusual," Thor managed.

"I like food with body. We're having shrimp curry tonight, by the way. I hope you gentlemen'll like it."

Mrs. Small passed through the dining room just then with a dustcloth. "India," she contributed in a satisfied voice. "Authentic."

Thor felt a sudden inclination to go off into a corner and have a quiet nervous breakdown. But he couldn't stay angry. He wanted to burst out laughing at the bemusement on Cody's face, even while realizing wryly that he himself was probably wearing much the same expression. Damn the woman—why'd she keep on knocking him off-balance like this? He felt like a yo-yo.

"You've been to India?" Cody was asking with keen interest in his tone of voice.

"Delhi," Pepper answered easily. "Beautiful place. Thor, I called Mom yesterday and gave her this number, so I'll probably start getting calls. Don't be surprised if my friends sound like nuts."

"That wouldn't surprise me," Thor said definitely.

Laughter lit her eyes. "I'm sure. Oh, and I've got at least a dozen clients coming today, so the place is apt to be noisy; they're all talkers, I'm afraid."

"Clients?" Cody looked bewildered.

"Dogs." Pepper smiled at him. "I'm grooming dogs for a friend of mine, and Thor's letting me use his mudroom."

"Oh." Fascination was beginning to grip Cody's mobile features. "You—uh—groom dogs?"

"She does everything," Thor told him ruefully. "And she's good at games. Don't play poker with her."

"She's that good?" Cody asked as if she weren't present.

"She cheats. Cardsharp."

"Imagine that." The blond man turned his thoughtful eyes back to Pepper. "An expert at sleight of hand, are you?"

Smiling, Pepper rose with her empty plate and started around the back of Thor's chair. Pausing for only a moment, she demonstrated marvelous legerdemain by neatly removing a coin from Thor's ear. Still smiling gently, she tossed the coin to Cody and went out to the kitchen.

Cody stared down at the quarter while Thor cautiously felt his ear.

"Thor," Cody said in a contemplative voice, continuing to gaze at the coin, "where *did* you find her?"

"I answered an ad in the paper," Thor said carefully, and then broke apart.

However he'd responded to Cody during the past years, Thor was clearly unable to be "not overly friendly" with Pepper's strongly felt presence raining absurdity on all of them. From breakfast the day was duly launched along those lines, and it would have taken a stronger man than Thor to resist laughter.

It began with the deluge of the "clients," all arriving within ten minutes of one another. Without Tim, her helper, Pepper had something of a struggle on her hands trying to get all the dogs into their wire kennels. Such a time, in fact, that one toy poddle and two Pekingese escaped her and invaded the den, where Thor and Cody were playing a game of chess.

"Grab 'em!" Pepper yelped from the doorway. "Chico eats pillows and Malfi's Rising Star *refuses* to be housebroken!"

Neither Thor nor Cody wasted time in wanting to know which dog was which: both lunged for the invaders. Thor scooped up a golden Peke that already had its teeth into a pillow on the couch, while Cody dexterously snared the tiny black poodle that was sniffing thoughtfully at the leg of the coffee table. Pepper cornered the remaining brown Peke near the fireplace.

"What the hell?" Thor managed, firmly removing the pillow from sharp little teeth.

"Sorry," Pepper gasped, trying not to laugh. "They got away from me."

"Obviously."

"Which is which?" Cody asked, subjecting his poodle to a critical stare. "Have I got Malfi's— What was it?"

"Malfi's Rising Star. Yes, you've got him. Thor's got Chico, and I've got Duchess. Whose move is it?"

Thor glanced automatically down at the chessboard. "Cody's."

"Move the bishop," Pepper told Cody. She tucked Duchess under one arm, Chico under another, and somehow managed to retrieve Malfi's Rising Star from Cody before leaving the room.

Cody stared down at the board for a moment, then decisively moved the bishop. He grinned at Thor. "She's right. Mate in three moves."

Thor made a rude noise and sat back down to try and win back the ground Pepper had cost him.

Their game was relatively undisturbed for a while, Thor getting up only once to check on the sound of the motorcycle that heralded Tim's arrival. Then the phone began to ring. Thor answered it since Mrs. Small was busy in the kitchen.

"Hello?"

"Hello there. Is Pepper around, or have you buried her?"

Thor took the receiver away from his ear to stare at it for a moment, then replied to the cheerful masculine voice. "She's here. Hold on a minute."

"Sure."

Thor yelled to Mrs. Small, who passed the message on to

Pepper. She came in the den with a harassed expression, drying her hands on a towel.

"I wonder why Noah didn't leave poodles off his ark?" she murmured despairingly to the two men, then picked up the phone before either could attempt an answer. "Hello? Oh, hi! No, I was just bathing Malfi's Rising Star. Don't laugh; he's a prize-winning poodle. Who? Oh, that was just Thor."

Thor, listening intently, lost his knight in an absent move and sent a glare toward Pepper. She smiled gently at him and went on with the conversation.

"Yes, Yes. What? No, that was Istanbul. Of course, I'm sure! Well, I bought the thing, didn't I? It was Istanbul. No, the sari came from India. What *is* this anyway? You taking inventory? Oh. Oh, I see. Well, tell Marsha that saris come from India and sarongs from the Orient. Yes. Okay, fine. See you." She hung up the phone, smiled faintly at the two men staring at her, and headed back for the mudroom.

"Istanbul?" Cody asked plaintively.

Thor sighed. "Don't look at me. I haven't figured her out yet."

They went back to the game. But they were destined to listen in on three more conversations, Pepper's end of them, anyway. None of them made sense. The callers were male, male, and female respectively, which was all that Thor could attest to. Unless, of course, he could offer his opinion that all three callers were holding onto their sanity by the skin of their teeth.

But Pepper's end of the conversations was intriguing.

"You did what? That wasn't very smart. Oh, really? Well, why did you listen to him? That's ridiculous! Just because she's from Hong Kong— I hope you decked him. Oh, good! Both eyes? Nice going, hero. Raw steak. Really, it works very well.

Of course, I'm sure. Oh, does she? Well, some of those ancient remedies are terrific, you know. No. No, I'll probably be down that way in a few weeks. Sure. Hey—call Cal and tell him; he'll get a kick out of it. Okay. Bye."

"No, I'm grooming Kristen's dogs. England. An English breeder. If you keep laughing like that, you'll hurt yourself. Of course, she doesn't realize—what a ridiculous question! Him either. A dog show. Me? In London. A friend of a friend, you know. Who? That was Thor. Don't bother; I'm taking all the best god-of-thunder jokes. I'm working on it. No, very nice. Look, if you called just to exercise your giggle box— What? Men have giggle boxes, idiot. And yours is upside down. Funny, that's funny. Right. Okay, you— What? Oh. Belladonna. Yes, the berries are poisonous. You need the whole plant? Let's see . . . Hemlock then. Seeds, leaves, and roots. Of course, I'm sure. Okay, bye."

"Hemlock?" Cody murmured uneasily. "D'you suppose he wants to poison somebody?"

"Beats the hell out of me," Thor said.

Cody reflected for a moment. "An ad in the paper, you said."

"Uh-huh."

"Oh, hi! When did you get back? Really? Did he give you that cute little chalet halfway up? Good. Wasn't the view terrific? Well, I'd think you could have stuck your heads out at least once! What's the use of being in the Alps unless you— Did you? That's something, anyway! Paris, huh? Who? Oh, did he? A running chess game. No, for six months while I was on the Left Bank. Didn't he tell you? No, they raided that club; that's how we met. I wasn't doing anything. I was just there. Overnight. Everybody else slept and we played chess. Did he say that? Liar! He only arrested me so I'd give him a game; nobody else was up to his weight. No, he never put it on the records. Did you tell him that? Well, I'll give him a call sometime. Sure. Don't mention it. Give him my love, okay? Bye."

By then Thor's game was in shreds. "Arrested," he muttered, staring across the board at Cody. "Good Lord!"

"Sounded harmless," Cody ventured cautiously.

"She's probably wanted for murder somewhere."

"You think so?"

"Hell, I— Oh, never mind. I concede the game, dammit. Let's try poker."

"You're the host."

Lunch turned out to be run-of-the-mill steak and salad, which prompted Thor to ask Mrs. Small sardonically if she'd run out of "Pepper's Authentic Recipes," a question she didn't deign to answer. Pepper turned up for the meal looking even more harassed, and accused Thor of trying to drive her to an early grave.

"I think you've got that backward," he told her.

"No, I haven't. You let Brutus and Fifi out hours ago, and they found something to roll in that smells terrible. Tim's gone home for lunch, and the pets have to stay out in the mudroom until I can wash them."

"So?" Thor was unsympathetic.

Pepper glared at him. "So Brutus is taunting Malfi's Rising Star through the wire and Fifi thinks she's being punished! She's almost hysterical!"

Cody choked on his baked potato, and Thor pounded him on the back with more force than necessary.

"Quit it!" Cody managed, eyes watering.

Pepper took her seat in something of a huff, but her normally sunny temper rapidly reasserted itself and she became cheerful again. "Oh, well. At least most of the clients are done. There's just Sunnydale to do, and none tomorrow. After today I need a break!"

"Don't we all," Thor murmured.

"Funny man. Did you beat him, Cody?"

"The chess game? He conceded."

"Was he a good loser?"

"Not really. He never is."

"Ah. I'd better keep that in mind."

"Really? Why?"

Thor tapped his water glass with his fork. "Hey, guys— guess who's here?"

"The god of thunder, breathing fire," Pepper murmured.

"Striking sparks with his magic hammer," Cody contributed solemnly.

"Why didn't my parents name me George?" Thor asked the ceiling.

Pepper subjected him to a critical scrutiny. "You don't look like a George. You look like a Thor."

"Thanks."

"Don't mention it."

"Do I look like a Cody?" Cody asked politely.

Pepper gave him the same critical appraisal. "Yes."

"Brief and to the point," Cody noted dryly.

"You asked."

"She's honest," Thor told his friend.

"A woman in a million, in fact." Cody was approving.

Thor winced. "Well, there's honesty . . . and then there's *honesty*."

Trying to hide her amusement, Pepper looked at him

gravely. "Would you like me to lie a little? I can, you know. With the best of them."

Thor looked as though there were quite a few things he could have said to that had Cody not been present. Instead, he said wryly, "Of course you can; you're a woman."

It was Pepper's turn to wince. "Damn, could I get you with that one! I hate blanket statements." Quite deliberately she added, "Besides, If you haven't learned by now not to stick any kind of label on me, then there is something badly wrong with your faculties."

Thor sipped iced tea and stared at her over the rim of his glass, refusing to be drawn. It was Cody who had a remark to follow hers.

"It occurs to me," he said consideringly as he gazed at Pepper, "that for all your little-girl voice and lack of inches, you are a formidable lady."

Pepper looked at him, totally deadpan. "Better men than you have learned that—to their cost," she said, and lifted an eyebrow at him.

After a moment, Cody turned a mournful stare on Thor. "My friend, you are down for the count."

Thor choked slightly, taken by surprise since he was unaware that Pepper had blurted out her true intentions to Cody after barely laying eyes on him. Before he could respond, Pepper did.

"The count is nine," she murmured, demonstrating a knowledge of boxing terminology. Rising with her cleared plate, she added a *tsk-tsk* sound and said, "Kayoed—and at his age too." She went away to the kitchen.

"An ad in a newspaper," Cody said slowly.

Thor could only nod.

"Classified?"

"Uh-huh."

"Did she come with Green Stamps?"

"If you want a bed to sleep in tonight," Thor said threateningly, "shut up."

"Uh . . . yes."

The rest of the day went smoothly—compared to the morning. Pepper finished the grooming of the last of her clients and left Tim to watch over them until their proud owners picked them up. She got Brutus and Fifi cleaned up, then went and took a shower herself.

When she came back downstairs, she found Thor sharing the den with two disgruntled pets. Brutus was sulking after the indignity of a bath, and Fifi was lying as close as possible to Thor's chair and looking nervous. Thor was absently shuffling a deck of playing cards.

"Where's Cody?" Pepper asked as she came into the room.

"Pestering Mrs. Small." Thor looked at her, eyes hooded. "It's a favorite pastime of his."

Pepper laughed. "It figures." She went over to sit on the couch, pushing Brutus to one side and ignoring his irritated grumble.

"I'm sorry about last night," Thor said suddenly.

Determined to keep it light, Pepper said, "Sorry you left so abruptly? Or sorry that it happened at all?" Belatedly she realized that this was their first moment alone together since last night.

He smiled a little. "Sorry I left so abruptly."

She shrugged. "Well, I did sort of hit you over the head, didn't I? I seem to have lost all ability to be . . . subtle."

Thor stared at her for a long moment. When he spoke, his words came slowly, consideringly, but his voice was raw around the edges. "Do you know . . . I've been through more emotions in the past twenty-four hours than I have in years. From amusement to absolute fury. And through it all—through it all, I've wanted you more and more with every second that passed."

Pepper swallowed hard. "You don't like it."

"No."

"I'm sorry."

"Are you? What about the chase?"

She glanced down as Brutus gave up his sulks and climbed into her lap. Absently she petted him. "I don't know, Thor. I just know that I'm sorry you feel that way. I feel as if . . . as if I've known you for a long time. I feel as if you should be my friend. But whenever I look at you and think *friend,* then I see *lover.* As if you can't be one or the other without being both. I've never looked at a man that way. I don't know quite how to deal with that."

Thor waited until she met his steady gaze, then said with odd gentleness, "Brave talk aside?"

Pepper smiled, recalling her arrogant remarks about chasing all the way to hell and knockout punches. "Brave talk aside. When you're small, you learn to talk big—or get run over. You also learn determination." Her violet eyes were direct. "I may lose this time, Thor, but I'll know why."

He nodded slowly, understanding what she was telling him. Win or lose, Pepper meant to find out why he avoided commitment. He could hardly blame her for that. Truth to tell, he wanted her to know. But he wasn't yet ready to tell her. And that bothered him, because he understood why. In the past he'd never hesitated to let a woman know why he avoided ties. Now he was hesitating.

Not because Pepper mattered too little . . . but because she mattered too much.

"Truce?" She was smiling at him. "I think we need a little breathing time, Thor."

"Things have been happening a bit rapidly," he agreed in a regretful tone.

"You can say that again!" She laughed unsteadily.

"Truce then. We'll slow the carousel before we both fall off."

Pepper grinned. "You know—between imagery, analogies, and metaphors, I think we've invented our own language!"

"I've always wanted to do that."

"Fun, isn't it?"

"Hello, all," Cody said, coming into the room.

"It's the one-eyed jack," Thor told Pepper.

"Better than a suicide king," she said solemnly.

"Not if jacks are wild."

"Are they?"

"One-eyed jacks and deuces."

"That sounds reasonable."

Cody cast a bewildered look down at the growling Chihuahua attached to one leg of his jeans, then apparently decided to ignore it since everyone else was. "Not to me, it doesn't. Have I wandered into a verbal poker game?"

"Speaking of which"—Thor briskly shuffled the cards he still held—"why don't we play a few hands? If, that is, Pepper'll push the sleeves of her sweater up and submit to a body search before every hand."

"Oh, that's cute!" she told him dryly.

"It was worth a try."

"Hey, fella, I don't have to cheat to win."

"Let's take her money, Cody."

"I'm game."

"Cut for the deal. Ten of clubs."

"Jack of diamonds," Cody announced. "Go away, Brutus."

"Queen of hearts." Pepper smiled. "I deal."

Thor looked suspicious. "You cut that card every time!"

"Makes you wonder, doesn't it?"

"Push back your sleeves, dammit."

"Will somebody get this savage creature away from my ankle?"

Pepper didn't win every hand. Just most of them.

With a truce declared and scrupulously honored by both sides, an odd sort of harmony settled into their relationship. It was aided during the first couple of days by Cody, who was, whether he was aware of it or not, a buffer who allowed them to find the distance they needed.

Since Pepper was free of her grooming duties on Wednesday, all three spent the day just enjoying themselves. They played chess and cards and charades indoors. They raked leaves outside because of the windy night before, finishing with the inevitable leaf-fight. All three were energetic, athletic, and competitive, which meant that they were exhausted by the end of the day.

Mrs. Small continued to lay before them various culinary examples of Pepper's travels, leaving palates in a state of perpetual shock. Brutus attacked Cody about every three hours—apparently on principle.

Cody left early Thursday morning, his only comment on the relationship being a private one to Pepper just before he went.

"Stick around, huh? You've been good for him."

His words were good for Pepper. He knew Thor better than she did, after all, and if he approved . . . well, it shored up her flagging confidence. In the meantime, however, the truce went on.

Pepper taught Thor to deal crooked hands at poker, argued furiously with him over which team was best on televised football games, and soundly defeated him at chess for four solid days before he discovered that he was able to psych her out by carrying on a ridiculous conversation all the while.

His favorite method was to conduct a guessing game as to how exactly Pepper had misspent the past years. Although still searching for the pieces to the puzzle, he kept it light and leaned toward the absurd. He might not have learned much about her past that way, but he beat her at chess.

"I know! You're a spy."

"It's your move," she said dryly.

"A double agent, probably."

"Smile when you say that."

"What's the going rate for spies these days?"

"Cheap. It's a buyer's market."

"No, really? I'd think the other way around."

"There's a waiting list for the spy school," she drawled.

"Maybe I could add my name to the list. Who do I see about that?"

"Your local spy-recruiter, of course."

"Put in a good word for me?"

"Not on your life. Move!" she ordered.

"There."

"Damn."

"Checkmate."

"Arrested in Paris, were you?"

"Eavesdropper."

"Always. Why were you arrested?"

"Jaywalking."

"Funny."

"Great comeback."

"I'll do better next time."

"Do that."

"If not a spy, you were a smuggler."

"Was I?"

"That was a dumb move. I think my guess hit close to home."

"Ridiculous."

"Admit it—I shook you that time."

"Not a chance."

"You're awfully small to be a smuggler."

"I fit into small places."

"True."

"Check."

"Ah. Wasn't a dumb move after all...."

"You know—something's just occurred to me."

"Did anybody ever tell you that you could talk the hind leg off a donkey?"

"Now, that's the pot calling the kettle black with a vengeance!"

"Funny man. What's occurred to your busy brain?"

"I don't know your last name."

"You don't know my first name."

"What? What's Pepper then?"

"A nickname."

"You mean I don't know either of your names?"

"Nope."

"I'm living with a lady whose name I don't know?"

"Looks that way, doesn't it?"

"Well, hell. Tell me then."

"Sorry. You waited too long to ask."

"I'll ask Mrs. Small."

"She won't tell you."

"I'll find your driver's license."

"It's in the van and you promised not to go in there."

"Dammit."

"Checkmate."

"What?"

"I've caught on to your little game now, guy. And two can play it. We'll see who psychs out who."

"Great. That's just great."

"We could arm-wrestle. I'm sure you'd win at that."

"You're a lot of help."

seven

THAT FIRST WEEK SLIPPED BY AND THEN A second one. Pepper received calls from her friends from time to time, calls to which Thor listened unabashedly and from which he learned absolutely nothing concrete. The clients came and were groomed and left. Meals continued to be exotic. The truce went on.

Since it was always her recipes and never her cooking that Thor sampled, he challenged her assertion of being able to cook on Mrs. Small's next day off. Pepper pulled out all the stops, whipping up culinary masterpieces that would have had the great chefs of Europe crying into their bouillabaisses. By the time a groaning Thor pushed himself away from the table that night, he willingly conceded that Pepper could, indeed, cook.

Thor complimented her solemnly on her "wonderful little feminine talents," which goaded Pepper into sitting up three nights running to knit a scarf for him. She presented the scarf and asked sweetly if he had any buttons that needed sewing on . . . socks to be darned?

He asked if she did windows, and got hit in the middle of his chest with a ball of yarn.

And the truce went on.

But it was wearing thin in spots.

Pepper was finding it increasingly difficult to be relaxed in Thor's company. She caught herself watching him with a fixed intensity, and had to bite her tongue more than once to keep from blurting out in plain words how she felt about him. She tossed and turned at night, restless, her body punishing her for sticking to her rules. When she looked at Thor, a desperate need to touch him haunted her.

There were times when she would have willingly and deliberately broken her rules, times when the need to belong to him—however briefly—tortured her. And it wasn't the fear of defeat that kept her from breaking her rules, but a new fear of what would happen afterward if she did. She had discovered that love was not a gentle emotion, and that it was not something she'd be able to put behind her without regret. When—if—she had to leave him, it would be bad. Very bad.

Toward the end of that second week their relationship altered in a far from subtle manner. And it was all Thor's fault. Whether he realized that she was wavering or was just following his own instincts, he'd apparently decided that a truce didn't necessarily mean a laying down of *all* arms.

Along those lines he employed the one weapon Pepper couldn't fight with her wits or her ability as a gameswoman, the one weapon that would break her in the end if anything did.

He began to act like a lover.

It was small things at first. A light touch. A playful slap on the fanny. A hand toying absently with her hair whenever he was near enough—and he almost always was. A kiss on her nose.

Then the light touches began to linger, and the kisses fell

on her lips more often than on her nose. He watched her like a cat at a mousehole, and his smile made her increasingly nervous. He smiled at her, she thought, as though she were chocolate cake . . . and it were time for dessert.

"You're staring at me."

"Of course."

"Why?"

"I like staring at you."

"It makes me nervous."

"Good."

"What d'you mean, *good*?"

"I want to make you nervous."

"Again, *why*?"

"I believe I told you once that these days a man needs every edge he can find or steal."

"Get Brutus off the coffee table, will you?"

"Changing the subject?"

"Why don't we roast marshmallows?"

"You're cute when you're nervous."

For the first time in her life Pepper had the uneasy suspicion that she'd painted herself into a corner. And though she was not a woman given to panic, Pepper was halfway there. Falling back on her wits, she decided finally to show Thor a few more puzzle pieces in the hope that it would distract him from his own strategy. And since she always felt uncomfortable talking about herself, the tactic called for a couple of her nutty friends.

It didn't take her long to choose between them. After casually asking Thor if he minded, she called Cal and Marsha Brenner and invited them to visit. They were more than willing to drive up from New Hampshire, mostly intrigued by Pepper's current residence and what she was doing there. Of all her friends they were the friendliest and most talkative, and she had no doubt that either of them would talk about her to Thor if he asked.

Pepper wasn't quite sure what she hoped to accomplish by the tactic. She told herself sternly that Thor needed to know more about her, but a wry little voice in her head said that she just wanted a buffer for a day.

She ignored the voice.

The Brenners arrived late on Sunday morning, driving their beat-up Mustang and radiating good humor. Introductions were performed, and all four stood for a while near the garage and talked casually.

Cal Brenner was average in height and build, with a lazy voice and rather penetrating blue eyes. His wife, Marsha, was several inches taller than Pepper and had copper-colored hair and green eyes. She was quite strikingly beautiful. Her voice was deep and rich and seemed constantly full of laughter.

The conversation was innocent and causal at first, consisting mainly of descriptions of the scenery along the newcomers' route from New Hampshire. But it took an abrupt and bewildering turn within moments of their arrival.

Marsha, who had been watching Pepper narrowly for some time, suddenly emitted what sounded like a gurgle of suppressed laughter. Then the laughter was gone as though it had never existed, and she was leaning forward slightly. Placing her hands on Thor's shoulders, she gazed up into his startled eyes with an expression of heartrending pity.

"Oh, you poor man!" she said intensely.

Thor stared at her blankly for a moment, then looked over at Pepper. She was leaning against her RV and gazing pensively up at the clear blue sky. Helplessly Thor turned his pleading eyes to Cal.

The other man stood with arms folded across his chest. Obviously taking pity on his host's bewilderment, he said gravely, "You'll have to excuse my wife. She's always wanted to be an actress; sometimes she gets carried away."

"I can't bear it!" Marsha wailed suddenly, turning away from Thor to prop an arm against the garage and rest her forehead on it. "I can't bear it—another free spirit shackled!"

A bit desperately Thor asked Cal, "What part's she playing now, Lady Macbeth?"

Marsha momentarily dispensed with the histrionics to tell him reprovingly, "You don't know your Shakespeare."

Thor shook his head slightly to clear the mists, then glanced at Pepper again. She was solemnly studying her fingernails and whistling softly between her teeth. He looked back at Cal. "D'you mind throwing a little light on the situation?"

Cal looked thoughtful. "Well, as I said, Marsha wanted to be an actress. But before Broadway or Hollywood could discover her, Pepper did. And Pepper gave her to me."

"I beg your pardon?" Thor asked, thoroughly baffled now.

"Threw her at me actually. Of course, she was throwing me at Marsha at the same time. A veritable clash of the Titans. It took nearly a year, and some fancy footwork, but our Pepper got the knot tied in the end."

"I'm still in the dark," Thor protested.

"She's a matchmaker, you know. Renowned worldwide. In fact, I personally know of one sheikh who's taken up monogamy because of Pepper. Shocked his entire kingdom. An Arab sheikh without a harem? Boggles the mind."

While Thor was still swimming through the seas of bewilderment, Marsha lifted her head and directed a stern glance at

Pepper. "Does he go to his fate blindly unsuspecting?" she asked.

"Oh, no." Pepper smiled gently at Thor. "He's been warned."

Marsha abandoned her role to turn around and lean back against the garage. "Boy, am I going to enjoy this! We ought to sell tickets; the whole gang would turn up for ringside seats."

"Somebody tell me what you're talking about," Thor requested, but he already knew.

Marsha smiled at him, devilment dancing in her green eyes. "Well, since my husband has been at great pains not to put the matter bluntly, I'd be glad to. You see, we have a slight advantage over you; we've known Pepper longer. So we know that once Pepper gets her hook into a fish, *he's landed*."

Thor looked from her laughing face to Cal's bland one, and then at Pepper. She was still smiling at him. "I see. I'm the fish."

Marsha nodded. "That's it. And what makes it so enjoyable for us is that Pepper has never hooked a fish for herself before. Her footwork this time should be well worth watching."

Dispassionately Cal said, "She doesn't look it, and God knows she doesn't sound it, but Pepper is the most dangerous woman I've ever met. Heart of gold, mind you, but ruthless as hell."

Thor stared at Pepper. "I think I should have paid more attention to that warning."

"Too late now," she murmured, and came forward to link her arm with Marsha's. "Come along, friend. Let's go and see what we can dig up in Mrs. Small's kitchen."

"Isn't it Thor's kitchen?" Marsha asked interestedly.

"No. His home and her castle."

"Ah. Lead the way."

They strolled off.

Thor stared after them for a moment, then looked at Cal. "And I thought Pepper was the only nut. I think there's a treeful of them. No offense."

"None taken." Cal grinned. "Welcome to the tree."

"It isn't an accomplished fact, you know," Thor reminded him, wondering if he should be worried that he felt more amused than trapped.

"Isn't it?"

Thor decided to avoid the polite question. He leaned back against the Corvette. "So tell me—since you've known her longer—about Pepper. One short paragraph, if possible." Thor was determined to find out everything he could from these friends of Pepper's, no matter how underhanded it might be to pump them.

"Can't be done, I'm afraid." Cal smiled slightly. "Unless you'd like the definition we've accepted for years."

"Which is?"

"That Pepper is an enigma wrapped up in a puzzle within a mystery—followed by a question mark."

"How long have you known her?"

"Ten years. She was three years behind me at Stanford."

"Stanford?" Thor blinked. "Well, well. She didn't mention that."

"Uh. Phi Beta Kappa. Summa cum laude."

Thor's eyebrows rose. "Didn't mention that either. What else hasn't she mentioned to me?"

"Probably most of her life." Cal shrugged slightly. "She's an odd one, our Pepper. Doesn't talk much about herself. What she does say is just mentioned in passing—people she's met, or places she's been. She doesn't try to be mysterious, she just thinks that other people are more interesting than she is. Our gang, the crowd formed during college days, has pieced together some things. But not much."

"For instance?"

Cal looked at him directly. "Does it matter?"

Thor met the steady gaze and realized that Pepper had loyal friends. And that this one, at least, wasn't going to reveal anything about his friend to a man with only a casual interest. "It matters," he told Cal, and knew then that it *did* matter. Dammit, it was no longer a game—if it ever had been. And, whatever it was, he was no longer certain that he wanted to win.

Without pushing or questioning, Cal simply nodded. "She was born and raised in Texas, but since she hasn't been back there in more than ten years, we assume she doesn't consider it home."

Thor was a little startled by this first bit of information. Texas? An odd coincidence. She certainly didn't possess a Texas drawl; in fact, her breathless little-girl voice had no accent of any kind. A result of her years of travel, perhaps? Before he could consider the matter further, Cal was going on.

"Started at Stanford at seventeen. Her father died about then, and apparently he left her an inheritance and told her to see the world. She always took off during vacations and holidays, bringing back gifts for the rest of us from all over the world. She never talked about her trips except for bits and pieces mentioned in passing. We learned not to ask questions about where she'd been. Pepper has a marvelous ability to head you off until you find yourself talking about something entirely different.

"Since college . . . I know a little, and can guess a little. She travels regularly now, out of the country more often than she's in it. She leaves the RV and the pets with her mother, who lives here in the East. If we want to contact Pepper, we call her mother, who usually has a number where we can reach her. And—well, she just goes."

"Alone?"

"As far as I know. She sometimes comes back with company though. She found Marsha stranded in London and brought her back. And several other members of our gang were discovered by her in various improbable parts of the globe. And I do mean improbable. Mae—who's now married to Brian, who was one of the founding members of our group—is from Hong Kong. Pepper brought her over to visit, she said, and had them married before the visa expired.

"Then there's Heather from Scotland and now married to Tom. And Jean-Paul, who came, of course, from France—"

"Jean-Paul?" Thor queried with all the American male's distrust of Frenchmen.

Reading the tone correctly, Cal chuckled. "You should meet him. He's an artist—a damn good one, as a matter of fact—and absolutely adores his 'Angelique.' He and Angela were married last year. Another of Pepper's matches."

"She sounds like the United Nations," Thor said in astonishment.

Cal shrugged. "What can I tell you? She likes her friends to be happy."

"And are they?"

"Oh, yes. Pepper has an uncanny knack for matching people with the right partners. Not a divorce or separation in the lot, and for some of us it's been a few years. She's batting a thousand."

Thor was silent for a moment, trying to fit pieces together and come up with a complete picture of a woman who was still largely unknown to him. Finally he shook his head. "The more I hear, the less I know."

Cal looked at him with a certain amount of sympathy. "Yeah, I know the feeling. There isn't much more I can tell you. She usually manages to drop in on us whenever she comes back to the States. We don't ask questions; she doesn't offer answers. In spite of her sometimes talkative ways, Pepper doesn't let a lot of herself out into the open."

Suddenly, and for the first time in his life, Thor felt a feeling so strong and so savage that he had to look away from the other man. And in that moment he was literally afraid to move or speak, because he didn't think he could be responsible for his actions or words. It had been building within him for long moments now, and he'd known it without recognizing the sensation.

Intellect struggled with two million years of instinct, and Thor wasn't sure which would win.

His scant knowledge of both Pepper and Cal told him rationally that theirs was a friendship and nothing more, but instinct as old as the cave fiercely resented the ten years they had known each other. Resented those years with an irrational and bedeviled jealousy.

Intellect won the struggle, but it left Thor feeling shaken and oddly out of his depth. He could neither forget nor ignore the jealousy, but he was at least able to shut it away in a small room in his mind where it chased itself in vicious circles. Not a solution, of course, but that way it wouldn't savagely attack Pepper's friend.

Thor dragged his thoughts from that subject and realized Cal was watching him curiously. But before the other man could question what, Thor surmised, had probably been a peculiar expression, Marsha stuck her head out the front door and called to them.

"Hey, you two! Pepper's found some stuff and she's going to make shish kebab. Think you heroes can start a fire in that monstrosity of a barbecue out back?"

"We'll do our best," Cal called back dryly. As she disappeared back inside the house, he looked at Thor. "We have our orders."

"Uh-huh." Locked room or no, Thor badly needed an outlet for the various types of frustration building within him, and that very emotion was reflected in his voice when he went on irritably. "Shish kebab. Dammit, is there anything that woman *can't* do? She cooks, sews, knits, and drives that monster RV of hers as if she'd driven a semi for years. She's got my 'vicious' stallion eating out of her hand. She plays the piano beautifully. She's a cardsharp. She knows enough about football to call the plays at a Super Bowl game, and enough about chess to be a grand master at the game—"

"She is," Cal murmured helpfully. "Bona fide. Won an international competition in Bonn a couple of years ago. Impressed the hell out of the judges since she was so young. Of course, an unkind soul could point out that she probably rattled her opponent by looking dumb and sweet, but—"

"But"—Thor interrupted with a goaded glare—"she was probably *born* a grand master." He released a sigh compounded of a groan and a growl. "She's not real. I don't believe in perfection, particularly in people. She has to have a fault somewhere—she has to!"

Cal frowned thoughtfully for a moment, then lifted a triumphant finger. "She's stubborn!"

Glaring at him, Thor muttered, "You're a lot of help."

"Sorry." Cal was smiling.

"Hell. Let's go get that fire started."

"Cheer up," Cal advised gravely. "It could be worse, you know."

"Yeah? How, for God's sake?"

"She might not have warned you at all. At least you don't go to your fate—uh—blindly unsuspecting."

"Dammit."

"Looked like they were having quite an interesting little chat," Marsha announced to her friend, coming back into the kitchen.

Pepper was chopping meat on the cutting board, and glanced up with a slight smile. "I'm not at all surprised, considering that little scene you and Cal were playing."

"Who was playing?" Marsha was cheerfully unrepentant. "Besides, it was a scream. Did you see Thor's face?"

"I saw it." Pepper laughed in spite of herself. "You ought to be ashamed of yourself, and so should I; the man must think I'm after his scalp by now."

"Well, aren't you?" Marsha asked with a grin.

"Not with a knife."

"So he keeps his hair but loses his freedom, huh?"

Pepper bent her head over her task and was silent for a long moment. Then, with unusual asperity, she burst out, "Is that what I'm doing—depriving him of his freedom?"

Startled, Marsha looked over from the sink, where she'd been washing tomatoes and onions. She turned off the water and slowly dried her hands on a paper towel, staring at her friend. "Hey, I was kidding, Pepper."

Pepper shook her head slightly. "I know. But the question's still there, Marsha. If I win . . . does he lose?"

"Is it a game?" her friend asked soberly.

"Maybe he thinks it is. Maybe he thinks that one of us can lose, and that we'll both end up with a nice little memory."

"But . . . ?"

"But . . ." Pepper sighed softly. "I don't think it'll end that way. In the beginning I thought that if I won, we'd both win. You know, in love and loving it." She laughed suddenly, harshly. "Vain of me, I realize. But I've always believed that happiness meant love and sharing."

"And now you don't believe that?"

"I don't know. It's . . . it's not a gentle emotion, is it? I never knew that." She smiled crookedly at her friend. "Now I understand what kind of wringer I put the rest of you through. Would an apology on bended knees make amends?"

Marsha smiled in return. "No need. People rarely fall in love totally against their will, Pepper; not one of us regrets your matchmaking."

"I'm glad," Pepper said simply.

"You won't get away with changing the subject this time," Marsha said conversationally. "For once, you're going to bend my ear—even if I have to badger you to do it. So. What makes you think Thor would lose if you win?"

"He doesn't want permanent ties."

"So?"

"So who am I to think he'd be happier tied to me?"

"Bad phrase, that," Marsha remarked objectively. "'Tied to,' I mean. Conjures up images of slavery. We both know that's not what you mean."

Pepper stirred slightly. "I know, I know. But if he values his freedom so much, isn't that what it amounts to?"

"He didn't seem to me to be rabid about his freedom."

"Not rabid. Just determined."

"Whatever."

"It's just that . . . well, what right had I to move in on him? To plunk myself down squarely in the middle of his life as if I belonged here?"

"Do you love him?" Marsha asked bluntly, in the tone of a woman who's sure of the answer.

Pepper stared at her fingers for a long moment, then lifted her gaze to her friend's face. "So much so that I couldn't bear for him to lose anything because of me. I want to add to his life, Marsha, not take away from it. And if that means I'll have to leave him with a nice little memory and a triumphant victory . . . then that's what I'll have to do," Pepper finished softly.

"Have you told him that you love him?" Marsha asked in an equally hushed tone.

"No." Pepper smiled a little. "I won't burden him with something he doesn't want."

Marsha stared at her for a moment, then said caustically, "If you ask me, you're being unnecessarily noble. What makes you so certain it'd be a burden to him?"

"He knows how I feel about love. He knows that if I feel love, I expect something permanent. If I tell him I love him, it'll be a burden to him. He's that kind of man."

"Has it ever occurred to you," Marsha demanded, "that he might just possibly be changing his mind about his desire for 'freedom' even as we speak? Has it occurred to you that perhaps he thought he wanted no ties only because he'd never found the right woman?"

"Yes, it's occurred to me." Pepper laid the knife aside suddenly, aware of the dangers of slicing anything with only half her mind on what she was doing. "It occurs to me constantly." She heard the hard-bitten sound of her own voice and was abruptly grateful that Marsha had stuck firmly to this subject; she needed to talk. "Don't you think I *want* that to be true? Don't you think I lie awake at night and wonder if I'll be able to leave him when the time comes? Dammit, Marsha, I want to fling my love at him! I've had to choke back the words a hundred times. I want to . . . to touch him whenever he's near me, and even more when he's away from me. It's hard to breathe when he's there and even worse when he's not."

She laughed unsteadily, a laugh that was a talisman to ward off tears. "I look at you and Cal, and think of the others, and I wonder—my God, did I do this to them? Did I, in my insufferable arrogance, put them through this hell because I thought I knew what was best for them?"

"Pepper—"

"And now this!" Pepper cut off her friend flatly. "Thor. I fall in love for the first time in my life, and I launch a campaign with all the cocky arrogance of a paper-pushing general! And if Thor's freedom is important to him and I win the battle, then he'll be caged. Caged!"

She felt her fingers aching and realized that she was gripping the edge of the counter as though it were a lifeline. With an effort she spoke levelly, almost neutrally. "Have you ever gone to a zoo and watched the cats? They pace. Constantly, endlessly. Do we have the right to do that to them? Animals should never be caged, even if they're given an illusion of freedom. And people should never be caged, even if the bars are formed out of commitments."

"We're all caged," Marsha pointed out quietly. "We're caged by jobs, by a way of life, by people who love us and those whom we love. There are limits to everything, Pepper, boundaries we all observe. You know that as well as I do. And if we had the choice, most of us would choose to keep the boundaries. Because there's something secure in knowing how far you can go."

"But is it fair to place someone else inside our own boundaries?" Pepper looked searchingly at her friend. "That's what bothers me. Thor has his own boundaries; is it fair to demand that he be limited by mine?"

Marsha returned the stare for a moment, then quoted softly, "'I am the master of my fate; I am the captain of my soul.' Thor strikes me as being both; he's his own man. If he is limited by your boundaries, it'll be because he wants to be—and for no other reason."

Pepper drew a deep, shuddering breath. "I suppose I'm selfish, but I want him inside *my* boundaries."

"You're not selfish. You're in love."

"And I'm afraid of losing." Pepper smiled shakily. "Funny,

that's something I haven't been afraid of in years. But I've never gambled like this before; there's never been so much at stake."

Marsha smiled a little. "Follow your instincts, friend. I haven't seen much of him, but I have a feeling that you and your Thor would be deliriously happy together. Go for it."

There was no more teasing that day about Pepper's matchmaking, and no real opportunity for Thor to learn more about her than he already had. But his sudden attack of jealousy had had more of an impact on him than anything Cal had told him about Pepper.

In that moment Thor had realized that it no longer mattered what and who Pepper was or had been. It wasn't important. What mattered was that, like a thorn or a splinter or a virus, she'd somehow managed to burrow beneath his skin. He was no longer *just* fascinated by her.

The other couple left after dinner, steadfastly refusing to stay overnight. They had apparently promised Marsha's mother in Bangor that they'd spend the night with her, and Cal professed himself in dread terror of offending his mother-in-law.

After they'd gone, Pepper sat on the couch absently dealing crooked poker hands on the coffee table and watching from the corner of her eye as Thor paced restlessly. She could feel the tension increasing moment by moment, growing within the room like a living thing. It made her so nervous that she mistakenly dealt a ten into a low straight flush. Swearing softly, she gathered up the cards.

"It isn't a game, is it?" Thor asked suddenly, quietly. He was standing by the front window, staring out. "It was never a game."

Pepper stacked the cards neatly facedown on the coffee table and then sat back, gazing across the room at his broad back. She wasn't surprised by his comment; her little voice inside had been telling her all day that the buffer of her friends had only postponed the inevitable.

Equally quiet, she said, "For me, no; it was never a game. The . . . methods . . . maybe. But I was serious from the start."

"Why me?" he asked, still without turning around.

"Ask me how many angels can dance on the head of a pin," Pepper said wryly. "I'd have a better answer for that."

He turned around, leaning back against the windowframe and looking across at her. She was somehow surprised to see that his expression was calm, his eyes thoughtful. As if his mind were somewhere else, he asked, "How did you get that scar?"

Pepper didn't even consider evasion. Or games. "I was carrying a briefcase full of gems and a man tried to steal them from me," she said calmly.

eight

PEPPER'S STATEMENT CERTAINLY CAUGHT Thor's attention. He smiled slowly. "I see. Did you rob a museum?"

She smiled a little. "Not quite. From time to time, I take jobs as a bonded courier. I don't need the money, but I enjoy the . . . the challenge of it. What I've carried most times was something small but valuable that the owner didn't want to entrust to any other method of transport. Stamp collections, old coins, heirlooms."

Making an innocent, empty-handed gesture, she said, "Now I ask you—do I look as if someone would entrust something valuable to me?"

"No," Thor replied dryly.

"The ace up my sleeve." Her smile turned rueful. "I haven't lost anything yet."

Thor nodded toward the scar on her hand. "But someone came close?"

Pepper rubbed a thumb across the mark. "Close only counts in horseshoes."

"What happened?"

"From the beginning?"

"Please."

"A wealthy American collector sold several of his finest pieces to an equally wealthy British collector. About that time there had been more than one jewelry theft on both sides of the Atlantic, and these pieces were very, very valuable. Couriers had been robbed en route; so the collectors decided on a shell game. They sent out several couriers along different routes, all but one empty-handed. I had the gems."

Thor crossed the room slowly to sit down on the couch beside her. "And?" he asked, obviously intrigued.

"There was a leak." Pepper sighed. "Only the two collectors were supposed to know which of us had the jewelry; we found out later that the buyer's valet had decided to go into business for himself. I'll pass up the remark about how hard it is to get good servants these days. Anyway, I made it across the Atlantic and into London in one piece. Unfortunately it was a foggy day in old London Town, which gave the would-be thief excellent cover and loused up my sense of direction.

"I must have run through most of the mews in the city—with him right behind me—before I finally located the buyer's house. And after a conspicuous lack of bobbies for more than two hours, there was one practically on the buyer's doorstep. And . . . well, that's all."

Thor reached over to cover the small, restless hand with its faint scar. "Other than this, did he hurt you?"

"He didn't get the chance!" Pepper grinned. "I'm small, but I'm fast."

Not returning the grin, Thor said slowly, "Dangerous work."

"Not really. Not usually." She shrugged. "I've been a courier for about six years; that jewel thing happened last year, and it was only the second time someone tried to hold me up."

Thor's hand tightened on hers. "What happened the first time?"

Pepper laughed suddenly as the memory flooded her mind. "It was hysterical really. You would have gotten a kick out of it. The poor guy wasn't after the old stamp collection in my case. He was just your average, run-of-the-mill mugger. I was carrying the collection from L.A. to New York, and had a one-night layover in Kansas City.

"I decided to visit some friends there, and I was walking to their apartment when this man yanked me into an alley. There he stood with this rusty pipe, getting ready to brain me. I don't know what made him hesitate, although he said later that it was because he hadn't realized until then that I was so small. Anyway, I had a few seconds to get good and mad, and so I pulled my gun out of my shoulder bag and—"

"Your gun?" Thor seemed equally fascinated and horror-struck.

"Uh-huh. I'm licensed to carry a gun, although I don't do so outside the States of course. It's a forty-five automatic. I've found that nothing makes a potential burglar or mugger more nervous than a very small woman inexpertly waving about a very big gun."

"Are you inexpert?"

"Of course not, but he didn't know that."

"Oh," was all Thor could manage to say.

"Anyway, as soon as he saw the gun he dropped the pipe and started stuttering and shaking. I was cussing him up one side and down the other, and the madder I got, the more he shook—it was really very funny."

"What happened?" Thor asked in the tone of a man who wasn't quite sure he wanted to know.

"I treated him to a hamburger," Pepper said gravely.

"You what?" Thor asked faintly.

"Well, he was hungry. We talked for a while, and then had a hamburger and talked some more. And then I took him with me to my friends' house and he slept on the couch. By the time my plane left the next day, he had a job training horses at a local stable. His name is Henry, and I drop in to see him about once a year. He tells everyone within earshot the story of how we met, and says he has a little Nemesis that makes him keep to the straight and narrow."

"I don't believe it," Thor murmured, staring at her.

"I don't see why not. Henry wasn't a very good mugger, but he turned into a first-rate trainer."

"Matchmaker . . . and mender of lonely hearts." Thor shook his head slightly. "Cal was right. You're an enigma wrapped up in a puzzle surrounded by a mystery—followed by a question mark."

"Cal said that?"

"Yes. After knowing you for ten years, he said that."

Pepper attempted a laugh that didn't quite come off. "I didn't realize I was so complicated."

"But you are." The arm lying along the back of the couch moved, and his free hand brushed a strand of silver-blond hair away from her face. "You are."

A subdued violence in her tone, she said suddenly, "But I don't want to be! Not to you! Thor, I'm *not* complicated! I'm ordinary!"

"I knew you were prone to understatement the first time I saw that 'van' of yours," he murmured with a tiny smile.

Pepper didn't return the smile. Having finally abandoned the "game," she never looked back. "I'm just a woman, Thor— no more and no less. Oh, sure, I've seen a lot of the world. I've seen things I hope to God I never see again, and I don't suppose ladies carry guns or turn muggers into horse trainers, but that doesn't mean I'm complicated. I laugh and cry and get mad like other women, and—*dammit!*—what's so complicated about that?"

Thor realized that she really wanted to know and he supposed that, from her point of view, she wasn't complicated, but he didn't quite know how to explain her uniqueness. Instead, he smiled suddenly and said, "Tell me your name."

She laughed in spite of herself. "Didn't you ask Cal?"

"I didn't want to admit to ignorance."

Pepper could feel Thor's fingers moving gently at the nape of her neck, and while the little caress sent her nerves jangling, it was also oddly soothing. She smiled at him and took a deep breath before announcing, "Perdita Elizabeth Patricia Elaine Reynolds."

Thor looked more than a little taken aback. "How much?"

A giggle escaped her. "There was a squabble over what to name the baby roughly twenty-eight years ago. My mother's sister, Perdita Elizabeth, and my father's sister, Patricia Elaine, both wanted the honor. They were both spinsters, and were mortal enemies from what I've heard; they both died while I was in my teens. The argument became so violent that my parents combined the names, literally flipping a coin to decide what came first. *Then* there was a threatened bloodbath over what to call me. One of my aunts—I don't know which, since both later claimed the inspiration—realized that the first letter of each name, with an extra *P* arbitrarily added, spelled Pepper. I've been called that ever since."

"Perdita," Thor mused. "That's not English."

"No. Latin or Greek. It means 'the lost one.'"

Thor stared laughing. "And you claim to be ordinary! Lord, Pepper, you've been unique from the moment of birth!"

Gazing into his smiling gray eyes, Pepper thought suddenly, *I've come home*. And there it was—the answer to the big question. Why him? Because she'd looked into those eyes, and the gooseflesh and thudding heart had whispered *home*. She had known that she loved him; until then she hadn't known why.

The restlessness that had tormented her for years seeped away in that moment. Before meeting him, she had tentatively planned to visit the Australian Outback during the winter and then see Venice in the spring. There was no hankering in her now to see either place.

Thor, his amusement fading away, saw something different in her violet eyes. A glow that was soft and deep and strangely mysterious. And it wasn't until he heard his own voice speaking that he realized something inside himself recognized that look.

"I can't ask you to break your rules," he said huskily.

"You don't have to." Pepper felt herself smiling, and knew that there was nothing of defeat in it. "I want permanence, Thor. But I know how to live for today. It'll be enough."

"Will it?"

"It'll have to be. Besides, I learned a long time ago that sometimes rules have to be broken. There's just no other way of dealing with them."

"Pepper—"

"Have you ever been seduced?" she asked seriously.

He blinked. "That's . . . that's a loaded question."

"No, I mean, really. Have you ever been seduced?"

"No. No, I haven't."

Slipping her hand from his, she reached out with both to begin slowly and steadily unbuttoning his flannel shirt. "Well . . . there's a first time for everything, or so they say."

Thor was silent and still through three buttons, his eyes locked with hers. "You don't know what you're doing," he breathed finally, his hands catching her wrists in a gentle grip.

Pepper chose deliberately to misunderstand him. "Well, I

admit that it's not something I've done before, but I've heard that every woman's a harlot way down deep. I think that's true; I don't feel at all like myself at the moment."

The hands on her wrists didn't attempt to stop her as her fingers continued their task. Instead, they slid up her arms slowly until they came to rest on the delicate bones of her shoulders. His fingers moved slightly, and she could feel the warmth of them through her own flannel shirt.

Pepper's fingers reached the button just above his belt and fumbled suddenly, becoming awkward and uncertain. *If he doesn't help me out,* she thought a little wildly, *I'll never forgive him!*

Whether he sensed her sudden confusion or simply lost patience himself, Thor did help her out. With an odd rough sound that seemed to come from deep inside his chest, he pulled her abruptly against him, his mouth finding hers in a surge of compulsive need.

Her hands slid slowly up his chest, feeling the rough brush of the dark gold mat of hair and the tautening muscles beneath. All her senses came almost painfully alive, sharpened, keen. The tangy scent of his after-shave, the crackle of the fire in the hearth, the hot demand of his lips, the thudding rhythm of his heart, her heart—all filled her being.

She rose up on her knees against him, her fingers tangled in his thick copper-gold hair, her mouth returning fiery demand for fiery demand and adding a helpless plea. She felt her breasts swell and harden against his chest, felt the fierce possession of his hands sliding down her back to her hips. And a reckless, desperate need flooded her veins with molten fury.

Thor's lips finally left hers, and she allowed her eyes to drift open, feeling boneless as he rose and lifted her into his arms in one smooth motion. She kept her arms locked around his neck, gazing into the silvery sheen of his eyes for a long moment.

Then her arms tightened and she buried her face briefly in the crook of his neck. She felt his rough breath stirring the hair piled loosely on top of her head.

"Pepper . . ." His voice was hoarse, driven. "If you're not sure . . ."

Her head lifted, violet eyes soft and impossibly deep. "Make love with me, Thor," she whispered. "I need you."

He kissed her briefly, his lips hard and possessive, then turned and carried her toward the stairs. As he started up them Pepper looked back over his shoulder and saw the dogs still in the den. Both pairs of canine eyes were watching their exit, but neither dog attempted to follow them.

How tactful, Pepper thought vaguely, then dismissed the dogs from her mind and concentrated on the feeling of being carried in a man's arms—this man's arms—as though she weighed nothing. Instead of feeling helpless, she felt strangely cared-for and cherished.

Thor carried her down the hall to his bedroom, going through the open door and kicking it shut behind them with one foot. He set her gently on her feet beside the bed and bent to turn on the lamp on the nightstand. As the lamp's soft glow spread over them and the huge four-poster bed, he straightened and looked down at her, his hands lifting to surround her face.

Pepper met his searching gaze with no hesitation, no uncertainty in her own eyes. And when his lips returned to claim hers, her instant and total response laid to rest any question he might have had about whether or not she wanted to make love. The probing of his tongue was answered by her own, her need echoed his, her desire matched his flame for flame.

His hands dropped to the buttons of her shirt, unsteady, impatient. The shirt was pushed off her shoulders as his mouth left hers to feather a string of kisses down her throat and along her collarbone, and Pepper flung the shirt aside to free her own hands. She tugged his shirt free of the jeans, helping him to shrug it off and let it fall to join hers on the floor. She nudged her loafers off, managing somehow to remove her socks as well, then stepped out of the jeans after he'd unfastened them and pushed them down over her hips.

Immediately her hands found his belt, unfastening it with unconscious familiarity. She slid the zipper down, and was on the point of pushing the jeans down over his hips when he groaned softly and brushed her hands aside. Obviously impatient, he stripped the remainder of his garments off, his eyes never leaving hers.

Absorbed, utterly unselfconscious, Pepper watched him undress. She thought dimly that he did indeed look like a god there in the lamplight; like a proud and pagan figure etched by the golden glow of a long-ago fire. And when he stood before her at last as raw and vital as man was intended to be, she was hardly aware of speaking.

"I knew that towel was a crime."

A curious expression that was half laughter and half passion lit his silvery eyes. "I wondered what you were thinking that night," he murmured huskily, stepping toward her. "You kept looking away from me."

Pepper caught her breath as his big hands began to smooth away her delicate underthings. "It frightened me," she gasped softly. "What I was feeling frightened me. It was too sudden; it happened too fast. . . ."

Thor looked down at her as the last scrap of satin and lace dropped to the thick pile carpet, his eyes flashing silver fire and then darkening to a stormy slate-gray. "And now?" he breathed, his hands finding her tiny waist and drawing her to him with torturing slowness.

"I'm not frightened now." The words were throaty, filled

with longing. Her arms slid around his waist as she closed the distance between them fiercely. "This is right, so right."

He caught his breath sharply, bending his head to find her lips with blind urgency. "God, you're beautiful," he muttered against her mouth. "I'm almost afraid to hold you, almost afraid you'll disappear when I touch you."

"I'm flesh and blood, Thor." Her hands molded the rippling muscles of his back wonderingly. "I'm real . . . a woman. Make me your woman, Thor."

Groaning, Thor reached around her to fling back the covers on the wide bed, then lifted her easily and placed her in its center, following her down immediately. Trapping her restless legs with one of his own, he raked gentle fingers through her silvery hair, sending pins flying, then spread gleaming strands across the pillow. His hands slid down her back as her arms locked around his neck, his lips trailing fire down her throat.

One hand stroked slowly up her rib cage, finding and surrounding her engorged breast. His thumb teased gently, rhythmically, until a hardened bud rose in taut awareness and pleaded for a more intimate caress.

Pepper felt an animal-like whimper rise in her throat as his mouth closed over the aching nipple, then was unaware of the sound when his swirling tongue sent shivers coursing through her body. Her nails dug into the taut muscles of his shoulders. She couldn't be still, couldn't bear to be still; fire was lancing through every cell, every nerve.

Her hands slid up to tangle in his hair, holding him closer as his mouth lavished attention on one breast and then the other. She could hear her own panting, shallow breathing, could feel her heart thundering in runaway need.

"Thor . . ."

"You're beautiful," he rasped against her flesh, teeth nipping gently, then tongue soothing. "God, how I need you!"

His caresses seared the sensitive flesh below her breasts, moved lower, and lower still. Pepper felt his fingers probing erotically, then the hot brush of his lips, and her senses spiraled crazily. Behind her closed eyelids, colors whirled in a kaleidoscope of passion, and a moan ripped its way from the deepest part of her.

Something grew within her, winding tighter and tighter, until she knew that it had to snap. It was hot and cold, sharp and dull, aching with a pain that was a pleasure almost too great to bear. Like a snowball or fireball rolling downhill, it gathered speed and size and filled her with its image, yet left her achingly empty.

"Thor!" Her voice vibrated with a pleading quality. She heard herself as though it were someone else and wondered vaguely at the desperation in that woman's voice. "Please, Thor..."

Her lashes, impossibly heavy, lifted as he rose above her, and desire-drugged violet eyes gazed up at him. She saw his lean face taut and masklike in an intolerable need, saw the slate-gray eyes flashing sparks of silver fire. And she saw the hesitation there, the uncertainty, and understood even before he spoke.

"I don't want to hurt you," he whispered raggedly, the words torn from him in his urgency.

Pepper pulled his head down, feeling the tension in him. "You won't," she murmured huskily against his mouth. "You won't hurt me. Love me, Thor—I need you so much!"

With a strange, rough sound from deep in his chest, Thor kissed her hungrily, fiercely. His mouth possessed before his body did, both making her his for all time.

Pepper felt him come to her as though he belonged to her, their bodies fitting as though time itself had decreed it. Her eyes widened, startled at the primitive feeling of being known, totally and completely, for the first time in her life. A little cry of surprise escaped her, surprise and wonderment, and her arms tightened around him in a new and instinctive possessiveness.

As if the act of possession itself were enough, Thor was still for a moment, gazing deeply and searchingly into her eyes. The touch of anxiety in his own eyes faded as she smiled and lifted her head to kiss him, and their lips clung together for a timeless second of eternity.

When Thor began to move, his gentleness and care touched Pepper almost unbearably. Knowledge welled up out of instinct as her body responded to his, matching his rhythm, possessing him as utterly as he possessed her. The hovering tension began to build again, winding itself tighter and tighter, a critical mass that had to find release. It gripped their bodies, driving them relentlessly, compelling them as if they were senseless moths to a fiery death. And the flame was too strong to resist, engulfing them both in an eruption that paralyzed their bodies and cauterized their senses. . . .

"Who," Thor demanded in a voice that sounded a single breath away from exhaustion, "seduced who?"

"Whom," Pepper murmured, snuggling a bit closer to his side and smiling with sleepy contentment.

"The question stands." He reached down to pull the covers up over them both, patting her hip along the way.

Pepper smothered a yawn against the warm flesh of his neck. "Why don't we just call it a joint effort, hmmm?"

"Suits me." He was silent for a long moment, one hand playing almost compulsively with her hair as though he couldn't stop touching her. When he finally spoke again, his voice was very quiet. "Have you caught me, Diana?"

She lifted her head, gazing at him with eyes that were still glowing softly. "You know I haven't."

Thor met her steady gaze for a moment, his own silvery eyes darkening with some kind of conflict. His hand cupped the nape of her neck and drew her forward, and he kissed her forehead softly before pressing her head gently down on his shoulder.

Troubled, Pepper moved even closer, needing to let him know that it was all right, that she understood. "I meant what I said before," she told him softly. "I can live for today, Thor. Don't worry about me."

"I have to." His arm tightened around her almost fiercely. "I have to worry, Pepper. Especially now."

She lifted her head again, holding the hand that had been stroking her hair. "No." A frown flitted across her face and was gone. "Thor, I'm a grown woman, and I've been responsible for my own actions for a long time. So if you're feeling responsible—well, don't."

His eyes were restless on her face. "There could be—"

"Repercussions?" She smiled a little and shook her head. "Not unless I'm one of the few women the Pill likes to trick. The doctor put me on birth control when I was sixteen. You know, my adventurous life-style and all that."

"Oh."

Pepper wondered suddenly why she had the feeling that her remarks had disappointed him. Was he, she wondered dimly, looking for an excuse to prolong their relationship? Did he *want* to be boxed in, with no other alternative? She wondered about his rules and what had written them.

The thought of having to leave him someday—perhaps soon—tortured her, but Pepper was determined that she wouldn't use a single "feminine" weapon to hold him. He'd be hers by *choice* or not at all. That fierce determination helped her to close the door on tomorrow.

"So you don't have to be responsible for me," she told him again quietly.

His restless eyes continued to search her own. "You told me to make you my woman," he said slowly.

Pepper hesitated, then nodded. "I'm your woman as long as you want me," she said with a simple, proud dignity.

Something like awe flickered in Thor's eyes, but his lips twisted slightly. "But I'm not to feel responsible for you?"

She tried to make him understand. "Thor, I think most women resent that phrase *belong to* because they've never had a chance to belong to themselves. They go from being somebody's daughter to somebody's wife to somebody's mother; they're never just themselves. But I *have* been just me. I've lived alone and taken care of myself. I've belonged to me.

"Don't you see, Thor? I belong to you now, not because you take, but because I give. It was my choice. You're not responsible for that; you're not responsible for me."

He sighed roughly. "So I just accept the . . . the gift and offer nothing in return?"

Pepper pulled herself forward far enough to kiss him. "Thor, stop feeling guilty," she chided gently. "I don't regret a thing; don't make me regret."

Thor hugged her suddenly, a rueful, half painful apology in his eyes. "I'm sorry, be—" He broke off abruptly, then went on so quickly that she wasn't sure he'd started to say something else. "I'm sorry, Pepper. If I had the sense God gave a mushroom, I'd be grateful that you see everything in black and white. If you've no complaints about this relationship, I don't suppose I should question it. And since you're satisfied . . ." He sent her a rather deceptively casual look.

She was smiling faintly. "I'm not going to fall into *that* trap," she told him wryly.

He grinned, honestly amused. "You'd think I'd have learned by now not to fish with you," he remarked in a dry tone.

"You'd think."

Still amused, but with a spark of puzzlement in his eyes, he studied her. "You're not about to pin me down, are you, Pepper?"

"No."

"Giving me enough rope to hang myself?"

"No."

He lifted an eyebrow at her. "If I told you to leave right now?"

"I'd leave. Right now."

"Without a single recrimination?"

"Not a word."

"Or a tear?"

She was still smiling. "You wouldn't see one."

"You'd just go?"

"I'd pack my things and go." Her eyes were calm and honest.

Thor did an abrupt about-face. "You don't have to sound so damn eager about it," he grumbled morosely.

Pepper started to laugh, wondering if he were half serious and yet realizing that she couldn't probe. The mood between them had lightened, and it had to remain light, she knew, or they'd get bogged down and begin heading toward an ending neither was ready to face yet.

"That wasn't eagerness," she told him solemnly. "That was sweet, womanly compliance with the master's wishes."

He brightened. "Oh, am I the master?"

"Don't let it go to your head."

"Just what kind of authority do I have?"

"Ultimate. Within reason," she responded promptly.

"That's a contradiction in terms."

"Not in my dictionary, it isn't."

"Maybe you'd better explain my authority, then," Thor demanded playfully.

"Don't tell me to shine your shoes."

"I see. Can I tell you to cook for me?"

"Yes. But if you say please, it'll taste better."

"Ah. Would you—uh—dance for me?"

"You have the heart of a Turk."

"I beg your pardon?"

"Harems."

"Uh. The question stands."

"Depends on the dance. And how you 'tell' me to do it."

"I begin to see what you meant by 'within reason.'"

"I thought you'd get it eventually."

"Request rather than command."

"I'm funny that way."

"I should throw away my bullhorn and whip, eh?"

"I would."

"Mmm. Diana?"

"Yes, Thor of the mighty hammer?"

"I have a request."

"Remember to say please."

Thor whispered a few words into her ear, and Pepper's expression was a bit dazed when she lifted her head.

"At least you said please," she mumbled.

It was a long while later when Thor's long arm reached to turn out the lamp on the nightstand. Pepper cuddled closer to him, eyes closed, her smile still a bit dazed. "Vitamin E?" she murmured in sleepy interrogation.

"Wheaties," Thor murmured, and pulled the covers up over them both.

Pepper dreamed of bees buzzing in her ear and automatically lifted a hand to shoo the pesky insects away. But her hand encountered a powerful masculine arm just as the buzzing stopped, and she decided muzzily to let Thor deal with intruding bugs. Drifting deeper into sleep, she thought she heard his deep voice talking to the bugs in low tones, but that was ridiculous because, Pepper told herself, people didn't talk to bugs.

Time passed, but Pepper didn't know how much. She just knew that something was wrong, something was missing, and the coldness and loneliness of its absence woke her up. She opened her eyes suddenly, wide-awake and disturbed. The room was dark, the luminous face of the clock on the nightstand proclaiming it to be just after four in the morning.

And except for her the huge four-poster bed was empty.

Pepper sat up and looked around. The door to the bathroom was open, and no light was coming from within; the door to the hallway was barely open, and only the dim hallway light was visible. She slid her hand across the bed beneath the covers, feeling the lingering warmth of his presence. He couldn't have been gone long then.

Where had he gone?

Not one to sit and wonder, Pepper slipped from the bed, not bothering with the lamp to find her flannel shirt still lying on the floor. She pulled it on and began to button it, opening the door to the hall and pausing for a moment to listen intently. Dimly she could make out a low voice coming from the den.

She went down the hall to the stairs, walking lightly on

bare feet, then down the stairs and to the doorway of the den. Thor was sitting half turned away from her, talking on the phone. He was completely dressed, and a jacket lay on the couch beside him. His face, revealed to her in profile, was expressionless except for a certain remoteness, and his voice was calm and level.

"Venezuela. Yes. No, they didn't know. Get the jet ready. I'll be there within an hour. Right." He hung up the receiver.

Staring across at him, Pepper's thoughts screamed inside her head. *Not tonight! Oh, please, not tonight! Not when it's so new and we're afraid to touch it....*

nine

THOR LOOKED UP AND TOWARD THE DOOR-
way, and saw her standing there. She was wearing only a flannel shirt that barely covered the tops of her thighs, looking
more sexy, he thought, than nine out of ten women could look
in sequins and feathers. Her hair was a little mussed from
sleep, but the wide, curiously bottomless violet eyes held no
drowsiness; they looked at him with a gentle inquiry that held
only as much curiosity as he would be willing to satisfy.

He wanted to move, wanted desperately to cross the room
to her and hold her. Wanted to explain what he didn't have
words for. Wanted to find words for the feelings tormenting
him. Wanted to smile at her and tell her that everything would
be all right.

He looked away.

"I have to leave." *Beloved*.

She came slowly into the room, halting at the end of the
couch and continuing to watch him steadily. "Do you know
when you'll be back?" she asked softly.

"No. Not really." *Beloved*.

Still steady, she asked, "Do you want me to be here when
you get back?"

His gaze moved swiftly back to hers. "Yes." *Beloved!*

An odd little sigh, almost soundless, came from her lips. "I'll feed Lucifer for you while you're gone."

"Thank you." So stiff, so brusque. *Oh, beloved. . . .*

He got to his feet and shrugged into the jacket as though the task demanded his utmost attention. He didn't look at her.

"Anything else you'd like for me to do?"

Tell me you'll miss me! "No."

She nodded slightly, and only the sudden clenching of one small fist at her side showed him that she wasn't as calm as she looked. He stared at the fist for a moment, then his gaze moved upward to her grave face. For an eternal second there was utter silence in the room. Even the two dogs, lying side by side in front of the cold hearth, neither moved, nor made a sound.

Thor started to step past her and head for the front door, but then something snapped inside of him. He turned suddenly and caught her in his arms, holding her with all the desperation he felt inside.

The relief of his sudden embrace was staggering to Pepper, and her arms slid beneath his jacket and around his waist eagerly. She could sense the emotions tearing at him, feel them in the tautness of his body and the strength of his arms, but understanding eluded her. She knew only that he was leaving her, and the fear that he would go without even touching her had brought agony.

He turned her face up with hands that weren't quite steady, his lips claiming hers with a ferocity that branded her as his—a strange, despairing possessiveness that seemed to deny its own existence.

And then he was gone.

Her lips throbbing, senses and thoughts in a whirl, she listened to the roar of the Corvette die away in the distance. Then a light—a candle—flickered to life somewhere in the back of her mind. It lit the area of darkness she had yet to find her way through, showing her a possible answer to the riddle of Thor's rules.

Pepper stood there for a long moment, and gradually everything began to make sense. Thor's reluctance to make a commitment, his constraint in the matter of his job, the impersonal house.

The house. She turned and left the den, spending the next half hour going through the house, room by room. She looked this time with eyes not searching for clues, but for confirmation. And she found it. Returning to the den, she sank down in a chair and stared into the cold, blackened remains of last night's fire in the hearth.

Granted, it was a guess. She could very well be wrong. But Pepper didn't think so. It explained the dichotomy. The man possessing the innate ability to care and to care deeply, to be sensitive. The man who avoided commitments, refused ties, and hated good-byes. It explained him.

Her puzzle was assembling itself with dizzying haste, the pieces falling neatly into place, and she was almost certain that the emerging picture was the right one.

What was his job? It occasionally took him out of the country—he'd mentioned Venezuela on the telephone. He'd told the person on the other end of the line to "get the jet ready." To Pepper's sharp mind that didn't necessarily mean what it would have meant to eight out of ten women—wealth; to her it meant haste, speed. Thor had been called to Venezuela, and he'd had to get there fast.

The job was dangerous. That much she was intuitively and instinctively certain of. And specialized. A man wouldn't be asked to leave his own country with all speed in order to handle a run-of-the-mill problem. Jean had offhandedly mentioned that Thor had been in Mexico at the same time she herself had been last year. Mexico? She'd read the papers; what had been happening in Mexico during that time? And then she remembered.

An oil well fire.

It had been a big one, she remembered. Three wells within spitting distance of one another, and all burning. And the situation had been complicated by the presence of terrorists who'd been determined to let the wells burn. The military called in ... The terrorists fading into the hills and taking potshots at anything that moved ... Valuable crude oil burning away ... And they'd called in—

A highly specialized team of firefighters! An American team! Men—she couldn't recall mention of women—trained to extinguish oil fires, chemical fires, any kind of more than usually dangerous fire where specialized knowledge was called for, technical skill demanded, and sheer raw courage—or stupidity—was required.

There was only a handful of such teams, Pepper was sure. A high-risk profession, often taking its members into remote areas and demanding of them the limit of endurance. And with present-day fears of terrorist takeovers, revolutionary coups, and "small" wars, any one of which could easily involve a very valuable oil field, it was a very dangerous profession.

She could be wrong about it, of course. But it seemed right.

And there was more to it all—she *felt* it! More to Thor, more behind his avoidance of commitment than dangerous work. She fiercely put from her mind the knowledge that he was, even now, on his way to carry on that dangerous work. Could it be ... ? No. No, just because she was sensitive to that, just because *she'd* been ...

But it fell into place so neatly, so logically. His father had ... and his mother? And perhaps because of that, he'd ...

It angered her. In fact, it made her damn furious! Because she could have been fighting it all this time instead of shadow-boxing in the dark. And the worst part was that she *understood*.

If she was right about it all, it was uncanny, really, her up-bringing and his so similar at the roots: Both had watched a father going into danger and a mother's terror. And from that common experience, each had evolved their separate and curiously dissimilar rules.

She was a gambler who knew better than to believe in certainty but wanted permanence. Brave, with an intelligent courage that saw the risk before taking the chance, Pepper had seen life in all its realities, all its painful, tawdry, reckless uncertainty. And she had felt the curious lure of danger, the excitement of challenge. She understood it because she'd inherited her father's courageous spirit, had absorbed the tragic regrets of the mother who had learned too late of years shadowed by crippling fear.

And so Pepper had promised herself never to look back with regret. She didn't shrink from danger or avoid risk. She reached out to people, gathering them around her happily and naming them friends. She satisfied her nearly insatiable curiosity, whether the result was a visit to an X-rated night spot in Europe or a period of study under the amused eye of a disreputable cardsharp.

She put down roots, however temporarily, wherever she went. She forged ties to people and places and things. Her friends were her friends, hostages to fortune with her knowledge and acceptance. And if fortune demanded a price to be paid, she would pay it then. She would not—*would* not—love one whit less just because that love could well be held, like the sword of Damocles, over her head one day.

And Thor? The root they had in common, she thought, had branched off in a different direction for him. He'd probably inherited a love of danger, of risk, from his father, and that recklessness was at odds with the sensitive man who'd watched his mother's fear. And being the man he was, Thor had chosen not to inflict that fear on another. He'd decided to go his own way alone.

It explained the house. Beautiful, a comfortable place to return to, but containing no memories. If he were to be suddenly wiped out of existence, there would be nothing in this house to cause anyone pain. It was impersonal with studied, deliberate care.

It explained Cody, the friend who was closer than Thor realized. Cody, who saw and respected the shield Thor carried to protect others from caring about him, and who came around anyway. The man who understood Thor and took care never to let him see that he *was* a hostage to fortune, took care never to let him know that a friend worried over him.

Because he'd have no hostages to fortune, and be no hostage himself—not Thor, the god of thunder—the reckless man could not be less than he was. And the sensitive man, held captive by his own choice, wouldn't let himself care.

Pepper wondered painfully what it had cost him. He was, she thought, a remarkable man not to have become embittered, not to have fallen back on sarcasm and coldness to shore up his shield. But he hadn't. He was quick and witty and humorous—at least with her.

And that, she realized, was the final piece of the puzzle falling neatly into place.

With her . . .

If she and Thor had met in some more conventional way, she would have seen him that first time with his shield up, his defenses strong. Instead, she had caught him off guard. The newspaper ad and then the story behind it had intrigued him, and he had gone to meet her against his better judgment. Their meeting...Brutus's attack...Impossible to be on guard with absurdity erupting all around you! And, the shield having dropped in surprise, it could never be raised quite so high again. Not with her.

And Pepper—blindly feeling her way—out of instinct or intuition or sheer damn dumb luck had stumbled on exactly the right methods to keep that shield partly lowered. She had challenged him, and with a streak of recklessness as wide as her own, he had accepted the challenge. It had amused him at first, she thought, intrigued him. The chase. But the chase had rapidly grown larger than both of them, and they had become caught up in it.

He had been a man alone. His housekeeper of five years had been a relative stranger to him, his home impersonal, his life ordered and limited. His only tie had been to a stallion named Lucifer who'd loved him and only him, and in spite of himself Thor had let himself care.

Lucifer was, perhaps, a beginning. A chink in the shield. And then she had barged into his life, bringing with her a neurotic Doberman, an attack-trained Chihuahua with inquisitive habits...and a puzzle. She had chipped away at his shield cheerfully, never realizing that he wasn't running from her at all, but from images burned in his mind.

Brutally abrupt good-byes. Fear-tainted absences. Desperate worry. And finally, the image that would haunt the kind of man he was: a woman in widow's black weeping in a darkened room.

Hostages to fortune. Himself a hostage to someone else's fortune, and he wouldn't be that, never be that, never that.

"Dammit," Pepper said, startling herself. She looked around, blinking, and realized that day had arrived while she'd been lost in thought. The dogs were quiet, heads lifted and eyes fixed expectantly on her. They're hungry, she thought vaguely. Breakfast time.

Then she heard the sound of Jean's VW, and the dogs raced to the front door to greet her. Pepper sat where she was, saying a quiet string of swear words she'd learned in various languages. Damn the man, anyway. How to convince him that he was already her hostage to fortune and always would be? And judging by that embrace just before he'd gone, that she was his hostage to fortune whether he knew it . . . or wanted it?

"He's gone?"

Pepper looked across to the doorway, meeting Jean's eyes. "He's gone. Venezuela. I think."

Jean nodded slightly, watching the younger woman with sympathy. "It's usually only a few days," she volunteered quietly.

"Yes." Pepper asked no questions, knowing that the housekeeper would understand. She'd hear the story from Thor or from no one. Period.

"I'll fix breakfast," Jean murmured. "And feed the dogs."

Pepper shook her head slightly. "I'm not hungry."

"You have to eat."

Looking across the room to meet concerned, motherly eyes, Pepper couldn't help but smile. "Okay. I'll . . . I'll go upstairs and get dressed."

That day passed, then a second and a third. Pepper groomed her clients during the day, helped Jean experiment with "foreign" culinary fare, and took care of Thor's horse and her own pets.

It was the nights that were bad. Jean had offered that first night to stay later than usual, but Pepper knew that she had a husband waiting for her at home, and refused to allow it. Any one—or two—of her friends would have been delighted to come and stay, but Pepper didn't even consider that.

She waited alone.

Watching television, knitting, reading, all were means to fill the time. A third night of automatically knitting while staring at the television produced a colorful afghan, which she defiantly tossed over the back of the couch.

It wasn't fear that tortured her during those endless nights. It was uncertainty. She couldn't know, after all, that Thor was even then in danger. She couldn't know. Except that she did. Her uncertainty, though, was all wrapped up in his work and his rules.

What right did she have to tell Thor that he was wrong about avoiding commitments? She had seen how fear could batter the mind and twist the spirit; she understood his reasoning. But she still thought he was wrong. And no special wisdom told her that.

It was just that she loved him.

His absence gave Pepper the time she needed to gather her thoughts and emotions and examine them as objectively as she could. And as the days passed she realized it wasn't only because she loved him and wanted to share his life that she believed his rules wrong. He was cheating himself, she knew, and cheating others as well. And no matter what happened between them, she meant to make him see that.

Pepper was curled up on the couch in the den watching a movie on television when she heard the Corvette. It would have been her fifth night alone.

As the dogs rushed to the front door she sat up slowly and used the remote control to turn off the television. Nervously smoothing the fine silk of her blue gown and negligee, Pepper steeled herself to stay put and not rush to greet him. She wanted to, God knew, but she was afraid. Because, while she'd had time to think during these last days, he probably had too. And she didn't know what conclusions he'd reached.

So she stayed put and listened to her heart thundering in her ears and the sound of his voice as he greeted the eagerly welcoming dogs. It wasn't until he spoke directly to her from the doorway that Pepper rose slowly to her feet.

"Well, two out of three's not bad, I guess."

She stared across the room at him, feeding the hunger inside of her with the sight of him. Dressed almost exactly the same as when he'd left, he shrugged his jacket off and tossed it on a chair, revealing a casual flannel shirt and jeans. He looked tired, she thought, but was blessedly whole and unhurt, and she took an instinctive step toward him.

But as he stepped into the room and into the light, she saw the look in his eyes and halted. She swallowed hard and forced herself to respond easily to his comment and not to the look that told her the ending was, perhaps, in sight.

"I didn't think you'd want a clinging sort of woman."

"What sort of woman are you, Pepper? No curiosity? No questions?"

"Both," she responded quietly. "I'll ask the questions if you're ready to answer. Are you, Thor?"

"Yes." He walked abruptly over to the window, showing her only a sharply etched profile against the blackened glass.

Pepper sat down on the edge of the couch, watching him. She took a deep breath, wondering if she hoped or dreaded her guesses to be confirmed. "Then tell me about your job."

He smiled a little, wryly. "Right to the heart of the matter. That's my Pepper."

"Tell me, Thor."

"I'm a partner in a small company," he told her quietly. "We specialize in dealing with fires. Oil and chemical fires; the kind that ordinary firemen just aren't trained or equipped to deal with. We fly all over the world, to remote areas and into cities and put out the fires. Sometimes we deal with deliberate sabotage, or duck bullets in some idiotic brush war, or fight diplomatic or bureaucratic red tape."

"And that's why you . . . you wrote your rules?" she questioned, sure now of the answer.

"My father and his partner started the company." Thor's voice was flat, tight. "My mother loved my father very much. When I got old enough to understand that—really understand it—I saw what it did to her. Having to say good-bye to him, time after time, knowing that each time could be for good. It made her old before the years caught up with her."

"And your father?" Pepper asked quietly.

"Dad." Thor smiled faintly. "He loved her. But this business . . . well, it gets into the blood. The challenge, I guess. The danger. He tried to spend time behind a desk—for her. But it didn't work for him."

Pepper waited silently.

"He was killed," Thor said abruptly. "An accident; they're common in this business. The explosives were unstable, more so than normal. He was too near the blast."

"I'm sorry."

Thor nodded slightly, then went on in the same flat tone. "Mom died a year later. Her heart, the doctors said. I think they were more right than they knew."

"And you went on with the business."

"I went on." He shrugged slightly, the movement rough. "Like I said—it gets into the blood. My father couldn't sit behind a desk. I can't either."

"No commitments," Pepper said softly.

Thor looked at her steadily. "After watching my mother die for twenty-five years, fear eating at her like a cancer? No. I can take the risk; I'll be responsible for me. But I won't torture another human being."

"Do you think you can make that choice?" she asked flatly.

Thor was silent, staring out the window again. The back turned to her was stiffly held, tension evident.

"Do you?" she repeated fiercely.

"It's my choice to make," he said almost inaudibly. "God knows, there are enough victims in the world; I won't help add to the list."

"You're suffering under an excess of nobility, Thor," she told him, letting scorn color her voice. He turned suddenly to face her—which was what she had wanted—and she went on quickly.

"It was never your choice, Thor! And, however this little game of ours ends, win, lose, or draw, I'll make you understand that!"

"Pepper—"

"All right, your mother couldn't take worrying about her husband; *my* mother couldn't take it either. Their men went into danger and it nearly destroyed them—did destroy your mother in the end. Well, it wouldn't destroy *me*! Not because danger frightens me any less, or because I'd care any less, but because I can handle it."

He looked puzzled. "Your mother . . . ?"

"My father was a cop." Pepper looked at Thor steadily. "He didn't have to be; his family was wealthy. But Dad was a cop down to his socks and through to his soul; it was in him to care about people, and he hated injustice. He loved his work. He also loved my mother. It took him two years to talk her into marrying him; she was terrified of being a cop's wife.

"Like your father, mine offered to try sitting behind a desk.

But Mom . . . was strong in some ways. She knew that she had no real right to use the emotional power she had over him. He would have quit if she'd asked; she never did. And she loved him too much to walk away from him.

"So I went through the same thing as you, Thor. Whenever he was on duty, I watched her jump when the phone rang, watched her pale when someone knocked on the door. I saw her cling to him that extra second before he left in the morning, and that extra second when he came home—safe. At first I was too young to understand or see anything out of the ordinary; I thought every kid's mother was nervous whenever Dad worked.

"Then I got older. And I saw then. I saw her bite her nails to the quick and pace the floor. I saw her watch television or listen to the radio with this terrible dread hanging over her if there was a report of police in a dangerous situation. And I got used to Dad calling her immediately because he'd known how it tortured her."

Thor had come forward, his strong hands resting on the back of a chair, almost gripping it, as he listened. "What happened?"

"He was killed." Pepper smiled a twisted smile. "But there was an irony about it. You see, Dad didn't die in the line of duty. His death was due to one of those senseless 'accidents' that fill up statistical sheets. He'd driven down to the local market for something—I forget what. A drunken driver swung wide on a turn and plowed into Dad's car head-on. He was killed instantly. The other man walked away."

She shook her head slightly. "We were at home waiting dinner for him when someone knocked on the door. It was funny: when Mom went to answer and saw Dad's partner standing there, she didn't suspect a thing. Dad wasn't on duty, you see. He hadn't even taken his gun with him."

"It must have been rough on both of you," Thor murmured, wondering at the uncanny similarity of their pasts.

"It was." Pepper lifted her chin and met his eyes levelly. "But both of us learned something very important. My first reaction was about what yours had been, that I'd never go through what Mom had, or allow anyone else to suffer because of me. Mom grew stronger. Not because the worst had happened and she didn't have to be afraid anymore, but because she realized how fear had cheated her all those years. She saw that their life together could have been so much fuller and happier if she'd only lived each day as it came instead of constantly dreading something she had no control over.

"And she made me understand that. She taught me that the worst thing anyone can do in this life is to regret—anything. Life's too short for that. Mom found out too late, but I didn't. I've been reckless more than once, and I've taken chances, but I've never regretted, Thor. And I don't ever intend to."

His hands tightened on the back of the chair. "And I don't intend to watch anyone suffer because of me."

Pepper laughed suddenly, a wry sound. "You believe that you can prevent others from caring about you? What about Jean? After five years d'you believe she thinks of you only as an employer, that she doesn't know you inside out? That she wouldn't feel grief if something happened to you? And what about Cody? He was your best friend until your father was killed, and then you shut him out. But he keeps coming around, doesn't he? He keeps coming around because you're his friend and he cares about you.

"And Lucifer? Oh, he's just a horse . . . but we both know animals feel. He loved you in spite of yourself, and you couldn't just walk away from that. And the dogs. Thor, both of them looked everywhere for you while you were gone, did you know that? They missed you."

She rose and went over to stand by the chair, staring up at him. "Thor, all of us give hostages to fortune, whether we will it or not. It isn't our choice to make. And we're all hostages to someone else's fortune. We can't protect those we care about from things we have no control over. We can't insulate ourselves or them."

"Pepper—"

Reaching up, she placed two fingers lightly across his lips to halt whatever he'd been about to say. "Think about it," she urged quietly. "That's all I'm asking, Thor. If you decide in the end that you'd rather not litter your life with . . . with hostages to fortune, then that's that. I told you I'd know if you took to your heels in earnest."

Her smile was a little twisted. "But you asked me for honesty, so there's something you have to know. If I walked out that door tonight, nothing would change. Like it or not, you're a hostage to someone else's fortune."

He reached out suddenly to pull her against him, his arms wrapping her in a tight bear hug. "When are you going to stop surprising me?" he asked huskily, his chin rubbing slowly in her hair.

Pepper slid her arms around his waist, the feeling of his hard body pressed against hers only beginning to feed her hunger. Instead of answering his murmured question, she asked one of her own. "Do you mind if I cling . . . just a little?"

"I'd need to have my head examined if I did," he whispered, almost to himself.

"Thor?"

"Hmm?"

"Welcome home. I missed you."

He went very still for a moment, then swung her up into his arms and started for the stairs. "I missed you too," he said gruffly.

"Pepper?"

"Hmmm?"

"Will you show me your home-on-wheels tomorrow?"

"If you like."

"I think it's time, don't you?"

"I've just been waiting for you to ask."

"Diana, matchmaker, mender of lonely hearts, goddess of the hunt, how did I manage to stumble across you?"

"You answered an ad in the paper."

He saw Pepper's home the next morning, saw the pieces of the puzzle beginning to fit neatly together. It was all there, as she'd said, but only to those who cared to look and knew what to look for. It was bright and cheerful and cluttered with memories. There were snapshots tacked up everywhere of the friends she'd made all over the world, mementos of the places she'd been.

Ties. Bonds.

Exploring like a cat with Pepper's smiling permission, Thor looked into closets and corners. He found evidence of her competitive spirit in trophies and awards. And he saw that the awards themselves meant little to her, since they were used merely to prop open doors or hold down papers, or were left to gather dust on the top shelf of a closet.

Small, custom-designed, and built-in cases held collections of jade and ivory, cheek-by-jowl with the crayoned drawings of children befriended along the way. Books on every conceivable subject were jammed into bookshelves and piled in corners, topped here and there by battered stuffed animals. A compact stereo system was surrounded by tapes and albums.

From the cheerful clutter emerged a portrait of a woman

who made friends and kept them, was intensely curious, competitive out of a love of challenge, had been everywhere—and probably seen everything—and had somehow managed to retain her enthusiasm for everything.

Everything, Thor mused silently, staring around him at her home. That was Perdita Elizabeth Patricia Elaine Reynolds. Honest, reckless, impulsive, humorous, wise, caring, lively one moment and reflective the next. How many women was she?

As many as I have to be, she'd said.

He looked now at her smiling face, the softly glowing eyes, remembered the night before and a passion matching his own. Like a thorn, she'd worked her way beneath his skin, but, oddly enough, there was no pain. And he wondered if it was too late for her to teach him what he wanted to learn.

He'd shut so much of himself away that he wasn't sure he could ever reach for those feelings again, sort through them, make sense of them. He wanted to reach out to her, but he wasn't sure how. And because she'd never told him what he needed to hear in simple words, he was afraid to try.

"Pepper?"

"Hmm?"

"Your home is . . . beautiful."

"Thank you. I hoped you'd like it."

The days passed, days filled with laughter and companionship. And nights filled with magic. Pepper taught Thor how to groom a hostile poodle, and worked determinedly at making his job a casual topic for conversation. She told him about some of her more absurd experiences and encouraged him to talk about his life before she'd landed in the middle of it. She played the piano for him, discovering that the instrument had been his mother's and that he couldn't play a note.

She cooked for him. She even danced for him. The dance was one she'd picked up on her travels, and was immediately dubbed the Dance of a Veil-and-a-half by a bemused Thor. It also led to a rather interesting evening.

A week. Two.

Pepper had her own reasons for not telling Thor that she loved him—although she thought that if the man didn't know by now, he was as blind as a bat!—but his continued silence on that subject, and the subject of whether or not they had a future together, unnerved her badly. Both her instincts and intuition failing her, she didn't stop to think that Thor had closed down that part of himself too thoroughly to be easily opened again.

Her only thought was that perhaps he was content with the undefined limits of their relationship.

But Pepper wasn't. True, she'd told Thor in all honesty that she could live for today. But she knew that every day she remained with him would make it that much harder to leave when she had to. And she still felt hope that he wouldn't want her to leave.

Wouldn't *let* her leave. . . .

So, closing her eyes and whispering a devout prayer to the patron saint of lovers, Pepper took the biggest gamble of her life.

ten

THOR STEPPED INTO THE LIVING ROOM AND halted, a sudden wave of coldness sweeping him from head to toe as he listened to Pepper talking on the phone. He found himself straining to pick up some nuance of hesitation in her tone, some regret...something. But her voice was even and unemotional. He could see her profile clearly; it seemed set and determined, and her eyes gazed across the room with a fixed intensity.

"Yes, Mr. Morris, I've talked with Miss James. Yes, I've thought about it, and—I've decided not to take over the business permanently. Yes, I'm...sorry too. No, I enjoyed it tremendously. I love animals. Well, I think it's time for me to move on."

For the first time Thor noted a hesitation, a wavering in her voice. But then it was even again.

"Miss James told you about me, eh? Yes, I'm something of a traveler. I'll probably be leaving the country after we get this business taken care of. No, it's just the equipment; I operated out of my...my home. If you could arrange to store the equipment somewhere until it's sold...? Yes. No, Monday will be soon enough. I'll bring the books by, and you can make sure that everything is in order. Two o'clock? That's fine. Yes. Yes, I'll be there. Thank you, Mr. Morris. Good-bye."

Pepper cradled the receiver slowly, her gaze still fixed on something that seemed far away and none too happy. Thor saw the worry-stone that had been absent these last weeks in her hand, her thumb moving with a methodical rhythm. Only that movement and the faraway eyes betrayed her.

"You're leaving me," he said suddenly, hoarsely. He slid his hands into the pockets of his jeans as she got up and turned to face him. His hands were shaking, and he didn't want her to see.

Pepper looked across at him for a moment, almost as though he were slowly coming into focus. Then she smiled easily, and he instantly recognized the curtain falling between them.

"I talked to Kristen this afternoon. I charged the call to a credit card, so you won't be billed for it."

"Dammit, Pepper," he muttered, swearing at her trivial aside. But she was going on cheerfully.

"It seems that the English breeder did have something permanent in mind when he swept her off to England; they're getting married in three weeks. And since he has all the grooming equipment he needs, she decided to sell hers. She offered me the business, but I decided to pass. I was just talking to her lawyer to arrange the transfer."

"Why won't you tell me that you love me?" he murmured, hearing the puzzled, raw sound of his own voice.

Pepper turned away suddenly and walked over to the window, staring out as though the distant pastures held a driving interest for her. "I thought I'd go to Australia next," she said lightly, tossing the words over her shoulder. "I've only been there briefly before—flyovers and one-night layovers. I'd like to see the Outback. And kangaroos and koalas in the wild. And then maybe a cruise. I've always loved the sea. I could—"

"Why won't you tell me that you love me?" he repeated

fiercely, nothing uncertain about his voice now. He saw the worry-stone still in her hand, still being worried methodically, unconsciously.

"Fifi will be happy with you here. I'll leave Brutus and the van with Mom; I always do when I'm traveling." She went on as though he hadn't spoken, but her voice was strained now, uneven. "Next week probably. My passport's up-to-date, and all my shots."

"*Dammit*, Pepper! Why won't you tell me that you love me?"

She whirled abruptly, showing him a face that was no longer calm. "Because you're not a man to cut notches on your belt!" she told him almost violently. Then she looked down and saw the worry-stone in her hand, flinging it toward the couch with a muttered curse.

Thor shook his head. "What the hell's that supposed to mean?" he asked roughly.

Pepper crossed her arms across her breasts and met his gaze, in control once more. "If you were that sort of man," she said in a calm voice, "and I told you . . . it would be a sort of trophy for you. You'd look back on it with enjoyment, and a kind of pride. You know"—she smiled crookedly—"another one bit the dust. Another scalp. Another notch."

"Pepper—"

"But you're not that sort of man," she cut him off flatly. "Don't you see, Thor? It'll be the past. And I'd rather nothing was said that you couldn't forget if you wanted to. Nothing to regret."

Thor moved toward her slowly, taking his hands from his pockets. When he stood before her, he held her eyes steadily with his own. "And what about you?" he asked huskily. "Will you have regrets?"

She shook her head immediately. "No. These past weeks . . . no, I won't have any regrets."

His hands lifted to her shoulders, the thumbs moving over her collarbone with a restless impatience. "Tell me that you love me," he said, his voice dropping to a dark and compelling rumble.

"Thor, don't make this any harder please. I told you that I wouldn't complicate your life. I told you that you wouldn't have to ask me to leave. But I didn't say I'd be happy about it. Don't make me regret."

"Tell me that you love me."

Pepper looked up into his taut face, the determined gray eyes. "Why?" she asked shakily. "You're *not* a man to cut notches in your belt. So why?"

"I have to hear you say it," he told her fiercely.

"You know how I feel." She felt the hands on her shoulders tighten almost convulsively, and saw a muscle leap in his rigidly held jaw. And the nearly drowned hope inside of her surfaced with a breath of new life.

"I have to hear you say it." His voice was ragged, shaken with a depth of feeling she hadn't dared to hope for.

He watched her face intensely, seeing her steel herself like someone fearing a slap. But when she finally spoke, her voice was quiet and sure, with a certainty that needed no intensity, no emphasis, to prove itself.

"I love you, Thor." She lifted her hands to touch his face, lightly, as if needing a tentative reassurance of reality. "I love you."

Thor saw the glow in her lovely eyes, the expression he'd seen before and never dared put a name to. And the coldness that had held him in its grip from the moment he'd entered the room finally released him. He caught her fiercely in his arms, holding her with a strength just this side of savagery. "God, Pepper! I was so afraid!"

His hands found her face, tilting it up urgently. He kissed her with a curious mixture of passion and tenderness, a delicate high-wire balance she gloried in because it meant that depth of feeling she hadn't dared to hope for. It meant—

"I love you, Pepper," he breathed unsteadily when his lips finally left hers. "I love you with everything inside of me."

She caught her breath, staring up at him, a sense of wonder filling her. The same wonder she saw in his eyes. Wonder and a giddy happiness, and a sense of wholeness she'd never felt before. Her arms slipped around his waist, and she felt the certainty of touching the other half of herself.

"Thor . . ."

His hands still framed her face, warm and strong. "Don't leave," he said huskily. "Stay with me."

She nodded, almost without being aware of doing so. "Who needs Australia?" she murmured. "Let the Aussies have it."

Thor gazed into the loving depths of her violet eyes, and a quiet laugh escaped him. "You and your chasing! You won after all; I'm trapped."

Pepper carefully stepped back until they were no longer touching. "There's no trap, Thor." She shook her head, smiling. "You're free. Tell me to leave; I'll go. I'm not asking for a ring and a promise."

He reached out to pull her abruptly to him once again. "But I am." His grin was crooked. "A ring and a whole basketful of promises. And I don't give a damn whose idea it was in the beginning."

She smiled up at him, more than content. But his next sober question surprised her; she honestly hadn't expected him to feel the need for a real commitment.

"Marry me?"

Pepper swallowed hard. "Thor, you don't have to marry me. It's enough that you love me." She laughed shakily. "You're *really* breaking your rules!"

"A very wise lady told me once," he said deeply, "that sometimes rules have to be broken. There's just no other way of dealing with them."

"Thor—"

"Marry me, sweetheart. I need you beside me for the rest of our lives. I need your humor and your strength and your intelligence. And most of all I need your love. I need to bind us together with every promise, every thread I can find. And—dammit!—I want it in writing! The kind of writing that you and I understand and believe in, the kind that means forever."

Pepper was vaguely aware that she wasn't breathing, but it didn't seem to matter very much. She could only gaze up at the man she loved more than life, and feel a deeply grateful awe that somehow—overcoming the stumbling blocks their separate lives had placed between them—they had found one another.

He held her even more firmly, looking down at her with the eyes of a man who'd doubted heaven...and found it against all odds. "I'm yours more than my own," he said quietly. roughly. "And I always will be. If you'd walked out that door, part of me would have gone with you. A large part. And I wouldn't have been able to forget even if I'd wanted to. You would have haunted me all the days of my life. Awake and asleep.

"Marry me, beloved. Stay with me...forever."

She swallowed again. "You're not worried about—about hostages anymore?"

Thor bent his head to kiss her very gently. "I'll always

worry," he murmured. "But the difference is that now I know how empty my life was without them."

"I love you," she whispered, "and I want to be your wife more than anything in the world!"

He held her fiercely. "I hope that means yes," he said unsteadily.

Pepper slid her arms up around his neck, pulling his head down and telling him in the best way she knew that it did indeed mean yes. . . .

It was some hours later and they were lying close together in the big four-poster bed when the conversation became rational again.

"Beloved?"

"Mmm, I just love that," she murmured, moved oddly by his rough-edged endearment; neither of them tossed around endearments lightly. "What is it, darling?"

He drew her a bit nearer. "Would you have left me?"

"I'm glad we didn't have to find out," she said softly.

He chuckled suddenly. "You were gambling, weren't you?"

"Well . . ."

"Oh, Lord. What have I let myself in for?"

Pepper snuggled closer, smiling contentedly. "The biggest poker game of them all, darling."

"With a cardsharp yet!"

"But aren't you glad I've got the winning hand?"

"In this game, beloved, I think we've both won."

"I know we have."

"And all the cards are wild."

"Only one-eyed jacks and deuces, darling."

"And the queen of hearts."

"True. She cheats, you know—the queen of hearts."

"Not a lady at all."

"S'terrible. Just terrible."

"Aces up her sleeves . . ."

"And love in her heart. . . ."

Pepper gave the concoction in the pan a last stir and tasted it critically. "There's *still* something missing," she said to her canine audience, then made a hasty lunge at the large Siamese tom who'd leaped onto the counter. "Not while I'm cooking, Tut!" she said, putting him firmly back onto the floor. "Blasted cat—why'd you have to eat the recipe card, for Pete's sake? Now I'll never know what's missing!"

King Tut cuffed an inquisitive Brutus without malice and then calmly sat down to wash a seal-brown paw.

"Some wedding present you turned out to be," Pepper told him darkly. "Cody and his bright ideas! Fifi, stop trying to wash his ears; you know he doesn't like it." The Doberman retired to a corner with an injured expression after being soundly cuffed by the disdainful cat, and Pepper sighed.

"I live in a nuthouse."

She glanced up at the kitchen clock and felt the warmth of Thor's imminent arrival filling her. Just another few minutes now; he'd called as soon as the jet touched down. One more dangerous assignment completed successfully, she thought, and let her mind wander back over the past year.

Once having taken the plunge, Thor had opened up wonderfully. He'd been concerned at first, she knew, watching her for any signs of the worry and dread both remembered from their respective mothers. But Pepper had been determined not to live in fear, and she hadn't.

And they had discovered that although the leave-takings were never fun, the homecomings had been wonderful. Pepper had worked to turn the house into a home, filling time while Thor's work claimed him and never letting herself brood.

There was nothing impersonal about their home now, nothing detached. Houseplants, knitted afghans, photos taken during the last year, and the items collected over Pepper's years of travel now filled the house. The home.

Leaning back against the counter, Pepper absently watched Tut playfully attack Brutus's tail. Thor had been immediately adopted by her friends during the past months, and Pepper had had the pleasure of watching him and Cody become closer.

Cody. Pepper giggled suddenly. She'd have to do something about Cody soon; he'd been footloose and fancy-free too long. He needed a wife to curb his mischievous ways. She thought of the peculiar sculpture that had been his gift on his last visit; he always brought something. The sculpture was a marvelous conversation-starter at parties, since no one seemed to be able to figure out what it was. It now graced the coffee table in their den, and Tut seemed strangely fascinated by it.

Still, Cody needed a home of his own. Pepper thought for a moment of the few unattached friends she had. Then she began to smile. Brooke, of course, and why hadn't she thought of her sooner? Perfect. Just perfect. Now . . . how to get them together?

She pushed the problem to the back of her mind, confident that she'd think of something eventually. A larger problem loomed in her thoughts, prodded by the slight ache in her lower back. Damn, the doctor'd told her to rest every afternoon, but with Thor coming home she'd forgotten.

Uneasily she wondered if Thor was quite prepared for yet another hostage to fortune, this one a scrap of humanity with his own blood flowing through its tiny veins. It was the final, most irrevocable commitment of all, and one they hadn't talked about. Unplanned, of course, and the doctor seemed a bit concerned about Pepper's tiny pelvis, but Pepper herself was deliriously happy with the news.

Knowing her husband, she felt certain that Thor would be, too, once he got over the shock. She decided not to tell him that the doctor had predicted a cesarean delivery after hearing of her large husband. She'd break that to him later. For now . . . Pepper took a deep breath and patted her only slightly rounded stomach.

"There's no going back now, sweetie," she said, and giggled.

She heard the roar of the Corvette then, smiling as all three pets took off for the front door. She turned down the burner under her Irish stew—authentic, Jean would say—and waited in the kitchen to meet her husband.

Thor came in a few moments later, casual in jeans and a sweater. Tut was riding in his accustomed manner on one shoulder, Brutus was tucked beneath an arm, and Fifi frisked happily at his side. The cat was nattering in his loud Siamese voice, Brutus yapping excitedly, and Fifi whining.

Laughing gray eyes met hers from the doorway. "One man's family," Thor said wryly.

"Is it my turn yet?" Pepper asked meekly.

"Are you kidding?" He set the cat and dog on the floor, patted Fifi with an automatically soothing murmur, and reached for his wife.

Emerging from the embrace with very little breath to spare for speech, Pepper managed to say happily, "I just love homecomings!"

"Mmm. Me too." Thor nuzzled her neck, breathing in the soft scent that was peculiarly hers. "You look very fetching today, beloved. I don't often see you in a skirt."

"I thought it'd be a nice change," she murmured, not telling him that only the realization that all her jeans were too tight had sent her scurrying to a doctor.

"Very nice." When the oven timer went off, he released her

with an obvious reluctance that delighted her. He sat down on a stool at the breakfast bar, watching her remove a pie from the oven.

"That smells good. So does whatever you've got in that pot."

"Irish stew."

"I'll gain ten pounds."

"If you haven't by now, you never will." Pepper turned off the oven. "Was it a rough one? It took less time than usual." They'd learned to talk about Thor's work, however briefly. It helped Pepper to know exactly what was involved in his work, and it seemed to help Thor as well.

"No, it was fairly simple. There was some high wind, but once it died down, we didn't have any trouble."

"Good."

Abruptly Thor asked, "Have you seen Cody lately?"

Pepper set the pie aside to cool and looked at him in surprise. "Yesterday as a matter of fact. I ran into him in Bangor and we had lunch. Why?"

Thor grinned slightly. "If I were a jealous man..."

"You know better than that."

"Thankfully yes, I do. Nevertheless, we'll have to do something about Cody. I'd think your matchmaking instincts would be revolted by his continued bachelorhood."

"They are, and I'm working on it."

Looking interested, Thor asked simply, "Who?"

"Her name's Brooke Kennedy, and you don't know her; I'll tell you about her later. Why'd you ask about Cody?"

Thor frowned. "Well, he left a package for me at the airport; I thought you might know something about it."

"What kind of package?"

Wordlessly Thor rose and left the kitchen, returning a moment later with the package. It was a white box tied with a bright red ribbon. He slid the ribbon off, removed the top, and propped the package up on the bar, revealing the contents.

Looking out of the box with bright button eyes was an average, ordinary, run-of-the-mill Teddy bear. Around its neck were two ribbons tied in bows, one blue and one pink.

Pepper stared at it, knowing that her mouth was open. Damn the man! How'd he guessed? She hadn't told him a thing! Then Pepper realized that she must have been dreamy-eyed and vague after hearing the doctor's news. Trust Cody to put two and two together, she thought wryly.

Thor was sitting on the stool again, gazing at the package with a frown. "I know Cody likes to add to the menagerie apparently, but why a stuffed bear, for God's sake?"

Turning off the burner under the stew, Pepper crossed to stand between Thor's knees, linking her arms around his neck with a smile. "Cody was just trying to steal my thunder, darling, and I'll strangle him the next time I see him."

"Steal your thunder?" Thor slid his arms around her, drawing her close. "What're you talking about?"

"Well, he couldn't have known for sure, since I didn't say a word to him, but he must have guessed. And you say I have a poker face!"

"Pepper."

"Well, I didn't want to tell you like this, dammit. I'd planned a cozy dinner with candlelight and wine and soft music—"

"Pepper..." Thor was beginning to look nervous. "Just what are you trying very hard not to come right out and say?"

"I'm pregnant," she said baldly.

"You're...?" Thor's nervous expression acquired a dazed tilt. "You're..."

"Pregnant." She spelled it. "And I hope you don't mind, darling, because I kind of like the idea. I mean, what's one more hostage? That front bedroom will make a marvelous nursery, don't you think?"

"Nursery," he murmured blankly. Bemused gray eyes stared into hers for a moment, then cleared suddenly. "Are you all right?" he demanded worriedly. "Why've you been cooking? Where's Jean? She should be doing this!"

"Jean's at her sister's house; the poor woman fell and broke her leg a couple of days ago, and Jean's helping out. And I'm fine, darling. You really don't mind about the baby?"

"Mind? I—" Thor cleared his throat strongly. "No, I don't— It's just that I've never thought about being a father."

"You have about six months to get used to the idea."

"Six months?" He swallowed. "That's not very much time."

"You won't need very much time." Pepper smiled at him lovingly. "Daddy's little man or Daddy's little princess—either way, you'll be a wonderful father, darling."

Thor hugged her suddenly, burying his face in the curve of her neck. "Damn you and your chasing," he said thickly. "Just look what you've gotten me into!"

"I think it's the other way around!"

He lifted his head, eyes suspiciously bright, and smiled at her. "I love you, you know. More and more every day. And I can't wait to meet Daddy's little whatever."

"Daddy's little hostage." Pepper kissed him tenderly. "I love you, Thor. I'll always love you."

Suddenly teasing, Thor murmured, "Even if I warn Cody you're after his scalp?"

"Even if you warn Cody. You know I play fair, darling. I'll warn him myself."

Thor lifted an eyebrow. "That sure of yourself? Just who is this Brooke Kennedy, anyway?"

Pepper told him, at length and in great detail, and her husband was looking a bit startled by the end of the recitation.

"She doesn't sound like Cody's type at all."

"She's perfect for him."

"The matchmaker's final word, eh?"

"I got you, didn't I?"

"You certainly did. Poor Cody."

"Save your sympathy. Cody'll be too busy to feel sorry for himself."

"Too busy?"

"Chasing Brooke."

"Oh, she'll run, will she?"

"In a wonderfully confusing circle. It ought to be interesting."

"Uh. Beloved?"

"Yes, darling?"

"You're dangerous."

"However—?"

"However, I have this curious love of danger. . . ."

About the Author

KAY HOOPER is the award-winning author of *Hunting Fear, Chill of Fear, Touching Evil, Whisper of Evil, Sense of Evil, Once a Thief, Always a Thief,* the Shadows trilogy, and other novels. She lives in North Carolina. Her next book, *Blood Dreams,* is coming soon from Bantam.